# PRAISE FOR
## *THE MITFORD AFFAIR*

**A *Good Morning America* Top Book for January**
**A *Town & Country Magazine* Best Book of January**

"Fans of World War II historical fiction will be fascinated."
—*Library Journal*

"An in-depth exploration of the complications and bonds of sisterhood. Benedict perfectly captures the anxiety and uncertainty of England's interwar years and serves as a timely reminder of the dangers of enigmatic autocrats. Fast-paced and eye-opening."
—Fiona Davis, *New York Times* bestselling
author of *The Magnolia Palace*

"In her latest book *The Mitford Affair*, Benedict plunges readers into a world of glamorous, charismatic young British debutantes and then turns that shiny world on its head. I was blown away—learning this true story of the Mitford sisters and the roles they played for and against the Nazis was nothing short of astonishing. Benedict delivers with all that readers have come to love and expect from her: nuance, élan, and the most delicious storytelling."
—Allison Pataki, *New York Times* bestselling author
of *The Magnificent Lives of Marjorie Post*

"Benedict unflinchingly peels away the giddy facade, revealing the tragedy beneath the one-liners in this close look at the

Mitfords' darkest hour: the family's embrace of fascism and flirtation with treason in the face of World War II."

—Lauren Willig, *New York Times* bestselling author of *The Lost Summers of Newport*

"Timely and suspenseful, *The Mitford Affair* is an immersive, spellbinding novel that illuminates the terrible allure fascism holds for some, as well as the courage and moral clarity that enable others to resist even when beloved friends and family succumb."

—Jennifer Chiaverini, *New York Times* bestselling author of *Resistance Women*

"Marie Benedict brings to life a dark chapter of World War II. Through grit and perseverance, three sisters—each more dazzling and intelligent than the last—work their way into the highest echelons of power. What happens when one no longer recognizes the siblings she was raised with? When caring turns to callousness? When love turns to rivalry? When the only choice is willful blindness or whistleblowing? One woman must decide whether to betray her sister or her country in this meticulously researched page-turner. Masterful."

—Janet Skeslien Charles, *New York Times* bestselling author of *The Paris Library*

"In a *Downton Abbey* meets *The Crown* epic, beautiful scale comes this unforgettable commentary on British society."

—Zibby Owens for *Good Morning America*

"This new novel by Marie Benedict takes one of the most fraught moments in the family's history and uses it as the basis for a fun, compelling, and deliciously mannered saga."

—*Town & Country Magazine*

"This engaging tale of genteel spies shifts easily between the sisters' perspectives and provides timely insight... Benedict's silky-smooth page-turner is sure to please her fans."

—*Publishers Weekly*

"Benedicts turns [The Mitfords'] remarkable story into made-for-Masterpiece historical fiction... Just try to stop reading."

—*Booklist*

# PRAISE FOR
# *HER HIDDEN GENIUS*

"Brings to life Franklin's grit and spirit... An important contribution to the historical record."

—*Washington Post*

"Marie Benedict brings human warmth and in-depth science to a novel on the life of Rosalind Franklin... Benedict is terrific at showing how male exclusivity operates and has researched the science in magnificent depth... A humanly as well as scientifically engaging read."

—*Financial Times*

"Benedict adeptly brings forward another accomplished,

intriguing, and unjustly overlooked or oversimplified real-life woman in a welcoming and involving historical novel."

—*Booklist*

"Benedict again illuminates an overlooked female historical figure, accessibly highlighting Franklin's scientific achievements and also depicting some of her personal life."

—*Library Journal*

"Marie Benedict has a remarkable talent for forcing open the cracks of history to draw extraordinary women into the sunlight. In *Her Hidden Genius*, Benedict weaves together molecular biology and human psychology to bring vivid life to Rosalind Franklin, whose discovery of DNA's exquisite double-helix structure takes on the narrative intensity of a thriller. Fans of historical fiction will devour this complex portrait of a brilliant and trailblazing genius and the price she paid to advance the frontiers of science."

—Beatriz Williams, *New York Times* bestselling author of *Our Woman in Moscow*

"Marie Benedict does it again, pulling another brilliant woman out of the shadows of history into an illuminating portrait for posterity. This eye-opening novel deftly explores the life of Rosalind Franklin—the wronged heroine of world-changing discoveries—and her singular pursuit of science. Educational and astounding. Brava!"

—Stephanie Dray, *New York Times* bestselling author of *America's First Daughter*

"What an important book this is. Through Marie Benedict's trademark insight and immersive historical research, Rosalind Franklin and her extraordinary legacy are beautifully restored to public recognition. So brilliantly sketched is this brilliant woman that you will find yourself both infuriated by the misogynistic battles she faces and inspired by the intellectual achievements she manages to secure regardless. A must-read for anyone interested in science or forgotten heroines."

—Kate Moore, *New York Times* bestselling author of *The Radium Girls* and *The Woman They Could Not Silence*

"Impeccably researched and beautifully written, *Her Hidden Genius* is a remarkable story of strength, perseverance, and achievement. Marie Benedict once again shines a light on women in science, vibrantly bringing Rosalind Franklin's genius to life in the pages of her novel."

—Jillian Cantor, *USA Today* bestselling author of *Half Life*

"Marie Benedict has given us an immense gift: a peek into the inner world of Rosalind Franklin, one of the most brilliant—and overlooked—scientists of her time. *Her Hidden Genius* describes the discovery of DNA in exquisite beauty, weaving the structure of the double helix effortlessly into a poignant and compelling narrative. This is Benedict's best work yet, a book that will break your heart, rattle your expectations, and ultimately leave you stunned by the sacrifices one woman made for science."

—Nathalia Holt, *New York Times* bestselling author of *Rise of the Rocket Girls*

# PRAISE FOR
# *THE MYSTERY OF MRS. CHRISTIE*

**An Instant *New York Times* Bestseller**

**A *USA Today* Bestseller**

**A Costco Book Club Pick**

"It's not a whodunit or even a whydunit, but a sort of how-the-hell-did-he-do-it? As Christie's first and best-known detective, Hercule Poirot, might say: Patience. All will be revealed."

—*Los Angeles Times*

"It's an empowering and wonderful tribute... *The Mystery of Mrs. Christie* reads like a modern domestic thriller in the vein of *Gone Girl* and *The Girl on the Train*. It's also a nod to classic whodunits that channels Christie's talent for writing unsolvable mysteries packed with puzzles, red herrings, and, most especially, unreliable narrators. Until the closing chapters, Benedict forces us to ask who is more credible: Agatha or Archie?"

—*Washington Post*

"[A] gripping historical fiction tale of true mystery."

—*Good Morning America*

"[A] clever reconstruction of Agatha Christie's mysterious 11-day disappearance in 1926."

—*E! News*

"*The Mystery of Mrs. Christie* is part domestic thriller, part Golden Age mystery—and all Marie Benedict! An absorbing and immersive plunge into the disturbed private life of one of the world's most beloved authors, who confounded police, journalists, and generations of biographers when she disappeared from her home, like something out of one of her own novels. But you just might find a solution to the puzzle here... (No Belgian detectives required. Knitting spinsters sold separately.)"

—Lauren Willig, *New York Times* bestselling author of *The Lost Summers of Newport*

"A winning whodunit from the thrilling life story of the mistress of whodunits, Agatha Christie herself, *The Mystery of Mrs. Christie* is a deft, fascinating page-turner replete with richly drawn characters and plot twists that would stump Hercule Poirot."

—Kate Quinn, *New York Times* bestselling author of *The Alice Network*, *The Huntress*, and *The Rose Code*

"What a read! Agatha Christie is so beautifully drawn, you could easily believe Benedict knew her intimately. Each page uncovers fresh layers of pain, rage, genius, and suffering, culminating with a firecracker of an ending. I loved it."

—Stuart Turton, bestselling author of *The Devil and the Dark Water* and *The 7 ½ Deaths of Evelyn Hardcastle*

"With twists, surprises, and an ending that packs a punch in more ways than one, *The Mystery of Mrs. Christie* is a whodunit infinitely worthy of its famous heroine. Benedict's exploration

of Agatha Christie's life and mysterious disappearance will have book club discussions running overtime. Quite simply, I loved it!"
—Lisa Wingate, #1 *New York Times* bestselling author of *Before We Were Yours* and *The Book of Lost Friends*

"Brilliantly constructed and richly detailed, *The Mystery of Mrs. Christie* is both a twisty mystery and an immersive portrait of the domestic and professional life of the legendary Agatha Christie. This is a must-read for fans of Agatha Christie."
—Chanel Cleeton, *New York Times* and *USA Today* bestselling author of *The Last Train to Key West* and *Next Year in Havana*

# PRAISE FOR
# *LADY CLEMENTINE*

**A *Glamour* Best Book of 2020**
**A *PopSugar* Best New Book to Read in January 2020**

"[A] fascinating fictionalized account of the consummate political wife."

—*People*

"[A] fascinating historical novel about Clementine, Winston Churchill's wife, keen political partner, and trusted confidant."
—*Christian Science Monitor*

"This outstanding story deserves wide readership. Fans of historical fiction, especially set around World War II; readers who appreciate strong, intelligent female leads; or those who just want to read a compelling page-turner will enjoy this gem of a novel."

—*Library Journal*, Starred Review

"A rousing tale of ambition and love."

—*Kirkus Reviews*

"Winning... The personality of Clementine reverberates in this intimate, first-person account. An intriguing novel, and the focus on the heroic counsel of a woman that has national and international impacts will resonate."

—*Publishers Weekly*

"With a historian's eye and a writer's heart, Benedict provides an unforgettable glimpse into the private world of a brilliant woman whose impact and influence on world events deserve to be acknowledged."

—Lynda Cohen Loigman, author of
*The Two-Family House* and *The Wartime Sisters*

"The atmospheric prose of Marie Benedict draws me in every single time. *Lady Clementine*'s powerful and spirited story is both compelling and immersive."

—Patti Callahan Henry, *New York Times*
bestselling author of *Becoming Mrs. Lewis*

"Benedict is a true master at weaving the threads of the past into a compelling story for today. Here is the fictionalized account of the person who was the unequivocal wind beneath

Winston Churchill's wings—a woman whose impact on the world-shaper that was WWII has been begging to be told. A remarkable story of a remarkable woman."

—Susan Meissner, bestselling author
of *The Last Year of the War*

# PRAISE FOR
# *THE ONLY WOMAN IN THE*
# *ROOM*

**An Instant *New York Times* Bestseller**
**A *USA Today* Bestseller**
**A Barnes & Noble Book Club Pick**

"A novelist that makes a career out of writing about 'The Only Woman in the Room'... In Benedict's telling, that story is a ready-made thriller as well as a feminist parable."

—*New York Times*

"In writing her narratively connected, fictionalized biographies, Benedict is not unlike an archaeologist digging up clues to moments of epiphany."

—*Newsweek*

"Benedict paints a shining portrait of a complicated woman who knows the astonishing power of her beauty but longs to be recognized for her sharp intellect. Readers will be enthralled."

—*Publishers Weekly*

"Once again, Benedict shines a literary spotlight on a historical figure whose talents and achievements have been overlooked, with sparkling results. *The Only Woman in the Room* is a page-turning tapestry of intrigue and glamour about a woman who refuses to be taken for granted. Spellbinding and timely."
—Fiona Davis, *New York Times* bestselling author of *The Magnolia Palace*

"Deftly portrays the fascinating life of a Hollywood icon whose scientific accomplishments have long been eclipsed by her sensuous beauty...follows a remarkable path of survival through the dangers of world war—and those at home, behind closed doors. A read as intriguing and captivating as Ms. Lamarr herself."
—Kristina McMorris, *New York Times* bestselling author of *Sold on a Monday* and *The Ways We Hide*

# PRAISE FOR
# CARNEGIE'S MAID

## A USA Today Bestseller

"*Carnegie's Maid* brings to life a particular moment in the ascendancy of Andrew Carnegie while enriching that moment with a sympathetic understanding of what it meant to be an immigrant living in poverty at that time. This would be an accomplishment for any book, but for one that cleverly disguises itself as a historical romance, it's an absolute treasure. The Carnegie legacy may be debatable, but Ms. Benedict's talent for bringing history to life is not."
—*Pittsburgh Post-Gazette*

"[An] excellent historical novel."

—*Publishers Weekly*

"With its well-drawn characters, good pacing, and excellent sense of time and place, this volume should charm lovers of historicals, romance, and the Civil War period. Neither saccharine nor overly dramatized."

—*Library Journal*

"In *Carnegie's Maid*, Marie Benedict skillfully introduces us to Clara, a young woman who immigrates to America in the 1860s and unexpectedly becomes the maid to Andrew Carnegie's mother. Clara becomes close to Andrew Carnegie and helps to make him America's first philanthropist. *Downton Abbey* fans should flock to this charming tale of fateful turns and unexpected romance, and the often unsung role of women in history."

—Pam Jenoff, *New York Times* bestselling author of *The Orphan's Tale* and *The Lost Girls of Paris*

# PRAISE FOR
# *THE OTHER EINSTEIN*

**A Target Book Club Pick**

"An engaging and thought-provoking fictional telling of the poignant story of an overshadowed woman scientist."

—*Booklist*

"Intimate and immersive historical novel... Prepare to be moved by this provocative history of a woman whose experiences will resonate with today's readers."

—*Library Journal*, Editors' Pick

"An intriguing...reimagining of one of the strongest intellectual partnerships of the nineteenth century."

—*Kirkus Reviews*

"Superb...haunting story of Einstein's brilliant first wife who was lost in his shadow."

—Sue Monk Kidd, *New York Times* bestselling author of *The Invention of Wings*

"*The Other Einstein* is phenomenal and heartbreaking, and phenomenally heartbreaking."

—Erika Robuck, national bestselling author of *Hemingway's Girl*

# ALSO BY MARIE BENEDICT

*The Other Einstein*
*Carnegie's Maid*
*The Only Woman in the Room*
*Lady Clementine*
*The Mystery of Mrs. Christie*
*Her Hidden Genius*

# THE
# MITFORD
# AFFAIR

A NOVEL

## MARIE BENEDICT

Sourcebooks and the colophon are registered trademarks of Sourcebooks.

Published by Sourcebooks Landmark, an imprint of Sourcebooks
P.O. Box 4410, Naperville, Illinois 60567-4410
(630) 961-3900
sourcebooks.com

Cataloging-in-Publication Data is on file with the Library of Congress.

Printed and bound in the United States of America.
WOZ 10 9 8 7 6 5 4 3 2 1

# CHAPTER ONE

# NANCY

*July 7, 1932*
*London, England*

T HE MELLIFLUOUS SOUNDS OF THE SYMPHONY FLOAT
throughout the ballroom. Servants pour golden champagne into the cut-crystal glasses. The fabled Cheyne Walk house exudes perfection down to the last detail, nowhere more than in its hostess.

There, at the center of the vast ballroom, stands the stunning, statuesque figure in a floor-length sheath of platinum silk, a shade that echoes her silvery-blue eyes. Her diamond-laden arms outstretched in welcome to her guests, she radiates serenity and unflappable, irresistible poise. If she were anyone else—someone I didn't know as intimately as I know myself—I would judge that sphinxlike smile a charade. Or worse. But I know she is precisely as she appears, because she is Diana, my sister.

I wrest my eyes from her and glance around the gleaming gilt and marble ballroom, expansive enough to easily hold the three hundred guests in attendance. As the dancers begin to pair up and then organize themselves, the revelers appear to emanate from Diana like the rays of the sun. It is a pattern that has repeated itself since our childhood; she always dazzles at the center, with us sisters fanned out around her like lesser beams. Never mind that the press considers all six of us Mitford sisters the very essence of the so-called Bright Young Things, she is the star.

The evening feels more like a celebration of the fashionable new home of Diana and her handsome, kindly husband Bryan Guinness, than a ball introducing one of our younger sisters, Unity, into society. *Where has Unity scampered off to?* I wonder, as I scan the crowded space for the spectacularly tall eighteen-year-old. Never one to abide by social dictates, she seems to have disappeared into the background instead of lapping up the attention as would be expected at an event in her honor. Finally, I spot her tucked into a shadowy corner, deep in conversation with our sister Pamela and our one and only brother, Tom, that golden boy of ours. Of my six siblings that leaves out only Jessica and Deborah, but they're too young to mingle in society.

Even though she pretends to be listening, Unity is clearly watching the other partygoers rather than engaging with Tom and Pamela. At least here at Cheyne Walk, she won't be required to curtsy twice and retreat backward as she'd had to do before the king and queen when she came out at Buckingham Palace. Poor Bobo, as we call her among ourselves, is not known for her grace, and we sisters had clutched one another's hands and held our breath until she'd completed the act without tripping and catapulting herself into one of Their Majesties' laps. Even then, she barely managed the feat without several awkward lunges and an initial backward step where her heel caught on her hem, sending a horrific tearing sound throughout the famous receiving room.

A shimmer of silver crosses the ballroom, and I observe Diana sashaying through the crowds. I think how alike Diana and Unity appear from a distance, both tall with their features blurred and blond hair flashing. Not so upon close inspection, and not only because Diana wears a seamless column of silver, while Unity sports a gray-and-white gown that is somehow ill fitting despite numerous trips to the tailor. For the millionth time, I give thanks that I was born with jet-black hair and green eyes instead of blue; I'd never want to come up wanting by comparison to Diana.

The music pauses, and I see Evelyn Waugh across the expanse. Delight and warmth course through me at the sight of my dear friend. Only the appearance of my unofficial fiancé would bring me greater happiness. But I know that's impossible, as Hamish declared himself unavailable for this particular function, providing yet another reason for my parents, whom we call Muv and Farve, to dislike him, apart from the multi-year, oft-delayed nature of our engagement. *What plans could your fey fiancé have made*, Farve wondered aloud using a most derogatory description, *that prevented him from attending the ball of his fiancée's sister?*

In my darker moments, I wonder whether I shouldn't have accepted Sir Hugh Smiley's proposal instead; banal though he may be, our union would have saved me from my current financial worries. And I'd have spared myself the constant muttering by Muv that it was time for me to stop my unseemly roaming around society, as I'm nearing thirty and still unmarried.

Evelyn glances in my direction, and I raise my hand in greeting, eager to have him join the gaggle of friends assembled at my side. These men—of which the poet John Betjeman and the photographer Cecil Beaton are but two—are my chosen family. Why shouldn't they be? The qualities that Muv and Farve disdain in me, along with most men of my acquaintance, are adored by these fellows, who revel in my well-read, quick-witted observations, particularly if they aren't appropriate. They are the only group to which I've ever felt I belong, and so, of course, Farve despises these "dandies." Even amid my five sisters, I've always been something of the outsider. With each sister usually paired off or teamed up—in childhood, Jessica with Unity, Pamela with Deborah, and Diana with Tom, like golden twins—I've often been alone.

Before I fix a bright smile of greeting on my lips for Evelyn, I run my tongue across my teeth to ensure that no slick of deep-red lipstick stains them. I smooth my gown, and then rehearse a few of the witticisms I've collected for him since we last met. Everything must be just so; none of us wish to risk Evelyn's humorous but biting censure. It's hilarious if wielded against those outside our circle, less so within.

But Evelyn comes no closer. In fact, he's changed course altogether, as if he's being pulled magnetically in the direction of Diana. A sinking feeling overtakes me, and I know this is my fault. Once, Evelyn had been my friend alone. When he was researching a book on high-society hijinks and asked to meet Diana, whose beauty and charisma had made her the star of her debutante season and catnip for the journalists, I made the introduction at a tropical party she hosted with her husband on board a riverboat called the *Friendship*.

I hadn't been worried; I knew that Evelyn planned on

disliking the young couple and making them the frivolous protagonists of his novel *Vile Bodies*. But all that changed when Evelyn came under Diana's spell. Now, he's so bloody mesmerized that I catch him wincing when I refer to my sister by the naughty nickname I've called her since infancy—Bodley, a play on the name of the publishing firm Bodley Head, because her head has always been too large for her body. This small imperfection is nearly imperceptible to others because her beauty is so overwhelming.

I glance away quickly, not wanting Evelyn or the others to catch me staring. Gawking simply isn't done; it reveals an unacceptable weakness. To hide my misstep, I say, "Looks as though Lady Tennant's trip to Baden did *not* provide the 'cure' the spa so widely advertises."

Even though this provokes the snickers I expect, I loathe myself for stooping low to achieve it. How I sometimes wish I had more weapons at my disposal than my barbed tongue and pen. But then my friends pile on with their own observations, each cattier than the last, until I cry with laughter. Only when I dab my eyes dry do I first notice it.

Diana stands at the center of a group of men, a common enough occurrence. But her gaze isn't upon a single one of them. It's not even on her doting, wildly wealthy husband. Those silvery blue, incandescent eyes of hers are fixed across the crowded dance floor at the last person I'd expect.

# CHAPTER TWO

# DIANA

*July 7, 1932*
*London, England*

D IANA STEPS BACK, AWAY FROM THOSE EYES AND INTO the crowd. Her guests part as she passes through, and some of the revelers reach out to shake her hand or kiss her cheek. Fingertips graze her shimmering silver dress. If she believed in false modesty, she could tell herself she's sought after only because she's the hostess of this lavish affair, where a grand mix of her family and society friends gather alongside other Bright Young Things. But she has never any use for such untruths; she is Diana Mitford Guinness and the world just makes itself available to her. It always has.

Amid the cacophony of voices, she hears Winston Churchill, husband of Cousin Clementine, rail on about a Stanley Spencer oil painting she has hung on the wall. Apparently, its depiction of the Cookham War Memorial is inaccurate, a fact of which only old Winnie would be aware. Diana blocks out his bluster—unusual, because she typically finds his political musings interesting, if disagreeable. She blocks out the sharp retort from his son, Randolph, as well; he's a great friend of her beloved and only brother, Tom, and she's long suspected Randolph fancies her.

Her handsome, adoring husband reaches her side. Aware of how striking they look together, Diana lifts her arms, heavy with diamond bangles, to cue the symphony and the dancers. Power surges through her as the musicians and partygoers follow her signal. All this is hers, she thinks for a fleeting, incredulous moment. The fabulously well-appointed Cheyne Walk home, complete with Aubusson carpets even for the children's bedrooms. The eighteenth-century country estate, Biddlesden, where they host any number of family and friends in season. Her two glorious little boys, Jonathan and Desmond, whom she's loved desperately from the moment they wailed themselves into her life. Her husband, Bryan, of course, heir to the Guinness brewing fortune and a barony. A veritable gaggle of friends, family, and acquaintances, always at the ready.

With all this, why is she so terribly bored? Not every minute, of course. Fleeting sparks of merriment present themselves in the form of diversions such as this one and the witticisms of dear friends like Evelyn Waugh. Occasionally, she derives satisfaction from reading a bedtime story to her boys. But a deep sense of aimlessness and unrest pervades her days.

*Never mind all that*, Diana tells herself. *How unseemly to think such thoughts.* She hasn't a right to be bored. There are Londoners right outside the gates on the brink of despair, sharing their disgust with her conspicuous excess in the face of worldwide depression. How dare she and Bryan spend their fortune on meaningless parties and acquisitions while so many struggle and starve with unemployment, they cry.

People think she's unaware—or worse, uninterested—in these angry throngs and their message, but she's not. Diana knows, down to a man, how many are assembled outside and precisely what they want. Beauty is not a barricade or a blinder to the truth. But what is she meant to do? Even the men of her acquaintance aren't prepared to dive headlong into the breach and shore up this floundering society, not even Bryan who has the money, the means, the connections, and the intellect to make a difference. And this knowledge sours her on him.

As the music slows, she feels the attention of the conductor and the dancers upon her again. Diana has nearly forgotten that the ballroom has paused, waiting for her to prompt the next dance. She raises her arm again, and the room animates, as if awakening from a collective slumber. As the strings play and the dancers twirl past her, Bryan, Evelyn, and a few select in the inner circle at the dance floor's center, she sees *him* again. Dark hair and eyes, he stares at her from the other side of the dance floor, his gaze never wavering even as one couple veers dangerously close to him. Her cheeks grow warm at the sight of him; she didn't think he would actually come. Sir Oswald Mosley, her M.

She returns his gaze, longer this time than the last. And suddenly, for the first time in recent memory, she feels very much alive.

# CHAPTER THREE
# UNITY

*July 7, 1932*
*London, England*

U NITY WISHES SHE'D BROUGHT HER RAT TO THE BALL.
Ratular would have fit perfectly in her handbag, and he would have provided a topic of conversation when an awkward silence descended, as inevitably happened. Not that the little pet would have had the chance to perform; indeed, no one seems to be interested in filling her dance card—even though the Cheyne Walk ball is in *her* honor, for God's sake. At the very least, however, Ratular, with his soft fur and ticklish whiskers, would have provided much-needed comfort. How she longs to crawl under the nearest table, as she does at home when the mood becomes too fraught.

Feeling uncomfortably constricted, she pulls at the strap of the gray-and-white Hartnell dress that Diana had specially designed for her this evening, not wanting her to wear her only other good ball gown—the one she wore for her Buckingham Palace presentation with the brand-new fur coat on top, all courtesy of Diana of course. No one else in her family has a spare pound to speak of. What an absolute brick Diana has been during this horrific deb season, Unity thinks. Much more helpful than her other sisters—not that her favorite, Jessica, who they all refer to as Decca, could do much as she was too young for society—but what of Nancy? Unity shoots her oldest sister a glance; she's preoccupied with her clever friends as usual, the ones with whom she *never* wants Unity to talk.

Blast, is that Nina Sturdee standing within earshot of Nancy? A shiver passes through Unity. The last thing she needs right now is a chat with one of her classmates from her short-lived days at Queen's Gate School, or St. Margaret's for that matter. Some hateful girl who might remember that the staff found Unity ill-suited for their institution and "counseled" her home to Farve and Muv, much to their chagrin. Unity has long known that the only reason Muv had made an exception from her insistence that her girls be educated at home was that she needed a break from Unity's *uniqueness*, as she put it. But tonight of all nights, she wants nothing more than to blend in—or stand out in the respectable, even attractive way she is meant to. No mean feat when she stands nearly six feet tall.

Just then, she sees Diana stroll to the corner of the room, where a cluster of young men are downing drinks as if their lives depend on it. As she leans toward the tallest, gangliest of the set and whispers in his ear, Unity studies how the other three freeze. It's as if Diana's very presence in their midst has caused an Arctic drop in temperature. How Unity longs for that kind of effect on men. Or on one man in particular.

The tall, gangly fellow tears himself away from his friends—with a modicum of reluctance, she notes—and walks toward Unity. He is smiling, and as he grows closer, she must remind herself not to return it. The fillings in her upper incisors make her teeth look gray and her smile menacing. More like a grimace than a grin.

The horns and violins begin to play as he asks, "May I have this dance?"

She nods, still very aware of her teeth and wanting to move to the lower lights of the dance floor before speaking. They begin to twirl around the ballroom, and she's grateful Diana selected someone over six feet. Aside from very recent house parties and three balls, her experience with dancing is limited to the twice weekly lessons Muv insisted upon, and she's not certain how smooth her steps would be with a partner shorter than her.

"What sort of music do you like?" he asks, one of those questions her dance instructor has suggested as appropriate chitchat. She wishes she thought of it first.

"I have a particular fondness for opera." She answers honestly, unable to fake the acceptable sort of replies the instructor recommended. This misstep makes her nervous, and so she blathers on. "German ones in particular. My grandparents were great friends of the family of composer Richard Wagner; that's why my parents gave me the middle name of Valkyrie." His face is blank; not at all the sort of awed expression she hoped for. Is it possible he doesn't know who Wagner is, doesn't know his world-renown stature? Perhaps he needs a bit of clarification, she thinks, and adds, "In honor of his most famous opera, the Ring cycle?"

"Ah," he says, then adds, "Interesting."

But his tone tells her that her conversation is the *opposite* of interesting; he finds her very dull indeed. So she tries a change of tack. "Do you like rats?"

He pulls away from her, staring at her face but not ceasing to dance. So she continues with the steps. After all, they are drawing close to Diana, and Unity does not want to disappoint her beloved sister.

But when they circle close enough to Diana to touch and Unity glances over at her for an approving nod, she realizes that her sister is oblivious to her presence. Diana is engrossed in a conversation with a man who is somehow familiar to Unity but she can't instantly place him—and they are standing inappropriately close. And then, in a rush, his name comes to her; he is that fascist gadabout, as Farve calls him, Sir Oswald Mosley. Why in God's green earth would Diana be talking so closely to *him*?

# CHAPTER FOUR

# NANCY

*January 24, 1933*
*London, England*

Are you quite certain, Bodley? You're so young to be making this decision—you are practically still newlyweds." I draw close to my serene little sister, searching her eyes for signs of hesitation or self-doubt. Even the tiniest apprehension might provide me with the opening for which Muv has sent me to get through. But all I see is the shine of excitement in her eyes; Diana has never been more beautiful.

"Oh, Naunce, you've been my staunch and often only ally in all this," she said, laughing, her voice a delicious chime as she uses the nickname she's called me since childhood. As if I'd told her an especially charming joke, instead of trying to peer into her heart and dissuade her from a most destructive path. "I'm old enough to have been married for five years and given birth to two boys, and as such, I'm plenty old enough to know exactly what—and who—I want."

I know she doesn't mean to wound me by calling herself "old" because she's managed to pull off the feat of marriage and childbirth by the ripe age of twenty-two when I myself have

achieved neither at twenty-nine. Thanks to Hamish St. Clair-
Erskine and his endless list of excuses and delays. But wound she
does, and I pocket this little injury for another day. We Mitford
sisters never forget. Only pretend to forgive.

"It's just that I'd hate for you to have regrets." I inhale deeply
from my cigarette, glancing around the small house she's leased
on Eaton Square, a far cry from her former palatial Cheyne
Walk house and her Biddlesden estate but reams better than
my flat. "Can't you just have a bloody affair with the man? Do
you have to divorce your lovely husband to run off and marry
him? I honestly think Bryan would rather scatter rose petals
over your adulterous bed than lose you forever."

That melodious laugh sounds out again, although this time
I swear I hear a hint of naughtiness. "Who said anything about
marrying him?"

For a split second, I am speechless, a state in which I
*never* find myself. When I do finally speak, I sputter. "Oh. We
all assumed—"

*Why the hell wouldn't we assume?* I think. If Diana dared to
leave her idyllic husband with his hangdog, worshipful attention to her, a rarity for his sex and class, why wouldn't the family
assume that it was for the fervent commitment of her damnable "M"? Why would we ever guess it was simply to slake some
lust? Muv and Farve's mortification over Diana's behavior—
which has led to a ban on us sisters seeing her, except for this
fruitless mission to bring her to her senses—will only deepen
when they hear this development, the first time they've singled
her out for disdain. I do not even want to think of the rage into
which Farve will fly when he learns of Diana's lack of marital

intentions. How many pieces of china will be sacrificed to his fury? I wonder. Certainly when we were children, many cups and plates had been smashed into smithereens when we committed the much less serious infraction of leaving jam dripping down the side of the jar.

Ever unflappable, Diana continues, "Naunce, darling, just because I've asked Bryan for a divorce does not mean I'm making wedding plans with M." Her usually ivory complexion has turned a bit pink at the mention of her precious "M." I loathe the way she refers to Sir Oswald Mosley—a facile political creature, charismatic to be sure, but known to jump party lines when it suits him and a notorious philanderer to boot. "You see, M has no plan to leave his wife. I will be happily satisfied with whatever time he can spare for me. And, in truth, I wouldn't mind a little more time to myself. Bryan had been quite overwhelming."

I am aghast. Why would Diana settle for crumbs? She could have the full and undivided cake from anyone else. Instead, she seems positively delighted at the thought of sharing her paramour with his wife of thirteen years, Cimmie, an heiress to the vast Curzon fortune, and whoever else may catch his fancy, which, by all accounts, could be any number of women.

Just as I am about to pose this very question, I hear a bounding down the stairs. Could it be Jonathan or Desmond? I thought the nanny had taken the boys to the park. The day is cold but unseasonably sunny, after all.

"Lady," a booming voice cries out from the foyer, and I know instantly who it is. Bobo. She's the only one who calls me "Lady" from time to time, and she is the loudest person I know.

Standing up to greet her with a kiss on each cheek, I see that she has squeezed herself into one of Diana's tweed sheaths. It is singularly unbecoming, and while I'm tempted to make a remark, I dare not lash out at this fraught juncture. One of Unity's tantrums would end this discussion in an instant.

"Bobo, did you not receive Muv and Farve's edict about Bodley here? She is to be considered persona non grata. We are not to be on speaking terms with her." I make light of our parents' instructions—I'm twenty-nine, so they can hardly dictate my actions, particularly since they don't support me financially—but Unity is still very much under their thumb. I'm surprised she's defied their orders.

She smiles, sharing those odd gray teeth with me. "I could hardly ignore Nard when I'm in London. Especially in her time of trouble." Gazing over at Diana with a near-worshipful expression, Unity uses her special nickname for Diana, the one reserved for when she's feeling tenderest toward her.

Muv and Farve had given in to Unity's pleas to live in London and try her hand at drawing while the social season continued, in the desperate hopes that it might widen her circle just enough to meet an interested suitor. I should have remembered that she would be in town more frequently than even the season demands, as her art classes on Harley Street would require it.

"And yet you ignore me and I'm in London as well." I half jest. Although I believe I *should* feel slighted that Unity hasn't reached out to me personally, I don't really enjoy spending time with her. Her moods are so variable and her interests so peculiar I find her tiresome. Not to mention I detest Ratular. Good god, who actually keeps a pet rat!

"You're too busy for the likes of me, Lady. What with your writing and all your chums," she says, plopping down next to Diana and reaching for her hand. How on earth does Diana connect so effortlessly with Unity? I wonder. What do they talk about when it's just the two of them? How strange it is to see Unity so often at Diana's side. Tom used to be her stalwart companion, during childhood anyway, but that's all changed now. He hasn't quite forgiven her for leaving his mate, Bryan, and our only brother has a full life of his own.

I decide to ignore the snub, and say, "Well, it's lovely to see you, Bobo. It seems an age since the holidays at Swinbrook."

Muv and Farve, along with our youngest sisters, Pamela, Decca, and Deborah, who we call Debo, live at Swinbrook House in Oxfordshire, a perfectly pleasant, sprawling country house, which we all loathe for everything it isn't—Batsford Mansion and then Asthall Manor, where we romped blissfully in turn, until Farve's finances dwindled due to poor choices and the general economic downturn, resulting in the move to Swinbrook. Growing up as we did, like a pack of feral cats in isolation with only each other for company since we tended to avoid vacant Muv and mercurial Farve, our setting very much mattered; it was everything.

How can I get the conversation about Diana's divorce back on track with Unity looming next to her? My thoughts barely settle on a tactic when the phone rings. A maid, part of Diana's "reduced" staff, knocks on the parlor door, and says, "Sorry to interrupt, Mrs. Guinness, but there's a call for Miss Nancy Mitford."

Who would be calling me here? The only people who even

know I'm at Eaton Square are Muv and Farve. But they wouldn't dare call here after taking such a strong stance against Diana.

I stub out my cigarette and push myself up from the celadon silk-upholstered chair. Diana's idea of sacrifice is different than most, I think, glancing around the sumptuous, bespoke furnishings.

Squeezing myself into the little telephone room off the foyer, I pick up the phone and offer a wary greeting. To my surprise, it's Hamish.

# CHAPTER FIVE

# DIANA

*January 24, 1933*
*London, England*

NANCY FLITS UP LIKE A BIRD, FLYING OFF HER PERCH ON an upholstered chair to take her call. The chair arrived in this new home on Eaton Square just three weeks ago from Cheyne Walk with the rest of the furniture. Bryan had insisted Diana take it all—hadn't she selected it in the first place, he'd asked wistfully—and honestly, he's been the bee's knees about this entire divorce business. She offered her gratitude for the furnishings but refused the Guinness jewels and art when he tried to send them to Eatonry, as she's calling her new house; they belonged with his family, she'd held firm, although she would miss the diamonds. Looking into his sweet, lovely blue eyes in that final moment, she'd wished she could stay the course with the marriage, but she knows her future lies with M.

The very thought of M sends shivers through her. From the moment they met—sitting next to each other last February at a dinner party given by the St. John Hutchinsons for Barbara's twenty-first—she'd felt an inexorable pull toward him. It began with his magnetic, powerful views on politics and the flaccid state in which Great Britain found itself. They were kindred spirits on that topic, maintaining that the current political parties and the men behind them were ineffectual and that a shake-up was needed. By the end of the conversation, she believed that Oswald Mosley was the man for the job, and told him so. And by the time he'd begun organizing the British Union of Fascists last summer, he'd won her over—mind and body. The memory of an illicit encounter they'd shared upstairs during a fête champêtre she and Bryan had hosted at Biddlesden flashes through her mind, and she feels a pleasant warmth pass though her.

Diana returns to the sunny parlor in her new home, where she's seated close to Unity. She's glad Hamish finally called, as she'd begun to tire of the way Nancy was circling round and round the topic of her divorce, finally asking about M in the cagiest way. Diana felt like telling Nancy that there was really no need for circumspection—Diana's devotion to M was no secret—and that she knew Muv and Farve had sent Nancy as a last-ditch effort to save her from social suicide. Their puppetry was plain enough. Why they thought Nancy would succeed, when the unified front of Farve and Bryan's father confronting M already failed, as had Tom's gentle pleading on behalf of Bryan, was anyone's guess. But Nancy usually avoided the entanglements of their parents' puppet strings with a deft hand, so she supposed Nancy was here as a show of support. Diana thought that was perfectly topping of her, not that it would make a whit of a difference.

Turning to Unity, Diana whispers, "Nancy thinks she's here to rescue me from myself."

A snort that Diana supposes is a chuckle escapes from Unity's mouth. She tries not to grimace at her little sister's ungainly ways.

"Do you think she would have come to Eatonry if she'd had any inkling of your plan?" Unity asks with an expression that could only be described as a sneer. Diana can see that Unity loves being in on the secret scheme for today, a revelation that only happened because she unexpectedly appeared on Diana's doorstep an hour before Nancy's planned arrival.

"Oh, I doubt it. She won't like the manner in which I'm rescuing her instead today—at least not at first. She'll thank me in the long run," Diana answers. Even though it's unseemly to admit, Diana has quite enjoyed this dash of subterfuge. How *tiring* it is to always be the passive, womanly ideal. She wants to *feel* and live and do, not simply sit and receive admiration, as Bryan was wont to bestow.

Then Diana hears a scream. She and Unity rise and race toward the telephone room. Diana hopes she's done the right thing by Nancy. She simply couldn't sit by and let Hamish keep stringing her along. The excuses for setting a wedding date served his purpose well, to be sure, but harmed Nancy immeasurably, especially as she neared thirty without a wedding ring. Hamish's delays were the perfect blind behind which he could hide his string of relationships with men.

Nancy has been deluding herself for years that Hamish's sexual predilections were something he could change on a whim. In fact, they are utterly unlike their brother Tom's dalliances with his classmates at Eton, fleeting and specific to those strange boarding-school circumstances, and Tom has now plunged into a series of flings with married and single women alike. Nancy deserves better than Hamish can give her, and in keeping with Diana's awakening, she cannot allow her sister to languish any longer. So Diana met with Hamish and insisted he break it off with Nancy using the fiction of another engagement, as Diana knew it would be the only explanation with enough finality for Nancy to let go.

When she and Unity reach the telephone room, the door is closed, but they can hear Nancy shriek through it. "What? Who are you marrying?" Her voice is shrill, and Diana feels momentarily sick. Has she done the right thing? She's ill-used to doubting herself, but Nancy's reaction gives her pause.

There is a brief silence, then Nancy yells again. "After all the years I waited for you, Hamish! I passed on other opportunities so we could be together. And now this!"

Then the telephone room grows eerily silent—until Diana hears a thud. She feels a rare wave of panic. Is Nancy okay in there? Is she upset over the loss of Hamish or the long, fruitless wait for him, the lost chances? What has Diana done?

Diana reaches for the doorknob to the telephone room but finds that it is locked. "Nancy? Nancy?" she calls out as she pounds on the door. "Open up!"

Nothing.

Unity takes a turn trying to rattle the door open and calling to Nancy—to no avail. Diana yells for the maid. "Do you know if there's a key to the telephone room door?"

As the maid pores through the kitchen cabinets, Diana and Unity scour the drawers in the drawing room, foyer, and dining room, without luck. After rooting through the library, Diana finally finds an enormous ring crammed with keys. "One of these *has* to work," she says to Unity.

Diana tries seventeen keys before the lock catches, and the door creaks open. There, her brilliant, confidant sister, always ready with a quip and impervious to the views and jeers of others, sits crumpled on the floor. Her face is wet with tears even though she's no longer crying, but that isn't what gives Diana a start. Her already pale complexion has turned ashen-white, and she is staring at the wall, trancelike.

Unity and Diana crouch down on the floor next to her and wrap their arms around her. Nancy neither bristles at their touch nor issues one of her famous gibes. She remains uncharacteristically silent, which may be the most troubling thing of all. Diana vows to keep her here at Eatonry until she's back to being Nancy again. A stronger, better version of herself, in fact.

Most of all, though, Diana *does* hope Nancy never finds out the undercover hand she's played in this, even if it's absolutely the best thing for her. Or if she does, that Nancy forgives her.

# CHAPTER SIX

# UNITY

*January 24, 1933*
*London, England*

U NITY'S ARMS ARE WRAPPED AROUND THE BONY SHOUL-
ders of her oldest sister. *How spindly Nancy seems*, Unity
thinks. One tight squeeze of Unity's strong arms and Nancy
would snap. Realizing that this thought is inappropriate, she
muses instead on what a relief it is—for once—not to be the
object of everyone's derision. Today it is the snide Nancy—
the one who mocks Unity's crushes and her social skills, while
Diana always listens patiently to Unity—who is subjected to
their pity. And Unity's mood lifts.

"Naunce," Diana asks sweetly, "will you allow us to take
you into the library? And get you a cup of tea? It will help
dry up these floods."

Leaning on her sisters, Nancy rises from the floor of the telephone room. As they stand, Unity hears a slight ripping sound. Did
that come from her dress? She hopes not; she'd borrowed it from
Diana today. The exquisite blue tweed dress shot through with
metallic threads does fit, if barely. When she tried it on—swiveling
this way and that—she'd hoped her eyes looked as silver-blue as

Diana's or that it somehow helped her approximate her sister's beauty. While she didn't see any evidence of such a transformation, she knows she'll keep trying, as she had earlier today by experimenting with Diana's makeup. After all, without fashioning a winning feature or witty banter for herself, how will she ever stand out among her many sisters? Other than for her tallness and, some would say, peculiar manner.

After Diana calls out for one of the maids to bring tea, they settle Nancy in that same upholstered chair in which she'd been sitting before the call. Diana scoots another chair close to Nancy and sits next to her, holding her hand. Whispering consoling and encouraging words to their distraught sister, Diana has her attention focused exclusively on Nancy. And Unity does not like it one bit. She didn't come to Eatonry to be marginalized.

She'd much prefer to have Diana all to herself. Barring that, she'd accept the ministrations of Diana's precious M. Just last week when she'd visited, Mosley had been standing at the bottom of the stairs, and he'd greeted her with a "Hello, Fascist." Unity knew that this was a high compliment from the founder of the new British Union of Fascists and took it as such. Given her own long-standing belief in the fascist political system and the view she shared with Diana that Mosley was the man the nation needed, she was, in fact, deeply moved. But because Unity still hadn't settled on what to call him—there was no etiquette rule book dictating how to address a sister's lover—she simply offered greetings.

"I have something for you," he'd said, reaching into his jacket pocket.

A present? Unity couldn't think of the last time someone had surprised her with a gift. She went down the final step to the foyer, took the wrapped parcel from him, and tore it open. A gold pin lay inside bearing the emblem of the British Union of Fascists, or BUF. Not only had she been accepted as a member into the BUF, but she'd been given elevated status, as signified by the gold pin. She was momentarily speechless, and when she recovered her voice, she screeched in delight.

"May I?" Mosley asked, reaching for the pin.

Not trusting herself to speak coherent words, Unity nodded. He drew close to affix the pin on her lapel. She smelled his cologne and observed the minuscule stubble on his chin, just below his mustache. Heady from proximity to Mosley—who Diana occasionally referred to as the Leader—in that moment, she'd actually felt like Diana.

But today, there will be no Mosley, no compliments, and no little gifts. Only Nancy. Sharp, uppity Nancy now morphed into sad, pathetic Nancy. Unity will have to console herself with not being the odd man out for once and wait for Diana's attentions to shift back to her. By the looks of things, it might be an interminable wait.

Then to Unity's great surprise, Nancy leans over to the chair where Unity sits at a slight distance from her sisters. Nancy squeezes Unity's hand and whispers, "Thank you, dearest. You've been ever so kind as well, and it means the world."

This unexpected affection stuns Unity into silence. Once she's recovered her thoughts if not her words, she wonders. Might this softening mark a metamorphosis in their relationship? A harbinger of a new closeness—in sisterly intimacy and maybe other sorts of kinship? Perhaps Nancy might even be brought round to a unifying cause, she thinks with a private smile, as her very own secret plan takes hold of her imagination.

# CHAPTER SEVEN
# NANCY

*April 28, 1933*
*London, England*

I GLANCE OVER AT PETER. THERE, READING THE PAPER IN MY favorite chair in Diana's parlor, behind a swoop of dark-blond hair that falls over his brow, sits my *fiancé*. How I love to say the word; I even enjoy thinking it. And I know that, in part, I have Diana to thank for this marvelous turn of events. If she hadn't coddled me at the Eatonry for a month—even assigning me my own bedroom—until I could stop moping about over Hamish, and then practically forced me back out into society, I would have never met Peter Rodd, banker son of the diplomat Lord Rennell, so brilliant that he actually studied at Balliol College at Oxford. We would have never become engaged.

After a month of despair pondering a life without Hamish, then fury at his cowardliness and his utter waste of my years, and finally relief, I began to see that I'd been deluding myself about him for some time—with thoughts that he truly loved me, that we could have a life together. Hamish would only ever love himself and, fleetingly, those men with whom he dallied. Never, ever me.

I am that pitiable woman no longer. Engaged to my social equal who might be more erudite than myself—in spite of his lofty Balliol education, I like to tease—I will no longer sit on that dark, dusty shelf where those of us that don't get engaged during our debutante seasons are relegated. And somehow, with Peter, I no longer have my old fears about marriage, that I'll get lost in the monotony of the nannies, cooks, and house-keeping, the schedule of children, and the moods of a husband. Perhaps that dread stemmed more from imagining marriage to Hamish than the reality of matrimony, I now think. This marriage *will* be a happy one, of that I plan on making certain.

In my quieter moments, when I'm alone in my flat with my bulldogs, Milly and Lottie, on my lap, a rogue thought sneaks in. Is the joy I feel about my marriage to Peter—in part—because it's my first triumph over the usually lauded Diana? Since she left Bryan for Mosley, she's no longer the toast of London but a pariah, while I'm being feted left and right for my engage-ment; quite the change from the indifference or peculiar looks I received when I announced I'd accepted Hamish's proposal all those years ago. Even Muv and Farve are pleased with me, although I know Peter isn't their ideal marital candidate. But they do believe he's a whole sight better than Hamish.

I hear Diana's light footsteps treading down the front stairs, followed in quick succession by the clop of Unity's. These days, they seem to travel as a pair, at least when Mosley hasn't beckoned Diana. If only Muv knew how flagrantly Unity defies her edict.

"Prod?" I ask. In Mitford tradition, my sisters and I had fashioned a nickname for Peter, and the shortening of Peter and Rodd to Prod was too delightfully easy and fun to say.

He looks up from his newspaper. "Yes, darling?"

"Ready to go?"

Peter leaps to his feet, and I think how dashing he looks in his black shirt. Sauntering over to him, I run a finger along his lapel. "You look so delicious in this uniform we might need to attend rallies more frequently."

He chuckles and says, "I could say the same about you."

As he leans in for a kiss, we hear Diana call from the foyer, "The car awaits!"

We pull away from each other, and I call back, "A moment, Bodley! I need to powder my nose." Then I whisper to Peter, "Pour us two stiff drinks for the car ride. I think we'll need them."

Unity yells back. "Heavens, Lady, there's no need to powder your nose. We are going to a political rally, not a ball." After my recovery from despair, Unity stopped the tender use of Nancy or Naunce for me and reverted more often to the nickname of "Lady," which she generally uses if I peeve her in some way. Occasionally I wonder what she finds offensive about me these days.

I disregard Unity and spend a moment before the mirror, powdering my nose and reapplying my lipstick. Then the four of us—all in black shirts combined with various elements of our normal attire—squeeze into the car hired by Mosley for us. Everyone looks positively dour, so I try to lighten the mood by saying, "Who could have guessed how well black becomes us!"

Diana shoots me a disapproving look. "Naunce, the black shirt isn't worn because the color flatters us. BUF members wear the black shirt because it is the symbol of fascism. It allows us to recognize each other and reinforce our belief that all men are the same regardless of wealth or social status." She doesn't mention the "coincidence" that the BUF's uniform is the same as that of Mosley's hero, Benito Mussolini.

My God, she sounds like Mosley. Over the past few months, I've spent hours and hours at Eatonry with the man, during which time I've become overly familiar with his views on fascism and the state of politics in Great Britain and on the continent. As Mosley likes to explain it, he founded the BUF to bring the country into the present by shifting away from the economic and social dysfunction of democracy to the more effective model of an autocracy. Mosley holds the governments of Italy and Germany in high regard, viewing them as excellent examples of what our country could become if ruled properly. In fact, he has just returned to London after a stint in Italy *with* Mussolini. Whenever Diana listens to Mosley drone on and on about his political plans, her eyes positively shine with awe. It is unsettling.

While I firmly believe that our country needs a change— we've got three million unemployed people, a financial crisis, and communism nipping at our heels, for goodness' sake— Mosley's views seem rather extreme. I'm more central in my thinking, and I'm not certain I'd have agreed to attend Mosley's big BUF rally tonight if Peter hadn't been so curious. And if Diana herself hadn't implored me to join her.

A man outfitted entirely in black greets our car when we arrive at Albert Hall and escorts us to front-row seats with militaristic precision. As we settle onto our chairs, I glance around at the other audience members. It is a veritable sea of black. But that isn't the only commonality among the rally-goers, by all accounts a fairly middle-class group but reportedly gaining in acceptance with high society. The audience is populated primarily by ruddy-cheeked young men, shot through with the occasional grim-faced, middle-aged man and the odd exuberant, youthful woman.

"Not what I expected," Peter whispers to me, having had the same look-round as me.

"No, they're not a pack of hooligans," I whisper back. I'd expected rabble-rousers.

"Shh," Diana hisses at us, as Mosley strides under a canopy of raised arms onto the stage. Her face is shining as she looks up at him.

His supporters break out into raucous applause at the very sight of him, their virile, dark-haired leader who sports a matching mustache. I even hear a few chants of "BUF," after which I notice several officials are dispatched throughout the crowds, presumably to ensure order.

Mosley stops strutting and stands with his hands on his hips staring out at the crowd, a stance which emphasizes his barrel-like chest. I'm guessing that his desire to emphasize his strong, almost leonine physique is the reason he selected a close-fitting black turtleneck for his "black shirt," instead of wearing a more formal button-down version like the rest of us.

I am mesmerized watching him move across the stage, intermittently pointing his finger and stomping his foot when he talks with his acolytes, as he readies to give his speech. This is a Mosley I haven't witnessed before, and for the first time, I have an inkling of what draws Diana to him. Of what draws *all* these followers to him.

Yet as he continues, his calculated movements begin to seem overdone. Suddenly all this orchestrated pomp and circumstance feels silly, and I begin to giggle. Diana stares over me, her lips a thin line and her brow furrowed and angry, as I desperately try to stop laughing. But then I catch a glimpse of Unity, and I no longer have to work at suppressing my mirth. Because the look of abject devotion on her face sends shivers through me, and fear takes its place.

# CHAPTER EIGHT
# DIANA

*April 28, 1933*
*London, England*

$M$ *WILL BE SO PLEASED*, DIANA THINKS AS SHE STARES UP at the stage from her front-row seat. Not only is she bringing the ever-loyal Unity to the rally as a family representative, but she has Nancy and Peter in tow as well. If only Muv and Farve would relent and meet with her and Mosley, she *knows* she could bring them round. They would see what she sees: that M knows the answers to the pressing questions of their age, how to address the inadequacies of their current government and society. For now, the only reaction she gets from Farve when she proposes such a meeting is an angry grumble, if he'll even take her calls, that is.

Her life before M seems positively frivolous. All glitter but no gold—excepting Jonathan and Desmond, of course. M has given her purpose beyond her wildest imaginings, and she is willing to do whatever she can to help him and his cause, the BUF. In fact, she'll do *anything* at all.

While she's seen the Leader give plenty of speeches before, it's never been on this scale and never with Nancy. Part of her wants to show off her lover's power and magnetism to her eldest, hardest-to-please sister. Probably some sort of effort to offset any residual reservations Nancy has about Diana's decision to divorce Bryan. Certainly Nancy's own happiness with Peter has softened her harsher views on M. Mind you, if Diana felt she could speak frankly, she would vocalize her own hesitations about the hapless and quite banal Peter. He may be clever, but his lothario reputation does not exactly recommend itself to a happy marital state. But such frankness isn't her right; she forfeited many prerogatives when she left Bryan.

A band is situated to the left of the stage, and as it begins to play as a prelude to M's speech, the rhythmic thump of the drums sends Diana's heart beating. Why are her nerves aflutter, when she barely felt a pang of anxiety over falling for M and leaving Bryan? Is it seeing her lover on this vast stage? Or is it the sense of being swept up into something larger than herself—into history?

Surrendering to the sensation, Diana shivers as she watches M march around the stage, a man of action unlike anyone else she knows, delighted that M's wife, Cimmie, chose not to attend this rally. It's the only way Diana can come. M's stride is sure and confident, never mind that thousands of eyes are upon him; he seems not only at ease in front of multitudes but in complete command of them. Longing surges through her, and she thinks about how his expert hands have touched every single part of her, exploring and sparking to life areas that had otherwise been asleep.

Is it his sexual prowess that ties her inextricably to him? Or is it the power and purpose that courses through him and reaches out to her, like the tentacles of an octopus? She doesn't know, can only acknowledge that his pull on her is undeniable. Even since their first night together, she has given herself completely to him and his cause, forcing herself not to ponder where she ranks in his life.

It hasn't been easy. Diana is used to being the center of attention, particularly with the man in her life. Bryan's existence had revolved around her entirely. Unlike every couple she knew, they'd lunched together at the Savoy nearly every workday, and even at balls, where it wasn't deemed appropriate for a husband and wife to stay by each other's sides, she'd catch Bryan staring at her from across the room. This unbridled adoration had been alluring at first, but as the years went on, it became stifling. Perhaps that's why the challenge of M appeals to her. He doesn't belong to her, and he's made plain that he never will.

His wife, Cimmie, will always have the official place at his side, he has told Diana, and this embarrassing fact was made plain to all the world when Cimmie accompanied him to Rome earlier this month and photographs of M and his wife alongside Benito Mussolini on the balcony of the Palazzo Venezia appeared in every newspaper. Even Cimmie's sisters—Irene and Alexandra, known as Baba—appear to have a greater hold on M than does Diana sometimes, and yet, this sacrifice is one Diana is willing to make for whatever time he can offer her. And who knows, perhaps when he sees her staring at him from the audience, cheering him on, he'll be swayed in her favor over Cimmie's.

The hall quiets as the band finishes, and M approaches the microphone, a single spotlight shining down on him. Diana's vision narrows, and her eyes meet his. For a brief moment, it is as if they are alone, bodies entwined, gazing into each other's faces, in her bed. He nods at her and then begins.

"Ladies and gentlemen, we are gathered here tonight to hear the policies of *British* fascism," M calls out, sending a very different sort of shiver down her spine than usual. She knows every word he's about to deliver; they rehearsed this speech together. And yet, on this stage, before this crowd, in his thunderous voice, the words sound entirely new. They enthrall her all over again, and the crowd along with her.

The rally-goers cheer, and Diana finds herself yelling alongside them, much to the raised eyebrows of Nancy. How wondrous it feels to lower one's defenses and get swept up in the fervor of the movement, particularly since M is at its center.

"The time has come for us to denounce those so-called leaders who blundered us into the crises of 1914 and 1931—squandering the promise of our beloved Great Britain. It is time for new hands to lift our dishonored flag and make it glorious again," he continues. For a solid thirty minutes, Mosley captures the attention of his followers with proclamations of how *his* authoritarian executive powers—should the BUF become the government—would address these crises by putting into action heavy discipline over society and the economy. He seems certain of the success of his course, destined for it. Diana is, of course, convinced and cannot imagine that anyone would feel otherwise.

Then he says the words he whispered on their first night together. But tonight she hears them anew and differently: "Let us begin our great adventure."

# CHAPTER NINE

# UNITY

*April 28, 1933*
*London, England*

How can Nancy and Peter giggle and sip at the drinks they brought while Mosley speaks? Unity is so tired of her family's political apathy, except Diana, of course, and Decca, who, for some ungodly reason, has decided that communism will be the savior of the English people, not fascism. Why do the others not realize that the world is on the precipice of change, that society as they know it will be decimated when that metamorphosis happens? Unity is determined to be at the center of the transformation, leading it and not allowing it to lead her.

Staring around the room at row after row of able-bodied, young fascist men, she tugs at her black blouse, the one she purchased specifically for this BUF rally; the front needs to be tucked in just so to emphasize her lanky physique. Muv wants her to spend the little money she has at her disposal on gowns for the season, but Unity knows that those pounds—their value decreasing rapidly in these depressed times—are better spent on her political endeavors. This movement holds the key to her future. She'll never shine in the social season, but here, she might just find a place.

Hers isn't a plan that transpired overnight, like that of Diana who has only recently "awoken" to the fact that something must be done about their country and that fascism is the way to do it. Unity's political dreams have been long in the making. Ever since she and Decca shared a bedroom at Swinbrook, their civic views had begun to form, perhaps being shaped in reaction to the other's perspective. As Decca became more and more strident in her passion for communism, Unity had felt certain that the answer to their country's ills lay in fascism, with her two heroes in particular, Mussolini and Hitler. *Only a firm, ingenious leader can direct Great Britain to success*, she would find herself yelling at Decca and then adding, *We can't possibly rely on the whims of the people. They can only be trusted to have freedom within the control of the state.*

At one point, the situation became so acrimonious that the sisters physically divided their bedroom in two with a line drawn down the middle—one side for communism and one for fascism—and each sister decorated accordingly. Decca had her communist library, a bust of Lenin, and copies of the *Daily Worker*, while Unity had Fascist insignias, photos of Mussolini and Hitler, an emblem of the new German swastika, and a record collection of Nazi and Italian youth songs. All this despite Farve's famous hatred of "Huns," his moniker for Germans since he fought them in the Great War, and his periodic orders for Unity to remove the Nazi items.

Some would call Decca a ballroom communist, but Unity respects her seriousness—any commitment to the nation's political future is better than none. And despite their disagreement, Unity adores her spirited younger sister and has always found their disputes to be more noble than the frivolous scrapes her other sisters got into, over clothes or hairpins or books. She and Decca might be political enemies, but in all other respects, they are the truest of friends.

As Mosley continues his speech, Unity takes the opportunity to study the crowd. Amid the black-shirted men, several of whom she gives lingering glances, a few women are scattered. Like their male counterparts, they sport black shirts in varying styles—some with rounded collars, a few with men's ties—but their seriousness is uniform. As she considers whether these women could be her tribe, more like her than the often-petty familial clan with which she's been saddled, one woman draws her attention.

Rather than black, this young woman has chosen a red cardigan. *Idiot girl,* Unity thinks. *How could she wear red, of all colors, at a fascist rally.* Red, the color of communism, the veritable antithesis of fascism. Could the girl really be ignorant of what she is signaling to the rest of the audience? Is she not fearful of the reaction she might elicit? The girl turns, and Unity nearly gasps at the striking resemblance to her sister Decca. What on earth would she be doing here? Unity shakes her head; she must have made a mistake. Muv would never allow her to attend a fascist rally, and Unity cannot imagine how she'd manage to sneak here.

But then she loses sight of the woman as Mosley's speech reaches its rousing crescendo. Defying the militia patrolling the aisles, a few bold men strike matches, and in the flickering light with Mosley's voice at full power, the space feels almost sacred.

An electric current seems to pass through the crowd, his res-
onant tone practically vibrating in the hall into her very being.
Unity is rapt at Mosley's words, even though she's read them in
his manifesto and heard them espoused at the Eatonry before.
But here, those same phrases seem to come alive. *Imagine*, she
thinks, *how mesmerizing such sentiments would be in Hitler's
expert, hypnotic telling.*

"I come to you with a new and revolutionary conception of
politics, economics, and life itself—" Mosley's voice booms, and
Unity can think of nothing but the vital role that she wants to
play. That she *will* play.

Destiny is pulling her toward that role. Destiny connected Diana to Mosley, revealing the fascist cause to her sister
through him. Destiny then brought Unity into contact with
Mosley and into the inner circle of British fascism. And soon
destiny will call her to leave behind this anemic British fascism
and to insinuate herself into the robust beating heart of the
cause—Germany.

# CHAPTER TEN

# NANCY

*September 3, 1933*
*London, England*

WHY DID I HARBOR THE TINY INKLING OF HOPE THAT my sisters would sacrifice a morsel of their own pleasure to help celebrate and plan my wedding to Peter? Why had I allowed the kindness and generosity of Diana when I was mourning Hamish to taint my thinking? *Stupid me*, I think, to have believed I could count on Diana, Unity, and to a lesser extent the rural-loving Pamela, to fete me in these last months of my engagement and usher me into the marital status for which I'm long overdue.

Instead, I'm left only with Muv, because Decca and Debo are too young for the role and Pamela has strangely volunteered to manage Bryan's three-hundred-and-fifty-acre dairy farm, despite the fact that Diana and Bryan are divorced, largely because she'd rather be off in the country by herself than anywhere else. I confess to never really understanding Pamela's rural bent, one of the reasons we occasionally call her "Woman" for all her womanly virtues, adoration of the country life among them. Whatever her reason, Pamela would certainly rather be at Bryan's dairy farm than at home with Muv and Farve. Diana and Unity, for reasons best known to themselves, felt compelled to travel to Germany.

"Darling," Peter calls over to me, holding up a piece of ornately flowered china. Of all the porcelain on display at Asprey, why on earth would he single out that plate?

"Yes?" I call back, trying not to wince at the atrocious piece. Surely, he's not asking me if we should select *that* as our pattern. Did he grab it because it was the easiest to reach on the shelf, and he's eager to get the cocktails I promised as a reward for this chore? It is the sort of Victorian china one might have found in the cupboards of Grandmother, the Lady Clementine Ogilvy, before she passed away and her belongings were scattered among her descendants.

"What do you think of this one?"

Oh no, that is precisely the question he's asking. "Honestly?" I venture.

"Always," he answers with that wry, handsome smile I fell in love with, although I know he doesn't actually want honesty in *all* topics. No man does. But, perhaps in this one matter, I can be frank. After all, thanks to the generosity of one of Peter's aunts who offered to buy our china as a wedding present, I'll be staring at these plates for the rest of my life. I don't want to wince every time I sit down to tea.

"I find it extremely disagreeable," I pronounce.

Peter guffaws, and I am pleased. My fiancé understands and appreciates my humor, something very few men outside my inner circle of friends seem to do. Most men, in fact, find my cleverness unpalatable. I lean over and kiss him—right here in Asprey—considering what a wise, if swift decision I made to accept his proposal. Even if it was meant as a bit of a jest when he first asked.

"Nancy," Muv interrupts us, tucking a dark curl back into her hat and smoothing the slightly Victorian ruffles at the bosom of her blouse. When she doesn't speak for a moment, I realize that she's signaling her displeasure at our display of affection. After all the fruitless waiting I did for Hamish, why doesn't she seem more pleased at my happiness? I would have guessed she'd be delighted that I'll no longer be an old maid. Is it just her general displeasure with me? She certainly dislikes the modest success I've had with my two lighthearted novels that explore the conflicts between the Bright Young Things and the older generation—*Highland Fling* about a Scottish house party and *Christmas Pudding* about a holiday spent in the Cotswolds—because she finds the similarity between certain characters and people we know to be unseemly. Especially my thinly veiled depiction of her.

There's no point in addressing her reaction head-on, so I use my well-practiced tactic of diversion. I point to an elegant, simple art deco set in the next aisle and remark, "Now that's rather marvelous."

———

China sorted and cocktails imbibed, Muv and I say our fare-wells to Peter and leave him in the bar at the Savoy. We have an appointment in Mayfair at Norman Hartnell, the designer whose modern styles I admire, particularly the way he utilizes structure as a base for his gowns and then overlays them with romantic, interesting details. There's a gown I'd like to try on, and I can't risk any bad luck at having my groom see the dress before the big day. Bad luck with men I've had in droves already.

We step into the stunning first-floor salon, all glass and mirrors in the art moderne style. I've already instructed the salesgirl to hang the gown in the dressing room so I can surprise Muv with it when I step out already in full regalia. This approach is my best chance at success, I've found. If I allow her to glimpse the gown I've already landed upon while she peruses others, she'll find any number of reasons to critique the one I've selected. And I need to curry favor, since she and Farve are covering the cost of the gown and reception—ceremony at St. John's Church on Smith Square followed by breakfast at the London town house my parents had leased for Unity's season, Rutland Gate.

While a salesgirl helps me into the chiffon, bias-cut confection, elegant and simple except for the crisscrossed bodice, Muv settles on the silk sofa, accepts a cordial from the salesgirl, and asks, "Will Peter be all right to return to the office?"

"What do you mean?" I answer, half-listening. I'm more interested in the gown than her question.

"He was well into his cups when we left him at the Savoy." Her voice has a pinched and prim quality, one that my sisters and I mimic when we're on our own. I am suddenly on high alert, as I now see where this line of inquiry is going.

"Nothing to worry about, Muv," I say. "He doesn't start his new position until after our honeymoon in Rome. No office to return to at the moment."

As soon as I say the words, I know I've made a mistake. I

hadn't told her that Peter left his job at the Bank of England and that he wouldn't resume work until January when we are back in London. He'd had a mad scramble to secure another post after he stomped off the job one afternoon.

"New position? What are you talking about? Doesn't he work at a bank?"

I force my voice to sound bright and cheery. "Oh, I didn't tell you about the opportunity he got at Hamburg Bank? It was simply *too* divine to pass up, and Hamburg even offered to let him start after the honeymoon!" While I couldn't wait to be married, in some ways, I was actually more excited about our honeymoon plans to stay at Peter's parents' apartment on the Palazzo Guilia in Rome than actually setting up house.

Muv doesn't reply to me directly, but I can hear a gentle grumble from outside the dressing room. Did I hear her mutter that she hopes this "job gap" doesn't devolve into another unpleasant conversation with Peter's parents over allowances? I almost felt sick listening to both sets of our parents haggle over who could pay the least, like Peter and I were a carpet at an Egyptian market they were hoping to get cheap.

*Time to distract her with this breathtaking gown,* I think. I step out of the dressing room and stand in front of Muv. Catching a glimpse of myself in the mirror behind her, I turn this way and that, pleased with the silhouette of the gown and the way the shimmering ivory shade enhances my black hair and eyes rather than clashing with them.

Muv's eyes narrow as she studies the gown and me in it. "Money isn't *that* tight, Nancy," she finally says.

I recoil at the oblique insult. "What on earth do you mean?" I ask, even though I know I shouldn't.

"It's awfully plain for a wedding dress."

I feel like crying. For once, I wish she'd consider my feelings, consider that I do indeed have feelings. Does she assume that because I'm quick with the barbs that nothing barbs me? When we'd searched for a wedding gown for Diana, Muv had been the essence of contentment and joy, complimenting my beautiful sister at every turn. Then again, there had been an audience watching Diana, since Bryan's mother and several Guinness cousins had also been in attendance.

I desperately wish Diana was here to temper Muv. The presence of my littlest sisters Decca and Debo could have helped soften her reaction as well, but they'd been prohibited from joining us since Muv and I are shopping for the intimate items of my trousseau afterward. Pamela had begged off, claiming she was too busy at the farm. And even though Unity's odd, unexpected sullenness can make for strange company, her buffering presence would have been preferential to *this*.

What is so important that Diana and Unity had to spend September in Munich?

# CHAPTER ELEVEN
# DIANA

*September 3, 1933*
*Nuremberg, Germany*

THE SYNCHRONOUS CLIP OF THOUSANDS OF BOOTS REVER-
berates inside her like the beating of her heart. Diana rides
the sound like a wave until it crests, with a roar of "Heil Hitler."
Breathless, she stares out at the *Parteitag*, the Nazi Party con-
vention, feeling alive with the promise of this unique German
form of fascism. *What stories I'll have to share with M*, she thinks.
If she is speaking to him on her return, that is.

Standing next to Unity on a stage reserved for the thousand
special guests, Diana watches as uniformed troops parade in
front of them in perfect unison. Even a group of brown-shirted
boys called Hitler Youth marches in step, and she is awestruck
at the sight. Unity reaches over and squeezes her hand, sharing
her amazement.

"How many soldiers are here?" she asks tall, square-jawed
Putzi Hanfstaengl, foreign press secretary to the new German
chancellor, Adolf Hitler, and the gentleman who invited them
to this event.

"Four hundred thousand," he answers, his English

impeccable. He'd told her that his mother was American and he'd gone to Harvard University in the States.

"I wouldn't have thought Nuremberg could serve as a base for so many soldiers." When she and Unity arrived a few days ago from Munich, Diana had been delighted by the ancient Bavarian town, with its peaked, red-tiled roofs and antiquated stone churches. This charm was enhanced by the fact that nearly every street sign and every storefront bore the red Nazi banners such that the town looked as if it had been wrapped up like a Christmas present. It was impossible to believe that this country could have ever been at war with Great Britain, that Farve himself had fought here.

"It doesn't. They were shipped from all over Germany for the rally by special train cars. All to celebrate the glory of our chancellor's victory," he says, a note of triumph in his voice. Hanfstaengl had been waiting for this moment almost as long as Hitler himself. After all, he and his family had sheltered Hitler after the 1923 putsch and stood by his side during his imprisonment, and when Hitler began to plot his rise, Hanfstaengl helped fund it and introduced him to all the right people in German society.

Shaking her head in astonishment at the effort, Diana gazes across the thousands of precisely arranged soldiers, appearing from this vantage point like the tiny metal toy soldiers Tom played with in his youth. Although, Diana knows these soldiers are no toys. They are living emblems of Hitler's power, and they make Mosley's BUF rallies seem like the efforts of a child. Not that she would *ever* say such a thing to her beloved.

*Thank God Unity had begged to go to Munich*, Diana thinks,

*and not only to witness this.* Diana could not have tolerated staying in London a minute longer. Ever since Cimmie died in
May—from a shocking, unstoppable infection after a burst
appendix—M has been inconsolable. While Diana understood
from the beginning that Cimmie would remain his wife, she'd
forced herself to believe that it was in name only. But the depth
of M's grief was astonishing, and Diana came to understand
that the depths of his feelings for Cimmie had been as well.
Where did this leave Diana?

Keeping her demeanor serene and even as always, Diana
had given Mosley a wide berth most of the summer, making
herself available for him when he asked but never requesting
more than he gave her. She maintained this approach even
when he privately confessed the guilt he felt over his many
betrayals of his late wife, and he alternated between this dour,
remorseful state and frenzied bouts of work for the BUF. But
when she learned that he was consoling himself not only with
her but with Cimmie's sister Baba, who'd had a romantic infat-
uation with M for some time—and worse, that he planned on
spending August on a motoring tour through France with Baba
while his three children holidayed with nannies, even though
M swore he would keep their relationship platonic—well, she
needed to get far, far away. Mosley needed to be reminded that
she was not a woman with whom one trifled.

Her initial encounter with Hanfstaengl in July came at a
most fortuitous time. She'd walked into a dinner at the home of
Mrs. Richard Guinness, a distant cousin of Bryan's, to discover
a man at the piano so enormous that he dwarfed the instrument
almost comically. But there was nothing comical about his talent.

Strains of Brahms drew her to his side, and when he finished, Mrs. Guinness began peppering him with questions about the Nazi regime. In a booming voice that matched his stature, he replied, "I am here to answer all your questions about Nazism in Germany and dispel all those rumors you've heard about violence and our treatment of the Jewish people. I formally invite everyone here to be my guest in Germany and witness for yourselves the wonderful changes that Chancellor Hitler is making!"

After that pronouncement and sweeping invitation, Mrs. Guinness introduced Hanfstaengl to Diana as a personal friend of Hitler's. He said that he'd heard about Diana and had been hoping to meet her. Diana's stomach flipped, wondering which of the many horrible rumors he'd been told, but he simply mentioned that he'd overheard she was a believer in fascism as well.

By the end of their conversation, he had extended a personal invitation for her to attend the first rally of Hitler's chancellorship in September as a special guest, along with an introduction to Hitler; she must see for herself what is happening in Germany, he'd said. Diana knew that M would be rife with jealousy over such a meeting, both personally and professionally, and decided that it might be just the thing. Unity's desperation to make the Munich trip was the final impetus, and when Bryan took the children for a summer holiday, Diana made plans for her and Unity to travel to Munich.

———

Diana stares over at Unity, whose eyes are shining. Already an ardent fascist, Unity does not need any further convincing

about the rightness of Nazi politics. But Diana can see from
the light in her sister's eyes that her appreciation of German
fascism goes beyond mere acceptance.

"The only thing that would make this day more perfect
would be to meet Chancellor Hitler," Unity muses dreamily.

Diana does not comment. Unity has already asked
Hanfstaengl once whether they'd have the opportunity to
meet Hitler, and Diana does not want to encourage her to
inquire again. When Diana accepted the invitation to the
rally, she imagined Hitler would be readily available for an
easy introduction, but now that she's observed the hundreds
of thousands of soldiers here today and that Hitler—who
she's only seen from a distance—is always heavily guarded,
she realizes how hard it will be to get access to him. Not to
mention, she and Unity are the only English people in the
special guests section, and she doesn't want to call attention
to their presence any more than Unity already has. The Great
War wasn't that long ago, and tempers may still be piqued
over losses and sacrifices that the war entailed. Farve certainly
loathes Germany with such vehemence that the Great War
could have happened yesterday.

But Hanfstaengl has heard Unity. "The chancellor will be
standing on this very stage, at this very podium"—he points to
the dais—"within the hour."

As Unity turns toward their host, Diana sees a familiar
ferocity on her face. Before she can intercede, Unity asks, "You
aren't playing with me, are you?"

Hanfstaengl bestows a beneficent smile upon her, and then
his expression turns serious. "About the chancellor, I never

joke. And, should the opportunity arise to make the introduction"—he hands Unity a perfectly pressed linen handkerchief—"I might suggest that you remove your lipstick. You and
your sister are two perfect specimens of Aryan womanhood,
but our chancellor does prefer a natural look—only the natural
adornment brought about by sun and sport."

As Unity presses the cloth to her lips, momentarily chas-
tened, Diana wonders if that is why she and her sister have
been invited to this momentous occasion—to prove that even
English "specimens of Aryan womanhood" are adherents of
Nazism. Just then, six decorated soldiers march onto the stage,
clearing a wide swath among the "special guests." Into that
opening steps a dark-haired man with a distinctive mustache
wearing a belted, light-brown uniform and a crimson armband.
From the roar of the crowd and his distinctive appearance, it
can only be Hitler.

Quiet descends upon the multitudes as he centers himself
behind the microphone. *How eerie that his very presence can
silence thousands*, Diana thinks, *but also how spectacular*. And
then he begins.

Although she and Unity can only observe Hitler in occasional glimpses from the side as he delivers his speech, the power
of his voice is undeniable. Diana watches as it transforms the
faces of the soldiers in the crowd. She doesn't need to understand every word to comprehend what this message delivers
to these people who've been brought so low by the Treaty of
Versailles and the worldwide economic depression: hope.

*Oh, how M will stew when he learns where I've been*, Diana
thinks, and then another thought occurs to her. Perhaps this

trip will not only serve as punishment for him, but as a means to secure *the* prominent position with her lover. Perhaps the connections she's made in Nuremberg can provide Mosley with access to the network of the most powerful fascist in Europe, the sort of contacts he needs to succeed, but that Diana alone can provide. From this moment forward, Diana is certain everything will change.

# CHAPTER TWELVE

# UNITY

*September 3, 1933*
*Nuremberg, Germany*

U NITY PEERS OVER THE PHALANX OF SOLDIERS SUR-
rounding Hitler to catch a better glimpse. Never has she
been so thrilled to be nearly six feet tall. But even so, she must
stand on her tippy-toes to get a good look. Suddenly a pair of
stern-looking officers part, and she sees him in excellent detail.
Her breath catches in her throat. It is actually *him*, the man
whose picture she's had on her wall for years. Hitler.

Then Hitler's voice rises as he slams his fist on the podium,
and Unity jumps. A ripple passes through the crowd at his
words, and Hanfstaengl's body becomes rigid. What is Hitler
saying? Unity wishes she spoke German, especially when the
crowd then breaks into a deafening roar. How will she ever connect with Hitler if she cannot speak his native tongue? In that
moment, she determines that she will learn. Perhaps here in
Nuremberg, or even Munich?

In order to immerse herself in German, she will have to find
some plausible rationale to convince Muv and Farve or, she thinks,
simply lie to them. *How easy it has been to fool them this past year,*

Unity thinks. If they knew how many hours she'd spent at the forbidden Eatonry in the company of her *verboten* sister, they'd go bananas. And if they had the slightest inkling that she and Diana weren't in Munich attending the opera, strolling through galleries, and studying Bavarian architecture, but instead standing on a Nuremberg stage designated for special guests at Hitler's *Parteitag*, well, they'd be one-hundred-percent certifiable—Farve, in particular, given his loathing of the Huns. How delicious.

Chuckling to herself in thinking about their reaction, Unity considers how adept she's become at spinning believable lies. How many outings has she invented with imaginary friends so she could scamper off with other fascists to share ideology and disseminate the Leader's BUF publication, the *Blackshirt*? Of course, to keep up the ruse, she always has to be home on time, attend the unavoidable social events, and take care to hide the pin Mosley has given her.

So far, Muv and Farve think she's just an ordinary deb like her sisters and other girls in their circle. Well, maybe not totally ordinary. Unity has never been called that. But she's fairly certain she can pull the wool over her parents' eyes one more time so she can master German in Germany; it will bring her one step closer to the union with Hitler of which she dreams.

Unity thinks back on the conversation she had with Hanfstaengl before Hitler arrived. She initiated the exchange when Hanfstaengl had become obviously irritated with her questions about meeting Hitler in person. To change the topic, she blurted out, "Did you know I was born in a town called Swastika?"

Diana rolled her eyes, and Unity winced. Had she made

another misstep? But to her surprise, Hanfstaengl's eyes widened. "Is that true?" he asked Diana, as if Unity could not verify the place of her own birth.

"It is," Diana said with a wry smile. "My parents had become entranced by the notion of gold-mining in Canada, of all things. They were living in a cabin in a mining community called Swastika when Unity was born."

Hanfstaengl nodded appreciatively at Unity while Diana spoke. Then he studied Unity as if for the first time and said, "Our chancellor is quite a believer in fate, and while I don't like to speak for our esteemed leader, I think he'd consider being born in Swastika a sign."

Unity felt her cheeks flush. Was it possible that, for once, she had done something right? That her oddness was working in her favor? And that her sense of her destiny and the actual future were beginning to align?

As Hitler's speech comes to an end, a uniformed photographer steps onto the stage, and Hanfstaengl motions for him to approach. "I think Chancellor Hitler would be most pleased to have a memento of your visit to his *Parteitag*. Would you be willing to pose?" he asks Diana and Unity.

Diana hesitates, but Unity leaps at the opportunity to place herself before Hitler, even if only through a photograph. "It would be an honor to pose for a photograph for the Chancellor."

Sensitive to Diana's reluctance without discussing it, Hanfstaengl arranges Unity alone in front of a group of highly decorated soldiers, right in the middle. Stepping very close to her, he pulls the collar of her black blouse out from her tweed suit jacket and spreads it wide. He then nods to the photographer to approach and, in English and German, calls out, "Please salute for the picture."

With a flash of light, the camera snaps the photo, and Unity experiences a rush of excitement. Will Hanfstaengl actually give Hitler this image and tell him the story of Unity's birth? Her stomach flutters at the thought. Unity simply knows Hitler is her destiny, and perhaps the wheels have been set in motion.

# CHAPTER THIRTEEN
# NANCY

*June 8, 1934*
*London, England*

P ETER, DARLING, MUST YOU ALWAYS BRING A COCKTAIL TO
the rallies?" Diana asks in that dulcet voice of hers. The
rest of her dinner guests have already left for the BUF rally, but
we three sisters are traveling together with Peter in a separate
automobile arranged by Mosley.

I hold up a silver flask and shoot her a mock-serious glance.
"Bodley, the cocktail is for the car, the whiskey is for the rally."

Peter laughs, and I feel like I've won a minor victory. These
days, tension runs high at Rose Cottage in Strand-on-the-
Green, a picturesque area of Chiswick that borders the Thames
and is dotted with attractive little houses, where my new husband
and I have settled. The months leading up to the wedding and
the ceremony itself were a sort of blissful dream. I didn't realize
how unreal they were and how ignorant I was until we arrived in
Rome, and our honeymoon began. Our days were spent pretending to sightsee, me in teetering heels and with a swollen ankle
and Peter in constant pursuit of a bar for a "quick one," until he
passed out by late afternoon.

Diana doesn't laugh along with Peter. Her expression is somber, and I suppose I should thank my lucky stars that Mosley isn't on the scene to give me a right proper lecture. "Fascist rallies and drinking don't go hand in hand. It sends entirely the wrong message," Diana says, as prim as the schoolteachers we never had. Our parents did not believe in formal schooling for us six girls; only Tom was sent off to Eton and Oxford. The rest of us muddled along with the occasional governess—until we drove her off—and free use of the extensive family library; amazing what one can teach oneself, and what one can't.

"Must they be mutually exclusive? If so, that might be a barrier to entry into full-blown fascism," I joke. I've grown a bit tired of all the sanctimoniousness at Eatonry as Mosley's fascism takes hold throughout ripe quadrants of English society, including a surprising number of aristocrats fearing the toll communism would take upon them and their fortunes should that movement gain footing instead. Although Diana's home isn't the BUF headquarters, sometimes it feels like it with Mosley's presence looming literally and figuratively. To Peter, I've taken to calling Mosley "Sir Ogre."

My husband is now doubled over at this exchange, which I'd meant to be humorous but not necessarily hilarious. I wonder if he finds it so amusing because the discussion involves his favorite pastime—drinking. What I glimpsed in Rome had taken firm hold within a month of our return to London, and Peter lost his new banking job for his repeated failure to return to work after his long, boozy lunches. Currently, we are living on my earnings as a writer and the pittance we receive from our families, although Peter insists on spending money as if we have access to limitless funds. We've already had the bailiff on our doorsteps to collect on Peter's unpaid debts, and we haven't even been married a year.

"You two." Diana shakes her head in disapproval but doesn't forbid the drinks. I guess she realizes they are a necessary adjunct to our attendance at the rally. And she does like to make a good Mitford family showing.

Unity marches into the parlor in full fascist regalia, complete with leather gauntlet gloves. "Good God, Naunce," she says, not identifying the source of her disapproval. But given her strident adherence to all things fascist—a mindset that's been magnified since her trip to Germany—I could have committed any number of offenses. No one can live up to Unity's expectations except perhaps her hero, Hitler, about whom she's been insufferable ever since she briefly laid eyes on him in Nuremberg. A fact, of course, about which my parents are oblivious. Farve would be apoplectic if he knew that his daughters had been in Germany in the company of Huns.

As usual, we've been assigned front-row seats to Mosley's spectacle, although tonight we are not in his usual setting, Albert Hall. As mainstream publications like the *Daily Mail* publicly back Mosley, the BUF membership has grown—both in numbers and in variety of associates—and Mosley has secured a larger venue, Olympia Hall at Hammersmith in London. He told Diana to expect over ten thousand attendees, and as I scan the soaring space brimming with not only the usual black-shirted young men and women but workers in their laboring garb and even entire families with their children, I believe it.

Peter reaches for the flask I've stored in my purse as the band trumpets patriotic songs and a line of men carrying black-and-yellow BUF flags march down the aisle. Does this mean Mosley will appear? We have been waiting nearly thirty minutes, and the typically orderly rally crowd has grown restless. As have I.

The lights begin to dim and the arc lamps swing onto the stage, creating that all-important dramatic circle of light into which Mosley steps. *Finally*, I think, *we will hear his speech*. I don't even care that it'll be the same rhetoric I've heard before since it'll move this evening along. At the sight of the BUF leader, the fascist salute pops out from many members of the crowd, but I also hear a surprising amount of booing. We had walked through a group of protestors—a mixed array of communists, pacifists, and Labour Party members—but I would have thought the Blackshirts would have prevented them from actually entering the hall. I suppose they could be sporting Blackshirt garb as camouflage.

The protests quiet as Mosley approaches the microphone, but as soon as he opens his mouth to speak, a chant breaks out from one of the galleries—"Out with Mosley, out with fascism!" The Blackshirts who had been lining the aisles break ranks and leap over chairs to reach the offending gallery. The objectors grow silent as the Blackshirts loom, and Mosley begins his speech.

But he does not manage to get more than a few words out before a woman screams, "Down with fascism!"

Within seconds, one of the arc lights swings, and the audience sees that the Blackshirts have pulled the woman's arms behind her back and are pushing her out of the hall. I'm surprised at the force with which they're handling this verbal protest, but the BUF has made no secret of its insistence on order.

Mosley tries to speak again, to no avail. This time, the hall seems full of whistles and hoots coming from all directions. The agitators must have carefully scouted out their positions to maximize the impact of their dissidence. Within seconds, Blackshirts are scattered throughout the hall, and I can hear the thud of blows being delivered and screams at the pain being inflicted.

Soon, the entire hall erupts, and Mosley is left alone on the stage under a single arc lamp, futilely trying to calm the audience as the lights rove, seeking out protestors. Anti-fascism pamphlets rain down on the rally-goers, and an arc lamp shines on a ceiling girder over 150 feet from the ground. There, a man perches, emptying bags of pamphlets onto the crowd and screaming, "Down with fascism!"

Blackshirts clamber up to the girders, and like ants, they assemble and converge on the man. But as he scrambles onto a girder the soldiers haven't yet occupied, everyone around me shrieks. Including me. Are we terrified that the protestor and the Blackshirts will fall to their deaths, or are we scared that we will be crushed in the process? I don't have time to arrive at an answer, because suddenly the hall echoes with the horrible sound of a scream and a crash.

People start to stampede out of the hall. My sisters and I are frozen, gobsmacked at this display of violence. But then, a crush of Blackshirts wielding nightsticks and chasing a gaggle of young men and women holding signs heads in our direction, and we start running. Peter grabs my hand and begins pulling me toward an exit sign.

"Diana! Unity!" I yell over my shoulder toward my sisters, but I lose sight of their faces as my husband yanks me farther and farther away from our seats.

"Nancy!" I hear Diana scream, but then her voice fades.

Just as we reach the exit doors, I feel a hand on the back of my jacket dragging me backward. I lose my grip on Peter's hand, and I hit the floor, feeling footsteps on my back. And then everything goes black.

# CHAPTER FOURTEEN
# DIANA

*June 8, 1934*
*London, England*

*I*S M *ALL RIGHT?* DIANA ASKS HERSELF IN A PANIC AS SHE remains immobile in her seat. Chaos has broken out all around them in Olympia Hall, and she cannot see the stage as the arc lights are scouring the crowds. All she can think and feel is a near-paralytic worry about M. He *cannot* be harmed. Too much depends on him. *She* depends on him.

How dare they lash out at M? Don't they understand that he cares about the people of Britain? That he alone has the power to save them from the sort of economic and psychological despair that overtook the people of Germany? They are *all* lost without him. He has a plan to end the overwhelming poverty and unemployment plaguing the nation; he has an agenda for developing Great Britain to its former glory; he has designs to unite Europe rather than fostering antiquated divides; and yet he wisely advocates Great Britain's military preparedness in any event. How can these upstart protestors—deluded with their notions of communism and pacifism—not understand this? They are every bit as bad as the weak, ineffectual British leaders currently in power.

Out of nowhere, Blackshirts appear and take her by the hand. As they help her to standing, their most decorated officer says, "The Leader has asked us to bring you to safety, Mrs. Guinness. He is waiting for you backstage."

They begin to tug her toward the steps bordering the stage, and she strains against them. "What about my sisters? We cannot leave them behind," she insists, glancing behind her to see an empty row of seats. She scans the floor in a panic to see if they got trapped underfoot by the crush of people fleeing the hall. But Unity and Nancy are nowhere to be seen.

What on earth has happened to them? Quite against herself, Diana feels like screaming. Nancy has Peter at least, for whatever that is worth. But Unity? She's on her own. If something happens to Unity, Muv and Farve will never forgive her, especially because they expressly forbade her from bringing Unity to this rally. And they are barely speaking to her as it is.

"Mrs. Guinness, we must hurry," the officer says.

She allows herself to be encircled by them. They move as one against the tide of fleeing people, up the small set of stairs, and across the empty stage. Just as they reach the dressing rooms at the back—where she assumes M is being guarded—a woman launches herself from a darkened hallway at her.

Wrestling Diana to the floor, the woman rips at Diana's hair and yells, "How can you align yourself with that disgusting fascist?" As her fingers rake across Diana's cheek, Diana thinks of her sweet boys, Jonathan and Desmond, and all she wants is to return to them unharmed. Who will mother them if she is gone? The last time they were together, they sat for a portrait by the Russian surrealist painter, Pavlic Tchelichew, who envisioned Diana and her boys all with long golden hair and enveloped by blue shadows. If only she could return to that tranquil moment.

With billy clubs, the Blackshirts beat the woman off her. Pushing herself to standing, Diana smoothes her hair and her dress. Her hands are shaking, but it simply will not do to appear anything less than perfect for M.

As one of the Blackshirts marches the woman off the stage, her hands cuffed behind her back, Diana says, "I am ready to be taken to the Leader now."

"Of course, ma'am."

Guarding her on every side, they escort her to a dressing room with more Blackshirts stationed outside the door. Nodding to each other, one of them pushes open the door, and she steps inside.

There, her beloved M stands. Hands on hips, his thumb tucked into the wide black belt that emphasizes his powerful chest, he looks every bit the leader he's meant to be. The leader she will ensure he becomes.

She rushes into his arms, burying her face in the crook of his neck.

"Darling," he says, tipping her chin up into the light, "what happened to your face? Did someone attack you?"

"It's nothing, darling. A simple scrape that your men prevented from becoming more." She beams at him. "All that matters is that you are safe."

"A little fracas can hardly deter me from my course," he answers with a chuckle, although it sounds forced. And she notes that his usually swarthy skin is pale. He *is* scared, but of course, doesn't want to appear that way to her. "The only reason I'm holed up in this room is to prevent the negative publicity that could come with *my* involvement in an altercation." He balls up his fists. "Although I'd love to get my hands on those protestors."

"Of course, M," she whispers, drawing very close to him. "Silly of me to even suggest that you might not be safe."

M wraps his arms around her until she can feel his desire for her. Even here, his need is great. But the chaos at their doorstep distracts him. "I just hope that this ridiculous protest doesn't shift public perception away from the BUF. We need the support," he says.

Diana is pleased that she has waited to reveal her plan. Because now is the perfect time for M to understand exactly what Diana can help deliver to him and his cause. And how indispensable she can be.

# CHAPTER FIFTEEN
# UNITY

*June 8, 1934*
*London, England*

U NITY STARES AT THE PANDEMONIUM UNFOLDING IN Olympia Hall. She finds the protests disrespectful and crass, but she is more disgusted at the BUF than the demonstrators. How could a political organization dedicated to order and authority have allowed potential dissenters into their key rally in the first place? Hitler would have excised the objectors like a surgeon with a tumor. By allowing his rally to be tainted by the protestors, Mosley has revealed his weakness.

Where have Nancy and Peter gone? Craning her neck, Unity stands and uses her height to see over the frantic crowds attempting to exit the hall. But there is no sign of her sister's distinctive hat or her husband's bare blond head, and when she looks back, Diana, who had been sitting in her usual serene position with her feet tucked under her and her hands folded elegantly on her lap, seemingly unmoved, is now gone. Thank goodness she hadn't brought Ratular with her tonight; he might have gotten crushed in this melee.

What should she do now that her sisters have disappeared?

It's hardly as if she can hunt down a telephone and ring up Muv and Farve for their help. They'd go positively mad if they knew she was here.

As she looks for the exits, a mass of people charges in her direction, and she becomes swept up in their movement. Her arms and legs tangle in those of men and women of all ages and backgrounds, even children, and she has trouble keeping her balance as they move en masse toward the nearest exit doors. But she knows that, if she falls, she risks more than injury. She is in danger of being trampled.

They pass under a balcony containing a row of private luxury boxes, and Unity swears she hears her name. Assuming it must be Diana, she turns back toward their seats, but her sister is still nowhere to be seen. Where the hell is Diana? Did she leave Unity behind in search of her precious Mosley? Unity likes to think of herself as self-sufficient and strong, but she's hurt and angry at being abandoned.

"Unity!" a voice calls out, and now there is no mistaking her name.

Unity scans the crowd, trying to find the source. Perhaps Nancy and Peter are ahead, calling to her. But then she hears, "Up here!" and Unity stares up at the balcony to see the shadowy profile of a woman in a red sweater. Could it be the same woman from that other rally? Certainly there isn't a hint of red anywhere else in the crowd, and it cannot be a coincidence.

Then the woman leans forward, illuminating her most unexpected face. It is Decca, her seventeen-year-old sister.

"What are you doing here?" Unity yells up at her, unable to make sense of her little sister—a communist to the core—here at a *fascist* rally. Is she actually here to protest? What would Muv and Farve make of this?

"Don't worry about that now," Decca says. "Just take the stairs to the right and meet us up here. It's safer!"

Unity spots a staircase tucked away under the balcony to the right, and given that everyone is desperate to exit in the other direction, it's empty. Extricating herself from the crowd, she races up the stairs. Her sister waits at the top, and Unity has never been so happy to see her. And relieved.

"Decca!" Unity practically screams as she reaches out to embrace her.

"Bobo, my sweet Boud," Decca says, using two of her nicknames for Unity at once and patting her on the back, "are you all right? You looked like you were in a tight spot. What are you doing here by yourself?"

"I should be asking you these questions, *little* sister. Muv and Farve would absolutely die if they knew you were here—protesting at that. And on your own!"

"I'm not on my own, Bobo. Cousin Esmond is here with me," she points to a familiar figure, who's been lurking in the hallway and only now steps out into the light. Esmond Romilly's mother, Nellie, is first cousin to Farve—as is Nellie's sister Clementine Churchill, wife of the politician Winston—making us Mitford children second cousins to the Romilly and Churchill children.

As Unity and Esmond greet one another, Decca continues. "Anyway, Muv and Farve would be every bit as furious to find you here."

"I hardly think so. I am the older sister, after all. And I'm not alone either. I came with Nancy and Diana."

"That's almost worse than me sneaking in here with Esmond," Decca laughs. "Nancy and Diana are old enough to know better, whereas Esmond and I are young enough to be forgivably stupid."

Unity knows she should be angry at Decca for participating in this demonstration tonight, but she cannot harbor a grudge against Decca, her Boud. Even if her beliefs are wrong, her heart is in the right place.

"Even if you came out to protest the rally? As part of the communist faction?" As soon as Unity saw Decca with Esmond, her presence made sense. While Decca's political allegiance to communism is no secret—*her half of the bedroom is practically wallpapered with the hammer and sickle,* Unity thinks—Unity has never known her to take action on her beliefs. But the sixteen-year-old Esmond is cut from a different cloth. He publicly proclaimed himself to be a communist at age fifteen, and since that time, he's launched a magazine espousing his views, written several magazine editorials, and formed his own political group and organized marches for them. Even though Esmond is family, Muv and Farve would be furious to know Decca has been here—especially with *him.*

Decca's cheeks flush, and Unity knows she's caught her out. But, in truth, they'd both be drowning in the drink if their parents found out. Decca replies, "And what if they found out you were here as a step in your grand plan to move to Munich and become a Nazi?"

"Well, I won't tell Muv and Farve, if you won't," Unity offers, more interested in protecting her own ability to fulfill her scheme than in thwarting Decca's machinations as a communist.

The sisters shake on it, and Decca adds, "We were never here."

# CHAPTER SIXTEEN
# NANCY

*October 4, 1934*
*London, England*

I AWAKE WITH A GASP, STARTLING MYSELF OUT OF THE recurring nightmare I've had since the violence at Olympia Hall. The sensation of being trapped underfoot, unable to rise or fully breathe, has permeated my dreams, taking a variety of forms and story lines. But no matter the narrative, the dreams always end in the same manner, with me struggling for air and giving a final ragged gulp before lurching to consciousness.

Sitting up in bed, I reach across the silk hand-me-down quilt from Diana for a reassuring touch of Peter's shoulder. But the bed is empty. I squint over at the clock on my nightstand and see that it is three o'clock in the morning. Where the hell is he? A better question might be, why am I angry or surprised? My husband's absence has become one of the only constants in my married life.

I lie back down, but after fifteen restless minutes, I know I'll never return to sleep. My mind is whirring with lingering memories of the dream and worries about Peter's whereabouts.

Should I work? I'm nearing my deadline for the draft of my new novel, *Wigs on the Green*, and we desperately need the money I'll receive upon submission. Peter has lost yet another job, and his primary financial contribution these days stems from the odd newspaper article he writes.

While I force my thoughts back to the novel, I pace Rose Cottage, pausing only to light a cigarette. Inhaling deeply, I circle the parlor, wishing for the soft glow of dawn and the reflection of its rays off the ripples of the Thames. I adore the way they dance on the ceiling of the little rooms of this house, making it feel like a boat en route to a faraway land. But how things have changed since we first moved here, when my mind was full of plans to be a wonderful housewife and build a safe little home with Peter. Now, I just pretend at the role, and it seems fitting that the prior inhabitant of Rose Cottage went by the name of the Great Sequah, a traveling entertainer from the Victorian age who dressed and performed as a Native American chief even though he was English to the core. We are both charlatans.

I settle at my elegant, diminutive desk, a castoff from Swinbrook, which I've set up in the drawing room in front of a great bay window that overlooks the river. Before I can even begin writing, I hear the pitter-pat of footsteps. My sweet bulldogs—Milly and Lottie—look up at me with sleepy, bleary eyes, as if to chasten me for my middle-of-the-night wanderings. But then they curl up at my feet, warming them as I return to the manuscript.

Like my prior two novels, *Wigs on the Green* is a comedy, and again, I draw upon the events and people in my life. But

this time, the issues hidden behind the frippery are those nipping at the edges of my conscience. The story revolves around
a fascist pageant play set in a placid English village with a
main character not unlike Unity, Eugenia Malmains, who
makes lively speeches on the village green about fascists called
"Jackshirts" because of Captain Jack, a leader of the fictional
Union Jack movement not unlike Mosley. Given my feelings,
I could not ignore the political backdrop that is unfolding all
around me, particularly among my own family members. My
desire to make fascism central to the book grew out of my *own*
evolving attitude about the political movement.

After the Olympia Hall rally and the violence the
Blackshirts inflicted at the slightest provocation, undoubtedly
on Mosley's orders, I could no longer even pretend to be in the
same political ranks as my sisters. Did we not live in a society
where free speech was guaranteed? Could Mosley not bear the
slightest critique of BUF and his rule? The strutting, postur-
ing, flag-waving, and shows of bravado I'd chuckled at privately
now seem menacing rather than humorous, and I felt an urge to
unmask Mosley and his dangerous army as hooligans through
my writing. I also began to wonder if I could use my writing as
a way to awaken my sisters from this madness.

But I knew from the start that I could not attack Mosley
and the BUF head-on. How could I come right out and say
that fascism is madness and Mosley and Hitler along with it?
Diana is Mosley's creature entirely, as is Unity in a different
sense. To go after Mosley would be to go after them, and I do
not want to alienate my sisters forever. So I devised this other
way—a comedic, sly exposé that pokes a bit of fun at British

fascism and, hopefully, gently opens up people's eyes to the peril it poses. They only need to look a little further, to Germany, to see what happens when a fascist leader is given any power.

Of course, when Diana found out about my topic, she became upset at the mockery she suspects I'll make of Mosley. She cares not a whit about how I might depict her or Unity, because in her mind, they are simple foot soldiers to the great Leader. But this is precisely what I want people to understand. Without the willing adherence of men and women like Diana and Unity, these fascist leaders have no power. We needn't become victim to their tyranny as is happening in Germany and could happen in Great Britain. Although, of course, that is precisely what my sisters want and why they don't want my book published.

Sometimes, I find my sisters incomprehensible. And not only because they are fascists.

Returning to the chapter I'd partially drafted, I review the exchange between my stand-ins for Mosley, the BUF, and Unity—Captain Jack, the Jackshirts, and Eugenia Malmains. I wonder if the new chapter goes too far in Eugenia's stated dedication to fascism. Does the speech I made up for her sound too strident such that it's no longer funny? Drawing from the well of my own experiences—as all writers do—I read the brief "speech" aloud and compare it to one of Unity's own diatribes. The similarity of tone and spirit is uncanny, and I decide to keep the language intact.

Suddenly the front door slams open, and I jump. "Prod?" I call out, furious with him for staying out until all hours without me. What happened to the evenings when we'd traipse back home at first light in our evening dress from a ball at Blenheim or late-night cocktails with friends, only to bump into the early shift arriving for work at Pier House Laundry a few doors down from Rose Cottage? Still, I'm of mixed mind, as I'd rather it be him than some marauder.

In stumbles my husband, looking less than handsome with his unruly hair, unfocused eyes, and shambling walk. "Is that you, Nancy?" he says, squinting at me as if seeing me through fog. Which, I suppose he is, in a manner of speaking.

"None other," I answer without glancing up again. I don't want to converse with him, keeping him awake any longer than necessary. Better that he goes to bed and sleeps off this stupor than I say something I will regret.

Jars bang and glasses clink as he fumbles around the kitchen. "Still dabbling in that silly book?" he asks.

"Indeed," I answer, unable to resist continuing, "we've got to pay the bills."

The kitchen is silent for a minute, then the sound of ice on crystal grows louder as he steps into the parlor. "Nice dig, Nancy. Pleased to see you're not taking out all your anger at me through Jasper Aspect. You're leaving some aside to dish out directly to me?"

Given that I *do* normally reserve my irritation for the pages of my books—the *Wigs on the Green*'s Jasper, for example, a side character who's in search of a wealthy heiress and resembles Peter, although my husband didn't do very well in the heiress department—I'm surprised that my emotions even register with him. And I'm particularly astonished he's able to articulate his complaint in his befuddled state. I know better than to engage when he's drunk so I keep my eyes on the page, willing him to leave and pass out on our bed. That's what he seems to do most nights anyway.

Finally, I hear the clatter of his footsteps on the stairs, and I sigh in relief. I'd closed my eyes to the negative signs about Peter before our marriage because I so desperately wanted to marry. And even now, when I can no longer ignore his flaws, I must do what I can to make this union successful. I do want children, after all, and I don't want the stigma of divorce from which Diana suffers daily.

But that doesn't mean I must stay utterly silent. I do have other avenues to share my voice. I turn back to a chapter that features Jasper, the ne'er-do-well, drinking philanderer, for whom I'm presented with material daily. Into his mouth, I place the thoughts I'm having—that marriage is such a dreadful gamble, one might be better off placing their bets on a horse.

# CHAPTER SEVENTEEN
# DIANA

*October 4, 1934*
*Munich, Germany*

A TINY PART OF DIANA LAMENTS HER DEPARTURE TODAY from this attractive little flat off Ludwigstrasse in the heart of Munich. She has enjoyed her weeks here, surrounded by Biedermeier furniture, tended to by an excellent maid and cook, and immersed in all things Nazi. Unity has served as an excellent guide, having used her months being "finished" at the exclusive school founded by Baroness Laroche to great purpose. Although, upon reflection, Diana believes that the most useful information Unity has gathered did not come from the school but from her own reconnaissance. How surprisingly resourceful her little sister has proven to be.

But Diana's scrumptious little boys await her in London and so does her love. *How pleased M will be at the progress I've made toward our goal,* she thinks. The connections she's made here in Munich and in Nuremberg at this year's *Parteitag* will serve him well in the months and years to come as they endeavor to build up the BUF to become the prominent governing political body in Great Britain. Having shared her scheme with M about the role she might play in uniting Great Britain and Germany in this common political cause by helping weave together the Nazi leaders with her very own Leader, she is elated that she will return home to him bountiful, delivering the first stage of their plan. No one else at home knows that this is the reason she came to Munich; as far as the family and even Bryan are concerned, she's come to check on her little sister while the children were with their father. Only Unity knows something of the truth.

Diana thinks how far she has come in the weeks since this year's *Parteitag*. When she and Unity arrived in Nuremberg from Munich on September 5, they did so without a single ticket to one of the many celebratory events and nowhere to stay. They had, of course, reached out to Hanfstaengl, as he'd been so very encouraging about their attendance the year before. But he'd declined their request for tickets so vehemently—he'd suffered a mighty backlash for his decision to bring the two heavily lipsticked British women last year— that Diana felt offended and they backed away.

Having no desire to spend the night in a train station if their efforts in Nuremberg proved fruitless, Diana would have given up right there and then but for Unity. Her sister had every intention of attending the *Parteitag*, tickets and hotel reservations notwithstanding, and would not allow Hanfstaengl's admonitions to stay away to deter her. Unity's persistence was a marvel, when not put to wayward purposes, of course.

Their train to Nuremberg left before dawn broke over Munich, but by the time they stepped onto the platform at their destination, the streets were already crammed with people and every cafe was filled beyond capacity. At the sight, Diana pulled a train schedule out of her purse and began studying return trains. Yet Unity appeared undeterred.

She turned toward Diana with a wide smile, so delighted she forgot to hide her gray teeth as she typically does. "How marvelous is this, Bodley! Aren't you thrilled that we came?"

Before Diana could reply, Unity grabbed her by the hand and pulled her toward a biergarten within view of the station. Why was she in such a bloody hurry? Diana wondered as Unity dragged her through the throngs, jabbering the whole way. Haste is hardly the Mitford way, hardly the way of any of their set. "Just think, if we stake out a position in the streets today and camp out there overnight, we will have the most topping view of the Führer for the parade in the morning. We don't need a hotel after all!"

Diana felt decidedly different and was about to say so when she saw two elderly gentlemen rise from their seats at a shared table—and understood Unity's haste. Empty chairs.

As they settled into them and ordered a beer from a passing waitress—never mind the hour—Unity began chatting away to their tablemates in German. Although Diana had received some German tutoring from Unity since she arrived and had plans to attend the Berlitz school upon their return to Munich, she couldn't make head or tail of the animated exchange.

Finally, after a particularly long chin-wag among Unity and their stablemates, Unity glanced in her direction and exclaimed, "Well, isn't that simply marvelous, Nard!"

"What is so marvelous, Bobo?" Diana felt perfectly comfortable using their private nicknames in public, because she assumed none of these common people spoke English.

Unity pointed to a grizzled gentleman with bright-white hair and a matching unruly beard. "He's one of the first one hundred thousand members of the Party," she practically screamed, clapping her hands in delight.

*What on earth is my little sister on about*, Diana thought to herself. But she didn't ask, because she could see from her over-eager expression that if she waited, Unity would tell her herself.

"See that gold badge on his chest?" Unity asked.

Diana nodded.

"Only members who joined the Nazi Party early—in the first hundred thousand—got that sort of pin."

"I was actually number one hundred, the hundredth person to join the Nazis," the man interjected in English, then glanced at the others at the table and—for their benefit—said, *"Parteigenosse Nummer Hundert."*

Unity's eyes widened, whether from the information he'd imparted or the fact that he spoke English, Diana wasn't certain. "One hundred!" Unity screamed in English. "Then you must have known the Führer in the early days."

The man beamed. "I did indeed, although our leader has come very far since then. It is wonderful to see two beautiful English girls here celebrating the Führer. Hopefully, you'll take the Führer's message home with you!"

He raised a glass to them, and they took sips of their beers along with him and the motley mix of ex-soldiers and Bavarian hausfrau-types at their table. "Where are you staying?" he asked.

When Unity explained their plight, the entire table expressed their horror that two young English girls would be left out on the street for the entirety of the *Parteitag*. The man reached for a tablet of paper and pencil from his inner jacket pocket, scribbled a few indiscernible words, tore the paper off, and said, "If you go to the Nazi office in charge of accommodations with this slip of paper"—he pointed to a little building with a red-tiled roof—"they will make sure you are taken care of." Unity launched into a stream of German that Diana assumed was thanks, because within moments, the entire table took turns embracing her.

*How fortunate that unexpected encounter proved,* Diana thinks as she finishes packing to return home. Not only did she get to experience firsthand the exhilarating speeches on all that the Nazis had accomplished in the past year—achievements in job creation, agriculture, industry, and infrastructure that were ignored by the British press in favor of accounts of Nazi anti-Semitism and violence, all translated by Unity—but she also met many influential Party members. When she and Unity returned to Munich, Diana set about fostering those relationships at dinner parties hosted at her Ludwigstrasse flat and with visits to the opera. All for M and the future of the BUF. What might her lover accomplish with the might of the Third Reich behind him?

As she packs her remaining dresses into her oxblood leather suitcase, Diana muses on her success. She shouldn't be surprised that her plans reached fruition. After all, when she sets her mind to a task, she manages to accomplish it. Since there is nothing in the world that Diana wants more than to secure her place at M's side, she will do exactly what is required to have him all to herself, providing something that no one else can give him, especially that miserable Baba. She will deliver the Nazi Party support to M.

# CHAPTER EIGHTEEN
## UNITY

*October 4, 1934*
*Munich, Germany*

G ERMAN CLASS ENDS FOR THE DAY, AND UNITY SPRINGS from her seat. Racing by the other girls boarding at Baroness Laroche's finishing school and the other English nonboarders who avail themselves of the Baroness's classes, she skips down the stairs and out the front door. She cannot risk being late.

"Fräulein Mitford!" a familiar voice calls after her. In the privacy of her own thoughts, Unity thinks of the owner of the voice as a jailer.

Unity turns back toward the Baroness's lovely family house in the formerly exclusive, patrician section of Munich, where the Baroness now offers schooling and boarding for affluent girls because the financial toll that the Great War took on her circumstances requires an income. Unity lives and learns here as part of the "finishing school" experience her parents have permitted. Ever since she and Diana attended the *Parteitag* last fall, she'd known her future lay in Germany. But it wasn't until Decca successfully advocated for a "finishing" year in Paris that Unity was able to convince Muv and Farve that she should have one as well, no easy task given Farve's loathing of the Huns. Unity thanked her lucky stars that her little sister didn't break their promise and divulge to Muv and Farve that she'd been acting on her fascist beliefs. Unlike Decca, Unity requested Germany, where—she fibbed—she'd spend time in a pleasant study of the German language and its culture as well as attending chaperoned social occasions. Muv was always relieved to have an appropriate place to deposit Unity.

"*Ja*, Frau Baum?" Unity answers with the expected deferential bow of her head. The proper display of respect is crucial in German society; this is one cultural lesson she's learned, at least.

"You left without asking permission." Frau Baum's expression is stern, as it must be when corralling the overexcited girls in her care. "Or informing us as to your whereabouts."

"*Bitte verzeih mir, Frau*. I will not let it happen again." Unity keeps her gaze on the ground and her head down.

"That's all well and good, Fräulein Mitford, but where do you think you are going *now*?" Frau Baum persists. She is nowhere near as easy to fool as Muv and Farve, but Unity has found ways.

She slaps her forehead as if she cannot believe she's forgotten to reply. In reality, she knows precisely where she is headed, as it is the same location almost every single day, but she is hoping not to answer. She prefers to tell the truth whenever possible, because she has found herself entangled in a sticky web of lies all too often, so she threads the needle of truth with her answer. "I am planning on taking a stroll in the Englischer Garten with my friend Ariel Tennant and her cousin Derek Hill."

This is indeed true. Unity does have such plans. But for the weekend, not today.

Frau Baum looks her up and down, an unmistakable skepticism in her gaze. She opens her mouth, and Unity suspects she'll order her to stay at the boardinghouse today. But then, from within the elegantly papered walls of Baroness Laroche's establishment, a shrill voice calls for Frau Baum, and Unity is set free.

Practically running down the cobblestone street, she slows as she approaches her destination and wipes off her lipstick. It would not due to arrive at Osteria Bavaria disheveled, out of breath, or wearing lipstick. Such a frazzled, tawdry state does not comport with the Nazi image of the perfect Aryan woman—statuesque, blond, cheeks ruddy from sun or sport, blue-eyed, proper, and mannerly. A Nazi might describe this sort of beauty as *auffallend*, and she imagines herself to be the embodiment of those qualities. Imagine! They even find her height attractive

By the time Unity reaches the corner of the small five-story stone building housing the restaurant and pulls open the door, the clock near the entryway strikes two o'clock. Even though Frau Baum delayed Unity, her arrival time is perfect. Glancing around the cozy, wood-paneled establishment decorated with framed watercolors and etchings, she notes that it's largely empty, as always, due to the post-luncheon hour, save for a few tables with patrons savoring coffee. Toward the rear, behind a wooden half-partition, the staff is arranging a table for eight with the osteria's finest china and silver.

*He is coming,* Unity thinks with a shiver. Perhaps today will be the day.

Nodding to the restaurant owner, Herr Deutelmoser, who's come to expect her at this time, she settles herself at a table for two near the front door. She pulls Rudolf G. Binding's novel *Der Opfergang* from her handbag and signals Ella, one of the waitresses, for a coffee; she alternates between novels celebrating various Germanic regions, books espousing Nazi ideals, such as Hans Grimm's book *Volk ohne Raum*, which she also carries in her bag, and a classic, dog-eared work by William Blake. Arranging her book, cup, and saucer so that she has an excellent view of the door, she begins to read, trying to immerse herself in the words.

The phone rings, breaking the silence of the restaurant. Herr Deutelmoser answers the call and gives a signal to his staff, kicking the osteria into frantic motion. Drinks are poured at the table for eight, candles are lit, baskets of bread are placed around the centerpiece, and menus are laid on each table setting. Then the staff positions themselves behind the chairs and waits to serve. Like Unity herself.

*How easy it was to ascertain the Führer's daily schedule*, she thinks as she watches the clock's second hand tick. When Hitler was in Munich, he lived at 16 Prinzregentenplatz, a city square in an affluent neighborhood. He usually had lunch later than most citizens, and nearly always at the Osteria Bavaria. A cavalcade of black Mercedes delivered him, his guards, and largely the same entourage most days: his official photographer, Heinrich Hoffmann, his press chief, Otto Dietrich, Nazi chancellery head Martin Bormann, and aides. Several well-placed tips and gentle persistence on her part had won her these tidbits of information and this regular proximity to her beloved Hitler.

The roar of the Mercedes sounds on the street outside. A door slams, and the restaurant door creaks open, the telltale black gauntlet of a guard appearing on the side of the door. Two armed officers enter first to clear a path. And then, finally, in steps Hitler, the leash to his Alsatian dog in one hand and a whip in the other.

Unity can hardly breathe. Even though she's laid eyes on the Führer countless times before, the effect he has on her is always the same. His neat uniform, his dark, well-combed hair, and his powerful blue eyes all combine to make her nearly swoon. Despite the sensation of being overcome, she keeps her eyes firmly fixed on him as he passes—in the off chance that someday he will meet her gaze.

After Hitler and his men settle at their table, she shifts her attention to her book and coffee, but only ostensibly. Throughout the course of their two-hour meal, she watches him under her lashes so as to avoid alarming him or his guards, all the while slowly turning the pages of her book. Gaggles of women routinely stalk and seek out the Führer—even offering themselves to him, naked under their overcoats— and Unity does not want to be associated with this unseemly conduct. Hanfstaengl has told her and Diana how much the Führer loathes this behavior. So she waits. Quietly. Mannerly. Patiently. Until *he* is ready for her.

Ella appears at her side, the sweet, gray-haired waitress in the traditional Bavarian dress who's always present when Unity keeps her vigil. But instead of topping up her coffee and asking if Unity would like a pastry, which she often accepts, Ella leans toward her and whispers.

"I thought you'd like to know, *Fräulein*."

"Know what, Frau?" Unity whispers back, nearly afraid to ask. Is it possible that this woman brings a message from Hitler's table? After all, she was just pouring drinks there. But Unity doesn't dare to hope.

"Today, the Führer asked me who you were."

"Truly?" Unity's heart beats wildly, and her voice trembles. Could this actually be happening? Could this be the moment of recognition that she's long sought?

"Truly," Ella replies with a small smile. "He asked me first, mentioning that he's seen you here several times. And when I told him that I only knew your first name, one of the Führer's aides said he believed you were an English girl here in Munich to study."

"Did he say anything else? Did he ask to meet me?"

"No, but his eyes lit up when the other gentleman mentioned you were English."

Unity reaches for Ella's hand and gives it a little squeeze. "Thank you. You cannot know what this means to me."

How Unity wishes Diana could be at her side. It doesn't seem quite fair that, on the very day her sister leaves Munich for London, Unity should finally be noticed by Hitler. During the weeks Diana rented a flat in Munich, her sister had waited with her, at this very table, for an opportunity such as this. Now, Unity is one step closer to her goal, a heady feat she accomplished entirely on her own.

# CHAPTER NINETEEN
# NANCY

*November 14, 1934*
*London, England*

THE SOARING, ARCHED GLASS CEILING DIFFUSES THE DAY-light, casting the Palm Court at the Ritz with a soft, warm glow. *No surprise all the ladies like to meet here at teatime instead of their clubs,* I think. The warm light is ever so flattering, making even the most decrepit doyenne look years younger and considerably kinder than her age or reputation would reveal. *Appearances can be deceiving,* I think, as I gaze around the busy tables among the gilt-topped marble columns and elegant swoops of several palm trees and count off the preening matrons who I know to be absolutely nasty behind the scenes.

I wonder if the light makes hay of the fine lines around my eyes and marionette etchings around my mouth I'm beginning to see in the mirror. Peter likes to comment on these symptoms of age when he's deep in his cups. Without thinking I trace my bloodred nail along the creases framing my lips.

*Stop,* I tell myself, *you cannot allow yourself to dwell on the rows and dark moments with Peter. Not today of all days.*

Today is a day for lightness and humor, at least outwardly—otherwise, I'll never convince Diana.

Just as I think about my lovely sister, in she steps. Although the ladies in the Palm Court pretend not to notice her, the entire tenor of the room changes as she enters and not only because she's notorious for having left the handsome Guinness heir and her perfect life for the *enfant terrible* of British fascism. It is as if, with each step across the marble parquet floor, a goddess has descended closer to the ranks of mortals. We all pale in comparison to her eternal silvery flame, and consequently, her presence sets off a flurry of adjustments to hair and garb as she passes through. Will I ever get used to the effect Diana has upon others? Upon me?

I stand, and we kiss each other on the cheeks. I wonder how the Palm Court patrons view us—my black to her white.

"How are things with Prod?" she asks, as the waitress pours her tea, to which she adds a squeeze of lemon. The timing of the question has been carefully selected so she needn't make eye contact at the moment of inquiry. Does she hope averting her eyes will prompt me onward to revelations? Somehow, I do not imagine that Diana wants the full truth, of which she is undoubtedly suspicious but perhaps not overly curious.

"If one cannot be joyful, one should at least be amused, don't you think?" I answer the best way I can manage without resorting to tearful confessionals, which I have no intention of doing. "And I have plenty to keep me amused."

"The boys still flitting around?" She doesn't need to list names for me to understand she's referring to Harold and John and Evelyn and the rest of the so-called Bright Young Things, although I wonder if our shininess has dulled over the past eight or so years since we received that nickname. The fellows used to inhabit Diana's abodes as well, until Mosley became a fixture on the scene. The Bright Young Things and Mosley are a cocktail that refuses to mix.

"Despite Prod's best efforts? Yes, indeed they are. Rose Cottage has become quite the home away from home for them." I sip my tea, hoping to mask my discomfort with this exaggeration. But I cannot stop myself from adding, "Perhaps that's why Prod is so often gone from home." I let out a rueful chuckle, and Diana shoots me a concerned glance.

"Are you quite all right, Naunce?"

Squaring my shoulders, I smile and say, "Quite." I will not put myself in a position to be the object of pity from a woman so pitied herself. Mosley's antics with his sister-in-law are well known and widely reviled—dalliances with the sister of one's recently deceased wife are the stuff of general loathing, even if it's just the stuff of rumors—and the disgust at Diana's situation has recently shifted to sympathy.

Diana nods. She doesn't believe that I am all right, and honestly, I wonder if I am. But if I allow her in, permit her to see how troubled I am and how alone I feel, I will never be able to accomplish the task at hand. So I change the topic to her own life.

"And how is Mosley?"

"Very well," she answers, her eyes downcast. Her cheeks turn a fetching shade of pink, and I marvel at the fact that, after two years and Mosley's rumored constant philandering, he still holds such sway over her. I cannot seem to forgive Peter his wandering eye, particularly since I suspect his hands and quite possibly other body parts have followed suit.

"He doesn't mind your trips to Germany?" I've lost count of the number of times Diana has traveled to Munich this year alone. What on earth requires her presence so frequently? *Surely she has enough fascism at home; she needn't travel abroad to get her fill,* I think. This is a topic we Mitford sisters—and even Tom occasionally, acting quite against the unbridled loyalty he once felt for Diana—discuss outside the presence of Diana and Unity. Could it truly be concern over Unity? While Muv's parenting was always offhand at best, Diana acts as if she's Unity's mother, not her sister, which we all find peculiar because she never had any interest in the role until recently.

"Quite the opposite," she answers, but does not elaborate. Pamela had bet me a half a pound that Diana wouldn't offer up the reason for her German jaunts, and in truth, I'm somewhat hurt Diana hasn't told me. Even though we have our petty jealousies and sibling rivalries, I think of myself as closer to Diana than to any of my other siblings. Never mind her childhood pairing with Tom.

"Is that because he approves of the purpose?" I bait her just a little. If I work too hard to extricate the information, she'll never offer it up. *But would a little gentle prying hurt?* I wonder.

She says nothing in reply, simply sips at her tea and offers me that serene smile. Once she becomes the inscrutable Sphinx, I know her reason is buried away like a mummy, and any effort I make will only serve to shovel more sand on top.

I continue as if she did respond. "Well, it's been topping of you to check on Bobo from time to time. Who knows *what* she might get up to if left to her own devices for too long."

Laughing, we reminisce over the various and sundry antics Unity indulged in during her debutante season, including orchestrating an appearance by Ratular at her final ball. Muv must have felt an incalculable relief when Unity was packed off to Baroness Laroche's.

We pause while our teacups are refilled, and by the time the waitress leaves, Diana's face has turned serious. "You are a trifle too hard on Bobo in *Wigs on the Green.*"

*Here it comes*, I think. The reason Diana has arranged this meeting. My latest novel, which I allowed Diana and Unity to read before it is finalized for my publisher.

"What do you mean?" I ask, all innocence although, of course, I know precisely what she means. I have been bracing myself for their reactions, because I can't very well publish the book without something of a say-so from them, can I?

"Oh please, Naunce. The unflattering character of Eugenia Malmains is a direct send-up of Unity," Diana says.

"There is a certain similarity, I admit, but Bobo says that she's pleased with the description of Eugenia Malmains— parallels and all." I answer cagily, not mentioning her vitriol at the depiction of fascism generally.

"That's only because you describe Eugenia as attractive— and we all know how thirsty Unity is for compliments. That flattery colored her judgment about the way you portray her allegiance to fascism."

"I hardly make her seem like more than a raving lunatic for fascism than she is. I mean, Unity stalks Adolf Hitler. What could be madder than that!" I exclaim, drawing the attention of nearby matrons. I lower my voice. "Eugenia is positively mild-mannered compared to Unity."

Diana stiffens, arching her brow. And I can see that she's about to launch into a little speech about Mosley, which is the *real* point of her objections to *Wigs on the Green*. I doubt she minds how I describe Unity's proxy, but she cares very much what light I might shed on Mosley and his movement. No matter how carefully I broach him.

She says, "I also object to your treatment of poor M."

"Mosley isn't in *Wigs on the Green*." I add, "I don't even use the term fascism or any terminology suggestive of Mosley or the BUF."

Diana scoffs at me. "Don't try to play me for a fool, Naunce. You don't even bother to mask Mosley as Captain Jack. And could you have even made an attempt at subtlety about the BUF? I mean, you call Mosley's Blackshirts Jackshirts? The two names even rhyme, for God's sake."

"*Wigs on the Green* is not a book about Mosley or fascism, Bodley. It's a folly about love and marriage and money that happens to be taking place during a time in which fascism is on the rise. It's just backdrop."

"You don't need to spell it out—you accomplish your goal of mocking Mosley without mentioning him by name." Her tone borders on the furious, but she is managing to tame her anger. For now. In a controlled, icy tone, she says, "I must insist that you not publish *Wigs on the Green*. I will not be able to maintain contact with you if you insist on releasing it."

How can she ask that of me and make such a terrible threat?

Doesn't she understand that Peter and I walk a razor-sharp line between socially accepted survival and penury, and that the slightest misstep could lead us headlong into destitution? Not to mention, her demand is rife with hypocrisy. Why isn't it every bit as important for me to share my views as it is to them to disseminate their fascist beliefs? Why is it acceptable for Decca to want to propagate her communist teachings—which are in *direct* contravention to fascism—but egregious that I should speak my own truth? And why is it somehow reprehensible for me to try to sway people with the only means at my disposal, my writing?

But I say none of that, because I know how those arguments will land. Instead, I say, "I have to publish the book. Peter and I need the money to live on. I don't have 2,500 pounds a year from an ex-husband to help support me."

Diana flinches at the reference to the generous amount Bryan pays to support her and the children. I feel cruel mentioning it, and I refrain from pointing out all the additional financial support Mosley provides her as well. It won't do to utterly alienate her, and I scramble to soften my words. "And anyway, all the references to the Jackshirts and Captain Jack are in jest, as would be plain to any reader. Even if they did make the connection. I would guess that the book would drive more people *to* fascism than away from it. But if you find particular sections objectionable, then perhaps you could identify them for me and I could consider striking them," I say with a small, conciliatory smile.

Diana does not smile back. Instead, she stands, putting on her buttery-soft leather gloves finger by finger. "I will take you up on your offer, Nancy, to review the book again. But if I find anything, my demand stands."

# CHAPTER TWENTY

## DIANA

*November 14, 1934*
*London, England*

T HE SHEETS ENTWINE THEIR LIMBS, UNTIL DIANA ISN'T
certain where her arm begins and M's ends. When their
bodies are this close, sweat-drenched and satiated, she wants to
prolong every second. *How fleeting are these moments of rapture
and union*, she thinks, *and yet, they are what bind me to him*. She
wants to freeze this moment as if they were butterflies under
glass, but M makes capture impossible.

"What did Nancy say?" M asks, his voice still thick and
his breath labored.

"That the novel isn't really about fascism, that we needn't worry.
That any reader will see the book as the fluff she intends it to be."
Diana doesn't know why she automatically reverts to her protective instincts when it comes to Nancy, even with her beloved. She
knows that Nancy's assurances are empty, that they *should* be concerned about her sister's portrayal of the BUF and Mosley. After
all, most readers will know of Nancy's connection to Diana—and
Diana's connection to Mosley—and assume that her words are
based in truth. And yet, the allegiance to her sisters pulls at her.

"Do you believe that?" he asks.

"I wish I did." She stays buried in his chest.

"So we must act. Let's file a libel suit like the one I brought against the *Daily News* for that damning article they published in the *Star*, claiming I had weapons at the ready to take over the government."

Diana doesn't answer at first. She has learned to pause, to make him wait for her answers, her presence, even her body. Only through withholding does M cherish that which he's eventually given.

"Hmm," she says, lightly running her finger in circles around his chest. "I'm wondering if it sends the wrong message to your followers to bring a libel suit against a work of fiction, particularly since it wouldn't be winnable." She could have objected on the simple basis that Nancy is her sister, but she knows this tactic will be more effective.

As her fingers descend down his chest, he closes his eyes and sighs at the pleasure she gives him. "Right as always, my exquisite goddess." His eyes open, and he looks at her. "But we must do something to stop Nancy."

"She's offered to let us edit out whatever parts of the book we find offensive before she delivers it to her publisher."

"She did? How did you finagle that?" he asks, impressed.

"I explained to her that I would never see her again otherwise." Diana still cannot quite believe she issued that ultimatum to Nancy, the sibling to whom she feels the closest aside from Tom. A life without Nancy's sharp tongue, bright wit, and bolstering companionship is one she cannot envision and hopes she need not experience. But it is a sacrifice she is willing to make for

M; she only wishes he would make a similar one for her. One in particular: Baba.

Wrapping his arms around her even tighter, M whispers into her hair, "You are a marvel."

"That's what they say," she whispers back and climbs on top of him. They kiss, and just as she loses herself in the feel of his tongue in her mouth and the touch of his hands on her breasts, he pulls away from her.

"I can't." He groans, then sits up, brushing her skin with his knuckles. "It's not that I don't want to, but I can't."

Diana cannot quite believe he is rejecting her advances. It is one thing to demur before a tryst begins, but it is quite another to deny her mid-intimacy, with her body displayed before him. She wraps a sheet around herself, as if peach silk fabric could protect her against his refusal, and begins to clamber away from him across the bed.

He reaches for her, but she does not allow herself to succumb. They tussle until she finds herself wrested into his arms again. She very nearly yields to him when he says, "You know I have to see Baba this evening. In less than an hour actually."

Diana stiffens. Is he really leaving this bed for a rendezvous with Baba? Months ago, she learned that M had allowed his relationship with his former sister-in-law to become sexual, a necessity, he claimed, to continue the financial and emotional support she provided for his children with Cimmie and no reflection on his feelings for Diana. She was able to compartmentalize and suppress her emotions about this limited betrayal because, she believed, M had compartmentalized his relationship with Baba. But this? Walking away from intimacy with

Diana for an assignation with Baba? As if he's conserving his sexual energy for *her*? The well-suppressed rage Diana feels for Baba—a fury that she has only allowed herself to direct toward *her*, never *him*—rises up, threatening to destroy her carefully constructed and cultivated facade of composure.

"Please, Diana, I will make this the last time. I promise." He takes a deep breath and then blurts out, "And I didn't want to tell you this, but she's been helping me with the BUF."

"What do you mean?" Diana's tone and body remain rigid.

"She's in a relationship with Count Dino Grandi, Mussolini's ambassador to London. And in her own way, she's been ensuring that Il Duce's favor stays with the BUF."

*Confessing this must cause him more pain than acknowledging his reliance on Baba for the children's financial support,* Diana thinks. Mosley always wants to appear strong and powerful, dependent on no one and nothing for his success. The fact that Baba has been bolstering his relationship with Mussolini—from whom the BUF receives significant funding, Diana recently learned—is not only surprising but ironic and disappointing as well. Because she too wants to deliver a foreign power to him.

Diana does not let herself speak; she needs to think and plan. Underneath her silence and motionlessness, she gathers her rage and the force of her will until she shapes it into the fine tip of a blade. With this weapon, she will make M hers alone.

# CHAPTER TWENTY-ONE
# UNITY

*November 14, 1934*
*Munich, Germany*

H ER FOOT TAPS IN TIME WITH THE CLOCK. AT FIRST, THE synchronicity was random, but as the minutes and then the hour pass, she does it intentionally. Unity does not want anyone to think she's overly anxious to see the Führer. He loathes the simpering, promiscuous acolytes who follow him around, and she wants to appear the opposite, which she imagines to be Diana.

In truth, Unity is nervous. She *always* is as she waits at the Osteria Bavaria. She lifts her cup for another sip of coffee, trying to keep it steady as her foot keeps tapping. She's afraid that if she abandons the repetitive motion, she might start some other more compulsive and less proper tic. As she had when Mum and Farve visited her last month.

She'd brought them to the Osteria Bavaria at the usual time, hoping to give them a glimpse of Hitler. While she and the Führer hadn't yet spoken, he knew who she was, and he nodded at her as he passed. She hoped this gentlemanly behavior would soften their view of Nazism. While Muv didn't object to the political situation in Germany or the Führer specifically—anything was better than communism, according to Muv, and she believed that the Germans had been unduly punished by the Treaty of Versailles—Farve had become even more leery than usual of the Huns on the heels of the actions Hitler ordered upon taking power, the Night of the Long Knives in particular, and the rumors Farve has heard about Hitler's treatment of the Jews.

That afternoon, to Unity's delight, Hitler did more than nod. He *bowed* in Unity's direction. The gesture so moved her that she leaped up, but fortunately, this overreaction went unnoticed by the Führer as he and his entourage had already moved on to their table.

Her cheeks warm at the memory of this impetuous action, and she thinks how lucky she was that Hitler hadn't witnessed it. Unity very much doubts he would take the next step of inviting her to join him for luncheon if he had.

She returns to her coffee and reading when Ella stops at her table, even though she'd just refilled her cup. Unity gives the kindly older woman a polite smile, and Ella pretends to top off her coffee while whispering, "I overheard him ask one of his guards to come over and ask you to join him."

Although Unity has dreamed of this moment countless times, she cannot believe it's happening. She discreetly smooths her hair and turns away to rub her teeth, making certain she has no lipstick on them. How fervently she wishes that she looked like the description Nancy gave her in *Wigs on the Green*, through the character of Eugenia Malmains.

A minute later, one of Hitler's special guards, a Schutzstaffel wearing his black uniform with a tan shirt, arrives at her table, saying, "*Guten Nachmittag*, Fräulein Mitford. The Führer would like to know if you would like to join him for luncheon."

Her voice trembles as she answers, "*Ja, ich würde so mögen. Danke.*"

Gathering her book and bag, she follows the guard to Hitler's table. She's envisioned this walk so often that it almost doesn't feel like the first time. Step-by-step, one plank of wooden flooring at a time, she approaches the men who tend to be with him most luncheons—photographer and politician Heinrich Hoffmann; the head of the Nazi Party chancellery, Martin Bormann; chief press officer Otto Dietrich; chief aide and adjutant Julius Schaub; Hitler's doctors Theodor Morell and Karl Brandt; and personal bodyguard Wilhelm Brückner. When she's close enough to touch the table, Hitler leaps from his chair to greet her. He smiles into her eyes, then bows before pulling out the chair next to him for her to sit.

Perching on the chair, Unity tries not to stare into his deep blue eyes. So close to him, she's in awe of his fair skin, his carefully brushed, fine brown hair and the elegant shape of his white hands. She waits to be spoken to, before speaking.

"We were discussing opera, Fräulein Mitford. Do you have a favorite?" Hitler asks.

Unity suspects that the men had not been discussing music at all, but instead that this question is a test. Would her reply be in keeping with Aryan dogma? Oh, she will not let Hitler down, certainly not with *this* topic.

"*Mein Führer*, there are many talented Germanic composers whose operas I admire, such as Mozart and Beethoven. But

I must confess to holding a special place in my heart for the work of Richard Wagner, his Ring cycle in particular."

Hitler straightens up in his chair, visibly pleased with her response. "You are a fan of Wagner? It is uncommon for a girl of your age."

Thus encouraged, Unity continues. She's rehearsed this exact exchange time and time again in her head, and now she recites from memory. "Oh yes, *mein Führer*. You see my grandfather, Bertram Mitford, was a dear friend of Richard Wagner's family, the composer's son Siegfried in particular. So I grew up listening to the great man's music, often in the company of his family." How liberating it is to share her actual enthusiasms and have them received favorably. Unlike all those boys she was forced to dance with during her debutante season who looked at her askance if she mentioned opera instead of jazz.

The entire table has grown silent. As if they cannot believe the words she's uttered. Unity had every reason to believe that her response would prove pleasing to the Führer, but from the frozen look on these men's faces, she isn't so certain. Has she said something wrong? Has Wagner fallen out of favor? She can't imagine that Hitler, who's long espoused the virtues of Wagner and sees the composer's operas as reflecting his German ideals, would have so drastically changed his mind.

"Your family is close with the Wagners?" His eyes are locked onto hers, and she feels the intensity of his gaze.

"*Ja, mein Führer*." She pauses, lowering her eyelashes and then glancing up at him through the fringe. It is a coy expression Diana occasionally does to great effect, and Unity has practiced it in the privacy of her room at Baroness Laroche's.

"In fact, my grandparents gave me my middle name in honor of Herr Wagner."

Hitler leans a little closer to her, until their hands practically touch, and Unity sees that the other men have done the same. Much, it seems, hangs on her answer to the question Hitler is about to ask. A shiver passes through her.

"What is your middle name?" he asks.

"Valkyrie. In honor of the second of the four parts of Wagner's Ring cycle. It was my grandfather's favorite," she says, then meets his eyes again. Staring into their depths, she experiences the most exquisite sensation of oneness with him.

*I could die right now*, she thinks, *and be happy*.

"*Die Walküre*," he repeats, adding, "the virgin warriors who selected the most worthy warriors and led them into Valhalla. The Valkyrie proved lucky to those they chose."

"Yes, *mein Führer*."

"Perhaps you will prove lucky to me, Fräulein Unity Valkyrie Mitford." His eyes are shining, and his hand grazes hers. "It is fate that our paths have crossed."

# CHAPTER TWENTY-TWO
## NANCY

*June 28, 1935*
*London, England*

W HY HAD I BOTHERED TO EXCISE THREE FULL CHAP-
ters of the book if Diana is going to cling to her anger?
At our tense meeting at the Ritz, I'd offered to edit *Wigs on the
Green* and cut out the sections she found offensive to Mosley
and his movement. She and her lover spent an unconsciona-
bly long time reviewing the draft manuscript, bleeding over
nearly every page with their red pens and fully expecting me to
acquiesce to their every demand. Never mind that their edits
could render the book unpublishable and Peter and I wouldn't
receive a single pound of the advance for which we were desperate. Diana has the audacity of someone who has always
gotten her way and wields her wishes like a righteous sword.

"Nancy?" A voice brings me back to the present. I glance up
to see John Betjeman standing at the front of the line of people
requesting autographs at my book launch. "Can I ask an old
friend to sign her latest book for me?"

"Only if you don't call her old," I answer with a wry smile
before leaping up to embrace John. "It's been too long, darling."

"Well, if you and your gorgeous husband didn't live in the positive desert of society out in Chiswick, we wouldn't be so bloody estranged!" he says with a cackle, and I laugh along with him. How I've missed all my friends, Evelyn in particular. Despite what I told Diana, my chums have never made a haven of Rose Cottage; it's too far away from central London, and Peter is too off-putting for them to spend much time there with me. No one wants to listen to him drone on about the merits of toll booths when he's inebriated. I've become quite estranged from my old chums, except for the odd drink here and there.

"You're one to talk!" I jeer back, then ask, "Where's Penelope?" Two years ago, John married Penelope Chetwode, the lovely, feisty daughter of a field marshal who'd been stationed primarily in India, in a secret ceremony, and they lived in the countryside of Berkshire or Oxfordshire—I could never remember which.

"Oh, you know Pen, she's always got her own cultural goings-on. Something about India, I think? But then it's always something about India." John hands me *Wigs on the Green*, glances at the line behind him, and calls out to the entire bookstore, "I hear it's going to be a runaway bestseller!"

Giggling, I watch as several browsers migrate over to the line from the stacks. I mouth, "Thank you," before settling back into my seat and reaching for my pen.

As I begin to write a personal note on the title page, John leans forward and whispers, "I also hear there's been a familial dustup over the book."

"Have you?" I say, not looking up, even though I'm desperate to hear the scuttlebutt.

"Oh yes, I hear the latest is quite the send-up of the Mosleyites and that the beautiful Diana is in a tizzy." He has a knowing smile on his face, the sort I've been known to sport when in possession of a particularly delightful piece of gossip. *Where had he heard this?*

I give him a sly glance and trot out the little seed I'm planting as a diversion from this sort of anticipated buzz. "Rumors like that would be good for sales, wouldn't they?"

I hear a sharp intake of breath, and then John says, "How deliciously wicked! You've started that little nugget yourself— what a devious, smart little ruse."

"I have my moments." I meet John's eyes and feel seen for the first time in months. This is strange and ironic because, of course, I've just told John a lie. He has indeed been privy to the truth about Diana.

Peter ambles over to us. "John, old chap, what a pleasure! Can I fetch you a cocktail? We've got a makeshift bar set up over here for friends and family." He points to the assortment of liquors and mixes he arranged on an empty shelf. It's the most helpful contribution he's made since we married, though the motivation for the undertaking is obviously to keep *him* in spirits throughout this book signing.

John winks at me and then says to Peter, "Why, aren't you a clever fellow?"

For a second, as I watch my husband chatter amiably with my old pal, I think how handsome Peter looks and how full of promise he is. Why must he let drink and women and laziness get in the way of his potential? There were moments over the past year when his behavior made me so furious and ashamed that I channeled all that emotion into my characterization of Jasper. When I dedicated the novel to Peter, had I done so tongue in cheek? After all, most of the repugnant views on women that Jasper expresses came directly from Peter's mouth. I feel I'm at a crossroads, but neither path ahead is terribly appealing.

I sigh, turning my attention back to the line. There isn't a single Mitford family member here, not that I expected Diana or Unity, of course. I'm not surprised Muv and Farve haven't shown either, as Muv has taken Diana's side in all this furor about *Wigs on the Green*, and at fifteen, Debo must follow their lead. But what about Pamela? Is she so smitten and busy with Derek Jackson—the quirky physicist and renowned steeplechase rider she's been seeing, who espouses an affinity with fascism such that the previously apolitical Pamela has suddenly claimed an allegiance—that she cannot make an appearance? And Decca certainly operates by her own set of rules despite her youth and is no admirer of fascism in any event, so why isn't she here? But of all of them, why is Tom's absence upsetting me so? My handsome, witty, even-tempered brother has always served as a steadying force in the ruckus forever flaring among us sisters. It seems that even the one Mitford I thought I could count on has withdrawn from me.

Most disappointing is the fact that the impetus behind the book—opening my sisters' eyes to the fascist horror unfolding before them—has had the opposite effect. It has driven them deeper and deeper into fascism and the men that embody it.

I return to signing books and making chitchat with the patrons of the venerable Hatchard's, the oldest book-store in England and one of my favorites. Glancing up from personalizing a copy of *Wigs on the Green*, I am astonished to see two familiar Mitford faces in line. Muv and Farve.

Although I long to spring up and ask them what changed their minds, I stay at my station. Some of these folks have been waiting upward of an hour, and after lambasting me for writing the book, my parents don't deserve special treatment.

I watch as they move one step closer to me, and when they finally reach the front, I say, "Fancy seeing you here."

Muv pulls her collar up high around her neck as if to ward off a chill I've brought into the room, and Farve clears his throat. Finally, he says, "We are proud of you, no matter your sisters' reaction." Not shocking that it's him and not her that's handed me the olive branch. After all, I mined family material for my earlier novels, and no one seemed to be bothered but Muv. Farve, in fact, seemed amused.

I notice Muv doesn't say anything. No compliments coming from her. I suppose I should be thankful that she's not yelling at me.

"Thank you, Farve." I stand up and buss him on the cheek. "Unity didn't seem to mind in the end, and one could hardly find a more ardent fascist." Unity sent the one letter in which she asked me not to publish the book, but since that time, our exchanges have been brimming with the usual light banter and Hitler sightings.

"Well, you don't see Diana here, do you?" Muv pointedly stares around the room. "You've upset her and Mosley terribly. You always treat everything as a joke."

"Should I depict everything as a tragedy instead? It's easier to approach life with a light touch than a heavy one. And anyway, I struck three chapters about Captain Jack from the book at their request, not to say demand, and now neither he nor his movement appear except a few oblique references. Yet Diana still refuses to see me."

"What do you expect? *Wigs on the Green* casts the Blackshirts in a satirical light. The fascist movement is nothing to laugh at; your sisters are quite dedicated to the positive changes the movement means to exact upon the world," Muv continues.

What on earth is Muv saying? Has Diana converted Muv to her cause? Or did the recent trip to Munich—where I hear Hitler nodded at her—change her thinking? "If it's as strong as they think it is, then a little laughter won't make it crumble," I say.

"There you go again, Nancy, always with the humor. Joking won't bring your sister to Hatchard's tonight."

"But my writing will pay the bills. Without my book income, Peter and I cannot make the rental payment on Rose Cottage. Something Diana doesn't have to worry about." I could darken the picture and elicit sympathy rather than ire from my parents if I told them what happened to money that I am foolish enough to bring home: Peter lifts it from my purse and spends it on drink or gambling.

Muv opens her mouth, then promptly clamps it shut. What can she or Farve say? Their own poor financial choices in investments combined with the worldwide economic crises have stripped their seven children of the cushion of family money, the sort most of our peers enjoy. And now, each of us must find our own way in the world.

Is that one reason why Diana's ostracism is so terribly

upsetting to me? Because, already, I feel cast adrift by my
parents, a feeling that's been compounded by Peter's dishon-
esty and betrayals? I simply cannot comprehend how Diana
can relinquish me in favor of her blind devotion to a man
who's placed her in a precarious position by taking her as his
mistress and refusing to marry her. A man for whom she sacrifices her family, when he will not forego a single one of his
own selfish pleasures for her, if the rumors about his sordid
relationship with his sister-in-law are true.

My goodness, how far will Diana go for Mosley?

# CHAPTER TWENTY-THREE

# DIANA

*June 28, 1935*
*Munich, Germany*

Castle ruins, autumnal fields, soaring church stee-ples, and the occasional snow-peaked mountain. The scenery of Germany appears much the same as France as it whizzes by Diana from her car window; the primary difference seems to be the language on the road signs. How wondrous and freeing to drive oneself from one country to the next all alone with the wind in one's hair and one's hands on the wheel.

*Surely,* she thinks, *this car is the best present M has ever given me.* On a recent getaway to Paris, he'd given her this Voisin, a sleek, silver automobile with a curved roof and long, outstretched front. She feels like an African cat racing across the savanna when she's driving it, and gratitude surges through that the car was ready for her to pick up in Paris when Unity summoned her.

Strange that Unity is now leading this charge. Her peculiar little sister has found herself in a position of power through persistence and obsession. Precisely when Diana most needed what she had to give, that prize for which she's been waiting since the first *Parteitag,* the trophy needed more than ever now that Baba is dangling a windfall of her own before M. Diana's enthusiasm at nearing her goal makes her irritation with Nancy—and her insistence on publishing her novel despite Diana's protests—fade away.

Diana had been finishing up a session with the Russian artist and mosaicist Boris Anrep at the National Gallery when the messenger arrived. Anrep had asked eleven friends to model for the nine Muses, plus Apollo and Dionysus, that he was depicting on a mosaic floor in the entryway to the famous museum. The chosen few were draped in togas and arranged in languid positions—Clive Bell as Dionysus, Virginia Woolf as Clio, Greta Garbo as Melpomene, and Diana as Polyhymnia, muse of sacred music and oratory, and so on—when a uniformed man clomped into the private space with an envelope for her, hand-marked "urgent" on the front. Her heart beat wildly for a moment, thinking something had happened to Jonathan or Desmond while in Bryan's care.

Apologizing to Anrep and the other models for the interruption, she'd removed herself to a quiet corner of the National Gallery and opened the envelope with tremulous hand. The note was from Unity: "Come to Munich at once. I've met HIM. And he wants to meet you." Excitement had coursed through Diana, and that very evening, she made her way to Paris to pick up the Voisin.

The landscape grows less bucolic and more urban, but in a very picturesque, Bavarian sense, if one ignores the occasional war-pocked area, of course. Gable-roof, Tudor-style houses arranged in groups around central squares and churches begin to spring up, until gradually, the swaths of fields disappear and the villages merge to become one sprawling city. Only then does Diana enter Munich proper, finding it as lovely today as she did upon her first visit. Does she adore the German architecture and setting because she and her siblings had been steeped in an appreciation for all things Teutonic from their youth, from their grandfather at least? Or is it because she grows one step closer to having M entirely for herself every time she travels here as she secures a more and more important place among the Nazi elite? Either way, the place holds great promise for her future.

The Voisin rumbles over the cobblestone streets as Diana winds her way into the city. She makes a few wrong turns, discovering that navigating Munich behind the wheel is quite different from roaming it on foot or in a taxi. Finally, the streets and buildings become more familiar as she nears the Schellingstrasse, and she's certain she's nearing her destination.

Then Diana sees it: the sign for Osteria Bavaria. Slowing the Voisin, she spots a large open space along a sidewalk and parks the car, thankful to locate an unusually large area to maneuver the long vehicle. Checking herself in her purse mirror, she brushes the ends of her hair back into their curl and decides not to reapply her lipstick. Hanfstaengl has shared Hitler's views on makeup, and her lips are naturally pink enough to give the effect she desires.

Stepping into the restaurant, Diana is greeted by the face of her sister staring at her from her usual table near the door. Unity springs up and wraps her in a too-tight embrace. "It's happening, it's finally happening," Unity practically sings into Diana's ear. She alone knows what this introduction may yield for Diana and M.

Diana coaxes Unity into sitting down at the table, where she orders two glasses of wine to calm *both* their nerves. Her heart is aflutter at the thought of what missteps Unity might make at this all-too-critical juncture if she's overexcited.

"Is he here?" Diana asks, glancing around the dining room.

Unity gulps at the wine and shakes her head. She gestures toward the large, semiprivate table where the Führer usually sits, and Diana sees that it is empty. Has she driven all this way, leaving her children in the care of the nanny for nearly a week, for nothing? What if Hitler has decamped to Berlin?

"But," Unity adds, "the table is set for his arrival. And Ella"—she nods toward the elderly waitress serving a table in the rear—"tells me that he is expected at his usual time. Two o'clock."

Diana glances at the cuckoo clock on the wall in the entrance. It is five minutes to two. She is relieved that she's not striding into the Osteria Bavaria *after* the Führer has settled at his usual table, thereby depriving the sisters of the critical chance to be invited to dine. Now she longs for that minute hand to race around the clock, so close she is to her goal.

As if she's willed it, the front door swings open wide, and two soldiers march in. Behind them, a dark-haired man in uniform follows, but his face is obscured by the guards. Diana freezes. Is it him? She does not want to appear overeager and crane her neck around, but the suspense is unbearable.

Finally, the man pauses and seems to turn toward their table, and his guards pause along with him. Gleaming black boots, visible between the guards' legs, step closer until Diana sees the familiar profile and mustache. It is *him.*

Does decorum mandate that she stand? Rarely at a loss, she is torn between what she imagines protocol requires and politesse necessitates, that the lady wait for the gentleman to pay his respects. In the split second of hesitation, the decision is made for her.

Hitler bows toward her and Unity, and says in German, "You must be Mrs. Guinness."

# CHAPTER TWENTY-FOUR
# UNITY

*June 30, 1935*
*Munich, Germany*

S TRAINS OF *DIE FEEN* FLOAT THROUGHOUT THE HALL. Unity knows that serious opera aficionados find this first of Wagner's operas to be overly simple and juvenile, with its focus on a fairy kingdom, but she adores the lightness of its music and, especially, the nature of its story. Unity wishes that Diana had been able to stay even one day longer to accompany her, but she understands her sister's obligations to her children. The notion of Ada, a half fairy, sacrificing her immortality in exchange for spending her life with the mortal man she loves, Arindal, makes Unity swoon. She cannot wait to discuss it with Hitler.

The chandeliers overhead brighten, signaling the intermission between acts, and Unity rises along with the other girls from Baroness Laroche's. They shimmy down the aisle, following Frau Baum to the foyer where refreshments will be for sale. These cultural outings to the opera occur every quarter, and the girls know to bring adequate funds for the sweets on offer.

"Isn't the story impossibly romantic?" Unity asks dreamily.

"Romantic?" Mary St. Clair-Erskine practically screeches.

Mary Woodise does along with her, then adds, "I can't imagine giving up my immortality for a man!"

"Especially not one as unsightly as this Arindal!" the first Mary giggles. The singer portraying Arindal is famously fat. Unity humors the first Mary most of the time, even though her brother Hamish broke Nancy's heart, but not at the moment.

"I can," Unity says, "because I would happily give up my life for the Führer." At the mention of her hero's name, she feels a pang of guilt that the travel for today's outing—a train from Munich to the town of Dachau followed by a brisk walk— required that she skip her usual vigil at Osteria Bavaria. She hopes Hitler will not forget her in her absence.

At the mention of Hitler, the girls glance around and then quickly change their position. "Well, of course, so would we," the first Mary corrects herself, saying, "but he is no mere mortal man." They would never want a passerby to overhear and possibly report them.

Frau Baum and her charges make their way to the little stand selling desserts, including Unity's favorite *Bienenstich*, or bee-sting cake, with its sweet honey-almond topping. The girls balance their sweets while attempting to find seating in the chairs grouped around the foyer. As they wind their way through the milling audience members, Unity bumps into a uniformed man, blond and fairly young.

Holding up her free hand in a gesture of apology, she says, "*Es tut mir leid, Offizier.*"

"*Nein, es ist meine Schuld, Fräulein,*" he apologizes and catches her teetering *Bienenstich* before it falls off its plate and to the floor.

They both laugh. She then realizes that this man is no ordinary soldier. His distinctive black uniform with a brown shirt tells her that he's a member of the Schutzstaffel. The SS, as it's known, is an elite unit whose primary responsibility is to guard the Führer and other high-ranking Nazis. And he's familiar to her. Unity knows exactly where she's seen him—at the Osteria Bavaria.

In that moment, he makes the connection as well. "Fräulein Mitford?" he asks.

"*Ja,*" she replies. "You are one of the Führer's special soldiers. I've seen you in his company many times at the Osteria."

"And I you." He bows to her. "You are a great favorite of our beloved Führer."

Her cheeks are hot, and she hopes the flush doesn't make her appear common or unladylike, but demure. The standards for proper Aryan womanhood are exacting. "I am fortunate to have spent time in the company of the Führer."

"He has often described you as that rare specimen of the perfect Aryan Englishwoman."

Deeply moved, Unity places her hand on her heart. A greater compliment she cannot imagine, and she's incredulous. "The Führer said that about me?"

The Schutzstaffel officer beams, understanding the import of his words to her. "He did indeed, Fräulein." His face then falls. "I must apologize to you again. I have been most impolite by not introducing myself to you. I am Unterfeldwebel Schwarz, one of the adjutants to the Führer," he says with a bow and a click of his heels.

"Pleased to meet you, Unterfeldwebel Schwarz," she says.

He points to a newly opened table near the window and asks, "May I sit with you while you enjoy your *Bienenstich*?"

Flattered and delighted to be showing off her connection to the other girls, Unity nods and follows him to the small bistro table with two chairs. They fall into easy conversation, primarily centered around Hitler and his likes and dislikes, in particular his favorite film, *Cavalcade*, about two English families as they navigate the Great War and the years that follow. When the conversation fades, Schwarz points out the window and says, "Do you see that building in the distance?"

She squints, trying to make out the structure in the diminishing daylight. "I think so," she says.

"That is the Dachau camp. I was lucky enough to tour it with the Führer last week, and we are quite proud of it." He smiles at her.

She gives him a close-lipped smile in return, and even though she's never heard about the Dachau camp, she understands she should say something encouraging. "You must be."

"We've made excellent use of an abandoned munitions factory. The building can hold many political prisoners who object to our Führer's command."

Now Unity comprehends the importance of the facility. "Of course, all who oppose our leader must be imprisoned."

"And so they are. There will be other sorts of prisoners there in the future—other enemies of the Reich—but we are pleased to have this prototype for similar prisons right here outside of Munich."

The overhead lights begin to flicker, a signal that they must return to their seats for the second half of *Die Feen*, and Frau

Baum appears behind Schwarz. Her eyes are wide at one of her girls talking to an elite Nazi. She would never dare interrupt any conversation with a member of the Schutzstaffel, but Unity can see she's torn. Propriety requires that the matron return her to their seats with the other girls.

But Frau Baum needn't worry. Schwarz takes the matter in hand. "May I escort you to your seat? It seems the opera is about to commence again."

Unity nods, thinking how Decca would laugh seeing her bold, unorthodox sister acting the part of circumspect Aryan girl, because they have never acted with modesty around each other. But then, Decca would understand better than nearly anyone that Unity is in the midst of achieving her child-hood dream.

As Unity walks into the concert area on the soldier's arm, he asks, "I would be most honored if you would be willing to see me again, Fräulein Mitford. For a meal, or perhaps a film?"

Unity's cheeks warm again; she would indeed like to go on a date with this attractive soldier, an ardent Nazi like herself. But would Hitler mind? Would it be awkward at Osteria Bavaria to take luncheon with the Führer while Schwarz looked on? She feels conflicted, and her face must reveal this emotion because Schwarz says, "Assuming our Leader does not object?"

Unity nods, grateful that he understands and shares her loyalties. "Assuming our Leader does not object," she agrees.

After Schwarz leads her to her seat and takes his leave, she's greeted by a barrage of questions. Who was the solider? Isn't he handsome? Has he got a girlfriend? What is his rank? Channeling her beatific sister Diana, Unity answers their questions patiently, holding back until she receives the very last one, the one she's been longing to answer: "How do you know him?" Mary St. Clair-Erskine asks.

Although Unity wants to jump up and down and shout to the world that she's dined with Hitler over twenty times, she lowers her eyes and says quietly, "Unterfeldwebel Schwarz is one of the personal guards for high-ranking Nazis, and I've met him several times while lunching with the Führer."

Frau Baum gasps, and the girls squeal. But before they can bombard her with new questions about Hitler himself, the second act begins. In the darkened hall, Unity feels the eyes of the girls and their matron upon her, and an unexpected power surges through her. She wraps that feeling of invincibility and importance around her like a cloak. It is the borrowed greatness of the Führer, and she will do whatever is necessary to keep it.

# CHAPTER TWENTY-FIVE
## NANCY

*July 12–13, 1935*
*Surrey, England*

I T ALMOST FEELS LIKE OLD TIMES. MUV AND FARVE ARE laughing with stately Cousin Clementine, who everyone calls Clemmie, while her cigar-smoking husband, Winston, knocks back whiskey with his son, Randolph, and Tom, who've always been close. Decca and second cousin Esmond stand in a corner, engaging in private chatter of some sort, while Debo is on the dance floor, fending off more invitations than she can accept. Even Diana is here. She hasn't spoken a word to me, but she's delightedly chin-wagging away with Pamela and Derek, and I wonder if her sparkle stems from the fact that Derek himself is aligned with fascism and now, to some extent, so is Pamela. Or perhaps it's simply that Mosley isn't here and so she can share her light.

Political upheavals, family discord, economic frailty, all could be happening somewhere else to entirely different people. Not here at Cherkley Court, the Surrey estate of Lord and Lady Beaverbrook, for their annual summer gala. Here, every guest glitters in a jewel-box setting that both stuns and impresses, from the immaculate, stuccoed estate itself with its vast hexagonal wings and Tuscan columns to the perfectly manicured gardens reached by wide steps extending from a lower terrace bordered by an elaborate parapet. I wish I still had access to Diana's closets so I could dazzle as vividly as the venue, but I've got to make do with an old navy gown, the bodice of which I had the local tailor rework. Still, I'm not fooling a single guest into thinking that this bias-cut Vionnet gown from 1928 is the latest in the 1935 Coco Chanel evening gown collection.

Where is Peter? We arrived in a hired car together, a silent ride during which he nipped at his ever-present silver flask. I suppose he's still smarting from our earlier row over his appalling, flirtatious display last evening with Mrs. Mary Sewell at bridge. I don't actually want him by my side at this gala, but I am concerned about his whereabouts and the mischief in which he might get himself on his own. Excusing myself, I walk out onto the loggia, thinking that perhaps he's come out here.

In a shadowy corner to the left, I see two figures moving. Their gestures seem agitated, and I wonder if they are fighting. I take another step closer. My heels clomp noisily on this otherwise empty section of the loggia, but the forms do not turn in my direction. But then my heel hits an indentation in the stonework and the scraping sound must have alerted them to an outsider's presence, because they separate and look over at me. And I see that the twosome isn't fighting but kissing, and that the figures consist of Peter and an unknown woman.

Pivoting away from them, I half run back into Cherkley Court. To my dismay, I walk right into the middle of a heated debate among Winston, Lord Beaverbrook, and Diana of all people. I will not give Diana—or Peter for that matter, should he return—the satisfaction of seeing me upset. So I light a cigarette with a shaking hand, grab a crystal flute full of champagne from a passing waiter, down it in one gulp, and ask, "What's all the fuss about here?"

"Ah, Mrs. Rodd," Lord Beaverbrook says, and I get the sense that he's about to pontificate. But suddenly, I cannot bear being called "Rodd." *Oh, the irony,* I think. After years longing for marriage, matrimony now feels like an odious yoke rather than an agreeable union.

I interject, "Lord Beaverbrook, I think we've known each other long enough that you may call me Nancy."

Diana raises an eyebrow, surprised I'm engaging in this level of familiarity with our esteemed host. The Canadian newspaper magnate and political puppeteer is a man of great wealth and power. He had served in Cabinet roles before founding the *Daily Express* newspaper, which caters to the conservative working class, although he'd never invite any of his readers to one of his parties. He's been a crony of Cousin Winston for as long as I can remember, but I've often found it perplexing how they became and stayed friends, given that they've engaged in some unpleasant political opposition in the past. Not to mention that Cousin Clemmie is no fan of Lord Beaverbrook, and she holds immense sway over Winston.

"I'll call you Nancy, if you call me Max," he says, his tone pleasingly jocular.

"As I was saying," Winston barks, clearly trying to return to the debate I'd interrupted. "We need to watch this Hitler fellow closely. He's already broken several conditions of the Treaty of Versailles from what my sources tell me, and he's amassing troops and weapons and munitions faster than we can count. For all intents and purposes, he's on the verge of waging war on the continent."

Lord Beaverbrook snorts and then opens his mouth to formulate his reply. Before he can speak, however, Diana chimes in. "I think you misunderstand the Führer's intent, Cousin Winston. He needs all that pomp and circumstance to lift his people's spirits, after decades of suppression after the Great War. His primary focus is bolstering the German economy to give his citizens jobs and homes. And I daresay he knows better than us what is important for his people."

Winston stares at Diana for several seconds without speaking. Silence is rare for him, and I brace myself for the tirade to come. "He's *the* Führer, is he? Is he *your* Führer? You know that the title translates to 'ultimate leader.' And that he achieved the title not by the vote of his precious citizens but by theft, usurpation, violence, and lies?"

Diana hesitates, and Lord Beaverbrook isn't going to let a conversational opening pass him by. He races into the void left by Diana. "That may all be well and good, Winnie, but it doesn't mean we've got to leap into war. We've barely just recovered from the last one. The British people simply do not have the appetite for fighting and loss, and you'd have the populace practicing military drills and manufacturing munitions in a mad haste toward rearmament. I think Chamberlain's got it right this time—let's keep the peace."

"You're willing to overlook how Hitler is treating his

Jewish population? And the rest he's got in store for them? My sources tell me that he's about to unveil a whole legislative system that will relegate them even further." He smiles a strange Cheshire cat grin at Diana. "But maybe those ideas go down well with certain of your family members, Diana. I hear that young Unity has been busy publishing her own anti-Semitic views in the German publication *Der Stürmer*—under a headline mentioning that she is *my* relative."

I gulp. It seems that word of Unity's misdeeds has spread. We heard the news directly from Unity herself, when she included a clipping of her published piece in a letter to Muv along with a translation. With evident pride, she informed us that she publicly proclaimed herself to be a "Jew hater." I felt sick when Muv showed me the letter. How could they let her stay in Munich, when this was the outcome? I asked. Muv acted as though she hadn't heard me.

Am I mistaken, or are Diana's cheeks flushed? Has my serene sister finally lost her legendary composure? She does not answer Winston's little taunt, and I wonder if she'd be more vociferous, even argumentative, if Mosley were here. For a moment, I've forgotten all about the betrayal I just witnessed on the loggia.

I'm eagerly awaiting Diana's response, when I feel a tap on my shoulder. I turn to see Peter standing behind me. "Can we talk?" His words are slurred, and his eyes unfocused.

My stomach lurches in disgust—at him and myself—but I nod. I have no intention of hashing it out with him here at Cherkley Court. I simply don't want him to embarrass me in front of such esteemed men and Diana. Perhaps my sister most of all.

We walk toward an empty corner of the room. "How could you?" I hiss. "Do you even know who that woman is?"

"I'm so sorry, Nancy. It's the drink. I promise to give it up." He stammers and sways, finally managing to get the words out. "Our trip to Venice will be the beginning."

We are meant to leave midday tomorrow for the first leg in our journey to Venice and the Adriatic. I had hoped it could be a fresh start after months of discord, but at the moment, I cannot stomach the idea of being alone with him for three whole weeks. "I don't want to talk about this here. We've got to get you home before you turn yourself into more of a cad than you already are. And take me down along with you."

Mercifully, Tom appears at my side. "Everything all right, Naunce?"

"Not really. I've got to get Prod home in a jiff, before he does even more damage to our reputations. Will you be a lamb and take him out of here? I'll see what I can do about rustling up a ride."

He squeezes my arm. "Of course. Come on, old chap," he says to Peter and leads him toward the foyer.

Before I depart, there's one thing I'd like to do. I glance around the room, searching for Diana. Where has she gone? The clock just struck one o'clock, and only the most elderly guests will have left so early. I don't know when I'll see her next, and I hoped to have a private word without Mosley present. Perhaps even make amends over *Wigs on the Green*, which has led Mosley to permanently ban me from his presence and whatever residence they share. No matter our differences, I don't want to lose my sister forever. I feel alone enough.

# CHAPTER TWENTY-SIX
# DIANA

*July 12–23, 1935*
*Surrey, England*

DIANA SLIPS OUT OF CHERKLEY COURT AS SOON AS HER conversation with Lord Beaverbrook and Winston comes to an end. She hops into her Voisin, thankful she had the foresight to drive herself and instruct the staff to keep the car in the front drive so she could make an easy getaway. Certainly she's relieved to escape from Winston's unexpected interrogation about Hitler and Unity and the Jews, but that isn't the real reason she fled. She and M have a rendezvous.

Glancing at her wristwatch, she realizes it's later than she'd planned to depart. She and M are meeting in the city for two nights before he leaves to take his children on summer holiday to Italy. She's determined to make those nights memorable because, although she's joining his group at the Rennells' villa at Posillipo in Naples for the second week, M will be there alone with his former sister-in-law for the first week. Diana aims to make Baba pale in comparison to her, both in what she can deliver politically and what she can do in bed.

Speeding along the back roads of Surrey, she sighs in relief when the city finally looms before her. Between Belgrave Square and Cadogan Place, five roads meet at a single, dangerous point, and she slows the Voisin to navigate the traffic, surprisingly heavy given the late hour. Out of nowhere, a behemoth black Rolls-Royce zooms through the intersection, directly into her automobile. She loses control of the steering wheel, and the car spins off the road, making a full circle before soaring off a hilly embankment bordering the road.

Time slows. She hears a horrible crunch and feels herself flying within and without the automobile, slowly as if the air has become as viscous as water. Her landing on the gravelly bottom of the embankment somehow seems as soft as a pillow, and she allows her eyes to close and drift away.

But not for long. Hands gently lift her, awakening her and carrying her away. She hears voices whisper and one woman stammer, "D-don't look at her, dear. Her face, it's t-terrible."

Diana is suddenly aware of a warmth in her hair and on her cheek. Lifting a single finger, a herculean effort, she touches her face. A sticky substance rough with tiny rocks trickles down from her forehead, covering her cheeks and nose. *Whatever could it be?* she wonders and drifts away again.

When she awakens, the light dazzles, such that she instinctively shuts her eyes. Lash by lash, she opens them, realizing that the brightness does not come from chunky rays of Mediterranean sun, as she'd hoped, but the stark whiteness of every object around her and the piercing overhead light. She is in a hospital.

She reaches for her face, hazily recalling the warm wetness she'd touched there. Was it blood? Instead of the smooth arch of her cheekbone and fine patrician slope of her nose, she feels rough thread and deep grooves and reams of bandages, and she begins to scream.

Wimpled nuns race into her room, and Diana understands that this is a religious hospital. "There, there, dearest. Your family is on the way." A doughy-faced nun pats her hand.

All Diana can think of is M. He will be concerned, wondering why she hasn't arrived. "May I have a telephone, please? I need to make a call," she says, or tries to say. The only word that sounds clear to her ears is *phone*.

"Hush, darling," the kindly nun says with another pat. "We can't have you getting overexcited. I'm sure your family can take care of all that. You must rest, as you've suffered a terrible accident."

Diana starts to protest, but the effort is too much, and the darkness descends. A day passes like this, or at least she thinks it's a day, pervasive dusk interrupted by brief snatches of consciousness in which glimpses of Muv and Farve and Debo and Tom and Nancy appear. But not M. Never M.

And then, without warning, she is suddenly, fully awake. She sits bolt upright in the bed, only to notice her father dozing at her bedside. "Farve," she whispers to the unexpectedly vulnerable, crumpled old man. "Farve? What's happened?"

His eyes flutter open, and he smiles. "Good to have you back, darling."

"Where have I been?" she asks, half-joking. She tries to smile, but pain spreads across her face at the effort. She abandons the expression.

"Where should I begin?" he asks, half-jesting himself as he

rubs the sleep from his eyes. "Let's see. It all began with an awful car crash. You needed two surgeries to repair your beautiful face. And thanks to the concerted efforts and generosity of Lord Moyne—"

What on earth does Lord Moyne have to do with her hospital stay? She interjects, "Bryan's father?"

"Oh yes, he was up in arms at the shoddy effort to put Humpty Dumpty back together again and insisted on bringing in the best surgeon in London, that New Zealander Dr. Howard Gillies. And thank goodness for his consternation because, according to all the experts, you'll walk out of this hospital every bit as lovely as before the crash. I don't think that would have been the case if we'd left in those rough, thick stitches."

She sighs in relief. "I owe him a debt of gratitude."

As Farve nods, a pressing question occurs to her. Did he say she's had two operations? She doesn't recall a single one, and to her, it seems as though she arrived at the hospital last evening. Or perhaps a day or two ago.

"How long have I been here?" she asks.

"Ten days, I think. No," he pauses, "eleven, if you count the day you arrived."

"Eleven days?" She is shocked.

"Yes. If you are worried about Jonathan and Desmond, please don't be concerned. Bryan has them—with Nanny, of course—and Muv and I have looked in. We didn't want them to see you like this, so we didn't bring them round."

Although she loves her boys, she knows that between Bryan and Nanny, Jonathan and Desmond are well cared for. No, that is not her primary worry. "What about M?"

Her father stiffens. He has never bothered to conceal his dislike of M and his disgust at the way he interfered in her marriage. "What about him?"

"He must be worried sick. Where is he?"

He hesitates and looks away, as if he'd rather not answer her question. "Diana, I don't know. He hasn't been to the hospital."

"What do you mean? Does he know what happened?"

"Yes. When you didn't arrive that first night, he called around to us—your mother and I, and your sister Nancy when we didn't immediately pick up—and, between us, we told him. But apparently, he had plans to take the children to Italy and decided to keep them."

She feels nauseous. M gallivanted off to Italy, with his sister-in law, while she suffered through two operations, in and out of consciousness, on her own? She steadies herself with measured breaths.

"Are you quite all right?" Farve asks.

"Yes," she says quietly, ashamed that she had to experience this disappointment in full view of her father. Thank God, Nancy wasn't the one who had to tell her.

To change the topic, she asks, "How much longer will I be in hospital?"

"I think the doctor mentioned something in the order of another month."

"A month?" She is stunned. She does the calculations, and the magnitude of the long hospital stay occurs to her. The second week of M's holiday is about to begin, the stretch where Diana was meant to arrive and overtake Baba—now and forever. If she does not get to Italy soon, Baba will believe she's taken Diana's place. And she has no intention of allowing that happen. No matter how she feels about M's insensitivity, she has made too many sacrifices for him and their future together to jettison it all over his temporary selfishness. Diana *will* win this fight.

"Farve, you've got to help me." Even though her entire body hurts—her face especially—she scoots closer to him. She cannot risk one of the nuns overhearing.

He sits forward on his chair, his usually stoic expression softened into apprehension. "Anything, Diana. Do you want me to call for a nurse? Do you need more pain medication? Or shall I ring your mother?"

"I need you to help me escape and get to Italy."

# CHAPTER TWENTY-SEVEN
## UNITY

*July 23, 1935*
*Hesselberg, Germany*

NEARLY FOUR WEEKS HAVE PASSED SINCE SHE'S SEEN THE Führer. Unity could count the days, even hours, if pressed, but no one asks. The girls at Baroness Laroche's, Frau Baum, and even the Munich friends she's made through Ernst Hanfstaengl's sister, Erna, can read on her face the long separation and confirm it in the newspapers reporting Hitler's presence in Berlin, Carinhall, Heiligendamm, and Rosenheim—everywhere but Munich. Having spoken to him, dined with him, laughed with him, Unity cannot bear being without him; it's like being torn away from her sense of purpose. Each day without contact, she feels more and more restless. And more and more reckless.

She craves Hitler's presence, and it builds up within her like a physical need. When Unterfeldwebel Schwarz asks her to a film during the Führer's absence, she decides she won't wait to ask Hitler's permission and accepts. In the dark and solitude of the movie theater, she imagines that it is *him* sitting beside her in the Nazi uniform instead of Schwarz. She leans toward him and kisses him, breathless with desire not for the boy next to her but the leader he's sworn to protect.

After amorous contact with Schwarz fails to slake her desires, Unity takes risks to draw Hitler's notice from afar, to ensure that he knows her dedication remains constant and profound. When Julius Streicher, in charge of Nazi propaganda and the publication *Der Stürmer*, asks her to share opinions on the Jewish population, she agrees, but only if his publication will change its public stance on Mosley and the BUF. Previously it had accused Mosley of softness toward the Jews, and Diana had asked Unity to do whatever she could to make the Nazis more amenable to partnership with the BUF. With Streicher's agreement in hand, Unity drafts a letter for publication, going further with her statements than she ever has before, beyond what she even believes—fiercely advocating for the removal of Jews from society in Germany and England and describing herself as a Jew hater.

On the heels of the reaction to her letter, Streicher asks her to speak at the Nazi festival at Hesselberg, and a delighted Unity accepts. The celebration is to take place at a historic Nordic site where pagan midsummer fetes took place, and the Nazis have invited the local people to wear traditional costumes paired with swastika armbands, while listening to speeches from key Party leaders.

She rides in a Mercedes-Benz in the middle of the motorcade to the Hesselberg rally, window down and wind blowing back her hair and sitting between two of the Nazi officials' wives she's come to know from dinner parties to which Hitler invited her in the spring, Magda Goebbels and Anna von Ribbentrop.

The crowds part for their imposing black vehicles like the biblical Red Sea, although Unity knows better than to make an Old Testament reference with this group of Nazis. She almost giggles at the way in which citizens, some of them weighed down by their regional costumes, scamper out of the way of the parade of Mercedes-Benz vehicles. Such is the might of the Führer.

With military precision, the cars approach the stage and park in a perfect line. The waiting Unterfeldwebel race to open their doors, as the band strikes up a rousing version of the Nazi anthem "Horst-Wessel-Lied." Unity squints into the bright sunlight as she steps out of the automobile and follows the senior Nazi officers and wives up the stairs to the dais, which is festooned with Nazi banners. She then strides onto the stage with a confident step—no more awkward debutante for her—and lines up alongside the luminaries to face the crowds. She is elated at her role in this pageantry, and it takes effort on her part to tamp down her smile enough to cover her teeth. *Not even Nancy would dare laugh at me now*, she thinks.

Studying the throngs of Hitler Youth, soldiers, and local citizenry carrying red Nazi flags flapping in the wind like a field of poppies, Unity notices that they grow more and more excited as they listen to vigorous speeches by Reichsmarshall Hermann Göring and Streicher, who punctuate their phrases with bangs on the podium just like their leader. Unity's nerves begin to agitate as she awaits her turn to speak. Will she honor Hitler properly with her words and delivery? Will he hear details about her enthusiasm and be reminded of her dedication? But when Streicher motions for her to join him at the podium, the applause and the cheers energize her, banishing all sense of anxiety. *This is for the Führer*, she thinks and begins.

Her black gauntlets on for effect, Unity salutes the crowd in the Nazi fashion, and they react with a great roar of approval. Galvanized, she calls out, "*Heil Hitler!*" She then leans closer to the microphone, and in her well-rehearsed speech, she declares her allegiance to the people of Germany and their strife, aligning with the Nazi Party as the means to raise them up. Then, she reiterates the more incendiary parts of her letter to *Der Stürmer*, which brings wild cries from the rally-goers and pats on the back from Streicher and Göring.

As Unity returns to her place in line on the stage, Magda and Anna beam in approval. *Strange*, she thinks. Here, amid the ranks of these Nazis, she feels as though she belongs, much more so than when she was presented at court to the Queen of England during her debutante season. These leaders and their wives have actually *chosen* her. She wasn't foisted upon them out of obligation or ancestry or inheritance as she was on her family, their society, or the Crown.

Overjoyed, she raises her hand in a final Nazi salute, and stares back at the cheering crowds, triumphant. *Surely, this will garner Hitler's attention and approval*, she thinks. Maybe even his love, supplanting Eva Braun in his affections. Unity prays that it will. Because if she doesn't have Hitler, what does she have? What will she have to offer Diana? Who is she without him?

# CHAPTER TWENTY-EIGHT
# NANCY

*August 20, 1935*
*Oxfordshire, England*

A M I A FOOL, AS EVELYN WILL SURELY CALL ME WHEN HE finds out over drinks later this week? Or have I simply let the golden Italian sun and warm waters of the Adriatic cast a spell on me, as they have on visitors for centuries? Because when Peter and I return from our summer holiday, I decide to stay in my marriage.

For the twenty-one days of our trip, Peter kept the promise he made at Cherkley Court, although he'd been inebriated and remorseful when he'd made it. While we rode in gondolas in the canals of Venice, dined on the terraces of palazzos, and swam in the sea, he stayed sober and attentive, his eyes and affection solely on me. It was the honeymoon we never had.

I only hope it will last.

———

Stones crunch under the tires as Peter pulls around the drive approaching Swinbrook House, the Oxfordshire home Farve built in 1926 when financial woes demanded he relinquish our beloved childhood family properties. We sisters even made up a mournful dirge about the family's downward spiral from Batsford Mansion to Asthall Manor to Swinbrook House. To the outside eye, I suppose Swinbrook looks rather grand, with its towering three stories, its wide, symmetrical expanse and its attractive vantage point on a hill. But to me, my sisters, and Tom, it simply cannot compare to the enchanted homes we lived in as children—castle-like Batsford Park with its 10,000 acres or Asthall with its forgotten rooms and rambling hallways, smaller but still vast at two thousand acres. Those places are the repository of our childhood memories, not this newly built, austere structure with its eighteen bedrooms. Swinbrook House contains no Hons' cupboard, that cozy, warm closet where we would hide and tell secrets; it is not a home to inspire magic.

As we approach the front of the house, I wonder about Diana. I'd sent her a letter from our trip, but received no reply. I suppose she's been healing from the accident, and I do hope the time has eased her pain. What will I face from her today? Will she still be holding on tight to her grudge about *Wigs on the Green*, or will her dangerous brush make her rethink petty feelings?

The towering front door swings open wide before we even knock, and Rosie greets us at the door with such enthusiasm I realize it's been an age since I visited Swinbrook House. "Mr. and Mrs. Rodd, what a pleasure!" With my parents always in the city overseeing the parade of sisters who've come out over the past few years, there hasn't been a need. But I should have returned to see the staff; after all, it was Rosie and Nanny Blor and several regular maids who offered the consistent love and affection that distracted Muv and mercurial Farve could not.

I squeeze Rosie tightly. How many days had she provided a refuge when the pawing and nagging of my sisters overwhelmed? How many nights had she soothed me back to sleep after a nightmare because I knew better than to disturb Muv or Farve, who went on legendary rants when we interrupted his bedtime?

We catch up on Rosie's family for a few minutes, and she then directs us to the terrace, where the luncheon will be served. "Your parents are already there, and some of your siblings," she says, guiding us to the terrace's wide glass doors. "And they've been waiting."

"I'd rather stay here with you," I say with a squeeze of her hand.

"Ah, love, don't I know it. But duty calls," she says with a nod and a gentle push.

We step out onto the stone terrace, which looks over the picturesque village, home to the Swan pub and not much else. Muv and Farve sit at either end of the long wrought-iron table as if they were in a formal dining room, with Tom, Decca, Debo, Pamela, and Derek settled on the chairs in between. Tom spots us first, stubs out his cigarette on the balustrade, and leaps up to greet us.

Putting a hand out to shake Peter's, Tom says, "Old chap, how've you been?"

"A sight better than when you saw me last," Peter says, referring to his appalling state at the Beaverbrooks' gala.

"Ah not to worry, chum"—Tom embraces me tightly—"not when you've put such a beautiful smile on my sister's face."

I grin at Tom, grateful for his words. It isn't often that I get a compliment in this company. No one else rises, so I make my way around the table, kissing each of them on the cheek. "Where is Diana? And Unity? I thought she was here visiting from Munich."

"Had been recalled from Munich, more like," Decca says under her breath.

"Such a brief visit," I add.

"It was long enough," Pamela mutters.

My sisters' comments aren't low enough to escape Muv's notice, and Decca and Pamela receive a scathing glance. "What?" Decca challenges Muv, something that's been occurring with more frequency. Passive she is not. "Are we going to pretend that as soon as Unity's antics hit the front page of the newspapers, you and Farve didn't insist she come home? And that once she was here, you couldn't wait for her to go back?"

Farve grumbles, and Muv changes the subject by asking, "Nancy, would you like a cocktail? Peter?"

I glance over at my husband, wondering if this will be the moment when his laudatory behavior will change. "A lemonade will do the trick for me," he says, to my great relief.

"The same for me. It looks refreshing."

I decide to change tack and inquire about Diana, who hasn't answered any of the letters I sent her. More than anything, today, I'd hoped to make amends with my sister; I've missed her. "I assumed Diana would be here as well, with Jonathan and Desmond." A terrible thought occurs to me. "She *is* out of hospital, isn't she?"

Decca and Debo giggle, and Decca asks, "You haven't heard?"

"Heard what?"

"Farve helped smuggle her out of St. George's Hospital just over a week after the accident," Debo says, well pleased to know the gossip for once.

"I thought she was meant to be there for well over a month," I say, confused. I'd actually postponed our trip to the Adriatic until Diana had successfully completed her second surgery. Only the doctor's encouraging words about her recovery gave me the comfort to leave.

"She was," Debo interjects, "but she couldn't bear to be parted from Mosley."

"I thought he'd gone to Italy with his children a few days after the accident."

"He had," Decca answers. I suppose it's her turn to divulge the scandalous news. "So Farve snuck her out of the hospital, helped her get a train to Naples, and from there, she flew to the villa."

"On her own?"

"Yes, with a fully bandaged face," Debo chimes in, not wanting to be left out of this scuttlebutt. Pamela, I notice, has been quiet; perhaps she doesn't want Derek to see this side of her family. She had, in fact, specifically asked us to refer to her as Pamela in the presence of Derek—never "Woman."

I am astonished. Even for Diana, even given her absolute devotion to Mosley, this is outrageous. And dangerous. But I am more flabbergasted that my father acted as her accomplice. I glance over at him, thinking about the eggshells that we walked on during our childhoods so as not to rouse "the Beast"; only when we felt daring—and terribly bored—did we have contests to see how far each of us could push him before his legendary temper emerged, a game Unity always lost. But his face bears its usual stoic expression, and he keeps busy carving the ham. What on earth prompted him to agree to such a rash scheme? I would ask, but I don't want to risk "the Beast" right now.

"Should we eat?" Muv asks, pretending as if a most bizarre exchange hadn't just taken place.

Peter and I are peppered with queries about Venice and the Adriatic over the meal, and I wait until a scrumptious dessert of Eton mess with strawberries is served to return the conversation to Unity. "So how *was* the visit with Unity?"

Silence reigns at the table. What in the name of God transpired while we were away? I have never known a Mitford family meal to be quiet. "What happened?" I insist.

Muv mutters, "Nothing."

Even Decca and Debo keep their eyes down and their lips sealed, until Farve finally says, "Well, she decided to practice her pistol shooting during the church fete."

"Pardon?" Did I mishear? Surely, he didn't mean to say that Unity shot an actual real-life gun during the annual St. Oswald's summer fair, a cherished event in which local ladies ran raffles and competed for best-in-show roses and sponges while children played ring toss and games of chance and the men swilled ale. He must have meant one of the games set up by the church ladies.

"Yes," he answers, still chewing a last bite of Eton mess. "Excused herself right in the middle of the Bakewell tart competition and began her pistol practice behind the church.

Of course, everyone came running. Thought someone had been killed."

"Where did she get a gun?" I am aghast and torn between laughter and tears.

"That's anyone's guess, but I'd surmise that there's no shortage of weaponry in the company she keeps," he says.

"We had hoped that a trip home might restore her to herself," Muv remarks.

"Maybe it did, Muv? Maybe Unity's 'self' is a swastika-wearing, pistol-toting Nazi?" Decca says, not bothering to mask the anger on her face. *How hard it must be to see her sister deep in the grips of fascism, the enemy of all Decca holds dear*, I think.

Muv doesn't answer, but I ask, "She wore a swastika armband while she was home?"

"Even to the church fete," Decca answers.

"Even to the Swan pub," Debo adds.

"Oh my God," I say, pushing back in my chair.

Farve says, "Winston says the Nazis are using her for propaganda, to encourage the English people to think well of them. You know, if one young English lady of high standing can be friends with Hitler and happily live in the 'New Germany,' you can as well. That sort of thing."

"Don't the Nazis realize that Unity could put people *off* them?" Decca snickers.

"Jessica!" Muv scolds.

I glance over at Peter, whose mouth is agape, which, I suppose, *is* the proper reaction to this conversation. His mouth finally shuts and then opens again as he speaks. "Why are we sitting around talking as if Unity's behavior is normal? Joking about it? It was one thing when she attended a few rallies of the British Union of Fascists with her older sisters. But now, stalking Adolf Hitler? Wearing a swastika in Swinbrook? Shooting guns at a church fete? Something must be done about her—*for* her."

I could kiss him. It is the first logical utterance about Unity that I've heard.

"Peter's right," I say. "We've got to do something to help her. Starting with getting her out of Munich."

"Yes," Peter echoes me. "Why was she ever allowed to return in the first place?"

Muv looks down her nose at us, because—of course—it is a subtle dig at her and Farve. "In proposing that we extricate Unity from Munich, you are suggesting that there is something wrong with her beliefs. Unity is entitled to her notions— whether or not you agree with them—just as much as you two are or, I dare say, Decca is to hers."

I've never known Muv to care about one's right to political views before, and I cannot help but wonder if she is motivated by a desire to *keep* Unity in Germany. Or perhaps she simply wants to pick a fight with me. Either could be true, or both.

"Muv, we aren't objecting to Unity's beliefs. We are concerned about her behavior. Supporting a political movement by casting a vote or even engaging in a protest is very different from moving to a foreign country, pursuing its leader, and then returning home in full fascist regalia with a gun," I say, as evenly as I can.

To my utter astonishment, Farve nods. "Nancy has a point,

Sydney." Muv's eyes widen, and he pauses before continuing. "But maybe we don't need to bring her back home just yet. What if we send over one of the children to lay eyes on her and the company she keeps? Report back?"

Muv considers his idea, and from the gleam in her eye, I see that she finds it far preferable to retrieving Unity. "Should we send Diana? She certainly knows her way around Germany."

"I'd hardly credit Diana with making good decisions at the moment," Peter says. "Didn't she just check herself out of the hospital to fly halfway across Europe to meet her lover? And anyway, shouldn't she still be healing from her surgeries?"

Decca and Debo snort, and even Pamela chuckles. Muv says nothing. How could she?

I pick up where Peter leaves off. "Not to mention, she's spent week upon week with Unity in Munich in the company of the Nazis and hasn't once sounded the alarm about Unity's behavior. It makes Diana an unlikely candidate to bring her home. And anyway, is Diana still in Italy with Mosley?"

"Yes, Diana is recuperating there. Perhaps there is nothing to be concerned about in terms of Unity." Muv's eyes narrow as she turns toward me. "Perhaps this is you picking on your sisters again because you don't share their views—as you did with *Wigs on the Green*."

How tired I am of being the brunt of her anger and dislike! Does Muv ever consider that the reason I'm sharp is because I needed to become a blade to survive this family? I want desperately to retreat from this controversy and return to the fleeting peace I found with Peter on the Adriatic. But how can I do that to Unity? If there is a chance she's at risk to herself or others,

I would never forgive myself if I didn't try to help. Particularly since it's clear no one else will.

Peter reaches for my hand and gazes into my face. He must see the conflict raging within me, the desire to flee up against the compunction to help. He rises to the occasion—becoming the husband he vowed to be—and speaks for me. "Why don't we send Tom?"

# CHAPTER TWENTY-NINE
## DIANA

*August 20, 1935*
*Naples, Italy*

D IANA GAZES OUT ACROSS THE BAY OF NAPLES TO MOUNT
Vesuvius, her eyes lingering on the island of Capri, which
juts out of the middle of the azure sea. How she adored her
day on Capri with M, just the two of them swimming, dining,
drinking, and making love on his thirty-foot, three-cabin yacht,
the *Vivien*, her recovering face dramatically shielded from the
strong sun with a few stunning wide-brim hats, of course. Far
from the ears of the children and the eyes of Baba. On that day,
as she stood next to M, Diana sensed that she'd won.

Her triumph had not been a foregone conclusion when she
arrived at the villa at Posillipo. She'd underestimated the extent
of her injuries and the toll of the travel, a flight from Croydon
to Marseilles, followed by a seaplane to Italy, and then a train to
this affluent area of Naples that sits on a verdant hillside with
dramatic views of the Bay of Naples. Weak and looking the
worse for wear, she'd arrived during the middle of an elaborate
formal dinner party that M was hosting for the Crown Prince
and Princess of Italy, who Baba had known since her youth.

The expression on M's face when the footman delivered him to Diana—half her face underneath a lovely silk scarf—had been priceless. "Diana, wh–what," he stammered, and then wrapped her in his muscular arms. "My poor, precious goddess, how did you manage it?"

"You've always said I was a marvel," she whispered into his neck, and he rewarded her with a most tender, delicate kiss on her wounded face.

Although M had excused himself from the dinner to settle Diana in one of the many guest rooms, she could hear Baba and M arguing in the hallway. The fury in Baba's voice snaked down the corridor into the lavish guest room and under the pressed cotton sheets where Diana lay, as if that anger meant to strangle her. And this pleased Diana greatly; after all, the purpose of her visit here was disruption.

Over the next three days, M kept the two women apart, no great challenge given Diana's need for rest and recuperation. A terrace overlooking the bay extended from her bedroom, and she was quite happy alternating between her bed and a chaise longue in the sunlight with her face shielded, interrupted only by periodic visits from her lover. She tolerated the notion of Baba and M together in such close proximity to her, only because she knew her presence in the villa was driving a wedge between them. She never complained about the time M dedicated to his former sister-in-law; Diana was playing the long game.

After three days of this arrangement, Diana heard Baba storming through the villa, ordering servants about as she packed her belongings. Loud shouts of "insufferable" and "intolerable" could be heard echoing up the stairs and down the hallways, whether these outbursts were for Diana's benefit or M's, she didn't know. By the time M returned from delivering Baba to the train station, Diana had already installed herself in the master suite, which her nemesis had only just vacated. And for the next several weeks, as they sailed and swam and dined and played with the children, the trip went precisely as she'd hoped.

———

"Darling," she says, wrapping her arms around his neck. "Do you have absolutely everything you need?"

"Well…" He nuzzles her neck, warming her all over, while carefully avoiding the few remaining plasters on her face. "How can I have everything I need if you won't be there?"

She laughs, beaming up at him through her lashes. "I'll be waiting right here for your return, and it will be only four short days."

"Four important days," he clarifies, then adds, "thanks to you."

Smiling beatifically—as if it was no small thing for her to arrange a luncheon in his honor hosted in Munich by Hitler himself—she says, "It is no less than you deserve."

"It might be the very thing to keep the BUF going strong," he says, in an understatement. After Baba left, M made another confession to Diana. Mussolini had been subsidizing the BUF to the tune of five thousand pounds a month for several years. The money arrived in mixed currencies via an agency with international ties, owned by an old friend of M's. But in the wake of the violence at Olympia Hall, membership in the BUF has been falling, and Mussolini's people have been telling him that British fascism might not gain the sort of traction they hoped for. Payments have decreased, putting the BUF's future at risk, especially when Mosley had lost the patronage of Lord Rothmere as well after the Olympia rally. M was ebullient when Diana told him she thought she had a solution, although, of course, she didn't mention that she hoped to solve two problems with the Hitler luncheon she'd orchestrated—bolstering the BUF and eviscerating M's need for Baba's assistance. M must believe he alone made the decision to leave Baba behind.

"Absolutely, darling. I know it will," she says with a long, languorous kiss.

Closing the door behind him, she grabs a bottle of champagne and a crystal flute and descends the hundred stairs that lead from the villa to the beach. Dusk has settled on the magnificent bay, and many of the boats have returned to the docks, leaving a vast expanse of unusually placid blue. Diana pours herself a tall glass of the bubbly, raises it in a toast to herself, and downs it in one draught. She then strips off her white silk dress and dives into the sea, triumphant in her primacy.

# CHAPTER THIRTY
# UNITY

*August 22, 1935*
*Munich, Germany*

*T*HANK GOD TOM DOESN'T ARRIVE UNTIL NEXT WEEK, UNITY thinks. Although her brother speaks fluent German, received his law degree in Berlin, and has long adored all things Teutonic, one can never guess what peculiar opinion he might blurt out. Unity cannot risk a misstep on his part, and given the odd circumstances around his visit and her strong suspicion that he's being sent by her parents to spy on her, she's deeply concerned about how Tom might behave amid a crowd of Nazis.

Tonight is special. She's been invited to several of the high-ranking Nazi dinners and outings in the past, although usually of a more public variety. *They do like to show me off, almost like a treasured prize*, she thinks with a smile. But this evening is the first time she's been included in the inner circle, perhaps because the idea for the event stemmed from her.

When she received Diana's letter about the BUF's financial problems in the wake of Mussolini's reduced funding, she knew her imperious sister was subtly asking for her help with Mosley. She felt indescribably moved by the fact that *she* could deliver something to her sister. *Incredible how easy it had been to arrange the introduction of Mosley to Hitler once I set my mind to it*, she thinks.

How meaningful that letter had been to her on the heels of her disastrous trip home. No one had appreciated her at Muv and Farve's house. In fact, they downright objected to her wearing the same sort of garb she did in Munich—all black with her beautiful little gold swastika pin or bold red armband and, occasionally if it was cool enough, her black leather gauntlets. Unity knew how striking she looked in her Nazi uniform, and she was positively downhearted that they objected to her clothes, rather than showered her with compliments as she'd expected. And that was nothing compared to the fuss they raised when she practiced her shooting at that tedious church fete at St. Oswald's. What was the problem with a little target practice when everyone was out of range? She wishes that all those narrow-minded English people—especially the ones that went running at the sight or sound of her at St. Oswald's—could see her now at the epicenter of Nazi power, being celebrated for her views and attire rather than reviled.

Unity glances around Hitler's flat, where he is hosting the private luncheon. She has been here four times before for small gatherings, and today, the art-lined apartment is festooned with bouquets of flowers as well as the arrangement of several tables with white linen, crystal, and silver around the parlor and dining room. The guest list is equally impressive; in addition to the usual upper-echelon officers, Hitler has invited some German aristocrats and luminaries, including the Kaiser's daughter, the Duchess of Brunswick, and some members of the family of the famous composer Richard Wagner. *Diana will be well pleased,* Unity thinks, *because if Mosley makes a good impression here, new funding may well come his way.*

"Fräulein Mitford," Winifred Wagner calls over to Unity. As she weaves through the guests to the widow of Siegfried Wagner, who'd been a friend of her grandfather's, she thinks how inextricably intertwined are her life and the Führer's, and how all these shared elements have brought them together to this destined juncture. She knows that she is part of something larger than herself, that she's found her purpose at Hitler's side.

"How lovely to see you, Frau Wagner," she greets Winifred in English with a warm embrace. Although Winifred considers herself German and had been adopted by a German relative at the age of eight, she was born in England to English parents. "I trust you've been keeping well."

"With the Führer in charge, how could we be anything but well?" Winifred beams over at their beloved leader, with whom she and her late husband had been friends for over a decade. In fact, rumor has it that, during Hitler's incarceration in the 1920s, the Wagners supplied the wrapped food and stationery upon which he wrote his autobiography, *Mein Kampf.*

"I couldn't agree with you more, Frau Wagner," Unity concurs.

"I understand you and our friend have been growing quite close," Winifred says with a knowing, almost maternal smile.

Much to her consternation, Unity feels her cheeks flush. She wouldn't want Winifred or anyone in Hitler's inner circle to think she had grand aspirations. "I am fortunate to spend time with our Leader."

"He favors you, my little Valkyrie. You should feel nothing but proud of that," Winifred says with a pat on Unity's arm. "In fact, he mentioned that he might like to host a special event for you at the Bayreuth Festival." The festival is an annual summer event in which Wagnerian operas are performed in a specially designed theater.

Unity cannot believe Winifred's words; it would be an unimaginable honor. "An event for me?"

Winifred drops her voice. "Yes, but perhaps he wants to make this a surprise. Let's keep it between us."

As Unity nods in agreement, Mosley passes by, whispering, "Hello again, my little fascist." Upon his arrival yesterday, they'd spent the better part of the day together, with Unity briefing him on all things Hitler. Today, she knows that Mosley must concentrate on forging relationships with the leaders here to convince them of the importance of the BUF to the overall Nazi mission. She's arranged for him to have a translator at his side to facilitate conversation with those not fluent in English.

Streicher has Mosley in tow, and they pause to talk to an official Unity doesn't recognize. While she listens to Winifred talking about the schedule for the Bayreuth Festival and alterations they are making to its famous stage, she eavesdrops on Mosley's conversations with these men.

"I think we'd like to see the BUF come more in line with our core beliefs," Streicher says to Mosley through an interpreter, and the other gentleman nods emphatically.

"We are already in such close accord with the Nazi ideology, I cannot imagine that would be a problem," Mosley replies, in as accommodating a tone as Unity has ever heard from him. "Is there a particular area you'd like to focus upon?"

Streicher smiles his strange, unsettling grin. "Well, the BUF has only hinted at the problem of the Jews. I think we would be well pleased to see the BUF come out with a public statement lambasting the manner in which the British Jewish community controls the press, the factories, the banks, even the cinema. If the BUF would be willing to go even further and call for an end to this Jewish corruption not only in England but in Europe, well"—the grin grows wider—"I think that would go a long way to convincing the Führer that our interests are aligned."

Unity notices the slightest flinch on Mosley's face, but he is quick to agree regardless. "The BUF would be honored to make a public statement that proclaims its kinship with the Nazi beliefs about the Jews."

Streicher folds his hands across his enormous belly and says, "Excellent, I was hoping you'd feel that way. Let us introduce you to our host, Herr Hitler. I think he will be most pleased."

As the men cross the room to the corner where Hitler holds court, Unity turns her full focus back to Winifred with a smile. She is certain that Diana will be pleased with her handiwork.

# CHAPTER THIRTY-ONE
# NANCY

*July 28, 1936*
*London, England*

S TAY CALM. KEEP EVEN. ADHERE TO A SCHEDULE. DO NOT
allow my feathers to get ruffled. No overtaxing myself.
This is the prescription I receive from my doctor after Peter and
I have been trying unsuccessfully for a baby for over two years.

This advice had been doled out to me before, but it isn't
until the kerfuffle over Unity and Diana over the summer that I
decide to commit to my doctor's instructions. It helps, of course,
that Peter has been staying on the straight and narrow; we seem
to have gotten in the habit of niceness to one another, which
may be more important than love in the end. His surprisingly
steady presence allows me to keep away from familial and political strife—admittedly made more challenging by the invasion
of Ethiopia by the Italian fascists, ratcheting up my fear about
Unity and the spread of fascism—and instead remain focused
on healthy endeavors.

The retreat from familial controversy and societal pressure
is made easier by my latest project. One that engrosses and
busies me, not to mention providing much-needed income, but

isn't particularly strenuous. It comes in the form of an unexpected commission from my cousin and friend Edward, Lord Stanley of Alderley.

The Stanley family of Alderley are not just relatives. They have long been a mainstay of British aristocratic life, and when Edward inherited the family castle in Scotland, he discovered a literal treasure trove of letters stretching over the centuries. He wants me not only to catalog the thousands of missives, but also to make historical sense of them, synthesizing them into a mirror of the past. I was his ideal candidate, he said, not only due to my writing talent but because of my close tie to the family, my understanding of their quirks and the vagaries of time. Farve's father—my "naughty grandfather," as we called him for his teasing ways and his sometimes condemnable behavior—had been married to Lady Clementine Ogilvy, a daughter of the Earl of Airlie who belonged to the Stanley family. So, through Farve's mother, I suppose I am a Stanley myself, and it's my own history I'm writing as well.

I feel an unfamiliar peace as I sit at my little desk before the bay window at Rose Cottage. With each yellowed, brittle page of Stanley letters I lift and study, I feel like I'm uncovering a part of myself and our collective past. Of all the delectable nuggets in the boxes, I'm particularly drawn to the mid-nineteenth-century exchanges between Maria Josepha, Lady Stanley of Alderley, and her daughter-in-law Henrietta Stanley. Maria, born in 1771, had been unusually bright and privately educated far beyond the norm, becoming known for writing about a daughter's right to choose a husband, and she shared those views with her daughter-in-law Henrietta, an advocate for women's education. I feel a kinship with these surprisingly modern ladies.

"Listen to this, Prod," I call out to Peter, who sits in his study, smoking and reading. "Maria applauded her daughter-in-law Henrietta for scolding her husband, John—who was Maria's son, of course—for not more vociferously defending women's rights. How utterly fabulous is that?"

"Sounds like something that would be written today, not seventy-five years ago," he calls back.

"Precisely," I reply. "I think modern-day readers would be interested to know that historical women shared their concerns and beliefs. They could learn a thing or two from these women."

"Are you thinking of writing just about Henrietta and Maria?" He asks the very question I've been toying with.

"Perhaps," I answer. "What would you think about a volume entitled *The Ladies of Alderley*?"

"Topping and very *you*," he says.

As I muse over this possibility, I reach down to rub Milly and Lottie, who sit at my feet as usual. Why couldn't my own family be more like these Stanleys, Henrietta and Maria? Using their intellect, societal position, and connections to advocate for positive change rather than fixate on putting fascists in power, here and abroad? I know from reading the newspaper and letters from Muv that Diana and Unity are in Munich for the Olympics. *What a colossal waste of talent and opportunity and what havoc they might wreak.* Should I be doing something more about my sisters and their dangerous views and companions, beyond writing fiction about it as I had with *Wigs on the Green*? I feel like I'm sitting on the sidelines of life as the world begins to fracture around me—while I wait for a child that may never come.

*Stop*, I tell myself. Thinking about my sisters and their political maneuvering will only make me anxious and rile my nerves, which have stayed wonderfully steady these past months. And very likely, nothing will come of their troublesome behavior, other than my worry. Instead, I inhale deeply and turn back to a delightful letter from Maria. Although their political world seems antiquated, it also seems wonderfully settled compared to today.

I hear Peter's footsteps as he walks into the drawing room. He rubs my shoulders and stares out onto the Thames, glistening in the gold-and-copper setting sun. "Beautiful light this evening."

I lean my head on his arm, thinking how marvelous it is to have someone upon which I can rely. It isn't something I grew up with, after all. "Should we pop out to the Bell and Crown for a pub dinner?" he asks.

If anyone would have told me five years ago that my ideal evening would soon be a day spent pawing through ancient letters followed by a pub dinner with my husband, I would have screeched. And Evelyn would have howled. But I don't see nearly as much of Evelyn anymore, and it sounds positively perfect. "Let's."

Do I miss the wild parties and heavy drinking of my days as a jeunesse dorée, or gilded youth? Am I longing to roar home at six o'clock in the morning still in my evening gown while regular folks are starting their morning work shift? Sometimes. But then I think how tiring and lonely those nights actually were, and I know that I'm content to retreat from the chaotic days and nights surging around us into Rose Cottage and the past. For now.

# CHAPTER THIRTY-TWO
# DIANA

*July 28, 1936*
*Berlin, Germany*

*THE SETTING IS IDYLLIC*, DIANA THINKS. A SPARE MINISTE-rial home decorated with flowers. A veritable phalanx of high-ranking Nazi officers surrounding them. Strains of Wagner floating through the warm summer air from the gramophone. A tunic of pale-gold silk over a long black velvet skirt. A bouquet of roses, chrysanthemums, and carnations. Not what every woman would wish for her wedding, mind. But perfect for M and Diana.

The ceremony has none of the grandeur and lavishness of her first wedding. There, she'd walked down the long, exquisite aisle of St. Margaret's Church in Westminster Abbey with the train of her gown held aloft by one of her eleven bridesmaids, before hundreds of aristocrats and high-society folks. The wedding made the cover of nearly every English newspaper, and they were heralded as the "It" couple of the decade. All a dazzling, empty facade.

This simple, private service is utterly different and, for that reason, perfect. She and M need the wedding to be secretive, particularly with the press interest in the increasingly controversial BUF and the consistent fascination with all things Mitford. Mosley is particularly concerned about the vengeful wrath of Baba if their union becomes known, and he cannot take the chance that she would attempt to smear him publicly and divert support and whatever money he still received from Italy or aristocratic acquaintances away from the BUF.

Diana and Mosley had discussed marrying in Great Britain, but that would not allow for any secrecy. Even if they managed to conduct the wedding privately, they would need to file the record of their marriage publicly, where it would eventually be discovered; journalists were constantly pestering them about a marital union, no one more than Winston's pesky son Randolph. Diana had raised this conundrum with Hitler during her more and more frequent trips to Berlin, a phenomenon that began when the Führer suggested a Berlin visit to Diana and they discovered how much they enjoyed each other's company at his private residence in the Old Chancellery.

Their evenings have been surprisingly casual and comfortable, sharing a simple vegetarian meal à deux and a film but nothing more; he has never initiated contact of an intimate or sexual nature, but instead has always been reserved and mannerly. Rarely do their conversations touch on actual politics—Hitler does not believe that is a woman's realm—but when they do, she acts the part of an ardent fascist. Even though she doesn't approach the vehemency of Unity or M, she and Hitler are in perfect accord in wanting peace and unity between Great

Britain and Germany. The most Hitler has expected in exchange for these cozy evenings is a description of what she has overheard about English-German relations, particularly if it involves Cousin Winston. This, she believes, is an innocuous enough tit for tat for his future financial commitment to the BUF.

"Mosley and I would, of course, like to marry," she said in reply to Hitler's polite inquiry about her future with Mosley, after explaining their unusual situation and leaving out the adulterous relationship between Baba and Mosley for fear of his reaction. The Führer can be unexpectedly moralistic, Diana has found.

"Naturally you want to marry. That is every woman's wish and in the interest of most men," he responded. Diana had heard some version of this several times before, an interesting view for a leader who advocates for the marital state and families so strongly but always has an excuse at the ready for not marrying his own mistress.

"Not you, Führer. You could never be placed in the ordinary category of 'most men.'"

He chuckled. Diana knew how much he enjoyed light, innocent flattery. "Well, my duties to Germany are such that I could never be the fully devoted husband and family man that is the Nazi ideal."

"Germany is the more fortunate for your dedication and sacrifice," she added and received a gentle pat on her hand for her efforts.

"But we must find a way to fulfill *your* wish. A woman of your beauty and standing should have the ability to marry when and how she wishes." He paused, and just as she was about to thank him for his kind words, he stood up. "What if you married here, in Germany? I could arrange special Reich permission for your marriage, and there would be no need to file anything publicly in England."

"You would do that for us? You would grant us that great honor?" She rose from her chair and faced him.

He reached for her hand and held it gingerly in his own pale palm. "For the Aryan beauty who will serve as the bridge between Germany and England? It would be my great pleasure."

———

Did Diana then use this kindly gesture on Hitler's part to place subtle pressure on Mosley to commit to a marital plan? Perhaps. After all, prior talk of commitment had consisted of evasion and vague promises on the part of M, and Diana had grown weary of his elusion. Not that Diana would ever nag or wheedle, and in the end, she didn't have to. Because Hitler did it for her.

Finally she stands before a registrar and M, ready to become his wife. *How long this day has been in coming*, Diana thinks, with a deep, satisfying sigh. If only her boys could be here; she loathed leaving them behind for the extended trip, of which the marriage will only be the first part, because the boys are old enough now to notice and track her absence, but it is necessary. This constant travel to Germany has become exhausting, but she knows she must maintain her status as one of Hitler's inner circle for Mosley's benefit. And for her own.

Her sole witness, Unity, catches her eye. Diana knows how

tickled she is to be the only bridesmaid and family member present, and Unity's off-kilter, slightly hysterical enthusiasm reminds Diana that she'll have to keep an eye on her little sister. Unity's access to the center of German power has left her a little unhinged, but there can be no real discussion of her return to England, as Muv and Farve have intimated. They'd decided to allow Unity to stay in Germany once Tom reported back that all seemed to be well with his younger sister. Diana needs Unity in Germany because she needs her access to Hitler. It would be strange for Diana to travel to Germany without the excuse of visiting her sister.

Diana looks past Unity to smile at her beloved. His dark hair, broad shoulders, and powerful presence are as commanding today as the night she first met him. The road to securing M has required more courage and abandon than she believed possible, but she never doubted her success. She has always believed in the force of her will.

So even though Reich Minister of Propaganda Goebbels may not adore Diana—he is suspicious of all the British—his Berlin home has become their wedding chapel and his Wannsee villa the site of their wedding breakfast, with no family to celebrate this union save Unity as her witness. Nontraditional, yes, but then the course Diana has charted is uncommon.

# CHAPTER THIRTY-THREE
# UNITY

*August 1, 1936*
*Berlin, Germany*

T HE PAGEANTRY IS BREATHTAKING, BEYOND EVEN WHAT Unity had witnessed at the various *Parteitage* she's attended over the years. The rush she experiences watching the Olympic flame entering the vast stadium, the showpiece of the newly built sports complex, to a crowd of over a hundred thousand spectators is indescribable. How proud she feels to be standing here in the special bleachers behind Hitler's podium on the opening day of the Olympics, an integral part of this new, powerful Germany—and key to ensuring the harmony between Germany and Great Britain. This, Hitler has assured her, is his goal as well.

The audience quiets as Hitler enters the arena. All eyes are on him as he accepts a floral tribute from a little girl, and Unity is delighted that the rest of the world gets a glimpse of the kindly Führer that she knows so well. The person behind the firm and powerful leader he presents everywhere else. Silence continues to pervade the stadium as Hitler mounts the stairs to the podium and prepares to speak. The audience thinks they'll receive a manic, dramatic speech—the likes of which they've seen on countless newsreels—but Unity knows he has chosen a different approach for this very public stage.

The Führer stands before the microphone, pausing before he begins. Calmly, slowly, and with minimal gesticulations, he says, "I proclaim the Games of Berlin, celebrating the eleventh Olympiad of the modern era, to be open."

The stadium is utterly still for a long second, expecting Hitler to say more. Unity has to restrain a giggle at the masterful, unexpected way the Führer has managed the world's expectations today. When finally he nods—a signal to start the parade—the audience breaks into a deafening cheer. And the parade begins.

The first of forty-nine nations begins its march around the track, passing first by the special stand of German and international guests in which Unity and Diana sit. Nearly 4,000 athletes, wearing the distinctive costumes of their countries, march and wave. Germany has nearly 450 contenders, with the United States as its fiercest competitor.

After nearly an hour of this procession, Unity and Diana follow the lead of those standing in front of them and sit down. But not the Führer. He stands at attention through it all, and Unity wonders if she's ever adored him more.

As Hitler offers each of the country's athletes the Nazi salute, Unity notices that only the Italians—Mussolini's representatives—actually have the courtesy to return the salute in kind. Great Britain's athletes refuse to use the gesture, and while Unity considers herself patriotic, she's embarrassed and ashamed at their disrespect. She wishes more than ever that

Mosley's efforts to make the BUF the prominent British political party had already been successful; if he'd been triumphant,
Great Britain's athletes would be using the Nazi salute here
today as well. Although she'd never tell Diana, Unity harbors
serious doubts Mosley will ever attain the same sort of success
as Hitler. But perhaps, just perhaps, Unity might be able to
move the dial in Mosley's direction. She fervently hopes so—
how else will she achieve her dream of an allied Great Britain
and Germany?

Through the din from the enormous brass band, Unity
hears one of the Nazi officials in the bleacher turn to another
and say, "Doesn't look like much of a boycott to me."

She knows they're referring to the public call for an Olympic
boycott by factions of the British and American communities
on the basis of the Third Reich's Aryan-only policies. What
really fueled the protest was the removal of certain Jewish
athletes from sports facilities and associations, particularly
heavyweight champion Erich Seelig from the German boxing
team, Daniel Prenn, Germany's top-ranked tennis player, from
Germany's Davis Cup team, and Gretel Bergmann, a world-
class high jumper, from her club.

The other official snorts, "The damned Brits and
Americans made that hoopla, and all they managed to do was
look like liars."

"No evidence of Jewish discrimination here in Berlin, is
there?" he says with a laugh.

"Our very own Goebbels made sure of that."

Unity recalls the flurry of activity in the months leading
up to the Olympic festivities with its anticipated thousands

of visitors from all over the ɣorld. The many signs regulating Jewish activities were scrubbed from walls, and the newspapers stopped lambasting the Jewish population and blaming them for every ill that befell Germany, past and present.

"Brilliant stroke to allow that Jew fencer Helene Mayer to compete for Germany."

"How could Germany be persecuting the Jews if they've got a Jew athlete representing them in the Olympics? Right?"

"Exactly, even if it makes me sick to see her out there saluting us."

Unity forces her attention away from the men, momentarily disturbed by their words. Why is she feeling this way, today of all days? She has espoused everything they stand for and far, far more. In conversations. In the newspapers. In rally speeches. She should be glorying in this day, but some latent part of her nags at her conscience. Refusing to listen to that voice, she silences it instead.

She suddenly feels eyes upon her. Did someone see her flinch at the comments about Helène Mayer? She must be careful. Other senior Nazis are jealous of her special relationship with Hitler, and she knows they're on high alert for any misstep. She will do nothing to jeopardize her relationship with the Führer. She will say and do whatever is necessary to further their tie and mission.

Surreptitiously she glances around. Diana isn't looking at her; she's trying to stifle a yawn. Unity knows Diana finds all this gamesmanship terribly dull—she's never been one for disc throwing and the like—but she does appreciate the importance of this spectacle, and even though Unity smarts over the à deux meetings between Hitler and Diana, she is happy to have her sister at her side. They make a formidable pair.

It is then Unity notices Eva Braun. Eva's enmity has been clear on the few occasions their paths have crossed, fueled no doubt by rumors spread by hate-mongers like Goebbels. Unity had assumed that once Hitler installed Eva at Berghof as his official mistress, any jealousy might lift. That she might understand they have different, albeit equally important, roles in the destiny of Hitler. And Unity will be the one to lift him up to his God-given place as the Supreme Führer of Europe.

# CHAPTER THIRTY-FOUR
# NANCY

*October 4, 1936*
*Kent, England*

HOW DO THEY EXPECT ME TO SIT HERE AND LISTEN TO this frivolous small talk? Chitter-chatter about wives and mistresses, the latest soirees, and who wore what. Don't they know how unimportant this all is? The pit in my stomach grows with each bit of examined minutiae. I want to scream, but instead I work up a paltry imitation of a smile for Muv and Cousin Clemmie and excuse myself from the tea table, leaving Debo and Pamela to handle the conversation.

I wander over to the window looking out on Cousin Winston's garden. As Clemmie tells it, the whole house is really Winston's idea—he purchased Chartwell on a whim years ago when she had just given birth to their youngest child, Mary—and she's never really claimed it as her own. The garden in particular belongs to him, and any number of half-started projects litter the expanse of green, including a half-built brick wall that apparently is also one of Winston's endeavors. I cannot quite imagine him in worker's garb, elbow deep in mortar and bricks.

Why did I come today and subject myself to this assault

of normalcy? As the months pass and my hopes of pregnancy pass with them, I have learned that I am safer with the past. The yellowed, stained Stanley letters. The tart, supportive exchanges between Maria and her daughter-in-law Henrietta. There, I can lose myself safely without fear of becoming annoyed or upset, without any assault on my thoughts or emotions.

If my situation doesn't improve—if I fail to get pregnant again this month—will I lose myself forever in the past? Will I forever exist on the periphery of life, watching from the outside? I can envision a future in which I spend the years sifting through these letters, churning out volume after volume of the Stanley family legacy. All the while, shelving my own sad future. Alone.

The smell of cigars permeates the air, and I turn to find Winston at my side. How does such a rotund man manage such stealth? Nary a floorboard creaked as he crossed the room to reach me.

"You lasted longer at the conversation than I guessed," he says with a thoughtful puff.

"What had you wagered?"

"Fifteen minutes." He glances at his wristwatch. "You stuck it out for twenty-three. Far better than I would have done."

"I don't believe you even joined us at the table."

"I'm a man who knows my limitations."

I laugh and say, "I believe your limitations are famous." As are his quirks. My sisters and I often muse on how the elegant, restrained Clemmie tolerates—even indulges—his peculiar needs and daily schedule here at Chartwell, including multi-hour baths and working in his bed and pajamas until after noon most days. Is this peculiar retreat from society more preferable to Clemmie than the humiliation she might endure in the more public spaces they used to inhabit? There, she faces scoffing and ostracism thanks to her husband's proclamations about the threat of the Nazis and the damage of England's ongoing appeasement under Prime Minister Chamberlain's leadership. People don't want to hear the truth; the fiction is so much more pleasant.

"You know, I've been wanting to have a private word with you for some time."

What on earth would Winston want with me? I always got the sense that he found me and my sisters unbearably frivolous, even though he certainly couldn't have formed that opinion based on extensive conversation with us. He always gravitated to Farve and Tom, usually with his son, Randolph, in tow. "You have? To what do I owe the pleasure?"

He pulls the cigar out of his mouth for a moment and uses it to point toward the window. "Should we walk through the garden? Weather looks like it'll hold."

"Sounds divine," I reply. What else could I say?

As we wander through Winston's garden with its view of the man-made lake, we discuss the grounds at first and his plans. Then, without any sort of segue, he says, "You know I don't know if I ever told you how much I enjoyed *Wigs on the Green*."

I stop in my tracks. "You read *Wigs on the Green*?"

He gives me a sly smile to the right of his cigar. "Why are you surprised? My reading appetites are vast and varied."

I smile back. "I would never doubt the breadth of your reading. It's just that *Wigs of the Green* is more fluff than anything, and it wasn't terribly popular with the family in any event."

He snorts. "I can imagine why. The pages were populated with Mosley and Unity, weren't they?"

I glance at him coyly. "I don't know what you mean. Captain Jack and Eugenia are entirely works of fiction."

He ignores me and continues with his intended conversation. "The views you shared on fascism in that book were anything but fluff."

"True enough. Writing is my way of expressing opinions. Women don't really have many other avenues of having our voices heard," I say as I amble at his side.

"I share your views." He stops walking and stares at me. "I've seen Hitler's boys at work, and I've been following his machinations through my sources. No matter what that idiot Chamberlain says, fascism is a threat to our country. Whether it's in Germany or homegrown."

"I'm no expert on German fascism, but I've seen firsthand the damage the English variety can do and has done." I pause and add, "I use satire and humor because they're the only weapons at my disposal, and the truth hits too close to home for several of my family members."

"I am concerned about those family members of yours, Nancy." He needn't name Unity and Diana to make their identities clear.

"As am I," I concur, wondering why Winston is suddenly interested in the welfare of my sisters. Admittedly, he's long had a fondness for Diana, who, together with Tom and Winston's son, Randolph, spent more time at Chartwell than the rest of us, but I don't think he harbors any special affection for Unity. Few do, outside our family.

"Do Diana and Unity ever tell you much about Hitler?" he asks. I'm unsurprised by the question. Winston's fixation on Hitler and his plans is well known, although a very unpopular stance with the Chamberlain administration, as well as the aristocrats drawn to fascism and the Nazis as a perceived antidote to communism.

"I can't say that Diana and I are particularly chummy these days. You might guess that *Wigs on the Green* has something to do with that. And Unity, well, she hasn't been to England much. She makes her home in Munich, not a place I'm dying to go."

"Ah, I see. Even though I no longer have the status that I once did, I still have ties to the heart of British power, and I worry that Hitler may be exploiting your sisters—Unity more than Diana. This will become more and more important in the days to come; I have it on good authority that Germany and Italy are considering an alliance."

I shiver at the thought of the two fascist powerhouses joining forces. "What do you mean that Hitler may be exploiting my sisters? For propaganda purposes?" I ask, perplexed. I can understand why someone might enjoy having the beautiful Diana on his arm at a news conference or public event, but Unity is a loose cannon in the best of times.

"In part. He certainly put them on display at the Olympics. Their presence among all those Nazis makes Hitler more palatable to the English. I suppose that's their aim. And Unity has served as his spokesperson against the Jews."

I wince at the unsavory reference. "Much to my dismay. What's the other part?"

"Extracting information from them."

"You think Hitler is getting valuable information from *Unity?*" I laugh. "She cares more about learning which desserts her precious Führer prefers than discussing military strategy. Even Diana is a stretch. It's not like Mosley has access to the inner workings of the government or key decisions about international policy—including Germany."

"Perhaps your sisters don't have ill intent. And perhaps your sisters don't realize the importance of what they may have heard in the company of English high society and what they have divulged or may divulge." He puffs on his cigar while assessing the landscape. "Or perhaps they do. You may be in a unique position to find out, or you could stay on the sidelines of the battle brewing and just write fiction about it."

I pause, not entirely sure what he's requesting and taken aback at his insight into my current state of mind.

Sensing my confusion, Winston continues, "This is an invitation, Nancy. To help steer the course of the world's future."

# CHAPTER THIRTY-FIVE
# DIANA

*October 4, 1936*
*London, England*

HOW POWERFUL HER HUSBAND LOOKS STANDING ON THE makeshift podium on Cable Street in the East End of London, speaking to the black-shirted BUF members about to continue the march from the parade they'd held on Royal Mint Street. *My husband,* she thinks again. How Diana adores thinking and saying that about M. Even though she's been married before, having *M* as her husband—linked to a powerful destiny through him—fills her with strange delight.

In that moment, M glances in her direction and his eyes widen in astonishment. He had warned her against coming, but she wanted to be here for this triumph. The day after he'd left their new home called Wootton Lodge in the north of England—a magical seventeenth-century stone house approached by a mile-long expanse of beech trees and nes-tled at the base of snowcapped Weaver Hill where her boys can toboggan nearly year-round and M can fish for trout in one of several lakes on the property—Diana had snuck away to London herself to surprise him at the rally. And now she watches as pleasure, then frustration registers on his face, seeing her at the periphery of the angry crowd gathering to protest.

The Jewish people of the East End, anti-fascists, and communist supporters alike have assembled to demonstrate against Mosley and this rally by the BUF. Diana estimates their numbers in the thousands. The BUF's public position on the Jewish community has stirred up their antagonism. Since Mosley's visit to Germany the summer before last and their marriage ceremony this past summer, the BUF has become more vocal about the dangers of the Jewish community, going from relative silence on the topic—Mosley made not a peep about Judaism in his manifesto *The Greater Britain*—to full-bore attack on the Jewish population. Just last week, M gave an interview in which he basically proclaimed that the so-called will of the people is determined by the Jewish financial sector.

Mosley had delivered precisely what Streicher had asked of him in their first meeting, and the BUF has been the recipient of the Reich's munificence in return. Although Hitler hasn't commented on this development—wanting the BUF's position to appear to have originated on its own—privately he has shared his pleasure with Diana, and she's pleased with what she has wrought behind the scenes, even if it's a touch unsavory. She only wishes that British citizens could see the merit of M's proposed social reform without voicing these crass positions, but she also knows that without Hitler's support, the BUF might cease to exist. Where would M be then? This stance is a necessary evil.

The crowd gets louder. Raising their fists and their signs

emblazoned with the words "Thou Shall Not Pass," the protestors scream, ordering the Blackshirts out of the East End,
a neighborhood with a robust Jewish population, the very
reason M selected it for this rally. The objectors actually tried
to block the march before it began, but the government agreed
with M's argument that he and his organization should be
allowed free speech and authorized this march. Even though
the decision-makers sided with Mosley, Diana knows there
are many politicians whispering about M's impatience with
the existing British government, but Diana wonders why M
should be patient when the existing system is failing right
before their eyes. The current system favors the old guard, not
the British people, and M has every right to act and take risks.
Never mind that the citizens of Great Britain loathe change.

"Get out of our neighborhood!" one young ruffian yells.

A chant of "Get out" takes hold, drowning out the BUF's
chants and songs. Then suddenly, objects begin flying. Bricks,
chairs, glass bottles, all soar over the throngs and land with
deafening crashes. New, different screams can be heard. Not
the battle cry of the protestors, but the shrieks of the wounded.
Diana sees blood trickling down the face of a young woman,
and she begins to back away until she hits the brick wall of a
butcher storefront.

*How wrong she'd been to ignore M's warnings*, Diana now
sees, as she ducks to avoid a glass milk bottle that a protester had
hurled through the air.. He'd told her that violence could break
out, and she'd nodded as if she agreed. But, as with everything,
Diana had followed her own plans, and tonight her agenda had
involved supporting him here. Danger or not. So here she is.

Glancing around, she doesn't see an easy path out of the crowd. But she does notice that swarms of policemen have arrived. Just as relief courses through her, she sees that the protestors are now targeting not only the BUF members but also the police, and some brandish chair legs wrapped in barbed wire. Are the protestors including the police in their ire because the government permitted the march in the first place?

Diana is trapped. By the protesters, the ineffectual police, the barricade blocking her exit, and even the BUF officers who cannot seem to get past the cluster around the podium where M still stands.

A huge paving stone whizzes by her head and smashes through the butcher shop window, sending shards of glass into the crowd. Diana feels a shove as people try to run. Stumbling, she very nearly hits the ground, but rights herself at the last second. Breathing hard, she knows she's just very narrowly avoided being trampled.

Looking over the heads of the throngs, she sees that M is talking with a man she recognizes as Sir Philip Game, the commissioner of the police. *What is he doing?* she wonders. Surely, Mosley cannot be acquiescing to the demands of the protestors or the government, should the officials experience a change of heart about the march. Such assent would signify a terrible weakness to Hitler, just when Mosley has managed to demonstrate strength and allegiance to the Führer. It would be a horrible development, undermining the very solidarity he's finally managed to forge. At her coaxing.

Fury threatens to take hold of her. Will M undo all the painstaking progress she's made with Hitler, all the endless coddling and gentle cajoling she's had to do to convince the Führer that Mosley is his man in England? Will M make a mockery of her efforts with his weakness?

At long last, one of M's men appears at her side and guides her down an alleyway, away from the fracas. But all Diana can think about is M and whether he's made an enormous misstep. Where is M, and what is he doing right now? What more will Diana have to do to prove to Hitler that her husband and his organization are one with the Nazi cause?

# CHAPTER THIRTY-SIX
# UNITY

*October 4, 1936*
*Munich, Germany*

U NITY PACES THE LENGTH OF HER NEW FLAT, AN ELE-
gant space bestowed upon her with the sweep of a hand
and a gentle kiss by Hitler himself. She'd clapped in glee at the
expansive parlor with its lovely view of the Englischer Garten,
leaping into his arms at the generous gift. Even though he
had waved away her gratitude—saying it was nothing, that
the Jewish owners no longer needed it—she saw the hint of
a smile peek out from under his mustache. And, as always, it
pleased her to please him.

But only one thing could give her pleasure now. The presence of her Führer.

Perching on the arm of the taupe settee that had come
along with the flat, she springs up again after a second. Even
the briefest rest eludes her. If Muv could see her pacing and
smoking and muttering to herself, she would describe her as
restless. But Unity knows that *restless* is too small a word to
describe the agitation she feels inside. She burns from within.

*Where is Hitler?* Even though she's aware that Germany and

Italy are in discussions to forge a treaty and she knows he's busy with that monumental effort, it does nothing to alleviate her nerves. She wants to track down one of his officers and scream the question that blazes inside her, day and night, but she knows her answers will not come if she howls. Such a public outburst isn't seemly for an Aryan woman. She must find another way.

Unity has not laid eyes on Hitler for two months, not since the Olympics, in fact. She has not spotted him around any of his usual places—*their* restaurant Osteria Bavaria, the Königsplatz where his official buildings border the square, his flat on Prinzregentenplatz, or even the beer hall he frequents with his military men, Hofbräuhaus am Platzl—and she has waited countless hours and days in the futile hope of catching a single glimpse of her love, her purpose. He has eluded her in Munich and even in Berlin, at his official headquarters and residence. The only place she hasn't sought him is Eva's flat on Wasserburgerstrasse, not far from Unity's own flat, and only because she fears repercussions from the notoriously jealous girl, who isn't afraid to take any measure to secure the Führer's attention. Even if that means making an attempt on her own life.

Why has he torn himself away from Unity? What has she done to warrant this punishment? Could he really be that busy? Tears trickle down her cheeks at the pain of this separation, the longest she's suffered and the only one without explanation or a single note from him. It is as if the tether connecting them is stretched near to snapping, and the pain of its elongation and the anticipation of a possible separation is intolerable.

Unity presses a fresh cigarette against the burning end of her old one, then inhales deeply of the new. If only she knew why he's stopped summoning her, she might be able to make amends. Did she make a misstep at the Olympics? With Eva or the Goebbels? She knows that Hitler's minister of propaganda does not care for her since she's an English citizen, but Diana's friendship with his wife, Magda, has softened that all-too-obvious judgment. Did Diana do something to offend the Fuhrer? She *had* nodded off quite conspicuously during the Olympic ceremonies and games. Perhaps the Führer thinks he can no longer count on the famous Mitford sisters for public shows of support.

Staring out the tall, arched windows of the parlor onto the top of the maple trees of the Englischer Garten, the leaves of which are turning a lovely golden shade, Unity tries to reason with herself. She imagines a conversation she might have with Diana, the only one always able to calm her fraying nerves and lighten her mood. *Oh, Bobo*, Diana might say with a silvery giggle, *you do know that Herr Hitler has a country to run, a Rhineland to remilitarize, a continent to conquer? His absence is not a silent signal that you've run afoul of his affection, but an indicator of his industriousness. Try not to take offense, dear.* And Unity might be able to laugh at herself. But, here, alone in her flat, she finds such lightheartedness impossible, and she only envisions the worst. Banishment.

A lone SS soldier marches around the outer periphery of the Englischer Garten, and a novel idea comes to Unity. She races to her bathroom, reapplies her lipstick, straightens her blouse, and then, scampering to her bedroom, she peels off her tweed skirt and dons her black fascist uniform jacket and skirt and slides on her leather gauntlets. Nodding in approval at her reflection in the full-length mirror, she then strides out of her apartment, down the spiral staircase, and out the front door to the pathway around the park's perimeter.

Pausing for a moment to ascertain the soldier's location, she walks toward him on the sidewalk. She keeps her gaze down and her head lowered as she careens in his direction. Just before she collides with him, she musters up the tears that have been simmering beneath the surface.

They bump into each other precisely as Unity had planned. Looking into the soldier's face with her tear-streaked eyes, she cries out an apology: "*Es tut mir leid!*"

"*Mach dir keine Sorgen, Junge Dame,*" he replies, not unkindly, and pauses to ensure she is unharmed.

"I've just been so terribly distraught about our Führer," she says in her unaccented German. *How the hours of study and practice have paid off,* she thinks. "I cannot consider anything but his safety and health."

The youthful SS junior officer, perfectly Aryan with his swoop of blond hair and blue eyes so light they seem translucent, stands up straighter, alarm registering in his expression. "Has something happened to our Leader? Was there an official announcement on the radio just now?" This soldier must know something of the rumors about Germany and Italy as well.

"No, no," she reassures him. "It's just..." Unity forces her voice to trail off, as if she simply cannot utter the next words.

"It's just what?"

"I had the most terrible dream about our beloved Führer,"

she whispers, tears running down her cheeks again. "If I could only see his face and confirm for myself that he is well, I could rest easy."

Relief softens his features, and a beneficent smile appears on his lips. "*Junge Dame,* I think I would have heard if anything happened to our Leader. I am familiar with his daily schedule, and all is in order." The smile turns proud. "I am, after all, a member of the Schutzstaffel."

The SS have only the reflected glory and power of the leader they protect and thus are nothing compared to him. Still Unity knows her reaction is a critical element of this little dance she is choreographing, and she must appear impressed if she's to achieve her aim. She forces her eyes to widen and her mouth to form a circle of surprise. Silently praying that her expression appears natural—artifice has never been her strong suit—she asks, "You are a member of *the* SS?"

"I am," he says, patting her shoulder. "And I promise you I would know if our Leader was in harm's way."

Unity places her hand over the soldier's. "Oh, how fortunate I am to have bumped into you." They laugh at her little joke, and she adds, "Still, I can't help but wish to lay eyes upon our Führer. I hope that doesn't make me sound greedy or unappreciative of your kindness."

"Not at all, *Junge Dame.* It makes you sound like a devoted Nazi, and that is a most attractive quality in a lady."

Unity forces her gaze downward demurely and says softly, "Might I invite you up to my family flat for tea as a way of thanking you?"

He glances over at the row of buildings bordering the Englischer Garten, pricey, imposing homes that only the wealthiest of Germans could afford. Or Hitler's favorites. "You live nearby?" He does not bother to mask his astonishment.

Unity points to her flat. "Just there." Knowing that he'd find it unseemly for her to live alone, she hastens to add, "With my parents and our housekeeper, although they are traveling at the moment."

He glances at his wristwatch and then at Unity. "My duties are nearly over for the day, and I suppose it would only be appropriate to escort you home, given your distraught state."

Unity nods and reaches for his elbow to steady herself. Together they walk in the direction of her flat, talking only of the Führer and Germany's glorious destiny. As they draw closer, Unity knows that she will do *anything*—sacrifice her body and soul, if need be—to insinuate herself into the confidences of this young SS officer to ascertain the whereabouts of Hitler. She must find her precious Führer and prove her worth to him again.

# CHAPTER THIRTY-SEVEN
# NANCY

*January 23, 1937*
*London, England*

I MOVE MY NEW MONTBLANC MEISTERSTÜCK FOUNTAIN PEN across my thick ivory writing paper, and the motion fills my bedroom with a pleasant scratching. The sound is a sight better than the clanging of pots in the kitchen by Mary, the maid, or Peter's angry slam of the front door as he marched off to "work," or wherever he pretends to go every day. What a relief to pick up my pen and drown out those objectionable noises, retreating into history with *The Ladies of Alderley*, away from ever-simmering quarrels with my husband and omnipresent worries over the fertility surgery that has relegated me to this bed for over a fortnight.

I return to the introduction to my tome. How difficult it is for me to condense the rich themes I see emerging from the lives of Maria and her daughter-in-law Henrietta, for whom I feel overwhelming familial pride. I mean, *my* ancestor Lady Stanley founded Girton College at Cambridge in 1869, for goodness' sakes, to give women a chance at a world-class education. How did my family go from that elevated perspective on women and education to my own parents' refusal to send us girls for any formal schooling, except for Unity who they couldn't wait to get out of the house? The mind boggles.

Closing my eyes for a brief moment, I ask myself what resonates most about the days of the Stanleys, and an answer comes to me. I am moved by the calm, settled stability of their political views, however old-fashioned and born from the sense of aristocratic entitlement. I'm moved by the way decisions were made out of a dignified concern for the citizens, including the women. It stands out in stark contrast to the chaotic, insecure grasping for political ideologies prevalent today, where fear of losing financial means is causing common sense and altruism to be lost. Do I adore writing *The Ladies of Alderley* because I long for a bygone England, so long vanished? I hadn't thought of myself as quite so staid.

With a flourish, I dot the final sentence on the last sheet of paper in the stack with a period. Placing my pen down on my lap desk, I study its black enamel and platinum exterior and shake my head at the thought that I almost returned this unexpectedly lovely Christmas gift from Peter. *You bought me a Montblanc Meisterstück?* I'd asked rhetorically of the German-made fountain pen, then added, *You might as well have placed a Nazi swastika under the Christmas tree with a bow.* Even Muv and Farve, no great fans of Peter, tsked at my barb on Christmas Eve, prompting me to apologize and accept the present. My anger stemmed more from his return to late nights of inebriated debauchery than fury over a German-made Christmas gift anyway. I'm fairly certain that my husband has yet to forgive me, and I know I haven't forgiven him. But I still need him. For a baby if nothing else.

I reach across the bed for a new sheaf of paper, but pain stabs my abdomen. Clutching at my belly, I panic. Have I damaged myself with so careless a motion? The curettage I underwent—necessary to remedy my fertility failings—requires rest and minimal movement to heal, or so my doctor told me. When I asked about the safety of writing on a lap desk from my bed, he waved away my query, as if so airy an activity could not possibly injure me. But the doctor underestimated the pull of my wandering, restless mind and the ability of my body to keep up.

The pain subsides, and my fear along with it. I remind myself that the doctor warned me there would be dull, nagging sensations as well as sharp, stabbing ones and that as long as it abated quickly, all would be well. And it *must* be well.

Inhaling deeply, I settle the fresh paper on my lap desk and begin writing again. A knock on my bedroom door interrupts me, and Mary calls out, "Ma'am?"

"Yes?" I answer, trying very hard not to sound annoyed.

"Sorry to disturb you, but you have a visitor."

A visitor? No one rang yesterday to inquire, but then, the Bright Young Things aren't exactly advance planners. Nor are they so young anymore, as I reminded Evelyn and Anthony Powell when they stopped by two days ago. They'd winced at the little jab, but they didn't retaliate because they knew it was fair. The first comment out of Evelyn's mouth upon entry to my bedroom critiqued my decision to undergo surgery for a baby that would only serve to tie me forever to the insufferable Peter; he'd said, in fact, that he always thought "I'd catch a better man." His words stung—mostly because they were true.

"Who is it?" I ask.

"Your sister."

I want to demand more specificity—there are *five* sisters from which to choose, after all—but I know my tone will reveal my irritation and I've already tested the limits of Mary's patience. We can't afford to lose her. In fact, on the sole income from my writing, we can barely afford her at all.

Without another word from Mary—or an assent from me—the bedroom door opens, and in steps Diana, resplendent as always. I am so shocked at her appearance here in my little house that I cannot speak. I have not laid eyes on her in weeks, not since Pamela's late-December wedding to Derek Jackson, that peculiar Renaissance man with passions for physics, riding, and fascism in equal measure, and we barely exchanged greetings then. The crowded nature of the nuptials made it easy for Diana to evade me, and in fairness, she was quite busy, as Pamela, with whom she was newly thick as thieves given Derek's fascism, often summoned her. Not to mention that the only thing on people's minds at the wedding was the king's shocking abdication due to his love for Mrs. Simpson; one could hardly imagine such a thing. *Who would give up a throne for a woman?* seemed to be the running question.

"Nancy," Diana says by way of greeting, with that silky voice of hers. I can always gauge her feelings toward me by the name she calls me. I haven't heard my nickname "Naunce" since I published *Wigs on the Green* nearly two years ago. An act she still perceives as a personal betrayal.

"Diana, what an unexpected treat," I say warily.

"Muv told me about your surgery, and I thought I'd pop

over to see how you are faring while I'm in London. Especially since Muv and Farve left with Unity to drive to Germany in her new car."

I'm tempted to ask why she didn't join them—given that she's always on one German jaunt or another—but hold my tongue. This olive branch of a visit is unanticipated, but very welcome, and I do not want the little reunion to end before it begins. I miss my favorite childhood companion. And reference to the political divide between us would certainly break that branch.

"It's very much appreciated." I gesture around the room, then down at my dressing gown. "On the mend, as you can see."

She glances down at the end of my bed, then over at me—an unspoken request for permission to sit. I nod, and she perches delicately on the edge. Even this movement of the mattress causes discomfort in my abdomen, and I wince.

"Are you quite all right, Naunce?"

Hearing my pet name brings a tear to my eye. I fuss at the tie on my silk robe so I won't have to meet her gaze. "As expected," I answer, then change the topic. "I miss seeing your boys. Are they enjoying the new house?" I was surprised when she decamped to Wootton Lodge, the estate in far-flung Staffordshire. Northern England is hardly the center of society, where Diana thrives, but I suppose it's convenient for Mosley's work in the Manchester area and keeping him away from the temptation of other women suits Diana.

Her face softens. "They miss you as well. M, in particular, loves to fish for trout in the plentiful lakes around the lodge." Her face assumes a dreamy expression at the mention of

Mosley. I'm struck by how this man continues to hold my beautiful, impenetrable sister in his thrall. What is it about him? "It's such a delight to watch him put down the heavy burden of leadership even a brief moment."

I don't comment that I'd asked after Jonathan and Desmond, not Mosley. That I do not care a whit about Mosley. Instead, returning the conversation to my nephews without my normal gibe, I ask, "How do the boys like it?"

"They're in their glory with all the woods and bluebell fields to romp about on horseback or foot in autumn and spring and the abundance of snowy hills to toboggan in winter," she answers with an almost beatific smile.

"Sounds ideal. How about you? Do you enjoy returning to the sort of natural splendor we had in abundance in our youth?" I ask with a laugh.

She smiles, then says, "When I am there, I do enjoy it. But I've been traveling a lot as of late. Helping M with his work."

Is Diana referring to her trips to Germany? Her only other travel consists of summer holidays, primarily to the Mediterranean. How interesting that she's describing her German travel as work; she used to pretend to go to Munich to look after Unity. Alarm bells ring, reminding me of that odd conversation with Winston, and I wonder. Is this confirmation of his suspicions? That my sisters are in Germany for more than a strange fascination with a fascist? The stakes seem even higher than they did at the time of that conversation, as Germany has been amassing alliances: first Italy in October and then Japan in November.

I study my sister, so icily lovely with her enigmatic half

smile. If I'm to proceed any further with this private inquiry, I will have to tread carefully. The Sphinx has always been notoriously ferocious in guarding its secrets.

# CHAPTER THIRTY-EIGHT

## DIANA

*January 24, 1937*
*London, England*

D IANA KNOWS PEOPLE ARE STARING. GAWKING AT HER
clothes and hair and jewelry and peering at her beautiful little boys. She wants to shield her precious children from
the unholy gazes and speculations; it's positively revolting
behavior for church. But she knows she cannot address the
other St. Margaret's churchgoers head-on—either through
words or actions—or she'll be labeled even more of a sinner
than she's already been classified for her divorce of Bryan
Guinness and so-called adultery with Oswald Mosley. She
cannot do that to the boys, and she reminds herself that it
doesn't matter, that, in time when their plans reach fruition,
their stares will be changed from revulsion into something
closer to reverence.

The minister begins the service, and she turns her attention to the altar. Keeping her hands on the nape of her blond
boys' heads, she forces herself to focus on the sermon. Behind
the minister looms an exquisite stained-glass image of the
Crucifixion from the sixteenth century, and this stunning

portrait entrances her until she notices that it also commem-
orates the union of Henry VIII and Catherine of Aragon, the
antithesis of the sort of union she desires with Mosley. When
the service ends and the crowd begins to disperse, she pur-
posely waits for the pews to clear before leading her boys down
the aisle.

"Diana, Diana," a voice calls out, one that sounds strangely
familiar. She pretends she cannot hear it, and she and the boys
continue their progress.

Footsteps thump behind her, and she feels a hand on her
shoulder. "Diana?"

In such close proximity, the voice is unmistakable. Diana
now wishes she hadn't come to church today or that her parents were here to serve as a shield. After all, it isn't often that
she attends and very rarely with the boys. But they are five
and six now, and given that regular services will be part of
their schooling, she wants them to feel comfortable with the
pews and the rituals and the long mass.

Turning around, she plasters on a smile and says, "Good
morning, Winston. Lovely to see you here."

"'Lovely' is a word used to describe you, Diana. Never me,"
Winston replies, his lips curling around his disgusting, unlit
cigar as he speaks. He reaches for her hand, which she must
disentangle from Desmond's sweet, pudgy little fingers. Then
the rotund man bows and places a surprisingly delicate kiss
upon the top of her hand. Diana must repress a shiver.

*How misguided is this man,* she thinks, *with his rants about
Hitler and the Nazis.* They are transparent, desperate attempts
to insert himself back into power. No wonder he's alienated

most of society and nearly his entire political party. He has no clue of what he speaks, and his diatribes will come back to haunt him. But she can say none of this. Not yet.

Her time will come—when Mosley is in power.

"What a coincidence to see you here. I was just thinking about your poor, troubled sister, as I walked from our flat to church today," he mutters as they proceed down the aisle, side by side after Diana arranges for Desmond to hold Jonathan's hand instead of hers. Winston and Clemmie have a flat near Westminster Cathedral, of which St. Margaret's is a part, and they occasionally use it when Winston leaves Chartwell for his tawdry political efforts.

"Which sister? I have many from which to choose."

"Are they all troubled? I would have thought that 'troubled' could only describe Unity."

"I suppose that's a matter of opinion and perspective," she answers evasively.

"On my walk this morning, I was contemplating the use to which the Nazi propaganda fellow Julius Streicher is putting Unity, the way he always describes her as Winston Churchill's relative."

Diana does not remark when he pauses. She can plainly see where he attempts to lead her, and it's a place she does not wish to go. No good will come of engaging with Winston now or admitting to anything. For her or Mosley.

"Aren't you terribly worried about your sister?" he prods, knowing she cannot stay silent in the face of such a blatant query.

"Why would I be? Unity has always been very firm and steady in her beliefs, and in Germany, she's not only free to voice them but has opportunities to participate in the cause to which she adheres."

"You aren't concerned that your sister has become a…a"—he stammers as he hunts for a word, unusual for Winston who's typically so glib—"companion of Hitler? Or a mouthpiece for him?"

Diana knows what Winston is hinting at; she's heard the whispers about Unity, in Germany and in England. That Unity exchanges sexual favors for information about Hitler and his whereabouts. That she has a string of SS officers with whom she's conducting illicit affairs. That she sometimes conducts orgies with the lot of them. That she's actually Hitler's mistress. Diana isn't naive; she knows that Unity may be having sexual relations with one or more of Hitler's guards. In fact, she's seen the evidence at Unity's flat. But the rest of the gossip—the multiple partners, the orgies, the mistress of Hitler—well, Diana deems it jealous rumormongering. At least that's what she tells herself.

"Why would Unity's *friendship* with Hitler bother me, Winston? I myself have spent considerable time with the Führer, at dinners and operas and festivals. And I've found him to be quite gentlemanly."

"You don't find his policies offensive? His actions?"

"Why would I object to policies that return Germany to a place of pride after languishing in shame after the Great War? Why would I find offensive economic measures that reduce unemployment?"

Sunlight blinds her as they step from the shadowy interior of St. Margaret's into the light of late Sunday morning. She must squint to look at Winston as he replies.

"What about his practice of placing his opponents in concentration camps? What about the Nuremberg Laws?" he hammers on.

Diana ignores his bait about the Jews and focuses on Hitler's treatment of dissidents. "Of course I believe that it's not right to imprison someone without a trial. We cannot just go around locking people up because they hold different sorts of views. But how can we criticize Germany for something Great Britain has done repeatedly? In Northern Ireland, in our colonies in India and Africa, to name but a few. Those who live in glass houses should not throw stones—didn't the minister make that reference in today's sermon?"

"Touché," Winston says with a chuckle. "But Unity has adopted Nazi anti-Semitism as her own and is now routinely quoted as describing herself as a Jew-hater. Doesn't it bother you that Hitler has influenced her to such an extent? I hate to think of what unpleasant actions she might take in the course of pursuing *his* goals."

Diana forces herself to laugh. "You clearly don't know Unity well, Cousin Winston. No one has a stronger will than Unity, and no one can force her to do anything she doesn't want to. Not Muv, not Farve, not her sisters, not Hitler. So I wouldn't waste my time worrying that she's being…what, Winston, hypnotized?"

"What about you?" Winston asks, studying Diana's face intently.

"Me?" Diana seethes, and she can feel her eyebrow arch in indignation. "You think *I* am susceptible to undue influence?"

His face flashes with righteousness, then impatience, and finally, humor. "Are you?"

"How dare you!" Diana spits out, then squares her shoulders and stares at the small, round, pompous man. She is galled that this imposter thinks that others like Hitler or even Mosley are capable of manipulating her, when, in fact, she is the one exercising all the power. It takes all her considerable self-control to maintain her calm exterior.

Winston does not reply, merely puffs on his blasted cigar and stares at her. As if she's a new species of mammal and he's trying to sort through the identifying features to assign her a Latin name.

Her composure restored, Diana smiles and says, "Cousin Winston, didn't you yourself once write that we should not judge a man until the whole of his lifework is finished and laid out before us? We are hardly at that stage—the entirety of Hitler's lifework isn't anywhere near complete and neither is mine."

# CHAPTER THIRTY-NINE

# UNITY

*January 25, 1937*
*Munich, Germany*

M UV'S LAUGH ECHOES THROUGHOUT THE LOFTY GILT
ceilings of the parlor. Farve accompanies her, and soon
their host does as well. Unity smiles at the sound, marveling at
her great fortune. Her most beloved people—Muv, Farve, and
Hitler—together in one place, their delight in one another evident and their merriment reverberating throughout the space.
Has Unity ever been this happy?

What a blessing it has been that Diana decided to stay in
London and not accompany her parents on this trip. While
Unity is grateful that her beautiful sister shares her passion for
the Nazi cause, Diana does prefer to be the only Mitford in the
limelight, and this often leaves Unity in the shadows. Why, she
often wonders, does Diana insist on monopolizing all the attention here in Germany when she's center stage everywhere else
in her life? Not to mention that she's got Hitler all to herself
during those visits to Berlin. Unity simply wants a few morsels
of Hitler for herself, and finally, today, she has them. It is as if
those long, painful weeks away from him never happened.

"Another éclair, Lady Mitford?" Hitler asks Muv through Unity, his hand already on the handle of the silver tray of strudels and éclairs displayed on the table between them. The Führer sits in a deep-plum upholstered chair next to Farve, while Muv and Unity perch on the matched set arranged across from them. Unity has spent several evenings here alone with the Führer, sharing delicacies and studying her sketches; as an artist himself, Hitler understands well how satisfying her notebook can be, and they bond over the manner in which art can be a powerful force in politics.

"How gracious of you, Herr Hitler. I would love another," Muv answers, and Unity translates. She pauses before taking one from the tray. "This *is* a special honor," she says to Hitler, knowing Unity will capture her words and emphasis.

Hitler offers the éclairs to Unity and Farve, who each dutifully take one. She doesn't think she's ever seen her blustery, mercurial father appear as cowed and humble. While Hitler's eight-room flat on Prinzregentenplatz is indeed luxurious and festooned with flowers, she knows it's the man who has impressed Farve and not his residence.

Unity had introduced them before, of course. Her parents have been in Hitler's company at two Parteitags and several rallies, and they've seen each other at Osteria Bavaria. But *this* is a horse of a different color. *A private invitation to tea at Hitler's flat,* Muv had asked, incredulous, *just us four?* Even Farve had chimed in, inquiring as to whether Unity had gotten the details straight. And when she informed them that it is an indescribable honor extended to a very, very few—only to those in the innermost of Hitler's circle—and that he postponed a trip to his mountain home to see them, Unity relished their awestruck reaction.

"I see where your daughters get their marvelously blue eyes, Lady Redesdale," Hitler says, gingerly placing the tray back down on the table as Unity translates.

Is Muv blushing? Unity doesn't think she's ever seen her mother blush before. When Muv positively titters in response, the suspicion is confirmed. Unity cringes. It's unseemly for one's mother to behave so flirtatiously, so girlish. Even if it is with the Supreme Leader. Perhaps especially.

Farve must see nothing inopportune about Muv's reaction because he ventures a quip. "They certainly didn't get them from me, *mein Führer*."

As Hitler chuckles, Unity realizes that this is the first time Farve has referred to Hitler as *mein Führer*—his Leader. He's come round on his views on the Nazi party; in fact, he'd vociferously agreed with a speech given by Minister Joachim von Ribbentrop during the London Anglo-German club banquet they'd all attended just before the holidays and Pam's wedding— but Farve has studiously avoided the all-important term. Has he fully embraced Unity's own views about the Nazis and her dream of an alliance between Germany and Great Britain? Muv certainly has.

"I am certain they benefit from your wisdom, Lord Redesdale, if not your eye color," Hitler announces with a slight pull on his mustache. "You have obviously passed on to your children the immense writing talent you displayed in the letter you wrote to the *Times* last spring."

*Now it is Farve's turn to blush*, Unity thinks as she tells her father what Hitler said. How very extraordinary. She cannot wait to tell her sisters. Decca especially. Even though she and her closest sister's political beliefs are polar opposites, Decca will be duly impressed by this gathering and devour Farve's reaction.

"Well, *F-Führer*," Farve says, and Unity sees that the title does not come naturally to him, "I've found the treatment of Germany since the war to be decidedly *un*-English, decidedly *un*-sporting, and I thought it was high time for someone to say so. Of course, I first presented those same views to the House of Lords."

All the Mitford siblings were astonished when their father trotted off to London to share his newfound perspective. Up until that time, he'd only ever exercised his right to sit in the House of Lords—a relatively new one since Farve was only the second Lord Redesdale—when his peerage rights appeared to be at risk.

Hitler sits up a bit in his chair, even though his posture is always erect, and nods. "For that, I am eternally grateful. We Germans do not have many champions in Great Britain these days." He will not say Winston's name aloud, but they all know of whom he speaks. The familial relationship between her and Winston never fails to embarrass her, and Unity is happy she needn't speak it aloud as she translates.

Farve glances over at Unity, then back at Hitler. "Unity has opened up our eyes to what's really happening in Germany. As has listening to your speeches, of course."

"I am glad of it," Hitler replies, letting silence take over the room. A silence that, it seems, he hopes Farve will fill.

Farve's face reddens, and Unity sees that it's not the earlier flush of embarrassment over Hitler's praise but ire. She hopes that her father's characteristic explosions do not make an appearance here. "I told all those self-important patricians and politicians in the House of Lords that they've got it all wrong. How can they pontificate about Germany when most of them haven't even been here to see with their own eyes how you've righted this ship!"

Unity shoots her father a look as she speaks his words in German. Even though he's saying all the right things, it simply will not do for him to launch into one of his unhinged tirades.

After he meets her gaze, his tone softens. "As just one example, Führer, their criticism of Germany's treatment of the Jews is simpleminded. I've seen plenty of Jews here, and they're handled with perfect respect if they follow the rules you've set out for them. You alone can assess the population of your country and determine who and what pose a threat—and if you feel that this is the safest way to manage your Jewish population, who are we to judge? And they've been given the opportunity to leave if they wish. We simply don't have the same insights you do, and it's unacceptable that some of my countrymen act as though they know better than you. It was time to set them straight."

Hitler's hand rests over his heart as Unity reiterates her father's sentiments in German, and tears well up in Unity's eyes witnessing the Führer so visibly moved. "How stirring, Lord Redesdale. We are indebted to your noble service." He glances over at Unity and adds, "It is more than I deserve given that you have already given us so much. You share your precious daughter with me here in Munich. The regular company of my personal Valkyrie not only comforts but inspires me to believe that, one day, we might achieve a Germany and Great Britain united in purpose. That is her fondest wish and mine as well."

It almost takes Unity's breath away to hear her beloved Hitler describe her dream as his own. This is her deepest desire, the one she whispers to him when they are alone. Although, in truth, they are never alone. SS flank him always, protective of Germany's greatest treasure.

"That is what we hope too. After all, *some* of us still recognize the historic ties between Britain and Germany—political, cultural, and blood."

Hitler practically jumps up in his chair at Farve's words. "Your words are as welcome and agreeable as one of Wagner's operas."

Beside herself, Unity interjects, "My father will help you however he can in Great Britain, *mein Führer*. He believes just as strongly as I do that we must find a way for Great Britain and Germany to have peace. If we can unite, we must be friends."

She turns to Farve. "Won't you, Farve?"

Unity knows who holds the power now.

# CHAPTER FORTY

# NANCY

*March 20, 1937*
*Saint-Jean-de-Luz, France*

WHY DOES IT FEEL AS THOUGH I'VE BEEN GIVEN THIS assignment because I've got nothing to lose? No social standing or title. No career of merit. No promising husband. Certainly no children. I suppose I should be thankful that the request got me out of the house and into the world.

Muv utterly and categorically denies this perception of me is the reason I've been "selected." Instead she says I am the perfect candidate to rescue Decca simply because I'm the only one whose politics—I'm a socialist democrat, if pressed—aren't abhorrent to my next-to-youngest sister, and thus, I have a better chance of bringing her back than anyone else. To everyone's horror, one of my sisters has turned full-blown communist and run away to Spain with Esmond Romilly, a fellow communist and son of Cousin Nellie, sister to Clemmie. It's to be my job to convince her to return home to the fascist bosom of our otherwise bourgeois family.

*How?* one might inquire. I have absolutely no idea. Decca might be more socially palatable than Unity—she was a pretty and popular, if reluctant, debutante—but she's every bit as stubborn. And by all accounts, so is Esmond, which may explain his decision to run away from boarding school to publish a left-wing magazine before joining the International Brigade to fight against fascism in the Spanish Civil War, with Decca in tow.

The whole bloody thing is preposterous and ill fated. But off Peter and I went to coastal France to meet the HMS *Echo* upon which the runaways had been prevailed to board, but only because the ambassador told Decca and Esmond that the Spanish refugees would be denied passage if they did not accompany them. A stroke of genius on his part, I must say. Now I stand amid the warehouses and rigging at the Jean-de-Luz port where the HMS *Echo* is docking, wondering how the hell I'm going to drag her home to Muv and Farve while diverting the attention of the reporters who've assembled near us.

"My God, is that them?" Peter points to the deck of the destroyer, where an impossibly young couple stands shoulder to shoulder with a dirt-streaked band of Spaniards. I was shocked when my erstwhile husband volunteered to join me on this rescue mission; I'd assumed I'd have to undertake it alone. *Have to keep an eye on the little missus in case she's in the family way*, he'd said with a wink, reminding me of the primary reason I stay with him.

Squinting up at the ship through the powerful Mediterranean sun, I try to make out the couple at which Peter points. Finally, I spot my lovely little sister with her dark hair and lithe figure. Even though the HMS *Echo* is fast approaching the busy French dock, her gaze is fixed on Esmond, and she stares up at him with starry eyes.

"The blasted girl is lovestruck," Prod whispers to me, in quite the most astute remark he's ever made.

While she has come by her devotion to communism honestly or, at least, as an understandable reaction to the fervent fascism foisted upon her by her childhood roommate, Unity, this romantic development will make my task immeasurably harder. I'm guessing Decca has doubled down on her commitment to the communist cause.

We stand there as the twosome saunter down the gangplank, hand in hand with only two small bags between them. Their carefree smiles disappear when I raise my hand in greeting and Decca sees me.

"You naughty thing, we've been worried sick! Muv has been weeping rivers. Floods."

"What in the bloody hell are you two doing here?" she asks, then proclaims to anyone who will listen, "This is an ambush."

I draw deeply from my cigarette before answering, trying not to lash out at her. "Well, darling sister, I would *not* be standing here in Saint-Jean-de-Luz if you hadn't forged a letter from friends inviting you to visit them in France but instead ran off with Esmond here"—I gesture to my second cousin, whom I've encountered occasionally through the years at holidays at Cousin Clemmie's and found unpleasantly combative—"leaving Muv and Farve positively frantic and sick with worry once they learned you weren't in Dieppe. Do you realize that, until Esmond's mother received a letter informing her of his whereabouts and your potential marriage, our parents did nothing but sit by the telephone, waiting for a call from you or the police? They thought you were dead."

Regret passes over Decca's face, until she glances over at Esmond. His stance and expression are positively defiant by contrast, and when she observes this, her features change to mirror his. She says, "What right do you have to foist your upper-class notions on me? I am over eighteen and should be able to choose what I want to do. I want to serve in the press corps in the Spanish Civil War with Esmond." Her words sound as if they came directly from Esmond's mouth. What has happened to my sister? Her face twists into an angry expression. "Was it you who arranged for us to get on this ship? The governmental push that practically forced us on board?"

Peter interjects, "Keep your voice down, Decca. There are reporters practically crawling all over the dock. Your little escapade has been headline news, and we'd like to keep this reunion out of the papers. Anyway, the governmental involvement was Esmond's mother's doing, not your sister's or your parents', so your anger is misdirected."

Esmond sneers at Peter and announces in a booming voice, "Let the reporters hear our story. More English people should be concerned about what's happening in Spain. It's a portend of the larger battle between fascists and communists that is unfolding on the continent around us, to which the Brits turn a blind eye in favor of easy appeasement."

The annoying young man is correct in my opinion, but this is neither the time nor the place for a heated political discussion. Plus his tone is unpleasant. We've got to get this personal situation in hand.

But Peter can't help himself and blurts out, "I've had just about enough of your pontificating, young man. Nancy and I aren't your enemies; we are simply here to check on your well-being and extend an offer of support on behalf of the Mitfords should Decca return to London. You should—"

This exchange is about to explode, which will not further the cause to which I'd been assigned. In fact, Peter staring down at the short young man and playacting at older brother will only cause Esmond—and consequently Decca—to dig in his heels more deeply; I saw his face flush at the mention of family financial support. We don't need any more obstinance here, but instead a little more of the sensibility of which I know my sister is capable.

I interrupt my husband. "What Peter means is that we've been worried about you and just want to have a little chat. There's a quiet café around the corner that serves the most delicious coq au vin. Can we invite you to a meal and a drink?"

Decca and Esmond's eyes light up at the word *meal*, and I wonder how long it's been since they've had a proper dinner. Without waiting for either of them to answer, I pick up Decca's bag and Peter hoists Esmond's over his shoulder, then we start walking the few blocks to the cafe.

I hear Esmond's voice behind me, calling out, "The only reason we're willing to speak to you is because you wrote *Wigs on the Green*. The rest of the Mitfords are Nazis."

Although I'm desperate to offer my mock-thanks, I stay silent. I'm grateful that I held my tongue because my sister falls in step with me, giving me the opportunity to ask, "How on earth did you two afford this adventure?" Muv told me that she and Farve had given Decca thirty pounds for the trip they thought she was taking with her friends, but that money must have run out some time ago. As far as I could tell, their only other income would have been the small stipend Esmond received from Reuters.

She half giggles. "You know I've always kept a stash of money for running away."

I giggle back, quite amused at the memory of Decca stashing away her money since she was practically a toddler. "I'd nearly forgotten." I think back on the many times that Diana, Unity, and I teased Decca about her secret pile of hoarded pence and pounds, always earmarked for her escape. It seems that money finally came in handy.

"Are you quite all right, Decca? We've all been worried about you," I say, wrapping my free arm around her bony shoulders. She's always been thin, but during her stint in Spain, she's grown positively skinny.

To my relief, she doesn't shake off my arm, but instead places her hand on mine. "It's been simply marvel—" She stops, realizing how it might sound to describe the Spanish war with such unbridled enthusiasm. "I mean, I adore being with Esmond and working together toward something larger than ourselves."

"Even if it means living with Esmond out of wedlock?"

"Especially," she answers with a devilish chortle. "Anyway, Esmond always says that marriage is such a classist, bourgeois construct."

"He would say that," I whisper to myself, careful not to alienate Decca or force her hand into another long speech about the wonders of communism.

We reach the café, and as we settle into seats at the marble-top bistro table, Decca asks, "Why isn't Unity being retrieved from Munich? Why do Muv and Farve only deem it necessary for you two to fetch *us*?"

"Damned good question," Peter mutters. I cannot blame him, as he's raised the question to my parents time and again, but such commentary doesn't support our argument at the moment.

I shoot him a look and answer as best I can a question I've asked myself over and over. "I suppose it's because she asked permission before she left for Munich and went through the normal channels—staying at an acceptable boardinghouse in the city center, embarking on a plan on studying German, and the like. She didn't secretly escape with a young man, while pretending to go on holiday with her chums."

Her eyebrows arch at my recasting of Unity's situation and her own. Then, with a glance at Esmond, she asks, "How can it possibly be acceptable that Unity is living on her own in a flat procured for her by the fascist Nazi leader of Germany from a Jewish couple who've very likely been sent to a camp? A flat where she not only invites SS officers whenever and however her fancy strikes but where she entertains Hitler himself? Yet somehow it's beyond reprehensible for Esmond and me to work in Spain on behalf of people who are being repressed and violently attacked by the fascists just because they have communist inclinations?"

I am rendered speechless by her question, and for a moment, so are Peter and Esmond. Decca has laid bare the inconsistent nature of my mission and the hypocrisy of our parents and others like them. I suppose Muv and Farve would explain it away by asserting that Unity is safe because any agreement Chamberlain reached with Hitler would be binding upon both countries—or that if appeasement is not to last, then perhaps Britain and Germany will align with Mosley at the helm at home—and Decca somehow is at risk. But this would be a lie. The truth is found in the chasm between their opinions on fascism and communism, which is created on the foundation of their own interests and fears. How very personal is the political.

# CHAPTER FORTY-ONE
# DIANA

*March 20, 1937*
*Berlin, Germany*

DIANA HAD THOUGHT HERSELF WISE TO BEG OFF THE trip to Munich with Unity and her parents in January. *Berlin*, she'd whispered to herself, *is the ticket*. Berlin is where she has Hitler all to herself, without Unity's obsequious and incessant nattering, and where she can wield the most influence over him. But has waiting to visit Germany until this secret spring trip been a smug, horrible mistake? What with Decca and Esmond all over the English newspapers now, headlines crying out "Another Mitford Anarchist," albeit a communist one this time? Even if Unity has been working to keep Decca's antics out of the German press, is their little sister's escapade going to undermine Diana's plan by alienating Hitler, who undoubtedly knows what Decca has done?

She paces around her suite at the Hotel Kaiserhof, twisting the strand of pearls at her neck round and round and watching the hands of the chimneypiece clock tick past. *The wisdom of my decision would reveal itself by evening, she thinks, when and if the Führer rings me back and invites me to his residence at the Reichskanzlei.*

She had followed the usual protocol when she'd landed in Berlin from London, calling his headquarters to inform his staff of her presence and availability. Typically, her telephone would be jangling by six o'clock with the invitation. Off she'd trot across Wilhelmplatz to Hitler's apartments where they'd spend the evening chatting pleasantly or enjoying a film. While Diana knows people speculate about their relationship, wondering how illicit and debauched their private time together might be, they'd be bored stiff with the fact that Hitler admires her from afar. He seems to view her as an example of perfect, untouchable Teutonic womanhood, enjoying her from arm's length only. She often wonders what she'd do if he actually made an overture.

By seven o'clock, she still has not been summoned, and dread begins to take hold. Does Hitler deem the Mitford name tainted because of Decca and Esmond's ludicrous adventure to help the communists in Spain? Does his failure to contact her today signal a permanent desire to distance himself? This would spell disaster for her strategy and her leverage with M.

Diana is tempted to take a page from Unity's book and stalk the Führer. His favorite haunts here in Berlin are familiar to her, and she could even make an impromptu visit to the Reichskanzlei. *If only Hitler could see me*, she thinks to herself. *All would be well between them.*

Suddenly the enormity of her situation strikes her. Here she sits, a woman alone in a hotel room in Berlin, her children over six hundred miles away alone with their nanny. She knows no one in the German capital except the Führer. Although she's always told herself she's in command, the reality is that she's at the beck and call of one of the world's leaders, one rumored to be ruthless and cruel. No matter that he's always acted the part of perfect gentleman.

What on earth is she doing? Are all these risks worthwhile? *How very strange it feels to question oneself,* she thinks.

Just then, her telephone rings. The clangor makes her jump, and by the time she races to answer it, she's practically breathless. "*Guten Abend.*"

"*Gnadige Frau, wollen Sie zu unshieruber common?*"

It is the call she's been waiting for. "*Es wäre mir ein Vergnügen,*" she answers dutifully.

She returns the handset to the cradle and begins racing around the room, making sure her clothes—a conservative pale-blue tweed skirt suit that nonetheless hugs her figure—and her face—a dab of powder but no lipstick or makeup—are perfect. Then, purse in hand, she descends the front staircase of the Kaiserhof Hotel and steps out onto the Wilhelmplatz. She must practically restrain herself from running across the vast, airy square into Hitler's lair.

Once across the plaza and safely in the Führer's rooms, she allows herself to sink into the deep cushions of the leather armchair. Diana then sips at her violet cordial and stares at the fire, pretending at relaxed contentedness. The red-orange flames dance in the vast hearth, casting the parlor in an enticing, warm glow. The scent of burning logs wafts into the air, and when she glances over the Führer, he looks as tranquil as she purports to be. Now is the moment.

They finish the comfortable, gossipy exchange they're having about mutual acquaintances, the sort of conversation Diana knows relaxes him. They return to their drinks and the fire, and she says in a teasing tone, "I hope Dr. Goebbels isn't still miffed at me. When we met last December, his irritation was evident, and I do loathe having anyone in your midst think ill of me."

Hitler gives her a wry smile. "How could anyone be miffed at the beautiful Diana Mitford?" Pausing, he pretends he's made a mistake. "Apologies, Lady Mosley."

Lowering her gaze in the demure manner he prefers, she replies, "You are too kind to me, *mein Führer*."

"Only speaking the truth, Lady Mosley." His smile remains. "It is acceptable for me to call you Lady Mosley, even though the rest of the world is unaware of your marriage, isn't it?"

Diana notes the pleasure it gives him to share a secret with her, and says, "Of course, Herr Hitler. I know my secrets are safe with you."

A black-uniformed officer appears from the shadowy corner of the room with two crystal carafes. After he refills Diana's glass and pours a fresh mineral water for Hitler, she returns to the topic at hand, the subject that brings her to Berlin. "So Dr. Goebbels has forgiven me for whatever sin I committed? Perhaps the fact that Lord Mosley and I inconvenienced him by marrying in his home? I do adore his wife, Magda; I hope he doesn't turn her against me."

"Impossible, Lady Mosley. Goebbels complains about everyone and everything, as I think you know. Certainly he has grumbled about the 100,000 pounds that the party wired to the Morgan Bank this past December for Lord Mosley's organization. But such gripes would never turn me against you. Nothing would."

She reaches out one long, manicured finger and runs it along the length of his sleeve. He shivers almost imperceptibly, and Diana knows she has her opportunity.

"I cannot tell you how relieved I am to hear that, *mein Führer*. Many a restless night has been spent worrying over the source of Goebbels's discontent, and it puts me at ease that his displeasure lay with the financial assistance your party has given to the BUF. Not me or my personal actions."

Diana does not say how crucial that December infusion of cash from the Nazi Party has been for Mosley's organization, an arrangement that has taken her over eight months of carefully crafted conversations and subtle pleas to achieve. Since Mussolini had largely eliminated his economic support, the BUF had plunged into dire straits, requiring Mosley to mortgage his own estate to keep the group aloft and then make serious cuts in his own budget, including moving his children into Wootton Lodge with him, Diana, and Diana's children. This infuriated his former lover, Baba, who didn't want Mosley or his children to have anything to do with Diana. Raising money for the BUF became ever harder in December when the government passed the Public Order Act that gave the police the right to call off public assemblies and marches, which had been a source of income for the organization. Diana shares none of this with Hitler, not wanting him to perceive the BUF as too weak to ally with.

"Never you," Hitler almost whispers.

"I feel much lighter, and I thank you for that," she replies. "I *do* hope you know that the BUF has the committed followers necessary to bolster the fascist cause in Britain and Germany, no matter what the British government does to try to undercut its power and its funding."

"The damn government. It's an outrage," he sputters while his blue-gray eyes blaze with fury. For a second, Diana feels afraid in his presence for the very first time. He must sense her discomfiture, because the patient, gentlemanly smile reappears. "Of course I know that the BUF and our Nazi Party share the same values and goals. Mosley has shown himself to be a true believer."

Diana could cry. She was never concerned about what Goebbels thought of her—raising his discontent served only to get Hitler talking about the BUF funding without her bringing it up explicitly—but she cares very much about Hitler's views on Mosley and the BUF. His statement is more generous than she'd dreamed and the perfect segue for her plan.

"You, me, Mosley, Unity... I believe we all share the same dream. The dream of a Germany aligned with Great Britain, however that transpires." She meets Hitler's eyes. "We want to ensure that the BUF is strong when that day comes so it can serve as your ally in Britain. But while we are grateful for your recent funds, we don't want you to think the BUF will depend on your party for its financial health forever. We have a plan to ensure our vitality."

A smirk is visible under his mustache. "What might that be, Lady Mosley?"

"Diana," she suggests.

"Diana," he repeats slowly, savoring the sound of her name on his lips.

"A commercial radio venture."

# CHAPTER FORTY-TWO

# UNITY

*March 20, 1937*
*Munich, Germany*

UNITY PORES THROUGH THE GERMAN NEWSPAPERS, national and regional. *Münchener Beobachter, Münchner Neueste Nachrichten, Berliner Tageblatt, Berliner Morgen-Zeitung, Berliner Abendpost, Neue Preußische Zeitung, Frankfurter Zeitung und Handelsblatt,* and even the *Bayreuther Tagblatt.* She has requested every publication, with the intention of scrutinizing every page to be certain her request has been granted. And so far, she has not seen a single mention of the terrible incident involving Decca and Esmond. This omission is an enormous relief, as Unity does not want it widely known that her sister is a communist. What would that do to Unity's reputation as an ardent Nazi, given that communism is its natural enemy? Hitler has kept his promise to bury the news in Germany.

But her mood darkens when she thinks of Decca. What happened to her poor sister that she went so far astray?

*Her leanings are not a surprise,* Unity thinks. She recalls their childhood bedroom; Unity's side was festooned with swastikas and the most handsome pictures of Mussolini and Hitler, while Decca had carved hammers and sickles into the glass windows on her side. Somehow those political lines down the center of their bedroom hadn't prevented their sisterly bond or the development of their own childish language, Boudledidge, understood by just those two and Debo a bit. The bond even withstood an ill-planned Mediterranean cruise last year, which Muv arranged to distract Unity, Decca, and Debo while Farve sold Swinbrook House and 1,500 acres of Oxfordshire land out of financial necessity. Even a difference of opinion over whether Unity should wear the swastika pin Hitler had given her in front of the Duchess of Atholl resulted in only a small skirmish, quickly forgotten and forgiven.

She wonders if Decca is jealous of her success with Hitler or even if it might have spurred her on. After all, the best Decca has managed to accomplish in her pursuit of communism is running away to the fringes of the Spanish Civil War in Esmond Romilly's thrall, while here Unity sits in the very bosom of Nazism, a close personal friend of the Führer. Not that she'd ever describe it that way to her sister—who had, in any event, described her flight as a grand escape in a recent letter—but Unity's mouth curls in a half smile at the thought of her triumphs.

A firm triple knock sounds at her front door, and she knows exactly who it is. She races to the door and answers it with the Nazi salute. There stands her beautiful, almost impossibly blond SS officer—Erich Widener. How fortuitous was their meeting last October in the Englischer Garten.

She gestures for him to step inside the shadowy flat, which grows darker as dusk takes hold of Munich. He scans the parlor, noting that every surface is littered with rumpled newspapers. "I see that my lieutenant delivered the papers you requested."

Reaching over to squeeze his hand, she singsongs, "Thank you. Your kindness is much appreciated."

He pulls her close and whispers into her ear. "It's my pleasure to do things for you, because I enjoy having you in my debt."

"I enjoy owing you something," she whispers back. "The act of repaying you is quite glorious. When I choose, of course."

Erich leans in to kiss her, but she turns her head in mock resistance. This push-pull of power is a familiar game between them, one Unity loves to play. As long as she wins.

Pretending to resist his embrace, she wriggles against him until he finally manages to press his lips against hers. Only then does she fully surrender. She inhales the scent of his cologne and the laundry soap used on his pristine uniform, and engulfs him in her mouth, arms, and hands until she's certain he's in her sway. Her ardor intensifies as she pretends this young man is Hitler.

Then suddenly, she pulls away. "I seem to remember that there was something else you were going to deliver to me in addition to the newspapers."

His eyes are shiny with longing, and he tugs her back toward him. "No, no, no," she says playfully, pulling away. "Not until you give me what you promised." Unity studies him as she resists his embrace, adoring the power she wields over him, *her* personal SS officer.

Unlike every other time they'd played this game before, he doesn't stop. Unity knows her own physical strength and believes she could stop him, but she also is confident that she need not take such measures. She need only reference the breadth of her authority as the Führer's special *Vertraute*.

"I don't think you want to do that," she says. The warning is clear in her tone even though she works to keep her volume low and even.

Erich stops, dropping his hands to his side. All the lust that had overtaken his features seconds before disappears, replaced by fear. "I'm...I'm sorry, Unity. I don't know what came over me."

Unity has to hold back her laughter at the expression of abject terror on poor Erich's face. *Funny*, she thinks, *how I enjoy witnessing fright and lust on his face in equal measure.* But she cannot indulge these feelings—particularly not the instigation of dread—as she needs this particular SS. He's proven immeasurably useful to her in procuring information so that she could be placed in the Führer's path and they could resume their relationship as if nothing had happened.

"No need for apologies, my dear Erich," she murmurs, doing her best to placate him. "I understand exactly how you might get carried away. I can get quite bewitched by you as well."

"Are you sure?" He reaches out to tenderly stroke her cheek. *Offending Unity could be tantamount to offending the Führer*, he is remembering.

"Positively," she says, intertwining her fingers with his. Then, with her free hand, she runs her fingernail up and down the front of his uniform. Dropping her voice so it sounds deep and suggestive, she asks, "So did you bring with you the little present you promised?"

"I did." He sounds relieved that she's returned to their little game, that she seems to have forgotten his overstepping.

"So don't keep me waiting any longer, and I won't keep you waiting either," Unity says as she slowly unfastens the silver buttons on the front of his uniform. "When will the Führer be back in Munich?"

"By week's end," he answers, his breath becoming quick and shallow.

"Where is he? The Rhineland?" She continues her progress down his uniform. *It is a logical guess*, she thinks, as there has been much to manage since Hitler marched three thousand troops into the region almost exactly a year ago—much to the chagrin of several European countries who maintained that it was a violation of the Treaty of Versailles.

"No. Berlin."

Unity pauses, trying to recall any pressing business that would require Hitler's presence in the capital. No mention was made at their most recent dinner, and she finds it strange that he'd return without an urgent reason. The Führer's preference for Munich over Berlin is well known.

"Why Berlin?" she asks, trying to make sense of it.

He stares at her. "Is it possible you don't know?"

She shakes her head.

"He is there to meet with your sister."

# CHAPTER FORTY-THREE

# NANCY

*December 28, 1937*
*London, England*

WE STEP OVER SOME RUBBISH OF INDISCERNIBLE ORIGIN and hold handkerchiefs over our noses to mask the smell. Peter whispers that he's about to gag, but in an effort to stave off my own nausea, I tell myself that it isn't rotting refuse but the scent of the briny ocean nearby. Even though I know it's far from the truth.

Decca's Rotherhithe flat *is* fairly close to the sea. But her building is decidedly slum-like, and the area bordering the actual ocean is a working dock, brimming with foul-mouthed sailors and warehouses that match their foulness in stench. I can hardly believe my little sister is living in these circumstances, and I now know Muv wasn't exaggerating.

When Peter and I hadn't been able to convince Decca and Esmond to come home with us from Saint-Jean-de-Luz, Muv and Edmond's mother, Nellie, traipsed off to Bayonne, where the young couple had decamped. Since Farve was apoplectic at the notion of his daughter living in sin with a communist, the mothers were determined to see the twosome

married, especially once they learned that Decca was pregnant. A wedding did indeed occur in the Harrods silk dress
Muv brought from London for the occasion. Afterward,
the mothers prevailed upon the newlyweds to return to
England—for the sake of the new baby—but they did not
realize the homecoming would not yield familial intimacy.
The couple chose a blighted area for their home, and Mitford
visitors were only permissible when Esmond left the flat for
his work at an advertising agency.

Peter lowers his handkerchief to knock on the flimsy
wooden door with a gloved hand. When no one comes to
answer, he tries again. Only then do I hear a tepid cry and a
voice calling out, "Hello! Who is it?"

Looking over at me in disbelief at my sister's informal
welcome—neither of us have ever lived in a home without at
least one maid capable of answering the front door—Peter's
mouth just opens and closes, uncharacteristically without a
sound. I take the reins and turn the knob. "Decca, it's Peter
and Nancy. May we come in?" I ask, stepping directly into a
room that I assume is the kitchen, given the presence of the
ancient-looking black stove and chipped enamel sink..

"In here," her voice calls out from another room. I am relieved
that the flat holds other rooms; perhaps they are an improvement
on this one.

Peter and I cross the tiny entry/kitchen in three steps into a
room that must serve as both bedroom and parlor. How would
one draw this conclusion? Based on the fact that a narrow bed
and crib sit in the corner nearest the fireplace, while the center
of the room holds two chairs and a settee, upon which my pale,

slender sister sits. Only then do I notice the chamber pot next
to the bed. My dismay at these impoverished conditions leaves
me speechless. How could they have chosen this for themselves
and their baby?

"Ah, good to see you, Decca." Peter manages to pull himself together more quickly than I do, even adding, "I say, is
that your little one in your arms?"

"Indeed." She arranges the pink bundle so that it faces us,
with pride evident on her face. "This is Julia."

At first glance, it appears as though Decca is proffering us
a pile of blankets. But then I spy a tiny, delicate face among the
folds, every bit as pink as the blanket in which she's swaddled.
Her eyes are closed, as are her rosebud lips, and an intense pang
of longing overtakes me.

I drop my purse onto the floor and reach for her. "May I
hold her?"

"Of course, Naunce." Decca stands and hands me the sweet
bundle. "Julia, this is your aunt Nancy."

I cradle the impossibly tiny baby in my arms, then lean down
to inhale her scent. "Heavenly, Decca. You did well," I tell my
little sister, thinking how easily she had this unplanned child; it
seems an unlikely miracle compared to the three long years Peter
and I have been trying with no success. But I can only be happy
for her when I see the rapturous expression on Decca's face as she
watches me hold her baby.

"Knock, knock." The unmistakable, dulcet voice of Diana
floats into the flat, and I see Decca's face fall. Once Muv was
given leave to visit Rotherhithe, Decca knew we sisters would
be descending upon her. After Esmond left for the day, that is.

In strides Diana, as cool and elegant as if she were entering the Savoy. Spotting Julia in my arms, she claps her hands and says, "Well done, Decca."

"Thank you," she says, accepting an intricately wrapped baby present. "You shouldn't have. We have all that we need."

Diana stares around the flat. "I hardly think so," she says, her exquisite nose scrunched as if a malodorous whiff had just passed beneath it. A distinct possibility, I suppose, between the baby and the neighborhood.

"Nancy," she says in acknowledgment of me. No Naunce today, but I do receive a warm smile. I doubt Mosley would be so pleasant. While he agreed to allow Diana to see me, he has maintained the official ban on me from his presence that he instituted with *Wigs on the Green*. Not that I mind avoiding him.

I return the greeting in kind. "Diana."

She makes no move to hold the baby. Instead, she prompts Decca, "Open the present."

Realizing that protests would not work with the imperious Diana, Decca tears open the thick, creamy wrapping paper and slices through the bows with a knife from her kitchen, if that's what the entryway space may be called. She lifts out an infant gown made from layers of ivory lace that could only be described as frothy.

Decca hands it back to Diana. "It's beautiful, Diana, but we cannot possibly accept it."

For once, Diana appears flustered. "Whatever do you mean?"

"I would never allow our daughter to wear something so bourgeois. It goes against my beliefs. Julia is perfectly fine in the sort of simple cotton outfit she's wearing now." She pauses, then adds, "And Esmond would never accept a gift from you—given what you and Mosley espouse."

The sisters stare at one another, and for once, I'm left without a pithy remark. Composed and firm, Decca has done what very few have managed to do—unsettle Diana. I wonder if Decca's reaction would be as measured and calm if she knew that, just last evening, Diana and Mosley were the toast of a reception at the German embassy, one attended not only by my parents and Peter's, but all of London's high society, including the Churchills. I'd felt quite a burst of love for Peter when he declined our invitation in Yiddish.

Into the void, I try to make peace between the sisters. "Diana, would you like to hold Julia?"

Her arms outstretched, Diana takes baby Julia into her arms and wanders into the kitchen. I hear her engage Peter in conversation, and soon the sound of cooing drifts in from the other room. Decca glances at me. "How can you stay so complacent with her, Nancy? I've read *Wigs on the Green*. I know you see—as clearly as I do—the horrors that will accompany the rise of European fascism, whether it's Mosley's homegrown variety or Hitler's savage version."

This is a question I ask myself. Except for the occasional flare of distrust and dismay at my sisters' behavior, I've tamped down my emotions over them. Over everything, really, the state of my marriage, the lack of a baby, the instability of our world. I think I'm afraid that, if I allow myself to feel even one of those things, then a tidal wave of emotion will overtake me. And I won't survive the deluge.

"I guess I don't have another belief system about which I

feel strongly, like you have communism. I simply know that I don't like the fascists." I say the only thing I can think of.

"You don't have to be a Communist Party member to fight against the sort of politics for which Diana stands." Her anger at Diana is unmistakable, but I don't hear her talk about Unity in a similar manner. "She's appalling."

"Do you feel the same way about Unity? If anything, I feel as though she's even more rabid in her adherence to fascism than Diana."

"My answer may sound strange, given that Unity has had that peculiar fascination with the Nazis since her school days. My God, no one knows that better than me—I had to go to sleep every night staring at pictures of Mussolini and Hitler. But no. I blame Diana for bringing her to Munich and giving her the access to the Nazis and then for exploiting the connections Unity developed for her own purposes—namely Mosley. She knows exactly how impressionable and extreme Unity can be, and Diana is the one who tied Unity's fate to Hitler's. Unity's obsession with Hitler and all things Nazi might have died a natural death otherwise." She shakes her head. "I could never forgive myself if I didn't take a position against fascism for Julia's sake. I cannot allow the world to become overrun by dictators without putting up a fight on her behalf."

Decca's words make me inexplicably sad and leave me feeling unbelievably ineffectual. "Maybe I can afford to be complacent because I have no one's future to worry about but my own." I toss off the remark, as I have so many like it.

My little sister looks at me with such sadness in her eyes that I realize I haven't covered up my own sorrow as thoroughly as I usually do. This sympathy is unexpected, and I am so unaccustomed to it that tears well up in my eyes. She reaches out and squeezes my hand, recognizing how this conversation has stirred up my own pain. Unspoken but very much understood.

Anger rises up unbidden alongside the heartache—and I feel a frozen part of myself thaw. Why do we never talk about what's really happening, both large and small? My grief over my barrenness. Our mutual worry about Unity's obeisance to the Nazis. Disdain for Diana's cultivation of Hitler for Mosley's sake and her exploitation of Unity for her purposes. My concern over Decca's hasty abandonment of youth for communism and motherhood. The great battle between fascism and communism brewing across the Continent, one that will call each and every one of us to account.

Why are we pretending at normalcy when these are anything but normal times?

I feel like screaming, but instead, I consider Winston's challenge of fourteen months ago. Will I choose the complacent writerly path, either hiding in the past or throwing out my opinions disguised as fiction, or will I dig into the underbelly of my sisters' activities and act with the courage of my convictions? I feel a spark ignite within me, and I know how I will answer.

# CHAPTER FORTY-FOUR
# DIANA

*January 1, 1938*
*Brandenburg, Germany*

M EIN FÜHRER, I BELIEVE IT IS YOUR TURN," MAGDA
Goebbels calls out, a cautious merriment in her voice.
Diana could almost hear her incredulous thought: *Is Herr Hitler
really sitting in my country home playing a parlor game on New
Year's Eve?*

"I believe that it is Lady Mosley's turn." Hitler nods in
Diana's direction, and even though they all know the Führer
is not playing by the rules, no one would dare say it aloud. For
reasons best known to himself, he wants Diana to go next.

"Of course, *mein Führer*, my mistake," Diana says, lowering
her head in apology. Magda squeezes her hand under the table,
and Diana has to stop herself from giggling. Of all the surprising
developments during her years insinuating herself into the Nazi
hierarchy, her friendship with the golden-blond, statuesque
Magda Goebbels has been the most astonishing. The unofficial
First Lady of the Nazi Party and center of the small coterie of
women Hitler admires, Magda is a canny, poised, social creature
not unlike Diana herself, but she is warm where Diana is cool.

Sometimes, Diana marvels that the woman who perfectly plays the ideal Aryan woman can also be so secretly shrewd.

"Let me think, let me think," Diana says, tapping one long fingernail on the tabletop even though she knows precisely how she'll answer this parlor-game question. Ever since Magda announced that they'd play Analogies after dinner, she began planning her response. Staring at the semicircle around the table—consisting of her, Magda, and Hitler's *Umgebung*, or little court—she gives Hitler a small smile.

Only then, once she notes how Hitler is leaning forward, awaiting her response, does she say, "The flower analogy of our Führer is a tiger lily." This is why he shuffled the game order, to see what Diana thinks of him. *Curious*, she thinks, how the soon-to-be world leader has his insecurities.

The *Umgebung* holds its collective breath, awaiting Hitler's reaction. When he smiles and then launches into a full-bodied laugh, everyone else does as well. These men have witnessed many of his tirades—explosions that led to violence, even against the inner circle—and thus their relief at his welcoming reaction is palpable. Diana, by contrast, has never doubted her ability to charm him.

After a few more turns, the game finishes. As if operating by a secret signal, two maids enter the parlor, one with a tray of éclairs and pastries and the other with a bottle of mineral water for the Führer and coffee for everyone else. As the staff begins serving, Hitler says quietly, "We are taking dessert in here rather than the dining room?"

For a second, the entire room freezes. Dr. Goebbels, the *Umgebung*, Magda, and the maids are rendered immobile by the Führer's small judgment, as if cast under a witch's spell in a tale from the Brothers Grimm. Magda is the first to reanimate. "Of course not, *mein Führer*, our staff misunderstood our instructions, and they will be chastised accordingly. We will take dessert in the dining room."

The guests rise and begin exiting the parlor, keeping an eye on Hitler's movements as always. With a wave of his hand, he instructs them, "You all go ahead. I'd like a private word with Lady Mosley."

Diana inhales deeply as the room empties and it becomes just the two of them. Silently, she prays that the reason for this moment alone with the Führer relates to her commercial radio proposal, and not something else. From Mosley's dark moods and mercurial outbursts, she knows that he cannot prop up the BUF much longer. Even the influx of cash that Diana managed to procure from the Nazi Party will only stave off the inevitable for a little while. And then where will she and Mosley be?

If only Hitler would seize upon her commercial radio idea, the BUF could soar once again. She and Mosley would be flush with cash, like the Conservative MP Captain Leonard Plugge, who'd obtained a French radio license and created the successful commercial station Radio Normandie. Although Diana's plans are much more ambitious. She hopes to knit together a network of German-based radio stations that would ultimately cover the entirety of Great Britain and offer light entertainment, something that isn't currently available but surely people crave. Diana hopes that Hitler might see not only the financial but also the political benefit of this scheme.

Diana turns the full power of her gaze on Hitler who sits

across from her in a tufted oxblood leather chair decorated with nailheads. Then she says, "I'm honored you'd like to speak with me, *mein Führer*."

"I've been thinking about your proposal."

It takes quite a lot for Diana's heart to race, but flutter it does. "The fact that you'd take time away from running Germany, forging alliances with other countries, and expanding into other Germanic areas to consider my little idea means the world." She placates him with the sort of compliments she knows he loves to hear, and her recitation of his litany of recent accomplishments—especially in the wake of the recent alliance of Germany, Italy, and Japan in the Anti-Comintern Pact—makes his eyes sparkle with pleasure.

"My advisors are not in favor of it," he says, studying her expression as he informs her of this. "But I think the plan shows promise that they cannot see, and I understand better than almost anyone the power of radio. Please, describe it to me again. Let me have the benefit of *your* vision."

"With pleasure. As you know, the BBC holds the broadcasting license for the entirety of Great Britain and Northern Ireland and fights any attempt to encroach on its airwaves. Yet, the BBC offers very little in the way of light programming, and we feel as though there is a ready market for it in Great Britain and Northern Ireland—a market for which advertisers would pay handsomely. If the BUF could construct a commercial radio system outside Britain while developing a strong foothold in this light entertainment market within Britain by playing the programming within Britain, then a dependable stream of cash could be raised for Mosley's organization and our investors. The ideal place to establish this commercial radio station—for both financial and political reasons—is Germany." She pauses and lowers her gaze deferentially. "But only with your blessing and permission, of course."

Hitler does not speak. Instead, his hands form a triangle as he studies her. Is he pleased with her short presentation, or is this the terrifying silence before the rendering of a savage judgment about which she's heard tales but never experienced? Diana doesn't know if she should continue or await a signal from him, and for only the second time in her life, something like fear overtakes her. The first time, of course, had also been with Hitler.

Diana decides to plunge forward in the direct manner to which he's accustomed from both her and Unity. Willing her voice not to quiver and reveal her nervousness, she says, "We have already put the corporate structure in place to shield Mosley's involvement from public view, not wanting to give any reason for British intelligence to investigate the radio station or us. All preparations in the event *mein Führer* decides that this plan is worthy."

"Wise, very wise," the Führer interjects, but before Diana can relax, he asks, "What would Germany gain by facilitating this radio-station arrangement other than the financial return on its investment?"

The question startles Diana. She had believed that the synergy between the Nazi Party and the BUF was plain, that she would not have to say aloud the prospect looming before them all. But it seems as though Hitler wants her to make the commitment explicit, and Diana did not make the sacrifice of her first marriage and her reputation to be married to a political leader who fails. Together, she and Hitler will make the BUF and Mosley succeed so they can join the Führer on that auspicious day when his party rules all of Europe.

"This would allow the BUF to be firmly in place when you—*mein Führer*—are ready to take the helm of Great Britain and Northern Ireland, providing you with a local government at your service." She pauses for dramatic effect. "As well as dedicated airwaves ready to communicate with and command your new subjects."

# CHAPTER FORTY-FIVE
# UNITY

*January 4, 1938*
*Munich, Germany*

V ERDAMMTES ENGLISCHES MÄDCHEN," UNITY HEARS A gravelly voiced man say from the library.

This voice is one she doesn't recognize, but given the number of unfamiliar senior Nazi officials at this gathering, that's no surprise. What does astonish her are the words being spoken—*the damn English girl.* There is only one English girl at this party tonight, so she knows they mean her. What has she done to enrage them? She knows her close relationship with the Führer makes some of them jealous, but to cast audible aspersions upon her is quite a different thing. And, because it is quite contrary to their leader's views, it is a dangerous thing.

*"Was sind ihre Motive?"* she hears in reply to the comment about her, and this time, she feels as though she *should* recognize the voice. It nags at the edge of her consciousness, as though she had a conversation with the speaker some time ago and his words have lived on in her mind, alive but faded.

The exchange continues to startle her. How dare someone question her motives? How could anyone have motives beyond wanting to support and admire Hitler? His success is all their successes—the success of the entire world, in fact—and she cannot understand why anyone would even contemplate another possibility. Aren't they all part of this grand quest together?

Pivoting away from the hallway near the library and back toward the parlor, she tries to turn her thoughts to this soiree, a sort of stand-in for a New Year's celebration since Hitler had spent the actual holiday with the Goebbels. She has worked hard to elevate her mood and forget that Diana had the honor of spending the actual day with him. But this sours her spirits, and her latent irritation over her sister's latest victory in the battle for Hitler's affection resurfaces. Unity pauses for a moment, trying to fix a smile to her face before reentering the room.

In that split second, the ongoing conversation drifts into the hallway, within earshot. "She certainly isn't in it for riches. The Führer pays for her apartment and travel, but those are things she could afford on her own." Ice clinks on crystal, and she realizes that the unfamiliar speaker is pausing for a drink. "Could she be spying for the British?"

*A spy?* They are accusing her of being a spy? How dare they! No one has shown more loyalty to Herr Hitler than Unity, not even his so-called officers. How can these men not understand her adoration of Hitler? Her belief in his greatness and the simple joy she feels sitting at his side? How can they doubt that she wants the same thing they all do: success for the Führer and accord with other European nations, including Great Britain? Fury starts to boil within her, and it takes every ounce of hard-fought restraint not to race into the library and pummel these two men.

"She *is* well connected in British high society, from where most of their politicians come. She's related to that annoying gnat, Winston Churchill, who is so determined to turn British political and popular opinion against the Führer. Perhaps he put her up to it?"

"Or MI5? It would explain how she knows Hitler's whereabouts and itinerary better than we do. How she's always waiting at whatever restaurant or teahouse he's planning on visiting has long been suspicious."

At this, Unity holds back from snorting in laughter. These so-called Nazi leaders are stupid and guileless. They have no idea how well informed Hitler's personal SS guards are and how close Unity has become to several of them, especially Erich. Perhaps it is *these two officers speaking right now* that Hitler does not—and should not—trust.

"We should assign a shadow to keep tabs on her. The Führer talks very casually in her presence, and I would hate to think she'd share his confidences with her English connections."

"The items he discusses in her presence are those he wouldn't mind reported back to England, I'd venture to guess. And anyway, I thought that shadow had already been arranged?"

"It seems not." A long pause ensues, and then an excuse is proffered. "The Führer has resisted it to date. He's too enamored of the eccentric English ways of these Mitford sisters to take seriously a suggestion that they could be dangerous. Their boldness, which he finds so off-putting in others, he somehow finds charming in them. And not at all a threat."

"A bit foolhardy, isn't that? Not to keep a close eye on them?"

Silence reigns for a long moment, and Unity is about to depart for the parlor when she hears one of the men hiss at the other, "Are you calling the Führer foolhardy?"

"No, no," the familiar voice rushes to defend himself, "I just meant that the decision to not tail Unity is a bit foolhardy, a choice which was undoubtedly handled by a lesser lieutenant. The Führer could never be described as careless. Never. And anyway, I know our Supreme Leader is behind the brilliant idea to use Unity as propaganda. Streicher put her to good use in that interview with *Münchener Zeitung* and the 'Letter from an English Girl' in *Stürmer*—"

"Don't forget about the rallies," the other officer interjects.

"Yes," the familiar-sounding officer replies, clearly relieved that the other echoed his remark, "she was masterful at the rallies and could well serve as a means of softening the English position on the Nazi Party. After all, if one of their own, a relative of Churchill at that, finds our government attractive—"

The other chimes in, "Who knows how many others might be sympathetic?"

"Exactly. It could make our reception much easier when we come rolling down the streets of London."

A flash of pride courses through Unity, before she remembers how this conversation started—with suspicion of her. And she remembers the traitorous comments the familiar man uttered about Hitler—that he was foolhardy. And she knows what she must do; that man deserves punishment for his treason, for his lack of pure faith in the Nazi cause and in Hitler himself. She only wishes that she knew who the perpetrator is.

"Putzi," the lesser-known voice inquires of the other, "how do you think the reception will be when we come rolling down the streets of Czechoslovakia or Poland?"

Unity stops listening. Her mind is alive with the knowledge

that the offending speaker is Putzi Hanfstaengl, the Nazi head of the Foreign Press Bureau. The same Putzi who distanced himself from Unity and Diana at one point when he found their makeup not in keeping with the Aryan ideal. She cannot allow this traitor to remain in the Führer's midst.

Not bothering to soften the clip of her footsteps as she walks down the hallway past the library, she steps into the parlor, awash in silvery damask walls and furniture offset only by the burst of color provided by bouquets of Hitler's favorite flowers, the white edelweiss, which has such symbolic meaning for him, and red hothouse roses to echo the Nazi flag. Unity feels like weeping at the thought of disrupting this tranquil scene with her news. How distraught will her Führer be?

"*Mein Führer*," Unity says to Hitler as she takes the upholstered chair at his side that he reserved for her.

"Where have you been, *mein Schatz?*" he asks pleasantly, glancing over at Magda Goebbels. "We've been having a most diverting conversation over which Munich teahouse serves the tastiest éclairs."

Unity knows how much Hitler enjoys these sorts of small exchanges with the cadre of women in his inner circle, and she is loath to change the subject. *But*, she reminds herself, *this is for his own protection and for the good of the party*. She steels herself for disappointing him and whispers, "*Mein Führer*, I have a grave matter to report to you. It involves Putzi Hanfstaengl."

As they continue their quiet conversation, Unity thinks how she might have finally won a battle for the Führer's love in the ongoing battle with Diana. She is revealing a traitor.

# CHAPTER FORTY-SIX
## NANCY

*March 24, 1938*
*London, England*

I SETTLE INTO THE HARD WOODEN CHAIR IN THE STRANGERS'
Gallery. From my front-row seat, I have a bird's-eye view of
the proceedings and, I hope, a good spot to hear the debate on
the floor. That said, there is one particular argument that I pray
I will *not* hear today.

Quite literally, I am a stranger to the Strangers' Gallery. I
have never had any desire to visit the House of Lords before.
Why would I waste my time listening to the pontification of
the same decrepit old men that linger on the periphery of the
dance floor at any given ball? If I'd wanted to be bored senseless
by them, I'd have accepted their invitations to dance years ago.

But today is different. Today, I'm desperate to stave off a
disaster. One I heard brewing over dinner with Muv and Farve
last evening, and one I hope my presence today will help avert.
This catastrophe did not start last night. No, not by a long
shot. I cannot say the precise moment it began, but if I were
to hazard a guess, I'd say it all began with my parents' first visit
to Munich to check on the ever-wayward Unity. Hints of this

possible calamity reared their ugly heads over the years, but in truth, the escalation happened bit by bit over time until it crescendoed not quite two weeks ago.

Beginning on March 11, less than two weeks ago, the BBC and newspapers began to report that Hitler had crossed the border into Austria with his troops, in contravention of all treaties. By Sunday, March 13, the papers began announcing a full annexation of Austria by Germany. Depending on the account one read, the Austrians were either dancing with joy at this reunion with their German cousins—their blood brothers, according to some—or experiencing terror and violence. I supposed both were probably true, depending on one's leanings and, quite frankly, whether or not one was a political dissenter or Jewish.

The subject of Germany's takeover of Austria, of course, came up with my parents, as Unity constantly reported to them on its glories and victories. Not to me, though, as I'm currently persona non grata on political issues because I dared to question her decision to live in a flat she'd taken over from ousted Jews. Over dinner at Quaglino's last night—one of the few restaurants Farve will visit while in London—Muv mentioned how "lovely" for Unity that she'd been able to witness the Nazis rolling into Vienna firsthand.

"How is it lovely to watch one nation be taken over by another?" I'd asked, shocked at her comment. How could her mother describe the brutal takeover of one country by another as "lovely."

Her right eyebrow raised at my question. "Lovely to see Austrians and Germans reunite and celebrate becoming one country. They are one people, after all." She sniffed. "No need to be so snarky about something so beautiful, Nancy. Always so bitter," she muttered.

Peter rallied to my aid. "With all due respect, some former Austrians may not be exactly celebrating." He was a wonder with my parents, if nowhere else.

"That's not what Unity has been writing in her letters, and she was there in Vienna from the very start. I think she'd know if the citizens looked happy or not." Muv sniffed again. "I don't know what lying rag you are reading, but any self-respecting newspaper should be printing the truth about the happy union of Austria and Germany."

Farve slammed the table with his fist, making half the restaurant jump. He usually managed to control his outbursts when we were out in public, but this conversation agitated him. "Blast it, Nancy," he said. He always directed his ire toward me even if he also felt it toward Peter. "Enough is enough. You haven't been to Germany; you haven't met Hitler; you are in no position to judge this reunion of Austria and Germany. If you heard how the Führer spoke about this plan, you would agree that his intentions are to chart a course that's right and fair. Anyone who disagrees is free to leave, but my understanding is that most Austrians are in favor of it. If we British could just stay out of Hitler's way and let the Germans conduct their own business, then we needn't worry about another blasted war."

"But what about—" Where has the father gone who used to rail about the Huns he fought during the Great War? Where is the father that used to chase us with his hunting dogs as we pretended to be those same Huns in the allegedly merry game he called "Child Hunt"?

He interrupts me before I can finish. "No buts, Nancy. Do not come in here spouting a lot of nonsense that you've read in some trashy newspaper. I am sick and tired of your sort of unsupported views, and I plan on voicing this opinion at the House of Lords tomorrow."

He tore into his steak, and Peter and I met each other's eyes.

After a few stifled attempts to talk him out of this rash action—*It's one thing to believe this nonsense and quite another to espouse it publicly*, I argued—I gave up and decided to come to Parliament today.

Do I really think Farve might halt or soften his diatribe if he sees me front and center looking down at him from the Strangers' Gallery? No, but I will never forgive myself if I don't at least try.

The gavel slams, and the session is called to order. "My Lords, we are called here today to debate the reaction by our nation Great Britain to the overtaking of Austria by Germany," Lord Snell announces in his nasally voice, then reaches for a glass of water before continuing. I am heartened by the fact that Lord Snell uses the word *overtaking* instead of the benign *annexation* that's so popular in the newspaper. It signals a deeper understanding of Hitler's actions, and Snell has been known for taking a hard stance against the growth of fascism and appeasement toward the Nazis.

Perhaps I am not to be alone in my hopes today.

My father stands before his peers, and my stomach flips. "I want to put forth a view today that I believe to be popularly held but little discussed." He clears his throat, and I see that Farve is nervous. Although he's spoken before his peers here before and hinted at his support for Germany, even he realizes that this is different. I stare at him, willing him to make eye contact with me and think again before he launches into this speech, but he is resolute and keeps his eyes fixed on anything but the Strangers' Gallery. Finally I cough very loudly, and he looks up at me, with recognition and recrimination on his face in equal measures as I slowly shake my head and place my hands in a pleading gesture.

When he clears his throat again and launches into his speech, I know my efforts are for naught. "I think we can all agree about the inevitability of Austria becoming part of Germany. Several of my fellow lords have mentioned it here today and in earlier sessions." He takes a deep breath—belying his ongoing anxiousness—then continues. "But what few have focused upon is the warm and ecstatic welcome that Herr Hitler received from the Austrian people when he arrived. I believe that most of the former Austrian citizens look upon the German Führer as their hero and are delighted to now call themselves Germans again. Never mind those few communists, Jews, and liberals who disagree. We should all be thankful that Herr Hitler was able to reunite these two countries without bloodshed or war, like the one happening in Spain right now."

Farve continues on. A rousing cry of huzzahs can be heard in the Strangers' Gallery, along with a fair share of boos. *Those boos are no surprise,* I think, *but I do find the huzzahs a bit astonishing.*

But the biggest shock is how much Farve's words sound

as though they come from Unity's mouth. Or, perhaps more accurately, Hitler's. Astonishing from a man who has hated the Huns with an intensity bordering on rabid all his life, followed in quick succession by his hatred of foreigners in Great Britain, frogs as he calls the French, Americans, and basically anyone save his children, wife, and a few country friends.

*My God*, I think, *how has my family become a megaphone for Hitler?* And how—and why—have Diana and Unity managed to do this? If I had never written *Wigs on the Green*, would my sisters have already tried to pull me in too? Especially when I'd once been willing to wear the black shirt?

Certain Mitfords have become like an insidious weed planted into the English soil with the hopes that we choke out the native plants. I must be a relentless gardener and assess this strange new growth. Must I rip out these weeds by the roots?

# CHAPTER FORTY-SEVEN
## DIANA

*March 24, 1938*
*Staffordshire, England*

S HE LIES ON HER BED, UTTERLY IMMOBILE. *IF I DON'T MOVE a single limb or even a finger*, she thinks, *perhaps the nausea will pass.* Perhaps it will lift its relentless grip on her and allow her to return to herself again, instead of the sick shell of a woman her pregnancy has caused her to become.

The sound of Jonathan and Desmond playing in the great lawn in front of the west entrance to Wootton Lodge drifts into her bedroom through the tiny opening in the window. Their laughter makes her smile, particularly since she knows they are under Nanny's watchful eye, and she turns her head toward the sound. A mistake. With the motion comes another wave of nausea, nearly forcing the use of the porcelain bowl at her bedside again.

She tries to tear her attention away from her own wretchedness and toward the radio program instead. The waves of Fred Astaire singing his hit song "They Can't Take That Away from Me" crest and wash over her before they recede, taking with them the image of the singer serenading Ginger Rogers on a foggy ship deck from the film *Shall We Dance*. Had she seen the film with Evelyn? She can't recall; how very busy the past year has been. Old friendships have faded away in the face of all her responsibilities.

An announcer's voice takes the place of the trumpet's final notes, bringing Diana back to the present and her physical discomfort. The news report exacerbates her distress, because she can feel the opportunities slipping through her fingers as she lies on her bed. As the broadcaster reiterates the exuberance with which the Austrian people greeted Hitler and his troops when they marched across the border nearly two weeks ago, there's no reference to the advance troops that rounded up thousands of dissenters and removed them to camps so Hitler's way would be easily paved. *Perhaps it's not common knowledge*, Diana thinks. After all, Unity has made her privy to many private details; her little sister has been in Austria since the Nazis arrived and, of course, has unparalleled access to Hitler himself. The report concludes with a summary of how the Nazis have now seamlessly shifted governmental power of Austria to Germany, with only mild verbal complaints by other countries despite the clear violation of the Treaty of Versailles.

How Diana wishes she was there. She knows well how pleasant the Führer can be when things are going his way, and nothing could make him happier than the successful reunion of his home country of Austria with his beloved Germany. If she were able to travel to Austria at the moment—without retching on everyone and everything—then she might be able to finalize the radio deal that M so desperately needs. Instead, here she lies, captive of her own body and this baby.

Of course, she wants to have Mosley's child, but the timing could not be worse. They haven't yet announced their marriage; they didn't want to face the personal and financial wrath of Baba, particularly when money is so tight and she continues to release Curzon funds at his request—barely. But now, with a baby on the way, they can hardly avoid it any longer. Mosley wants Diana to have *his* baby, not just raise Guinness children. She finds this endearing and, of course, welcomes anything to tie her to this elusive man forever.

Still, Mosley seems not to understand how instrumental Diana is in securing his future. Does he not understand that without her machinations in Germany, the commercial radio venture—which could not only sustain the BUF now but make the BUF integral to the Nazis in the future—would not be happening? That, in fact, his tie to Hitler and the Nazis would not even exist? That Hitler told her himself that, after Austria, she would have "her wavelength"?

All those long, exhausting trips to Berlin and Munich where she's deployed her charm and intellect to inveigle a relationship between the Nazis and the BUF have made Mosley viable when the inevitable comes to pass—another Nazi *Anschluss*, this time between Germany and Great Britain. Otherwise, M might have been relegated to the backwater of history. Or worse. And Diana will not have that.

She sighs, commanding the sickness to go away with the force of her will. Her endgame is growing closer, and that, more than anything, brings her peace.

# CHAPTER FORTY-EIGHT
# UNITY

*March 24, 1938*
*Vienna, Austria*

U NITY KICKS OFF HER SHOES, THROWS OPEN WIDE THE doors to the balcony off her room at the Imperial Hotel, and stares out at the Heldenplatz. The Square of the Heroes—so named for those soldiers that liberated the people from Napoleon in the nineteenth century and the Turks in the seventeenth—extends before her, vast and wide. Tonight several clusters of citizens dot the center, and soldiers guard the perimeter, but she recalls the 250,000-person-strong crowd that covered every inch just days ago, cheering for Hitler. Exhilaration courses through her at the thought of the masses sharing in the Führer's magnificent glory.

Extending her arms as Hitler did on a balcony not far from this one several days ago, she imagines for a brief second all that adoration is for her. Then she twirls and twirls on the balcony until she feels quite dizzy and collapses in a laughing heap. How pleased she is that she raced from Munich to Vienna to be part of the *Anschluss*, to witness history firsthand. After all, strangers stop her throughout Vienna, asking if they can kiss her hand because the Führer has touched it. She feels a bit like the Austrians worship her as well, and she's reveling in the sensation.

For some weeks, she'd known something was coming, particularly once Austrian Nazis pressured Chancellor Kurt Schuschnigg to appoint several Nazis to Austrian governmental positions. Then came the urgent meetings within Germany. The whispers among the high-level officers that broke off when she came close. Hitler's exultant mood. But no one would tell her the details, not even her precious SS Erich.

When she finally received word on March 11 that Schuschnigg had been forced to resign and Hitler arranged for his man Arthur Seyss-Inquart to take his place, she knew that military action would not be far behind. Yet even she hadn't suspected it to happen so soon. Late the next day, on March 12, she got word from Erich that the Eighth Army of the German Wehrmacht was entering Austria.

Without even bothering to pack a bag, she hopped into her car and raced to join the tail end of Hitler's procession, her foot on the gas pedal the entire way and her prized golden swastika prominently displayed on her lapel should she be stopped. Trailing behind the official cavalcade, she followed Hitler first over the border to Braunau, then onto Linz, and finally arriving in Vienna not far behind him. Watching her beloved Führer greeted by cheering citizens of the former Austria, some holding bouquets and wreaths for him and others waving Nazi flags, brought tears to her eyes. She knows how long this reunion is in the making.

Despite her close relationship with Hitler, she hadn't

expected any sort of special treatment when she arrived in Vienna. A park bench would have sufficed for a bed, in fact. She simply wanted to be in Austria for this momentous event. But when one of the Führer's guards spotted her, he must have informed their leader and arranged for a room at the Imperial Hotel, not too far from his own. And when Hitler readied to deliver his speech before the throngs at the Heldenplatz on March 15, he invited Unity to stand on the balcony alongside his most important Party members.

Unity had never been so proud. Hitler delivered the speech he was born to convey—explaining how the Reich has entered Austria as a liberator to return his German homeland to its rightful place as part of the German nation, how together they are becoming a "greater Germany." Studying her precious idol in such close proximity, she wept at the sight of his happiness.

As soon as the revelry died down that evening, she sat at the white-and-gold desk in her ornate, red-damask-lined hotel room and reached for a sheet of Imperial Hotel stationery, even though she was a bit tipsy from several glasses of celebratory champagne. "Farve, you'll never guess where your Bobo has been these past few days," she wrote, and then proceeded to detail the procession across Austria and the ecstatic welcome of the citizens. She urged him to share this account as "the British newspapers will undoubtedly tell a very different tale, a false one full of violence and harm that never occurred." And then she proceeded to write a similar letter to Cousin Clemmie's husband, Winston, the one who's been stirring up so much trouble for poor Hitler. Unity must do whatever she can to change the awful British perception of the Führer, so the destiny of Great Britain and Germany can be aligned and she will not be riven in two.

She hears a knock at her door and turns away from the balcony toward the sound. Even though she knows there are Nazi soldiers lining the corridors, she still wonders about the rumors of dissenters. She hasn't seen a single protestor, but that doesn't mean they haven't gone underground. *Stop*, she tells herself, *you sound as paranoid and negative as Nancy or Decca, when instead, you should have utter faith in Hitler and his plans.*

Inhaling deeply, she walks to the door and opens it wide. "*Mein Führer*," she practically squeals in surprise. Recovering her composure, she bows a little and says, "I'm so honored to see you. I know you've been extremely busy with the *Anschluss*, and I never thought you'd have time for me."

"I always have time for *meine Walküre*," Hitler utters in his very nicest voice.

Unity places her hand over her heart. His use of her pet name always moves her, making the right words of reply evasive. She so wants to please him.

He speaks into the unusual silence. "Especially since your father, the esteemed Lord Redesdale, spoke so highly of the Reich today in the House of Lords. He gave a powerful speech in support of the return of Austria to Germany."

"He did?" This news went beyond Unity's wildest imaginings. She knows that his visits to Germany had changed Farve's anti-Hun views considerably, but she never thought he'd take such a public stance with his peers.

"He did indeed." His smile is wide and unmistakable under his mustache. "In that speech, he referred to wondrous firsthand accounts of the Austrian people welcoming our troops. Accounts that, I suspect, came from you."

Unity gazes into Hitler's eyes, but she can't keep the contact. Unbidden, a line from Shakespeare comes to her, one Decca or Debo must have uttered in their endless nattering from his plays: *Dazzle mine eyes*. No one has ever regarded her with such admiration and fondness before; certainly not her parents or sisters, who have always seemed to regard her as peculiar or burdensome. Unity will do *anything* to earn this marvelous adoration from her beloved Führer again.

# CHAPTER FORTY-NINE
## NANCY

*September 27, 1938*
*London, England*

M Y HAND HOVERS OVER THE BRASS DOOR KNOCKER AT
26 Rutland Gate. I do not want to be here. I want
to be back in my bed, under layers of covers, still wearing
my nightgown at noon. Or sitting on my sofa, in slacks and
a sweater, with a glass of brandy, Bordeaux, champagne, or
sherry—whatever is closest—in my hand at five o'clock, only
to return to bed a couple of hours later. These are the only
places I've been able to tolerate for the past few weeks, and
my own is the only company I've been able to stand, other
than my dogs. I am not ready for this onslaught of family
and apprehension.

But needs must.

When I lost the baby earlier in the month—the only miracle that's ever seen fit to grow in my womb in three years—I
gave myself two weeks to mourn the loss of the unborn child
just beginning to form in my belly. Fourteen days to cry and
drink and smoke and indulge any reclusive or destructive
whim I might have. Fourteen days before reentering life for

good and putting behind me these years on the shelf as I tried desperately for a baby.

I ignored calls and notes from my family and friends, even Evelyn, and while I didn't officially banish Peter from our house, he found plenty of other beds in which to sleep, some of which belonged to other women. I did not care; our marriage of convenience hinged on politesse and our ongoing efforts to have a child, not love. I wanted to wallow in my grief alone, particularly since I knew it would be considered excessive compared to the loss of an actual child. My poor sister Decca lost her baby, Julia, when the infant contracted measles late last spring. The death of her sweet baby prompted Decca and Esmond to move to America this summer, although they ascribed it to the intolerable political developments in Europe. How Muv and even Farve cried over the emigration of their next-to-youngest and the loss of the baby that Farve never even saw, as part of his so-called punishment of Decca for her actions.

My fourteen days just ended, and now I must live up to the spark that ignited within me, the one I fanned into a small flame after the *Anschluss* and Farve's upsetting speech to the House of Lords. Last spring, before I became pregnant, I had started to make lists of Diana's trips to Germany and snippets of overheard conversations about her activities as well as Unity's—poring over old letters and reviewing discussions—as I tried to make sense of their schemes and assess any danger they might pose, while Winston's invitation reverberated in my mind. But when I *finally* conceived this summer, I took my doctor's advice very seriously and took to my bed. Those efforts came to naught, and now I've got to make good on my intentions regarding the insidious actions of two Mitford sisters. Today begins my new plan.

I lift the knocker and let it drop. The thud is loud, but no one comes to answer the door. I rap with my gloved knuckles, hard as I dare. Why isn't a hallboy or parlor maid answering the door? I know that Muv and Farve's finances are in terrible shape after several large losses—the Swinbrook estate and thousands of acres of land were recently sold, in fact, to help offset mounting debt—but have they gotten rid of even the most basic staff?

When the door remains unanswered, I walk around the front of the four-story stuccoed building, a nineteenth-century detached house in a fashionable part of Knightsbridge. The entrance is to the left, so I walk over to the expansive bay windows in the center and to the right. There sits my family, oblivious to my arrival. I rap on the window, until Diana turns my way.

After she motions that she'll meet me at the front, I walk back to the Tuscan closed porch that houses the front door. Diana swings open the door, and all that registers at first is her resplendent smile. How happy I am that we are pleasant to one another again, that she's been able to compartmentalize her anger over *Wigs on the Green* to afford us a relationship, albeit one outside Mosley's presence. But then I am afforded a full view of my sister, and I feel as if I've been slapped.

She is very pregnant. I'd been informed of Diana's pregnancy, of course, and she and I exchanged a giggly phone call over the summer when we believed we'd have children fairly close in age. But I haven't actually seen her for some months as she's been at Wootton Lodge or in Germany and I've been following doctor's orders and lying low, and the sight of her belly—her hand caressing it lovingly—is almost more than I can bear. It is a painful, almost physical reminder of my private sorrow.

Stretching out her arms, she coos, "Naunce." I allow myself to be enveloped by her. But when I feel her round belly against my flat one, I have to extricate myself.

"How is Unity?" I ask, without making mention of Diana's condition. I don't trust myself to discuss it unemotionally.

"You shall see for yourself momentarily," she says as we begin walking into the parlor. At the sound of our footsteps, Unity, wearing full Nazi regalia, pushes herself up from the settee and gives me a Nazi salute, ignoring Muv's protests that she's meant to be resting. "So good to see you, Naunce. I'm so sorry about, about—"

I interrupt her, not wanting her to speak aloud the loss. Sitting next to her, I reach for her hand and say, "Thank you, Bobo. Now sit back down and rest like Muv says."

We arrange ourselves in an awkward tableaux in the parlor, with Unity resuming her supine position on the sofa. My little sister, who cannot stop herself from prattling on as she fiddles with her gold Nazi swastika pin, says, "Oh, Naunce. Diana was just telling us the *most* amusing story. Do continue."

"Well, would you believe that my chef, Grimwood, and my butler, James, gave notice on the very same day and the exact same time?" Diana asks in her drollest voice.

"You don't say," I reply, hoping I don't sound as sarcastic as I feel. Does Diana not realize that Muv and Farve's circumstances are so reduced that they are operating with skeletal support? That

I certainly don't have a staff, aside from one jack-of-all-trades maid? Sharing the terrible burdens she suffers from her less-than-attentive enormous staff may not be the most sensitive conversation topic. In fact, as soon as Muv and Farve relinquish the lease on this London house, they'll make their primary residence a small Scottish island Farve purchased on a whim, called Inch Kenneth, and give up this London residence. I haven't made the trip yet, but Debo—out visiting friends this afternoon—describes it as murderous.

"You haven't heard the most amusing part, Naunce. D-Diana, tell her," Unity practically screams. She never did have any ability to modulate herself.

Diana glances over at Unity with a cool expression, and our little sister immediately stops talking. I wonder if that's how Diana keeps a handle on Unity in the fraught Nazi environment.

"They actually both handed me their notices from the floor of the kitchen, where I'd gone to hunt them down when neither surfaced upon the arrival of several guests. I hardly expected to find them lying on the linoleum floor, shards of Dresden china all around, and each of them sitting in a pool of their own blood," Diana announces and then waits for laughter, although I fail to see the humor in it. I do my best to muster a smile.

"A terrible fracas had broken out between the two men, leading to the fight and the double resignation," Unity chimes in, by way of explanation.

Diana continues the thread. "Neither could stand the idea of working with the other, so they thought simultaneously quitting was just the ticket."

Muv chuckles, "Can you imagine?"

Diana laughs along with her. "I swear it took more nego-tiation savvy to get Grimwood and James to stay at Wootton Lodge than it took to persuade the persnickety German minis-ters for our commercial radio deal."

*Ah, here it is,* I think as I watch my sister's ivory cheeks redden at the slip. *A commercial radio deal with the Germans.* This is the source of all the whispers over the past year or more and maybe the explanation for so many trips to Germany. What is this radio deal, and who is it between? Some company controlled by Diana and, I'm guessing, Mosley as well as some German governmental entity? I hardly think this is an auspicious time for a new business arrangement between a British company and the German government over radio—an area controlled by the BBC in any event and heavily protected by the British government. After all, hasn't Prime Minister Chamberlain been in Germany for weeks talking first with Hitler and then with Mussolini and the French premier Eduoard Daladier—all in an effort to reach an agreement to avoid war between Great Britain, France, and the Soviet Union on one side and Germany, Italy, and Japan on the other over Germany's annex-ation of western Czechoslovakia? There must be more to this than what I'm gleaning at the moment, and I'll have to review my timeline and notes about my sisters' activities with this new information at hand.

"Never mind about that." Diana changes the subject quickly, realizing her mistake. "Let's hear how you are feeling today, Unity."

"Almost completely healed," she answers with a slight cough. Unity had developed pneumonia during her annual visit to the Bayreuth Festival this summer, and it became so pronounced that Muv had to travel to Germany to tend to her.

"We'll see what the doctor says about that," Farve grumbles, with good reason. He's the one who had to run off to Nuremberg a few weeks after Muv returned from Bayreuth to fetch Unity when she came down with a serious case of the flu at the *Parteitag*. He thinks, probably rightly so, that she never quite healed from the pneumonia and that made her susceptible to the flu.

"Anyway, Hitler's physician, Doctor Morell, said he would treat me on my return to Munich. And I could not be in better hands," Unity says brightly. Hitler had put his personal doctor at Unity's disposal in Bayreuth, and she's unduly proud of this fact.

"Lot of good that did you the first time around. You got sick a second time," Farve barks.

"I am fine. And I'm going back, whether you like it or not, Farve," Unity barks back at him.

We ignore Farve and continue discussing Unity's health and the assessment of a local physician. The medical consensus seems to support Unity's desire to return to Munich within a week or so. But a persistent question resurfaces, with even more urgency than ever. Why would Muv and Farve permit her to go to such a politically unstable and aggressive country at this time? A country that may well be at war with Great Britain if Chamberlain cannot broker peace? Imagine what Winston would say. Good thing Peter isn't here; he'd raise bloody hell with Muv and Farve—Diana as well. The more I think on it, so should I. Haven't I committed to take action?

"Do you really think it's wise for Unity to return to Germany?" I ask.

The entire group looks at me as if my head has turned Medusa-like. As I gaze right back at them, I realize that they each have their reasons for allowing, even encouraging, Unity to traipse back into the spider's web. Muv and Farve cannot quite manage the single-minded, unruly Unity here, and Diana needs the access to Hitler and senior Nazi officials that Unity can help grant her, not to mention the cover of propriety for so many visits.

No one answers until Unity blurts out, "Stop talking about me as if I'm not here. Nancy, I know you still hold some *Wigs on the Green*–type views about the Führer and I've forgiven you for writing them down in that terrible book, but I haven't forgotten."

The fury in her voice is real, and I must tread carefully with Unity. "It has nothing at all to do with Hitler's views. But it does have everything to do with the political and military unrest on the continent. What if Chamberlain can't broker peace? You would be stuck behind enemy lines, and I do worry about my little sister." I look over at her, seeing the lost, lonely girl she'd been.

A smug smile appears on her lips, and I see that her anger has abated. "Naunce, you needn't worry about me. I am safe in the heart of the Nazis. Hitler and his men will defend me to the bitter end. After all, I am their Valkyrie."

Her imagery is disturbing, but I risk her ire and alienation if I tell her. As I consider what I should say next, she exclaims, "After all, *mein Führer* is about to become ruler of us all. Just wait until everyone sees what he'll do after Czechoslovakia."

As I look around the room to gauge the reaction to Unity's words, I see that only Diana appears unsurprised. Before I can ask what she means, Diana's nanny pops her head into the room. "Ma'am," she says to Diana, "the children have a question for you."

"Coming," Diana says, then pushes herself to standing. As she slowly makes her way out of the room, she says, "Perhaps I shouldn't have brought Jonathan and Desmond over to see Aunt Unity. They've been quite the nuisance."

"Nonsense!" Muv cries out, just as Unity exclaims, "Not at all! I needed to see them!"

With Diana gone, the room quiets for a long moment. Suddenly it occurs to me that I'd like to see the boys as well. I leap up, saying, "It's been an age since I've seen Jonathan and Desmond. I'll just pop in."

I stride down the back hallway toward the study where I'm guessing Diana's boys have been holed up with the nanny, as I haven't seen or heard them since I arrived. The study door is open just a creak, and I push it open a bit without announcing myself, hoping that I'll give the boys a pleasant surprise. Mosley's ongoing dislike of me means that I'm not in the boys' presence often enough, and for a worrisome second, I wonder if they'll remember me.

As I peer through the larger opening I've created, I see that Diana is kneeling next to her boys, correcting the way they are standing. What is she doing, especially in her condition? Then she abruptly stands up and issues a command: "All right, boys, now that you've got the proper form, let's hear it."

She steps back, affording me a full view of Jonathan and

Desmond. The adorable towheaded boys have their hands on their foreheads in a salute gesture. What on earth is happening here? They finish the salute and then call out, "Heil Hitler!"

Clapping excitedly, Diana smiles broadly at them and says, "That was perfect. We just needed that little tweak for it to be right. And we do need it to be right for when the Führer arrives, correct?"

After the boys nod their heads vigorously, she asks, "Have I answered all your questions about the proper greeting for our Führer? If so, I'll return to your grandparents and your aunts."

I want to scream at the disturbing sight I've just witnessed, but I clamp my hand over my mouth instead. I back away from the door as quietly as I can, willing the floorboards not to creak. As I turn to walk down the corridor into the parlor, I see the boys' nanny standing in the shadows. For a second, our eyes meet and I freeze, but I force myself to pretend nothing untoward had just happened and resume my stride. As I pass her, though, she gives me the strangest glance, and part of me wishes that I could stop and inquire. But I cannot.

Once inside the parlor, I make a loud show of taking my leave. I want Diana to hear these exchanges from the hall; I need her to believe that I've been here the whole time. What might she do if she thought I witnessed that treason? Of what do I believe my sister capable?

# CHAPTER FIFTY

# DIANA

*September 27, 1938*
*London, England*

DIANA CLOSES THE FRONT DOOR TIGHTLY BEHIND NANCY. It takes a significant push to hear the lock click, but instinctively, she shoves a little harder against the door to be certain. Her nerves are stretched taut, near to the point of rupturing. Nancy's visit to their parents' London home in such rare, close proximity to Unity has proven to be riskier and more treacherous than she thought possible.

She loves her older sister, of course. In some ways, she is the dark to Diana's light, the other half of her. But the political and personal divide between them has expanded over the years, and that has made an intimate relationship with Nancy almost impossible. Because ingenious, hypervigilant Nancy is the only one who might be able to suss out the entirety of Diana's plan. And she simply cannot have that.

Lingering in the front hallway, she wonders what Nancy might have overheard in the few minutes before she exited. *Stupid*, Diana thinks. Why didn't she insist on walking Nancy out? Rubbing her belly, Diana knows why: the exhaustion of this ill-timed pregnancy is making her sloppy.

She reviews the discussion that took place in the parlor after Nancy's dramatically staged departure, after her older sister had dispensed embraces all around, even to the ever-resistant Farve and ever-icy Muv. Unity returned the conversation to Hitler annexing the entirety of Czechoslovakia regardless of the terms to which Chamberlain, Mussolini, Daladier, and the Führer might agree. From the many dinners Diana has had in Berlin with Nazi leaders, she knows well that Unity is correct. But to reveal this sort of information to a wider group—British governmental leaders, even—would force Diana's hand, and turn her and Mosley into British spies or traitors in a blink, instead of the well-timed commercial and political partners they hope to be perceived as when Hitler's inevitable domination transpires.

Fortunately, Diana recalls that she'd been dismissive of Unity's rambling about a Czech takeover and changed the conversational topic. Even though she didn't know Nancy was hanging about, she had not wanted her parents to know anything about Hitler's plans to undermine any agreement Chamberlain might secure, any whispers she might have overheard. Her parents have been so wonderfully supportive of the Nazi regime, especially Farve with his speeches and his letters, and she doesn't want to jeopardize that in any way. They will need to maintain a united front in the days ahead, and she'll have a lot of convincing to do once Hitler marches into Czechoslovakia.

*What a relief,* she thinks. *My comments were innocuous.* She exhales audibly, and then she suddenly remembers. Just after Nancy bluffed leaving and Diana successfully dismissed Unity's chatter about the Nazis in Czechoslovakia, Muv had asked Diana if she could return to Germany with Unity when she left, perhaps pair that travel with the work she'd been doing to negotiate the commercial radio station. And Diana had replied that she could not because the baby was nearly here and, in any event, she'd nearly finished with the necessary permissions and permits to set up the station in Germany to transmit light entertainment in Belgium and parts of Great Britain. *Damn it,* she thinks. What *would Nancy make of that if she overheard?* Perhaps more importantly, what would she *do* with it?

Diana tries to imagine the scene. What had Nancy done while she loitered in the front hall? Put her gloves on slowly, finger by finger? Sorted through her purse as though hunting for something? Carefully applied her signature bloodred lipstick in the hallway mirror? What would she have done if Diana had come upon her spying? Most importantly, why was she curious enough to eavesdrop?

"Diana," Muv calls from the parlor, interrupting her thoughts.

"Yes," Diana calls back, not wanting to rush unless absolutely necessary. Although two or so months remain before her baby is born, she already feels huge and ungainly.

"There is a call for you."

Who knows that she is here? The staff at the London townhouse she and Mosley are letting?

"Who is it?"

"Mosley."

At the sound of her lover's name—her husband now, she still sometimes forgets—she hastens to the telephone table. He must have grilled them to locate her. Taking the handset from Muv, she turns toward the corner for a modicum of privacy.

"Hello, darling," she half whispers.

"You didn't mention you and your boys were going to Rutland Gate today."

"I didn't want to bother you with unimportant details of a visit to Unity and my parents," she says, careful to keep Nancy from the conversation. Mosley still perceives her as an enemy, probably always will. "And I know you are busy preparing to go to Paris."

Although Diana had struck the primary terms of the radio deal with Hitler's men this summer, she didn't want M to feel as though he hadn't played an important role. Even though they both knew it would have never happened without her. So when it came time to secure the finer points of the organizational structure, Diana suggested that Mosley and their lawyer meet the German negotiators, businessman Dr. Johannes Bernhardt, investment banker Kurt von Schroeder, and Hitler's aide Captain Fritz Wiedemann in the German side of Paris. She knew these last details of the deal might be tricky, given that the German government can only give a broadcasting license to a German company, a rule which their lawyers worked around by creating nebulous entities, and given the tight restrictions on programming. That way, M would stay out of harm's way from British intelligence and, more importantly, wouldn't feel emasculated by her triumph.

"I *had* hoped to review the outstanding contract terms with you before I left this evening," M says, making his displeasure evident. "You have insisted on handling most of the negotiations to date, after all."

Diana bristles. Only through her most charming and brilliant tactics has their radio plan gotten this far. To suggest that she is somehow monopolizing the negotiations for her own personal pleasure is ludicrous and insulting. But she says none of this. She knows how Mosley would view this sharp reaction, and she has no intention of alienating the one man she wants above all else, largely because he is the only one who has never capitulated to her wiles. Not now, when they are finally about to secure all they want as a couple—financial security, ready cash flow for their political group, and the right to sit at Hitler's side when he conquers Great Britain—and all she wants as a woman—to be Mosley's wife and bear his child.

Mosley has insisted on keeping their marriage a secret these past two years, outside of the immediate family, of course. Initially he was fearful of alienating Baba. As time went on, it became clear that his relationship with Diana would corrupt that financial tie regardless of their marital status, but by then, they had another reason for secrecy. The commercial radio negotiations were well underway, and Diana needed to ensure Mosley had no official link to the deal so the curiosity of British intelligence wouldn't be piqued. But now, bursting with his child and the radio deal nearly sealed, the time is nigh.

"The boys and I will be back to the flat in a tick." Diana swallows her discontent and promises Mosley a hasty return home to coach him on the radio deal.

# CHAPTER FIFTY-ONE
# UNITY

*September 27, 1938*
*London, England*

U NITY RISES FROM HER SICKBED SETTEE AND TRIES TO
grab the telephone from Diana's hand.

"Stop," her sister cries out, swatting her away like an irritating gnat. Unity loathes being treated this way, by Diana of all people. It takes her back to her childhood, where she felt strange and lumpish compared to her divine sisters. Despite the intermittent jealousy she now feels over her sister's beauty and charm, not to mention the easy way she's managed to forge a relationship with the Führer, Unity admires her sister, even worships her to some extent. And Unity had come to believe Diana felt some of the same feelings about her, appreciation at the very least.

"But I want to talk to Mosley," Unity whines, hating the sound of her voice but unable to stop herself. She misses Hitler terribly and wants him to know his Valkyrie will return to Germany soon. "I have a message for him to give to Captain Wiedemann when he sees him in Paris. An important message that Captain Wiedemann needs to pass on to *mein Führer.*"

"How does Unity know I am going to Paris? And who I'll be seeing?" Mosley says to Diana, but his voice is loud enough for Unity to hear through the handset. "What have you been telling her?"

His words startle Unity. Why wouldn't he want her to know about his trip and what he's doing there? Aren't they all on the same side? The side of the Führer and fascism? The side trying to get Great Britain to understand that peace between Unity's birthplace and her adopted homeland of Germany will serve both great countries well? That together they deserve to rule all of Europe?

"Shh," Diana whispers to him. She begins to back away from Unity, as far as the telephone cord will reach.

"Don't tell me to shush." Mosley is practically screaming now. Never mind that Diana has retreated to the corner of the parlor with the phone, his voice is audible. Not only to Unity but Muv and Farve as well, who are staring at Diana.

"She can hear you," Diana hisses.

"I don't care if bloody Hitler can hear me. You are my wife, and I won't have you telling me to be quiet. Certainly not for damned Unity."

"We cannot afford to alienate Unity," Diana replies in a hushed tone. "And in any event, you shouldn't speak about my sister that way."

Having utterly disregarded Diana's wish to back away, Unity stands close enough to observe her sister's exquisite face fall and her always-erect posture slump. How dare a man like Mosley speak to her sister this way? He is an ersatz fascist at best—hadn't he switched parties three times before settling on fascism?—and does not deserve her. Unity knows well that it is Diana who has true faith in Hitler and the Reich, manifested through Unity of course.

Unity is beginning to think that Mosley might not be a worthy partner to Hitler. That perhaps someone else would better serve the Führer when he and Great Britain reach their alliance. Perhaps Diana. Perhaps Unity herself.

A cold determination courses through her, and she turns away from her sister. As she walks toward the telephone table, she can hear her mother's voice calling to her, urging her to sit back down on the settee. Even Farve begins to call her name when Unity starts coughing. But she has no intention of retreating. She needs to protect her sister and protect her countries—Germany *and* England—all in one fell swoop.

Unity approaches the telephone. As she stretches out her index finger toward the black Bakelite phone base, she can hear her sister yell, "No!" But she will not be stopped and presses down, disconnecting Mosley from Diana. No one will stand in her way.

# CHAPTER FIFTY-TWO

# NANCY

*August 2, 1939*
*Perpignan, France*

S EÑORA, SEÑORA!" MEN CALL AT ME THROUGH THE BARBED-
wire fence. Hands jut out between the lower portions of
the fence without the knifelike edges, trying to grab my sleeve
or the fabric of my trousers. The desperation exuding from the
refugees is tangible and heart-wrenching.

"*Lo siento, señores,*" I call back with one of the few Spanish
phrases I've managed to nail down between duties. I wish I
could offer them more. Apologies are so very futile when their
bellies are empty and their futures uncertain.

I cross the squalid camp to the women's section, where they
too sit behind a barbed-wire fence as if they're criminals when,
in fact, their only crime is escaping into France from Spain,
away from the mass executions being conducted by the fascist General Francisco Franco and his armies. Staring at these
filthy, emaciated women, many with children hanging on their
flimsy cotton dresses or dangling from their thin arms surrounded by the family dogs and farm animals, I wonder—for
the millionth time—how they crossed the formidable Pyrenees

mountains to escape. Once these poor, wretched people finally made it over the border, how could France not welcome them with open arms? While I suppose the French are more preoccupied with preparing for war against Germany than the onslaught of refugees and should be credited with not sending them back to Spain, by placing these wretched folks in limbo, volunteer masses are needed to care for them. And there are dwindling resources as we attempt to find a country that will embrace these impoverished, famished multitudes.

Approaching the aid worker guarding the gate, I lament the fact that all I have are messages from relatives in the men's camp rather than food. Despite the fact that I have no supplies, the women gather around me with broad smiles as I step inside the gate. For propriety's sake, the refugee camp organizers separated men from women, effectively splitting up families, immediate and extended, and the ferrying of messages between the two camps by me and two other aides is their only method of communication. I understand the reasons behind the separation of the genders, but it seems unduly harsh at a time that's already unimaginably hard.

Mangling the Spanish pronunciation of many surnames, I am halfway through the distribution of letters when I feel a tap on my shoulder. "Nancy?" a familiar voice asks, and I turn to see Peter.

To my surprise, in the spring, my husband had traveled to Perpignan to help the hundreds of thousands of refugees fleeing from the violence of Franco's fascism, an act of altruism born out of the frustration of inaction. It took me a few months before I summoned the courage to join him, inspired by his newspaper articles and many letters describing the deplorable conditions here. I was also looking for purpose in the wake of my miscarriage and in the absence of additional clearly damaging evidence against my sisters that would have prompted me to stay in England and continue to gather information about them. It wasn't enough that Diana was turning her children into Nazi Youth. At least I don't think so. Not yet.

If I'd come here to spend time with Peter rather than provide aid, I'd have been sorely disappointed. Peter *did* greet me at the train station with a distracted kiss on the cheek, before immediately handing me off to another aide with instructions to help distribute rations to the refugees at suppertime. Since then, his responsibilities have kept him away from me most days and nights, and the London gentleman who'd seemed aimless except for his evening cocktail plans is positively alive with meaning here in Perpignan and integral to the efficient running of the refugee camp. He is almost unrecognizable, but I wonder how long it would take the routines of London to wear away this patina of purpose. How long would it take to wear away mine?

"Yes. Do you need me for something?" I answer, handing over the remaining letters to the guard.

"I'd like you to assign refugees and their families to cabins and bunks on the ship bound for Mexico. We've got a list of the souls that will be on board, and their names are in order of priority, based on the date of arrival here in the camp. But someone's got to do the trying work of finding space for them." He busses her cheek. "Do you mind giving it a go? No one is more of a whiz than you at organization."

"Nice try at flattery," I say with a wry smile.

He returns the smile, giving me a glimpse of Peter from the Savoy bar, the late-night cocktails with Evelyn, the last dregs of any soiree, and then he's all business. "Good sport, Nancy." He pats my arm as if I'm a colleague instead of his wife. "We don't want brawls breaking out once they board."

Studying me as if really seeing me for the first time since my arrival over a month ago, he says, "Why don't you close your eyes for a couple of hours? You look absolutely knackered, and you've got until tomorrow afternoon to assign the cabins and bunks."

His suggestion is surprisingly compassionate. If I'm not careful, I could end up falling for *this* Peter, an entirely different fellow from the one with whom I exchanged wedding vows and share a house back in Maida Vale, where we'd moved after Rose Cottage. I could end up wanting to stay married to *this* Peter.

"If you insist," I say.

"I do," he says, giving me a kiss on the top of my head and then responding to the questions and requests of Donald and Humphrey, his two assistants who have been patiently waiting for him.

I squeeze his hand in farewell and wander through the twilight toward the volunteers' area, where a makeshift village of tents has been assembled. *What a beautiful spot for a holiday this southern French coastal town might make*, I think, with its glimpses of the azure Mediterranean and the stunning orange-brick castle that dominates the horizon. Except for the fact that refugee camps have taken over the periphery of the town and the coastal areas, of course.

I reach my tent, stopping only to wash my dirt-encrusted hands in the basin of fresh water some thoughtful volunteer placed on a communal table. As I scrub beneath my appalling nails—how Muv would sniff—I wonder how my sisters and, more recently, Tom can support the sort of regime that spawned this human catastrophe of hundreds of thousands of displaced, desperate refugees. A regime more concerned about power and ideology than the citizens it's meant to govern. Would Diana and Unity continue praising their precious Hitler if they witnessed the suffering mothers and children I just left behind in the women's camp? If they saw with their own eyes the hundreds of babies, many of which are camp-born or will be ship-born?

*Stop*, I think. If I allow myself to speculate on how Unity and Diana can wave that damn Nazi flag with relish and possibly undermine their own country by sharing confidential information with the man who will soon be our enemy, I will never get the three meager hours of sleep allotted to me. *Stop*, I command myself again, when insidious notions creep in about the business and strategic alliances Diana is forging to assist Hitler in his planned rule of Great Britain. *Stop*, I whisper aloud when I chastise myself for only being able to gather high-level, rather harmless information about Unity and Diana—lists of places they've gone, dates of travel, Nazi officials they've met, and the like, but nothing substantial linking their fascist beliefs to anti-Britain activity—and then failed to muster the courage to share it with Winston anyway. But then this thought prompts another spiral: Why do I want to find out something damning about my sisters?

I try to calm down and refocus on the three hours for sleep, all that can be spared. It is three hours more than I had last night, and three hours more than Peter has had for nearly forty-eight hours.

I ignore the journals stacked up next to my cot, where I'm mapping out a novel in which I try to make sense of the political madness swirling around me and my sisters' part in it. I am too knackered. Instead, I peel off my sweaty clothes and wipe myself off as best I can, wondering when attempting to spy on Diana and Unity ceased to be enough for me in the war against fascism. When did I need to do more to change the trajectory of this terrible era, beyond amassing information on my sisters' suspect German business deals and writing novels about it? I cannot identify the hour or even the day, but one morning, I awoke and the spark turned into an irrepressible compulsion to join Peter in Spain to help with the refugees from Franco's war. I wanted to get my lily-white hands dirty with the real work of helping victims of fascism, beyond half-heartedly collecting information about my sisters' whereabouts, beyond scribbling fictitious characters struggling with similar issues. Perhaps, as I assess how far I'll have to go to stop my sisters from spreading the Nazi tyranny, I need the stakes to be real and to see them for myself.

# CHAPTER FIFTY-THREE
# DIANA

*August 4, 1939*
*Bayreuth, Germany*

**M**ORE TEA, LADY MOSLEY?" HITLER ASKS, OFFERING Diana the sweetest smile. Sometimes it's hard for her to believe that this kind gentleman with the most impeccable manners is the same person who so boldly and unexpectedly violated the Munich Agreement in March, the accord that had temporarily allowed Chamberlain to return home a hero and a peacekeeper. Regardless of the terms of that four-way pact between Great Britain, France, Italy, and Germany, in which Hitler agreed to be satisfied with "reclaiming" the Germanic part of Czechoslovakia called the Sudetenland, he'd taken over the rest of Czechoslovakia a few months later—to the horror of the world.

"That sounds delicious, *mein Führer*. Thank you," she answers, holding up her porcelain cup, a fine china with delicate gold etchings of a swastika. How does Hitler manage to ensure that his custom-made Nazi china is available at the restaurant of the Goldener Anker hotel where he stays while in Bayreuth for the Wagner Festival? Perhaps the hotel keeps a ready supply.

As Diana watches him pour the aromatic liquid, she wishes that she was home snuggling her sweet-smelling eight-month-old Oswald Alexander, whom they call Alexander. He's at such a delicious age, even though his arrival into this world was anything but delicious. She and Mosley had no choice but to publicly announce their marriage upon his birth, and the news riled up a tempest of unexpected proportions. Baba's dismay and outrage was anticipated, but the shock and upset of poor Nicholas, M's son, was painful for them all. Diana had grown to care for Mosley's children, and while they didn't necessarily return the emotions—Baba had planted too many evil step-mother fairy tales in their heads—his boys adored Jonathan and Desmond, and that warmed her heart.

As Nicholas's Easter holiday from boarding school grew closer, he'd calmed down, and Diana thought herself in the clear. She hunkered down for a nice long stretch at Wootton Lodge with her three boys and Mosley with occasional pleasant visits from his other children—until Hitler decided to occupy all of Czechoslovakia in a thumbing of the nose to Chamberlain, Mussolini, and Daladier. Even though she'd anticipated this action, it struck the nation and those around her hard. And while Prime Minister Chamberlain didn't react with a war proclamation or anything of the sort, a sense of foreboding had overtaken the nation, and Mosley became unraveled. Only the enthusiastic, larger-than-ever crowds at his July meeting at Earls Court Exhibition Hall—a demonstration for peace instead of war with Germany—could placate him for a brief time.

But then Mosley returned to perseverating over the financial stability of the BUF. Would the radio deal go forward if war was declared? How would he maintain the BUF until Hitler took over Great Britain—because M knows they're coming, believes that the German military is unstoppable—without the funds thrown off by the radio station? These questions were the constant refrain at Wootton Lodge, and no number of conciliatory words could ease her husband's distress. Poor Alexander had to be placed in the nanny's care while Diana traveled to Germany to work her magic once again. So here she sits.

"Are you looking forward to the opera tonight?" she asks, trying to muster excitement or, at least, genuine-sounding enthusiasm in her voice. In truth, she finds opera terribly dull, and the Führer's love of the tedious music is one of the most off-putting aspects of these trips. When will she be able to raise the issue for which Mosley sent her: to discover whether the radio deal is complete, the station underway, and the arrangement intact regardless of the vagaries with the Munich Agreement?

"Ah yes," he replies, a reverential tone in his voice. "*Der Fliegende Holländer* should be inspiring."

As she, Hitler, and Unity chatter about the performance this evening and the splendor of the lavish decorations on the Festspielhaus, Diana thinks how different the festival is this year. The mood is more subdued, and the apple-cheeked, blond young soldiers who'd been ubiquitous in years past are fewer in number. Several of their ranks have been replaced by bandaged and hobbling soldiers brought here to be inspired by Wagner in their recovery, and while she doubts that the heavy-handed productions of Wagner are what the doctor ordered, she also knows that no one declines an invitation from Hitler.

"And it will be a balm to have you two ladies as my special guests," he says with a gracious nod and smile at each of them. Diana knows that it does indeed give him pleasure to appear at the Bayreuth Festival with the aristocratic Mitford sisters—what with the family's close ties to Richard Wagner himself—on his arm. "Your presence here helps soothe my heavy spirit and gives me hope for a peaceful future for Great Britain and Germany."

Unity clutches Hitler's arm. The Führer's welfare is always paramount to her, Diana knows well. "Are you quite all right?"

"Oh yes, *meine Walküre*, there is nothing wrong with my body. It is only my spirit that is weighed down."

"I would do anything to help you," Unity says plaintively.

"I know," he says, patting her hand with his free one. "But I believe that this area is outside your purview. You have beseeched me on this topic time and time again, and it pains me that my sacred duty calls me to do something that will upset you."

*What on earth is he talking about?* Diana thinks.

Unity seems to understand, as her eyes widen and she cries, "No!"

Hitler's eyes dart to his guards, who've scanned the tearoom. The few other guests have not glanced in their direction, even though Unity's shriek must have been audible. They don't dare.

What is her sister privy to that causes such alarm? What next step are the Nazis about to take? She can't ask; eagerness would suggest an inappropriate interest. Still Diana prays that, whatever Hitler has ordered his troops to do, blasted Winston will not be proven right. That in seeking appeasement, Chamberlain guaranteed war.

The Führer reaches for Diana and Unity's hands. Once he holds one of each in his grasp, he lowers his voice and says, "For your own safety and protection, I am telling you something that is otherwise secret and known only to my top generals and ministers. You must both return to Great Britain after tonight's performance. Soon it will not be safe for you to remain in Germany."

A chill passes through Diana. She now understands all this circular, vague talk.

Even though he need not elucidate, he does. "War is inevitable. It could happen within days or weeks. Regardless, the only safe place for *meine lieblinges* is home."

"But you promised peace between Great Britain and Germany! And this is my home!" Unity wails, then begins sobbing, a pathetic sight.

What will become of the radio station upon which so much depends? Can they operate the business in these circumstances? These are the refrains running through Diana's mind. After all, the British government has no idea about their arrangement with the German government. War need not absolutely forbid their commercial radio-station venture.

Hitler releases Diana's hand and places both of his surprisingly pale, elegant hands around Unity's. "I know that. Of course, I do. You have proven yourself to be a true Nazi and the *Walküre* of Germany. But the government of your homeland neither wants to take the olive branch that I've extended time and again nor does it want to acknowledge the Germanic destiny to bring back together all its far-flung homelands and peoples into one united nation. Great Britain does not even want me to gather together the German people who were put under the control of the Polish government by the Versailles Treaty. Even with my protection, *meine lieblinges*, it could prove unsafe for you to stay here."

Unity's chest heaves as her sobs deepen, and Diana wonders whether there is more than mere concern to Hitler's urge that they leave. By sending Unity home, is the Führer sending a message to Great Britain that he is in earnest? Does Unity's return become his ultimate propaganda?

But Diana is calm, whether he has ulterior motives in ushering them out of Germany or not. She knows what she must do to achieve her ends.

She turns to face Hitler and says, "I refuse to believe this will be the last time I'll see you, *mein Führer*. Lord Mosley will continue to crusade for peace, and regardless of his success, I am certain that you will prevail and that we will meet again in Great Britain when we are all united as one. Mosley, Unity, and I will be waiting for you, at the ready to assist at your side."

Does Diana see a tear in Hitler's eye? When nothing trickles down his cheek, she wonders if it is a trick of the sunlight. Either way, he announces, with what seems like an overwrought show of bravado, "That is my greatest hope, my beautiful Lady Mosley. Until then, we still have *Der Fliegende Holländer* and tonight."

# CHAPTER FIFTY-FOUR
# UNITY

*August 4, 1939*
*Bayreuth, Germany*

U NITY REMEMBERS EVERY DETAIL OF THE EXACT MOMENT the world went dark.

A slight breeze cooling the humid afternoon on the patio of the Goldener Anker hotel restaurant. Steaming cups of tea somehow refreshing despite the heat. Heaps of Hitler's favorite treats on a silver tray. The bucolic landscape of Bayreuth offset by the vivid crimson of the Nazi banners and flags flapping in the breeze. The smile on her sister's face and that of her precious Führer.

She recalls how she felt in the minute leading up to the horrifying news.

Euphoria at the honor of this private gathering with the Führer before the opening night of the Bayreuth Festival. A surprising lack of jealousy and resentment at Diana on sharing this special occasion with her, perhaps because her sister was unusually reserved. Anticipation at the literal spotlight that will shine on her and Diana tonight at the *Der Fliegende Holländer*, when they proceed into the box reserved for Hitler's special guests. The peace of achieving her life's goal.

But then the announcement came. Her precious Führer spoke the words that she'd been dreading, phrases that she'd begged him never to utter. And then everything went black.

The next clear memory she has is exiting the Goldener Anker hotel. Her arm is resting on Diana's shoulders, and her sister seems to be bearing her weight. Unity feels completely slack, drained of the electric life force that courses through her when she's in the presence of the Führer. Where is he? Two of his guards are marching in front of them, but she doesn't see their leader anywhere.

"Has the Führer gone?" she asks Diana, her voice unexpectedly raspy and worn. As if she's been screaming.

Diana looks at her with eyes askance. "Don't you remember?" Unity shakes her head. Not trusting her voice.

"You lost all sense of yourself when he told us we must leave Germany. Cries. Sobs. Floods. The whole terrible bit. When those escalated into screams and worse, the Führer gave your arm a final squeeze and left the table. Then his guards ushered us out." Diana tsks. "Really, Unity, I understand why you are upset, but you cannot do that to the Führer. His citizens could become highly agitated and alarmed if he's made an English girl positively shriek."

"That's what I did?" Unity croaks. The moments after he urged them to leave are blank.

"That's *exactly* what you did. Right before you got down on your knees and begged him to stop his military action before he starts it."

"Oh my God," Unity whispers, mostly to herself.

Diana is silent as she leads Unity away from the guards and

the hotel. Guiding them toward the Hofgarten, the oak-and-beech-laden park that meanders through Bayreuth, she does not stop until she reaches a clearing free of any onlookers. Only then does she explode.

"Can you imagine what those German aristocrats at the tables around us must have thought? There is really only one interpretation." Diana stares at Unity. "That he has shared with us the worst and most secret news. That Germany is about to go to war with Great Britain. Why would you want to put Hitler in that position when he's trusted us with that confidential information?"

"I am sorry," Unity whispers.

Diana's disgust is evident. "It isn't me to whom you need to apologize. It's the Führer. And I suggest that you seek him out and make a formal application for forgiveness before the festival this evening."

"I will."

"If he will see you, that is. After these histrionics," Diana mutters, in the longest, most outward display of anger Unity has ever witnessed in her usually serene sister.

*A sort of madness must have descended*, Unity thinks. But how could she have allowed it to go so far? To compromise her beloved Führer? Only her abject dismay at having the two countries—the two peoples she loves and considers her own at war could have driven her to such an unhinged display.

"We are lucky to be alive, Unity. Don't you realize that many people have been killed for much less?" Diana seethes.

This pronouncement should make Unity fearful, and she suspects that is Diana's intention. But the opposite occurs.

Unity feels a wave of relief at the idea of being erased from this pain. It has been her only constant companion and friend for more years than she can remember. Only her time with the Führer provided her with a release from it.

Unity knows what she must do.

"If there is war, which I still pray the Führer can avoid, I will not be able to bear it, Diana. I will not be able to watch my two homelands slaughter one another. I will not be able to endure the belief that I could not prevent it from happening, that I couldn't convince the Führer of another oath. And I will not survive the separation from him. If war comes, I will have failed." Unity turns to face her sister, releasing all the poisonous feelings of covetousness and jealousy that have eaten away at their relationship over the years and allowing herself simply to experience pure love for this sister of blood and belief. "Diana, I will kill myself."

# CHAPTER FIFTY-FIVE
# NANCY

*September 3, 1939*
*Inch Kenneth, Scotland*

I PACE THE RATHER BLEAK, WIND-WHIPPED HOUSE THAT now serves as my parents' home on Inch Kenneth, a remote one-mile-long island in the Inner Hebrides of Scotland that Farve purchased impulsively when he had to sell Swinbrook. I can only imagine that it must have been a glorious, sunny day when he took the plunge into island ownership, because while this grassy hill ringed with craggy rocks and beaches is indeed magical on those rare bright days, it is beyond desolate on the typical rainy ones. But I suppose desolation suits us all right now.

Smoking cigarette after cigarette, even though not one of them provides the desired relief, I refuse to leave this room. This is where the radio receives the best reception, and I must hear the news announcement. The ultimatum that Prime Minister Chamberlain issued to Hitler two days ago expired at 11:00 a.m. Five minutes have passed since that deadline, and Germany has not replied. Instead, the Third Reich continues its assault on Poland, which, to my way of thinking, is the same as issuing a flat-out rejection of Chamberlain's command to withdraw. Yet I won't give up hope entirely that peace can be achieved until I hear the words spoken aloud— either way—on the BBC. *How the radio has become our lifeline*, I think.

Finally the radio crackles to life with urgency, interrupting a musical interlude, and Muv and Farve race into the room. I glance at the chimneypiece clock, and I see that it is 11:15 a.m. Chamberlain's voice fills the parlor, and I feel unmoored when he announces his disappointment that his "long struggle to win peace has failed." I know that can mean only one thing to this most strident advocate for appeasement. We are at war.

Muv screeches, and Farve collapses down onto the sofa. I am frozen in disbelief. Even though I've understood for some time that war was inevitable, it's one thing to know it intellectually and explore it as I write the novel I began in Perpignan—called *Pigeon Pie*—and quite another to accept it emotionally. Horrific futures play out in my mind, and only the burning of my fingers from the lit cigarette I've been holding brings me around.

*Peter*, I think and race for the telephone. In his last letter, he shared his plan to join the military the very moment war is announced, as he's too old for conscription. Is he already lined up at some dreary recruitment office? One would hope he'd use his network of school chums, but one never knows with my husband. Ever since he returned from Perpignan a few weeks ago, he's been quite the zealot for world change. I would like to wish my husband farewell in person—though he's more companion than husband these days—but the telephone might

have to do. I would also like to check on Tom, who's been too
near the side of the fascists for my liking these days, and of
course, dear Evelyn.

Rushing past the housemaid and cook crying in the corner
of the main hall, I reach the telephone room, only to discover
that Muv is already on the line. "Please, Diana, I've called
Munich but Unity's line is not in service according to the operator. I'm—I'm"—she stops speaking because sobs have taken
hold—"so terribly worried about her."

A pause ensues, then Muv says, "Of course, I understand
that this was her choice, that no less than Herr Hitler himself
urged her to return home. But that doesn't soothe my concern
for her well-being, and—"

Diana must have interrupted her, because Muv stops mid-
sentence. Her face grows redder as the seconds pass, until she
bursts out, "How dare you! You were certainly willing to call
and write your sister when it served your purposes, but now that
reaching out to Unity might put you and Mosley in harm's way,
you don't want anything to do with your poor, high-strung—"

Diana's voice has become so loud that I can hear her yell
through the handset into the hallway. I cannot make out the
words, but whatever she's saying, it has muted the edge of
Muv's sharp anger. "I understand that you have to protect your
family, and I know that you're pregnant."

Pregnant? Diana is pregnant *again*? No one told me. I
did not think that any news could send me reeling beyond
Chamberlain's announcement, but I was wrong. I lean against
the wall to steady myself.

"All right, darling. I will let you know if we receive word. I'll have your father telegraph her since the phone lines are down. Be careful in the meantime."

Muv pivots away from the telephone and bumps directly into me. "Are you quite well, Nancy? You look positively green. Of course, this declaration of war would set any one of us off." Then, before I can even answer, she rambles on. "I am so worried about our little Unity, so lonely and scared behind enemy lines. Not that Hitler is *our* enemy, of course."

All the worry and anger that has been simmering beneath the surface—over the war, my family's sick fascination with Hitler, now Diana's pregnancy—explodes. "What in the name of God are you talking about, Muv? Great Britain is at *war* with Hitler. Our country and our citizens are in grave danger!" I yell.

"Oh, Nancy"—she swats me away—"Hitler appreciates the British people and our way of life. Our nation will be fine. I am more concerned about what the British or German people might do to Unity in Germany."

"Have you not seen what's happened in each of the countries Hitler takes over? The Czechs? The Poles? Muv, in Perpignan, I saw firsthand the horrific things that fascists do to people. Make no mistake, Hitler will do those things to the British citizens and worse to the soldiers."

Muv's voice grows louder. "You don't know Hitler, Nancy. And we'd be better off under his command than with our leaders. Do you know what the current government will ultimately do to us? Institute some sort of socialist world order that will rob us of what little money and standing we have left—or worse, let the communists take over. You'll see."

"I hope I *never* see Hitler in control of Great Britain." I match her volume.

Farve stands in the doorway to the parlor, watching us. Muv and I freeze for a moment, and I wonder what he'll say. He's been uncharacteristically silent since the Nazis crossed into Poland and Chamberlain issued the ultimatum, although I've heard bits of negative grumbling about the Third Reich ever since they invaded Czechoslovakia in violation of the Munich Agreement. Will Farve continue his strange support of Hitler and side with Muv, or will he return to some semblance of sense?

"Not sporting of the old chap," he mutters, and as he walks away from us, I hear him say, "Damn Huns."

I exhale. At least one of my parents hasn't teetered into the abyss of Nazi worship. But I've still got to deal with Muv.

"We must not win this war," Muv seethes. "For ourselves, of course. But especially for Diana and Unity. What will become of your sisters if Great Britain wins? I mean, Diana and Mosley are here in England, but they've publicly aligned themselves with fascism generally and Hitler specifically. We must follow their lead and do all we can to make sure the right thing happens. And Unity—" She cannot finish her sentence.

Her words stun me into silence. Not only is she placing the needs of her two favorite children above the rest, as always, but she's putting them above what's best for the entire nation. And urging me to commit treason—like her and my sisters, apparently—in the process. I will indeed ensure that the right thing happens, although I define *right thing* very differently than Muv does. No more perseverating on sharing the information I've gathered on Diana and Unity, limited though it may be, with Winston. Because Diana and Unity's beloved Führer is now Great Britain's sworn enemy, after all.

Having issued her edict, Muv is finished with me; she has more important tasks to tend. Walking away, she calls to Farve. "David, we need to send a telegram to Unity."

Alone in the entryway, I hasten to the telephone, but I'm not planning on calling Peter first. Pulling open the drawer underneath it, I slide out Muv's address book and scan for a particular telephone number. I'd delayed sharing this information because I wasn't quite ready and did not yet have damning documentation in any event, but it's not "right" to hold out any longer.

After several failed fits and starts with the local operator, I finally hear the phone ring in the handset. "Hello?"

I recognize the voice, thank God. "Cousin Clemmie, it's Nancy Mitford Rodd. I apologize for interrupting you at what must be a terribly upsetting and busy time. But I need to speak to Winston."

# CHAPTER FIFTY-SIX
# DIANA

*September 3, 1939*
*Staffordshire, England*

DIANA CANNOT LOOK AT MOSLEY. IF THEIR EYES MEET, he will know that she's witnessing him at his most dejected. His spirit could sink so low he might never rise. She cannot allow that sort of anguish to overtake her; she's made too many sacrifices to permit failure. No, she will ensure that Mosley ascends, as she has always done.

Chamberlain continues to drone on over the radio, but Diana's mind is elsewhere. It isn't here in the seemingly cozy, wood-lined library at Wootton Lodge, with the birds chirping and the flowers blooming in the lawn just outside the French doors. It isn't listening to the momentous announcement of the prime minister on the BBC alongside Baba, Mosley and his other children Nicholas, Vivien, and Micky, and her boys Jonathan and Desmond, all of whom have decamped to Wootton Lodge for the duration of the war, along with a consolidated roster of nannies and, of course, baby Alexander who remains in his nursery. *The war...* She can hardly even think the word to herself.

Instead, her thoughts are fixed on strategy. How can she and Mosley stay safe while at the same time readying themselves for Hitler's certain victory, that wondrous time when Mosley can finally lead after a negotiated peace? M has assured her that England's military is no match for the German war machine, and Diana is counting on it. Not that she wants to engage in sedition, mind, but she needs a two-birds-with-one-stone sort of scheme to determine how their radio station might fit into the plan.

The broadcast ends, and the group begins to disperse, each to their own cares and concerns. Diana absentmindedly pats a crying housemaid's shoulder as she passes, and then whispers calming words into the ears of Jonathan and Desmond, who appear perplexed and terrified at the same time. Treading lightly, she skirts around Mosley and Baba, who are deep in conversation, having achieved a measure of civility for wartime, if not forgiveness.

Quiet and solitude are what Diana needs to work out their next steps. Mosley has already taken one bold misstep that she fears she must manage carefully or end up sidelined for the entirety of the war. On September 1, upon the issuance of Chamberlain's ultimatum to Germany, he published a statement in which he proclaimed that the war is really about Jewish finance and then urged his members to carry on the work of awakening the British citizens to the importance of peace. Those words might please Hitler, but they will not be popular with the wartime people of England, or their government. *Has the statement already invited the scrutiny of British intelligence?* she wonders.

Stepping into the parlor, Diana sees that Vivian has settled there, so she retreats to the drawing room, only to find Baba gone and Mosley standing there, staring out the wide windows onto the manicured lawn. As she tries to tiptoe out—backward, in fact—the ancient wooden floorboards creak, and Mosley turns.

"Ah, Diana, just the person I want to see. I've been musing on the turns of phrase for a public statement by the BUF."

Normally Diana would encourage the exchange and offer to record his thoughts, largely so she could soften and manipulate the message. So it pains her to say, "Are you sure that's wise, my darling? In light of Chamberlain's announcement?" She cannot bring herself to speak the phrase *declaration of war*. "Perhaps in a few weeks' time."

Mosley widens his stance and places his hands on his hips, as if he's onstage and she is one of his supplicants. "The BUF followers will be looking to me for guidance. We've been forging a path for peace for years now, and they'll be conflicted between what our country is asking them to do and what their conscience and their political party demands."

"I see." She perches on the edge of the pale-blue sofa and makes herself small. Instinctively, she knows how to manage this situation, but she wishes she didn't have to engage in the protracted performance to make it happen seamlessly. *No matter*, she reminds herself, *it's necessary.*

She continues. "You always know best, darling, and if you feel the BUF needs your direction, they must have it. Even at the cost of your own freedom."

Alarm registers on his face. "What do you mean? The cost of my own freedom?"

Waving her hand around as if his freedom is no match for his beliefs, she says, "Well, surely, as a fascist organization, the BUF is now on the intelligence community's list, and they'll be closely monitoring our activities and public statements. What is safe to announce in times of peace may be considered treasonous in wartime, after all. But I know your commitment to your followers trumps personal concerns and that you will make the right choices on the BUF's behalf."

Diana knows that Mosley has no intention of sacrificing his freedom for the BUF. As she hoped, her words make him rethink a rash statement. He asks, "So would you modify our earlier statement?"

"Hmm." She pretends to consider his question. Careful not to criticize his earlier proclamation, she says, "I think I'd steer clear of describing this as a war of Jewish finance, given that Great Britain has now officially entered the fray. Perhaps instead you could acknowledge the war and instruct the BUF members to follow the government's commands. That will help put British intelligence off our scent."

"Brilliant, darling, as always." He nods in agreement with her suggestion.

"But you might be able to intimate that the BUF could continue on the organization's work and fight for peace? Or would that be threading the needle too closely? Surely there isn't anything unlawful about advocating for pacifism?"

"No, I think that's just the ticket." He busses her on the cheek, then strides over to the desk to fetch his fountain pen and paper and begin drafting. Chuckling to himself, he mutters, "Even if we want peace for less than pacifist reasons."

"Will you excuse me, darling? I really should see about Unity," she says, although she has no intention of reaching out to Germany at the moment. She can only imagine how such an action would be perceived by British intelligence, who are undoubtedly monitoring the phone lines. Anyway, in her heart of hearts, if the pronouncements Unity made on Diana's last visit to Bayreuth are true, Diana believes her little sister is no longer reachable.

"Unity?" Mosley asks, his eyebrows knitted in confusion.

Has he forgotten about her sister? The one that has proven so useful for their cause? She's been integral to the survival of the BUF and its future, and Diana cannot quite believe that Unity has slipped Mosley's mind. Will Diana fade from Mosley's consciousness one day if she outlives her usefulness?

"She remained in Germany, even after the Führer urged us to leave if you'll recall?" Diana reminds him.

"Ah yes," he says, without looking up from his paper. *How disappointing he can be*, she thinks.

Disquieted, Diana mounts the spiral staircase toward her bedroom. As she reaches the landing, she hears the shattering of glass in that direction. She runs toward the sound, worried that the baby has evaded a distracted nanny and harmed himself.

Throwing open the door to her bedroom, she is surprised to see Baba. She wants to ask what the hell the miserable ex-sister-in-law of Mosley is doing in her inner sanctum, but she reminds herself that they'll be holed up at Wootton Lodge together for months, if not years. And then Diana sees, piled in the room, the blackout curtains that Baba must have been installing. Or at least, Baba wants Diana to believe that's the reason for the invasion of her private space.

Diana asks, "Is everything all right? I heard a crash."

Baba glances down at the floor, where shards of glass litter the carpet. Where on earth is all this glass coming from? It is then Diana sees the source. The autographed, framed photograph of Hitler that Diana keeps on her nightstand has fallen to the floor and smashed beyond repair.

"It was an accident," Baba says by way of explanation, without an apology.

But Diana can see that this is no accident. And she understands that, for the foreseeable future, she will be facing enemies not only from without, but from within.

# CHAPTER FIFTY-SEVEN
## UNITY

*September 3, 1939*
*Munich, Germany*

U NITY TURNS THE DIAL OF THE RADIO UNTIL SHE HEARS the final click. All these many days of listening to the broadcast have finally come to an end. She feels a mixture of relief that the long wait is over and fear that she has reached the inevitable conclusion.

Forcing her hands to stop trembling, she enters her bedroom and opens her wardrobe. She selects her most formal Nazi uniform, the one she saved for rallies and special occasions with Hitler. Slipping on the black blouse and skirt, she buttons up the fitted jacket and then secures the golden swastika pin on the lapel. The perfect Aryan image reflected in her mirror pleases her, and she smiles as she applies her dark-red lipstick, her one small act of rebellion.

She walks over to the dining room table, where she has stacked the telegrams from Muv and Farve, unopened because she couldn't risk any momentary weakness from their pleas, and a single telegram from the British consul ordering her to leave Munich. She picks up the letters she's written to Diana and her friend Baroness von St. Paul, who will outlive any war and can be trusted to follow Unity's final instructions to the letter. These she must place in the mailbox before—well, before.

Only then does she slide a key from her pocket and open the locked drawer of her writing table. There lies her most precious possession, the tiny, pearl-handled Walther pistol that Hitler gave her for her protection. She'd cried upon the receipt of this most thoughtful, generous present.

*How pretty its pearlescent handle looks in the sunlight*, she thinks when it catches a ray of sun streaming through the open window as she slides it into her purse.

Glancing around her flat, she muses on how happy she's been here, serving the Führer, becoming part of his glorious plan, however small. Even though she failed Great Britain miserably in not preventing the war, she has no regrets about her relationship with Hitler. The wishful part of her longs to stay in this German limbo, but the more logical part of her knows she can no longer serve two masters. There is only one path now.

Breathing deeply, she takes the telephone off the hook and puts on her black leather gauntlets, finger by finger. She then opens her door and descends the stairs, stepping out onto the bright, sunlit Munich streets. Squinting for a minute while her eyes adjust, she wanders the familiar route to the Englischer Garten, one of her favorite places in all of Munich.

Strolling along the pathway near the River Isar, she doesn't rest until she finds the perfect bench. There, under the shade of a beech tree without a single other citizen in sight, Unity finally sits and takes a deep breath. With the dappled sunlight making a pattern on her black uniform, she reaches into her matching black purse and slides out her beautiful little pistol. *I do not regret a single moment*, she thinks. Then placing the instrument carefully on her temple, Unity pulls the trigger.

# CHAPTER FIFTY-EIGHT
# NANCY

*September 4, 1939*
*London, England*

I THOUGHT I'D NEVER ARRIVE BACK IN LONDON. After my argument with Muv over the declaration of war, I'd insisted on leaving Inch Kenneth immediately. Not that Muv fought against my wishes, mind. In fact, she was so eager to be rid of me that she offered to drive me to the small dock where I could get a ferry to take me to the Isle of Mull. This was only the beginning of the long, disjointed journey back to London, followed by a long drive across Mull, then a boat trip to the coast of Scotland, and finally an overnight train from Scotland to London. No small wonder that Debo has begged off visiting the island ever again. At one point in our car ride to the dock, Muv threatened to toss me out of her vehicle and force me to walk if I didn't stop maligning *her* Hitler.

When I finally step out of the train station into London proper, bedraggled and exhausted from the sleepless travel, I feel as though I've entered an entirely different city from the one I left only two weeks ago. Despite the fact that it's Monday morning, the usual rush of black-hatted businessmen racing to their offices is less of a rush and more of a trickle. Certainly I had expected to see changes in the buildings—places of entertainment shuttered, as Chamberlain had ordered, for example—but the sight of boarded buildings, blackout curtains on nearly every window, and posters detailing air-raid protocol in the event of the dreaded bombing startles me.

I raise my hand to hail a cab, which seem to have become as scant as the usual London crowds. To my surprise, a man approaches me. "Mrs. Rodd?"

"Yes," I answer warily as I glance over at the unfamiliar fellow. He looks like any number of businessmen strolling down the street, wearing a black homburg hat and a matching overcoat. Who is he? And how does he know me? Peter could not have sent him to meet me, as it would be nearly impossible to accurately estimate my arrival time given the number of connections it took from Inch Kenneth, not to mention how frequently those connections went awry. "And you are?"

"Your cousin sent me."

What is he talking about? Is this some sort of inappropriate, ill-timed prank? Or is it something more nefarious? "You'll have to be more specific. I have loads of cousins."

"The cousin who's married to—" Here, the man pauses, visibly uncomfortable. "Clemmie. That's all I've been authorized to say, Mrs. Rodd."

"Ah, I see." This must relate to the phone call I made to Cousin Clementine about meeting with Winston. But we'd never arranged a fixed time.

"You placed a phone call to her, trying to make an appointment with her husband, if I'm not mistaken?"

"Yes?" I answer, but feel uncomfortable saying more. This is all rather cloak-and-dagger, even for Winston. "But we never made any firm plans."

"This is because he's just been named Lord Admiral of the Navy and cannot leave the war preparations. He has sent me here to fetch the information you referenced in that call." His voice is so low I can barely hear him.

"Lord Admiral?" I blurt out in shock. Governmental leaders have either mocked or reviled Winston for some time, due to his unpopular views especially on Germany, and those leaders are still in power. But as I think about it a bit more, it turns out he's been right all along, and I suppose those same governmental leaders must acknowledge that in some way.

"Indeed."

"Ah, I see." All the pieces are fitting together rather nicely, but just to be certain, I ask, "If you are who you say you are, then what exactly are you picking up from me?"

His brows furrow, and, for the first time, he seems less than absolutely confident. Then his face settles, and he says, "Let's call it the Itinerary."

I need to be certain before I hand him anything. This is information about Diana and Unity, after all. "Of who?"

"I don't think you want me to say specifically, so let's just call it the Sisters' Itinerary."

I nod, satisfied. "The documents are in my purse."

I set my luggage down on the ground and begin to rifle through my purse. He places a hand on my arm and says, "Not here. Why don't we head over to the tea shop, sit at the counter and order tea, while you just slide it over? A bit more subtle." He practically whispers.

Without talking further, we walk to the dingy train-station tea shop. Once our tea is poured and we take a few sips, as surreptitiously as I know how, I pass him the handwritten list of Diana and Unity's trips to Germany, their schedule there as best as I could parse it together, the names of the Nazis they met with, and any comments I recall either of them making about Hitler or his plans. Other than that, I don't have more to go on than my suspicions, which I can hardly list in a report, and I cannot make mention of Diana's radio-station reference as I have no documentation. It could have been an offhand, misunderstood remark by Muv.

An enormous wave of guilt washes over me as I watch him tuck the papers into his inner coat pocket like a news-paper. *Have I made a mistake?* I ask myself as I watch him exit the shop without a word. I'm left with my increasingly cold cup of tea and a sinking feeling in my stomach. Did I do the right thing? Do I really believe that my sisters would act against the interests of our country to further their fascination with fascism and Hitler? How can I suspect Unity and bring her under suspicion when we don't even know where she is or if she's all right?

My luggage in hand, I step back out onto the London street, thinking how I need to know more before I continue down this path with Winston and his unnamed lackey. After all, if I discover that I've got this all wrong, I can always call Winston and explain. At that thought, an idea suddenly comes to me. Today presents me with an opportunity I may not have again. So when I hop in a cab at the station, I give the cabbie not my home address on Blomfield Road but Diana's address—129 Grosvenor Road.

---

"Good morning, Mrs. Rodd. I am sorry to say that the Mosleys aren't in residence at the moment," Diana's housemaid, Dorothy, says. She seems nervous, but perhaps it's the anxiety all Londoners are experiencing.

Their absence is the precise reason why I'm visiting Grosvenor Road, although of course I don't say that. "Thank you, Dorothy. I do know that the Mosleys are at Wootton Lodge…" I had learned this from Muv during my stay at Inch Kenneth. "But when I told Diana I'd be near her London home, she suggested I swing by to pick up a few items."

"Of course. I apologize for the state of the place." She gestures for me to enter, glancing back at the hallway strewn with black fabric, and now I understand why she seems apprehensive. "We're hanging the blackout cloths as the government ordered. In the event Lord and Lady Mosley return to London. We'd have made it more presentable if we'd have known you were coming."

"Please, there is nothing to be sorry about," I say as I step into the foyer. "How could you have known I was coming? Things are so hectic at Wootton Lodge that I am certain Diana forgot all about it."

"Then you won't mention that the foyer is in disarray?" Dorothy asks.

"I was never here," I joke, realizing how incredibly fortuitous the timing is.

"Thank you, Mrs. Rodd. Please make yourself at home," she says and gestures to the interior of the lovely, well-appointed home.

"Thank you, Dorothy. Please don't let me keep you. I can show myself around," I offer, and she looks relieved to return to her work. In truth, Dorothy is late in installing the blackout curtains, perhaps another explanation for her nervousness. Regulations requiring that all windows be covered at night to prevent any illumination for enemy aircraft were instituted three days ago.

Given Mosley's ongoing abhorrence of me, I haven't exactly been a regular visitor here. I'm invited only when he's absent, and given that Diana and Mosley usually travel to London together, that is rare. Still, I have a sense of the general layout, and I certainly know my sister well enough to discern where her hiding spots might be. We'd spent more hours than I could ever count in the Hons' cupboard with each other and secrets for company during our childhood. But what I am looking for, I'm not exactly certain.

Sweeping through the drawing room, parlor, and dining room, I spend no time in these spaces because Diana would never hide something in public areas where any servant could stumble upon it while cleaning. I decide to head upstairs, and as I cross into the foyer, I bump into another servant. As I offer my apologies, I realize that I know her; she's the girl from Rutland Gate with whom I witnessed Diana giving her boys lessons in the Nazi salute. "Aren't you the boys' nanny? I would have thought you'd be holed up in Wootton Lodge with the rest of the family."

The girl, who couldn't be more than twenty with mousy-brown hair but striking blue eyes, answers, "Lady Mosley felt we had enough nannies and governesses at Wootton Lodge, what with all the other children and their minders there as well, so she sent me here to help board up the house and to assist when they come to London."

Her eyes well up a little at this, and I suppose she'd much rather be in the countryside where it's deemed safer. "I see," I say, patting her on the arm and offering what little I can. "I'm sure you'll be perfectly fine here in London. The government has things well in hand."

"Thank you, ma'am," she says with a bob, meeting my eyes for the first time with something like gratitude.

"Will you excuse me?" I ask, as I mount the wide staircase and head to the next floor. I linger in Diana's bedroom first, a flowery, silken affair. I try not to think about the antics she and Mosley get up to in here as I paw through drawers, under the bed and mattress, and sift through the purses and hatboxes perfectly organized on her shelves. To no avail.

*Her private study*, I think. Treading carefully down the hallway to the exquisitely decorated little sunlit study, I sit at her writing desk, imagining Diana sorting through her correspondence and replying with her Montblanc fountain pen in her elegant script. The thought of the beautiful, brilliant Diana makes me pause. Am I really hunting for incriminating information about my own sister? Do I want to find something that might confirm my suspicions that she has harm against

Great Britain in her heart, or uncover nothing and rescind my statements to Winston?

Pushing back from the desk, I see an array of silver frames on the little mahogany table next to the gray silk-upholstered chair in front of the fireplace. I wander over, expecting to see images of Diana's children and perhaps a photograph or two of us sisters. Instead, I am barraged by pictures of Diana and Unity with Hitler, Goebbels, and decorated Nazi officers I cannot identify. There are my sisters giving the Nazi salute, smiling against a backdrop of soldiers, and even sharing a meal with the Nazi leaders. Even though I've heard about their closeness to these monsters, I have a visceral reaction to seeing Diana and Unity in their midst. It makes plain their priority and allegiance.

Never mind our squabbles over the years, I love my sisters. But I cannot allow them to inflict their tyrannical views and to take steps to make Great Britain a slave of the Third Reich, Diana particularly. Emboldened, I return to Diana's desk and search through every corner of every drawer. What am I looking for exactly?

When these efforts yield nothing other than writing supplies, lipsticks, and her address book, I run my hand along the underside of the desk and I find it—a private, locked drawer. Pulling a pin from my hair, I kneel down and begin to pick at the lock, a skill I learned at Diana's side when we would scour through Muv and Farve's belongings as children. The lock springs, and I slide open the drawer. A stack of heavily marked-up typewritten papers sits inside. At first, I can't make sense of them as most are in German. But as I study the English documents scattered throughout and the handwritten comments in English in the margins of all the documents, I begin to get a sense of their purpose—Diana *is* attempting to set up a radio station through her German connections. Why? What would happen if Diana and Mosley got ahold of airwaves and suddenly someone other than the BBC—a governmental entity—controlled some of the messaging the British people received? Perhaps worse, what if my fascist sister and brother-in-law had an easy means of communicating with the enemy?

As the terrible possibilities begin to unfold in my mind, I realize that I *must* take some of this documentation. All my records on Unity and Diana's travels to Germany, Nazi meetings, and the damning conversations I've heard over the years pale in comparison to the incontrovertible evidence on my lap. This is the sort of evidence that Winston has long suspected might be in Diana's possession. I decide that taking a few key pages rather than the entire pile will be less likely to raise Diana's suspicions should she return to London and glance in this drawer. Although, I wonder as I select the pages, am I ready to hand them over to Winston? There would be no turning back—for Diana or me. Could I simply hold on to them for now, while I wait and watch? But how long can I truly wait, given that the Nazis and all the death and destruction they'll bring to bear are knocking at Great Britain's door.

A footstep sounds outside Diana's study, and I realize I have to act. No more hesitation, no more second thoughts. I tuck the chosen papers away in my purse, slide the secret drawer shut, and step out the door.

# CHAPTER FIFTY-NINE

# DIANA

*September 4, 1939*
*Staffordshire, England*

MOSLEY IS STEAMING MAD, AND EACH STOMP HE MAKES around Wootton Lodge heightens Diana's unease—because a furious Mosley is an unhinged Mosley. And they cannot afford any more mistakes.

"How could the authorities allow wholesale destruction of King's Road?" he screams as he marches around the drawing room where Diana patiently awaits the simmering down. M's powerlessness to stop the wrecking of the BUF's main London office on King's Road only prompts him to exert his power elsewhere, at home for example. She had provided him the opportunity to dominate last night in bed, but even those exertions have not slaked his thirst for movement and authority.

Diana assumes Mosley does not actually want her to answer this question. Even if he did, she would refuse; the explanation is obvious and upsetting. Mosley and the BUF—long proponents of fascism and even Hitler—have become the public, accessible targets for the British people's rage. The authorities like it that way. They would rather the citizens direct their animosity toward the BUF offices than anywhere else. And as the war escalates, this will be just the beginning.

"Where is the so-called order and control that this damned government claims to institute? I see neither hide nor hair of it! Hitler wouldn't stand for such insubordination. Neither would the BUF if we were in charge!"

Diana nods, tuning him out and tuning in the reports continuing to pour in on the radio. Announcers are detailing the war status of other countries—France, Australia, and New Zealand declared war as well but a surprising number have remained neutral, including the United States. There are updates on the military action in Poland as well and on Chamberlain's new war council, but they stay focused on the shocking German decision last night to torpedo a British cruise ship. The SS *Athenia* was bombed as it crossed the Atlantic from Glasgow to Montreal. Over one thousand civilians were on board, and only now are the rescue teams assessing the casualties.

*Why did Hitler choose the sinking of a civilian ship as his first military action involving Great Britain, only eight hours after the declaration of war?* Diana wonders. It doesn't make any sense, particularly from a man with his military genius. The Führer knows that it will make it harder to woo the British people later, when he's brought Great Britain under German rule. Consequently, she's inclined to agree with Mosley that the sinking of the SS *Athenia* might be the work of the British, a ploy to turn worldwide opinion in the British favor. She is wise enough to utter such sentiment only to Mosley, though, since it borders on heresy.

The constant ringing of the telephone interrupts the radio and Mosley's ranting. Diana has instructed one of the housemaids to take the calls, but to interrupt them only for an emergency. Otherwise, she and Mosley would spend the entire day either answering Muv's relentless questions about Unity or dealing with minutiae from BUF staff.

Mary peeks into the drawing room, clearly wary of the still-pacing Mosley. "There is a call for Lord Mosley. It's from the *Times*."

"The *Times* isn't on my list of emergencies, Mary," Diana says, trying to keep her tone even.

"But—but—it's the *Times*, Lady Mosley. And they said it was urgent."

Diana wants to vent her anger on this girl, but she supposes she only has herself to blame for trusting a simple local girl with a momentous task. "Mary, please just tell the reporter that Lord Mosley is busy and that—"

"No," Mosley barks. "Tell them I'll be right there."

*God no*, Diana thinks. In his current temper, Mosley will say all the wrong things and invite the scrutiny of British intelligence. But if she tries to hold him back, his fury will only mount, making his statement that much more incendiary.

As Mosley walks into the foyer, Diana changes her seating in the drawing room. Mosley would never allow her to hover, but if she situates herself just so, she should be able to overhear his side of the interview. "You want a statement on behalf of the British Union of Fascists about the sinking of the SS *Athenia*?" he asks.

The reporter must have answered the question in the affirmative because Mosley says, "All right then, I'll give you that, as long as you print the BUF's official position."

Leaping to her feet, Diana moves to the wall next to the foyer. She must capture every single word Mosley utters here.

"Yes, it is a tragedy. Of course, I recognize that," he says. "But until a full investigation is conducted, how do we know it isn't an intentional act on behalf of the British government, designed to bring the neutral countries into the war?"

Diana reels. How could he say this to a *Times* reporter? To suggest publicly that the British government planned the killing of its citizens, including women and children? It's one thing to say it to Diana or one of his party cohorts, and an entirely different thing to make it the centerpiece of a public message.

The room starts to sway, and a wave of nausea overcomes her. *What to do, what to do...* The refrain takes hold of her thoughts. She's worked so hard and so long to secure a brilliant future for Mosley—even going so far as to use her own sister for that purpose, a sister whose whereabouts are now unknown. Even now, even as Diana worries about him stepping over the line to subversion, she's racking her mind for ways to hold on to her triumphs: the close relationship with Hitler, the stability of the BUF, and the radio station, which is, of course, integral for the other two prizes. All for him. All for them.

Mosley's voice reaches a fever pitch as he argues with the *Times* reporter. Unsure whether this situation or her pregnancy is to blame for her nausea, Diana can't control it either way, and she races to the bathroom, barely making it on time. Finished, she crouches on the cold tile floor, doubting herself for the very first time in her life. Has she begun to lose control?

# CHAPTER SIXTY

# NANCY

*October 4, 1939*
*London, England*

N ANCY, THE LORD ADMIRAL IS HERE TO SEE YOU," HAZEL
calls out to me.

"Very funny. And the Queen of England is waiting for
you in the loo," I reply to her, not even bothering to look up
from the street map of London at my curly-haired, brown-eyed
fellow driver.

I know I've got to become more proficient about the
routes if I'm going to maintain my position with the Air Raid
Precaution group. The national Air Raid Precaution organization has created local groups to help shield the population
from air raids. We educate the citizens about protocol, distribute equipment, and respond to emergencies and calls for
help. My job is to ensure that the team arrives safely, and I am
desperate to keep the role because Peter seems so proud of me
when he describes the work I'm doing.

Moreover, the abundant free time of this Phony War—as
the newspapers have taken to calling this period of military
inactivity—allows me to concentrate on writing *Pigeon Pie*.

This novel focuses on a scenario close to my heart—a socialite volunteering in the war effort who discovers a Nazi espionage ring under her nose, spies who use radio propaganda to help their cause. Does this challenge Oscar Wilde's famous phrase about life imitating art with greater frequency than art imitating life? Time will tell.

My posting will change if I don't improve my track record on the road, and the thing I'll miss the most about the Air Raid Precaution group is Hazel, who's able to bring levity to the bleakest of situations. But even she can cast only so many of my accidents behind the wheel in a rosy glow. She tries to defend me by challenging my detractors to drive an Air Raid Precaution car on the pitch-black streets to pitch-black destinations. Who wouldn't have an accident or two? She always jests. It's an argument that has lost steam.

"No, really," Hazel insists, and for once, her voice sounds serious.

When I look up from my maps, her face is a study of solemnity, and behind her, in the doorway to the garage, stands Winston. How out of place he looks in all his Admiralty regalia in this dirty motor garage, the place where I've worked in a chambray jumpsuit since the day after I returned to London from Inch Kenneth. The day we lost contact with Unity. The day everything changed.

I almost laugh at the incongruous sight of him. Almost. It's hard to believe that, after all the animosity between Winston and Prime Minister Chamberlain, Winston was appointed to the Lord Admiral post in charge of the navy the day Chamberlain declared war, the very same post he'd held during the Great War. I suppose that a significant con-cession needed to be made, since Winston was proven correct in all his predictions about Hitler and his intentions. And Chamberlain was proven utterly wrong about the possible success of appeasement.

"To what do I owe this pleasure, Lord Admiral?" I ask with a little curtsy, one I hope doesn't appear too comical in this grubby jumpsuit. I am in earnest. I haven't seen him or his man since that day at the train station, but I've been reading about his military decision-making every day in the newspapers.

He snorts. "Why does the title Lord Admiral sound so peculiar coming from your witty Mitford lips?"

"That isn't my intent."

"I know, Nancy," he chuckles. He begins striding out the door, calling back to me, "Take a walk with me."

As I turn to tell Hazel that I'm stepping out for a few moments, I realize that she's staring at me with her mouth agape. My social status and connection to the leadership and aristocracy of the country have never come up in conversation, and it's been a glorious relief to keep it quiet. To just be Nancy. From Hazel's expression, I see that I'll have some explaining to do on my return.

His personal guards in tow, Winston and I step outside onto the dusky pink streets, still alive with the activity of labor-ers returning from work and mothers and children scampering home for tea because nightfall is an hour away. Once the sun fully sets and the darkness takes hold, these roads will be empty. But for now, soldiers dot the streets as well, as do military vehi-cles, but the most constant reminder of war is the boarded-up and blacked-out windows.

"How's the war treating you?" he asks.

"It's not exactly what I thought a war would look like—all loud bangs and sirens in blackness interrupted by fiery bursts. This may sound odd but I feel like we are on the sidelines of a children's game waiting for the team leaders to pick sides before we can begin. Germany chose Italy, and England picked France, but now we have to wait and see where the rest of the players land before we can start in earnest," I say as I pause to light a cigarette.

"Nancy, you do have a way with words and images," he chortles. "I understand your husband has become something of a hero in wartime, working tirelessly at a First Aid post after that brave work in Perpignan. And look at you, driving for the local Air Raid Precaution group. Clemmie has our girls doing war work as well," he says. But Winston never makes small talk for small talk's sake. Is this little exchange to show that he's keeping tabs on us? On me? Even though he hasn't reached out?

"It seems that war brings out the best in Peter," he continues. "Tom and Randolph as well. I understand Tom's left behind some of his less savory views to join the Devonshire Regiment, and Randolph is in the Fourth Queen's Own Hussars, my old regiment."

"Good luck to them all," I say, trying to sound bullish when, in fact, I am terribly worried.

"It's been good to see Peter this way. Peace seems to bring out the worst in him. I recall one night he crashed the Other Club…" His voice trails off, and we both know that he needn't finish his sentence. Winston could fill in the blanks with any number of nights and any number of bad acts on Peter's part. Astonishing how war has changed my husband. For now, we are enjoying a rekindling of the romance we once shared, at least on those rare nights our paths cross. I know, however, that it's fleeting.

"He's about to be commissioned into the Welsh Guards. Age will not stand in the way of his determination to fight."

"Bully for him," Winston says, then takes a long drag of his cigar. "Sorry I couldn't meet you in person at the train station that day."

"Yes, but"—I glance at his uniform—"more important duties called. Like running the navy in wartime?"

The weeks since I delivered my lists to Winston's man have given me ample time to consider my course, particularly now that I have the pilfered documents from Diana's study in hand and time to review them. The aid of a German-English dictionary helped confirm my suspicions that Diana is involved in a scheme to start up a radio station in cahoots with the Nazis. More shocking to me—although less pertinent for Winston—is Diana's disturbing callousness when it comes to Unity. At a recent family dinner after Muv and Farve returned to London to help find Unity, Diana seemed utterly resistant to assisting our parents locate our younger sister; she seemed, in fact, uninterested, which I find incomprehensible given the time they spent together in Germany. Was it all a facade to help Diana achieve her aims? Icy disinterest for one's at-risk sister isn't grounds for condemnation, but it does make me less inclined to view Diana's behavior in a favorable light.

He chuckles at my remark. "True enough. But I don't want you to think I've forgotten about you. Or your sister Unity, for that matter."

"Muv has been pestering Cousin Clemmie with letters and phone calls, and I *am* sorry. We've all told her there is nothing you can do. Once Great Britain declared war, any power the British military had to gather information or influence German affairs diminished."

"True," he puffs, "but only to some extent. We do have a powerful intelligence network. Even in Germany."

"Still?"

"Still. And I've been making inquiries about Unity."

I am both relieved and confused. Relieved that someone with power is actually searching for my silent, seemingly missing sister. No other governmental representative wants to spend a second of their time trying to locate a girl who's publicly declared herself to be a Nazi. But I wonder, why is Winston sharing this development with me rather than Muv?

"Oh, thank you," I say with a gentle squeeze of his arm. "Have you heard anything at all?"

"I assume you've heard the rumors that she's in a concentration or detainment camp of some kind?"

In the dizzying weeks after the declaration of war, this terrible possibility surfaced, leading to a hysterical Muv and my parents' relocation to London to have greater access in helping to bring Unity back. "We have, although—perhaps wishfully—we discounted them as the rumors came through unverified sources."

"You were wise to disregard the camp stories. That's pure gossip. I have heard something else, although you'll have to keep it between us two."

"Of course."

"It's more likely that Unity is in a hospital."

"A hospital? Did she come down with something? She'd been ill last year, and I always thought she went back to Germany too soon." Worry seizes me, and I clutch his arm. "Or was she wounded in a military action?"

"That's what I am trying to ascertain. She's alive, at least. Of that I can assure you."

"That's some small comfort," I sigh. "Is that why you came to me instead of my mother?"

"That's one reason. I know I can trust you to keep it quiet until I have the information confirmed through less sensitive channels." He puffs on his cigar again, and I wonder how the fastidious Clementine handles that stinky accessory. "The other relates to your meeting with my man at the train station and the lists you put together for me."

I nod, not trusting myself to speak. Because I am not certain that I'm ready to share the most damaging information—the documents I stole from Diana. I worry that it might affect his willingness to help search for Unity, but more than that, it is a line I'd be crossing from which I cannot return. But can I really wait much longer? What if Diana has been busy helping pave the way for Hitler?

"Now that we are at war with the dictator your sisters consider a close friend, I appreciate that you trust me enough to share information about your sisters once your concern heightened. And I was wondering whether you have found anything else that you might be willing to pass on to me—or, if not, you might consider keeping close tabs on Diana."

I notice he very carefully avoids the word *spy*. Is this

request the expected payment for his assistance with Unity? I am not certain I am ready.

"I would consider it."

"Excellent. You can expect contact from some of my people in the upcoming days, and when you are ready, they will be as well." He studies me, then adds, "I know this isn't easy, Nancy. But if it's any consolation, your sisters put themselves in this situation, Diana in particular. Although Unity's lunches with Hitler and her anti-Semitic newspaper letters haven't done her any favors. MI5 is already investigating both Diana and Mosley for treasonous activities. They already had been, in fact, before war was declared."

"Diana has been under investigation by MI5?" I am incredulous, although part of me wonders why I should be. I've suspected for some time that Diana was more than simply an admirer of Hitler. But to know that MI5 thinks the same somehow changes the situation inexorably.

"Yes, the government has been concerned for several years that if Mosley garnered enough public and financial support for the BUF, he could challenge the establishment—making Great Britain easier to conquer or turn into some sort of puppet state. The government wants to ensure that the BUF doesn't turn into—if it hasn't already—some sort of pro-Nazi fifth column. So, for some time, it's been under surveillance. And so has everyone connected with it, your sisters in particular given their Nazi ties."

"No," I utter. I've contemplated many scenarios regarding my sisters and the Nazis, but never this precise one.

"Yes," Winston says, with a mournful look in his eye. *This cannot be pleasant for him either,* I think for the first time. "Mosley, Diana, and Unity have been watched since September of 1934, and Diana has been deemed the smartest and most dangerous of them. In fact, the foreign intelligence service learned about Diana's marriage to Mosley years before she divulged it to you all. Did you know that they held the ceremony at the house of one of Hitler's right-hand men, Joseph Goebbels, who is the minister of propaganda, and that Hitler served as best man? That's how close your sisters are to the heart of our enemies."

"My God." I eke out the words, feeling woozy at the idea of Hitler in my sister's wedding party. I wish I had somewhere to sit down, even for a moment.

"It's a bitter pill to swallow, I know, especially when we're talking about your own family. My family as well." He stretches out his free hand to shake hers. "Welcome to the Special Operations Executive. Or as my agents call it, the shadowlands."

# CHAPTER SIXTY-ONE
# DIANA

*October 4, 1939*
*London, England*

T HE BENTLEY SPORTS TOURER VEERS AROUND EACH BEND in the road. The two-seater barely clings to the surface of the gravelly road, forcing Diana to brace herself, but she doesn't care. She relishes the distance and the speed, and finds the countryside more beautiful than ever. Does the danger of war heighten appreciation of one's homeland? With the passing of each kilometer, she feels lighter, less weighed down by guilt. Guilt she hadn't even known she was carrying until this morning.

She'd awoken with the strains of *Götterdämmerung* pounding in her head. The dark, foreboding music and lyrics of the opera she'd seen at the Bayreuth Festival with Unity chased her all morning as she dined on her daily breakfast of soft-boiled egg, coffee, and fruit, soaked in her bath, applied powder and lipstick, and put on her ivory cashmere sweater and pale tweed skirt. By the time she descended the stairs and greeted Baba and the children, all just down from the nursery for a romp in the garden, she felt as though Unity herself was whispering in her ear. *Come find me, Diana. Where are you? How could you have left me, knowing what I planned?*

"Stop," Diana finally said, shaking her head as if shaking off Unity's entreaties. Only when Baba looked over at her from across the drawing room did she realize that she said the word aloud.

Trapped at Wootton Lodge for the past few weeks with an anxious Mosley, the poisonous Baba, a gaggle of children cared for by battling nannies, the constant stream of horrific war news, and anxiety over possible interest by the British authorities, was it any wonder she felt ready to splinter? Was it really a surprise that concerns over Unity crept in from time to time? *Perhaps guilt does not account for her state, but rather nerves*, she told herself.

When Mosley strode through the drawing room a few minutes later, a sheaf of papers for a meeting in hand, she saw the answer to her dilemma. "I'll go with you to London," she announced, jumping up from the sofa.

"London?" Baba asked. "Haven't we just left the capital for our safety?"

"Are you sure, darling?" Mosley asked, glancing at her belly. Diana could hear Baba make a noise of disgust and look away.

"I couldn't be more so."

———

Mosley parks the Bentley in front of their Grosvenor Road town house. The usually bustling street is quiet, and parking spots are unusually abundant. Even though London is subdued due to the threat, Diana feels more comfortable here than at Wootton Lodge. Is it the looming presence of Baba at Wootton? Or does the otherwise welcome quiet at Wootton Lodge allow in the whispers of her guilt over Unity?

"Welcome home, Lady Mosley." Dorothy greets her with a bob. The girl looks skittish, but then Diana supposes that nerves are aflutter everywhere in London.

"Thank you, Dorothy." Diana hands her the cloak she'd draped over her shoulders during the ride.

"Darling, I'll be in the library working on my speech," Mosley calls over to her from the arched entryway.

"I'll just pop up to my study to gather a few materials. Then I'll help." How good it feels to return to their usual routines, in which Diana serves as sounding board and mellowing influence. Instead of the restless waiting at Wootton Lodge, the horrible anxiety of inactivity.

Stepping into the gray silken cocoon of her study, Diana immediately relaxes. She crafted this space as a refuge from the rest of the world and even instructed the staff to leave it alone, except when absolutely necessary for cleaning. This study and the little writing room off her Wootton Lodge bedroom are the only places where she can fully relinquish her tiring facade of serenity.

She settles at her desk, where a stack of correspondence sits, awaiting reply. Sorting through it, she notes that only one letter requires a quick response and puts it aside. Then she pulls open the drawers where she stores prior speech drafts. As she does, she notices that the locked drawer on the underside of her desk is not fully closed shut. Is it possible the force of her tugging on the speech drawer dislodged the locked one?

Crouching down on the floor, she studies it. Only upon close observation does she see tiny scratches on the lock pad. Who has been in her study and in *that* drawer? Panic sets in as she retrieves the hidden key, slides it in the lock, and opens the drawer. The marked-up agreements from the commercial radio deal remain inside, to her great relief, along with the receipt for the money the Nazis paid the BUF. She picks them up and flips through the pages, not noticing any change.

But there is no mistaking the marks on the lock pad. Is anything else askew? She glances around the room. All seems in order, until she sees that the photographs on the table near the fireplace have been rearranged. Is she overreacting or has someone been in here?

After locking the radio agreement papers back up, she grabs the speech for this evening. At the bottom of the staircase, she spots Dorothy in the dining room and discreetly asks, "Oh, say, Dorothy, has anyone been in the house during our absence?"

Dorothy's cheeks flush as she answers, "Other than the usual staff, there's only been your parents, Lady Mosley."

"My parents?" *Strange, Muv never mentioned stopping in at Grosvenor Road*, Diana thinks.

"Yes, Lord and Lady Mitford took respite in the parlor a hot afternoon last week when they were in the vicinity."

"No one else?"

"Not that I recall, ma'am."

"Diana," Mosley calls to her, and Diana leaves Dorothy and this line of inquiry behind in the foyer, passing the former nanny Jean along the way. Even though the girl is relatively meek and keeps her eyes down when she sees Diana, her upset is evident over being relegated to London while the rest of the family stays safe at Wootton Lodge.

"Where are my notes?" he barks as she steps into the library. Rifling through his desk drawers, he is making an absolute mess of things. "I don't want to say the same exact damn thing I did last week."

Even though she'd had misgivings about Mosley holding a rally in wartime, he insisted on making speeches to "his people," beyond issuing a formal statement in which he claimed that the war was actually started by Jewish international financiers and that the BUF should continue fighting for peace. To her astonishment, more than two thousand people assembled to listen to his speech last week. To her even greater shock, the audience members and Mosley himself greeted each other with the fascist salute, despite the fact that Diana had begged him to use a different form of greeting. M had accused her of pandering—at the precise moment when they should be doubling down—and she thought, but didn't say, that her views haven't changed, only the level of her cautiousness. Why doesn't Mosley see the need to fly low for now?

"I have them here, my love," she says, handing him the papers she's brought from her study.

Voices sound in the front hallway, distracting them for a moment. General Fuller pops his head into the library. "Thought I might find you here, old chap. Getting ready for the rally tonight?" The brilliant military expert on armored warfare became a key member of the BUF on his retirement, as he'd become frustrated at the slow pace with which the British government moved in modernizing the armed forces. He often popped in, particularly before an event as he preferred to enter the rallies at M's side.

As Mosley crosses the room to shake the general's hand, Fuller spots her and says, "Apologies, Lady Mosley. I don't know how I missed you; your beauty illuminates every room."

"You are too kind," she replies.

The general rubs his hands in anticipation. "Should be a rousing crowd tonight."

"Hopefully every bit as enthusiastic as our last rally," Mosley adds.

As Diana looks on with a pleasant smile, she debates mentioning her suspicions about the study when she and Mosley are alone again. Should she really trouble him with a far-fetched conjecture? While Diana finds it plausible that British intelligence is interested in them, she cannot imagine that agents have broken into their home and pawed through their belongings. Surely the staff would have rung them up at Wootton Lodge immediately to report such a transgression. *No*, she thinks, she'll keep her hunch private for the moment— and focus on the more immediate threat Mosley might pose to himself. And to her.

# CHAPTER SIXTY-TWO
# NANCY

*October 28, 1939*
*London, England*

L ET ME SEE IT." I RACE INTO RUTLAND GATE, PAST THE housemaid opening the front door and past Farve standing motionless in the hallway as if he's been stunned by a blow. Perhaps he has, in a manner of speaking. Perhaps Unity has forced him into this stupefied state.

I practically run into the drawing room. There Muv lies prostrate on the sofa, her head in Debo's lap to my surprise. I don't know why I didn't expect to see Debo here, since she lives here and not on desolate Inch Kenneth. But she's so rarely here when I visit that I don't think about her as living at Rutland Gate, even though my parents have taken back the lease for a time. I suppose she had been spending her days before the war gallivanting as any young society girl should, although now—like most of them—she volunteers for the war effort instead.

Muv clutches the paper to her chest, her hands gripping it like a life raft. She does not move when I enter. She doesn't even open her eyes.

"I need to see it myself, Muv," I tell her. Debo shakes her head in silent warning.

My mother does not release the paper. "I read it aloud to you over the telephone. That should suffice."

"Muv, please"—I reach for it—"let me read the telegram for myself."

I peel away her fingers, one by one. Walking over to the table lamp, I hold to the light the brief message telegraphed by Janos von Almasy, a friend of Tom's, and a Hungarian citizen so he's able to travel into Germany.

The few terse words of a telegram deliver the news for which we've been waiting for weeks, long days as we waded through a slew of rumors and incendiary news reports where I couldn't mention what Winston had told me. "Unity is in hospital, ill but recovering. Damage done by self-harm is mending slowly. Efforts to move her from Munich are halting," I read aloud.

To myself, I reread the words several times. Writer that I am, I can see how Janos carefully chose the word *self-harm*. How he must have labored to find just the right euphemism to soften the blow of the actual word—*suicide*.

Unity tried to kill herself. My poor, misguided sister. How alone and despondent she must have been to believe that suicide was her only avenue!

I collapse on the upholstered chair across from the sofa, realizing that Farve entered the room at some point and settled on the edge of the sofa near Muv. "Self-harm?" I ask, although we all know it's not really a question.

"Perhaps it doesn't mean what we think it means. Janos is a Hungarian, after all. Eastern Europeans aren't known for their command of the King's English," Muv says. "They're forever mixing up words."

Even in her despair, Muv cannot resist a slur. And I cannot resist a retort, try as I might. "Janos is part of the royal family of Hungary and educated at Cambridge; he may well have more precise King's English that we do. In any event, I can't think of many other ways to interpret 'self-harm.'"

Farve snorts, which I take as a sign he might be recovering himself. An important development as we may well have significant work to find out more, and we may need Lord Redesdale to do it. Not the gobsmacked Farve.

Muv resumes crying and, as usual, blames me for her misery in its entirety. "Why do you always have to be so difficult, Nancy? Here I am, sick with worry over your little sister, and you want to split hairs over the English fluency of a Hungarian national."

Never mind that she started it.

Debo rolls her eyes and gives me a sympathetic glance. Perhaps I am being overly harsh with Muv. Now is not the time for my reactions. I know this on some level, but I cannot stop myself.

"I apologize, Muv. It's just that I worry that we leave ourselves ill-prepared to assist Unity to pretend otherwise," I say.

Farve roars. "What possible difference does it matter since we have no way of helping? We can't even bloody get her out of Germany."

The front door slams with a shudder. Farve leaps up to see what ill-mannered servant allowed such an affront at this terrible time. I expect to hear yelling, but instead I hear the silken voice of my sister and the sweet chirp of my nephews talking.

"Diana darling, we are in the drawing room," Muv calls out to her, all "darling" and sweetness when I did not even merit a greeting.

In glides Diana, as elegantly outfitted as ever in a pale-blue dress and matching hat. Was she already so immaculately attired in an ensemble suitable for cocktails at the Ritz when Muv called her with the news about the telegram, or did she take care to don the armor of a lady before she set out? In her wake come Jonathan and Desmond, accompanied by the nanny, the mousy-haired girl that I thought had been demoted from nannying to housework. Why did Diana bring her children over today of all days? And then it dawns on me; she's using them as a shield to soften any blows coming her way for refusing to assist in the efforts to find Unity.

I've seen Diana intermittently since I stole the radio-station document. Diana and the children seem primarily to keep to Wootton Lodge, making visits challenging given my work schedule. And even on those occasions when they are in and around London, Mosley is practically omnipresent, and I am not welcome. It's made it difficult to "keep an eye" on Diana as Winston requested.

"You look flustered, darling. That can't be good for the baby," Muv coos, after greeting the boys and then shooing them off into the library, quite against Diana's wishes.

At the word *baby*, Diana automatically caresses the tiny swell of her belly. I feel an all-too-familiar pang at the gesture, and I have to turn away. Only Debo notices.

As Diana perches on the edge of one of the straight-backed Hepplewhite chairs farthest from me, she explains. "There is a veritable phalanx of reporters outside Rutland Gate pummeling me with questions about Unity. We barely made it through."

Muv's hand flies to her mouth. "Oh dear" is all she can muster.

"How in the hell did that riffraff hear about Unity already? We just got the telegram ourselves," Farve yells.

"They've got spies in all the telegraph offices and telephone exchanges. I understand the newspapers and magazines pay handsomely to the operators and messengers who can deliver information. They probably knew before we did," Diana explains.

My stomach flutters at the word *spies*. Diana did not glance in my direction, but I couldn't help but feel accused. I haven't decided whether I should turn over the radio-station documents although I'm not quite certain for what I am waiting. After all, we are already at war.

Pushing Debo away, Muv rises from her supine position to offer Diana tea from the tray delivered by the maid. "Diana, darling, you and the Führer are so very close. I feel as though he will help us get Unity out of Germany if *you* ask him."

Diana squirms in her chair, unusual for one so composed. I'm guessing this is exactly the sort of request she was hoping to avoid by arriving with her boys in tow.

Finally she says, "I don't know what you're talking about, Muv. We are at war with Germany. It's not as if I can pick up the telephone and ask to be connected with our enemy, only to ask a favor."

Farve mutters, "Damn Huns," before Muv can answer. It's such a relief to hear his old, familiar hatred of the Germans return. Such a contrast to Muv's ongoing preference of Germany over her own country, even though her son and sons-in-law are off to war to defend it.

Muv persists. "Come now, Diana. I know you have the means to reach Hitler. If you could only let him know—"

Diana interrupts, "I don't know what on earth you are talking about, Mother." Muv looks taken aback; Diana only ever calls her *mother* when she is furious.

"Why are you playing dumb?" Muv asks, her eyebrows raised. "Just the other evening I heard you say something about your means of communicating with him about your radio—"

"Enough, Mother." Diana's voice is loud, perhaps louder than I've heard it before, and it sounds oddly strained. "I have no method of contacting the leader of Germany, with whom we are at war, need I remind you. And even if I did, I would not dare use it and put myself and my family at risk."

"Even for Unity?" Muv appears shocked, and Debo's eyes have widened. "She's your family as well as Mosley and your boys."

"Even for Unity. She made her choice when she decided to disregard the Führer's clear instructions and stay in Germany. Anyway, I've suspected that she might take the route of"— Diana pauses, searching for the right word, and then settles for the same one Janos von Almasy selected—"self-harm since this summer."

Muv stands up and stares at Diana. Debo looks incredulous, as does Farve.

I do not feel surprise; I feel rage. "Why didn't you tell us? We could have gone to Germany and dragged her out of there before the borders closed and it was too late. Here in England, we could have kept her safe from herself!" I scream.

Diana's posture is now ramrod straight. "Nancy, you know better than most how laughable your comment is. No one has ever been able to keep Unity from herself. I could not sacrifice myself by trying then—and I will not do it now." She pointedly rubs her belly.

My rage is replaced by shock. Mosley, fascism, and her intimacy with the Nazis have changed Diana; that I've known for some time. But to refuse to take measures to stop your own sister from killing herself? Who is this person masquerading as my sister? What monster has taken hold of Diana?

I cannot be in the room with her a second longer. Standing up, I am about to storm out of the room and out of Rutland Gate altogether, when another idea comes to me. Leaving Diana to fend off Muv's ongoing barrage of requests, I head toward the kitchen instead of the foyer, as if I'm giving instructions for tea. Then I stop in the library where the nanny and boys are hiding out.

The girl sits on the floor with the boys, playing some sort of card game. "Miss?" I interrupt them.

She stands and looks at me with those remarkable blue eyes, and I question myself. Should I really take this step? What if she reports back to Diana? But then I resolve myself to the task. After the display of abject coldness I just witnessed, I must take the risk. After all, it is only mildly perilous compared to the lengths our men go to in war—Peter and Tom among them.

"Just thought I'd see if you and the boys would like anything. I'm arranging for tea."

The boys clamor for sweets, while the nanny gently calms them down. "I'm fine with anything, Mrs. Rodd. Thank you," she says quietly, as the boys return to their card game.

"I'll arrange it," I say and move to leave. Then, as if I've just thought of it, I ask, "Apologies dear, but what is your name again?"

"Jean, ma'am."

"Jean, I remember you well from another visit here with the boys," I say, awaiting her response to assess how—or if—I should proceed.

She doesn't reply. Instead, her gaze shifts to the floor, as if she's embarrassed of what we both witnessed. This is the reaction for which I hoped, one that provides me with an opening.

"Jean," I whisper, reaching for her hand. "I can only imagine the disturbing things you've observed in the Mosley household as you serve as nanny to these two beautiful boys. Activities perhaps made even more upsetting now that war has been declared against Germany. If you ever need someone to talk to about anything troubling you've seen or hear—"

Jean interrupts me with a low whisper. "I overheard Lady Mosley tell Jonathan and Desmond that they needn't fret about the war because she knows it will be over very soon. Then she told them that's why they must keep practicing their salutes for the Führer." Tears well up in her eyes, and she asks in a quivering voice, "Is Germany about to invade England?"

My God. How could my sister be saying such things to her

children? Even if she believes it? Even if there is something she knows? Even if she's part of the plan? A shiver passes through me.

Poor Jean is terrified. But I hope she can summon the courage to do what I'm about to ask of her, so that Diana and Mosley don't have the power to wreak havoc on us all.

# CHAPTER SIXTY-THREE
# DIANA

*October 28, 1939*
*London, England*

THE WALLS ARE CLOSING IN, BUT IS SHE THE ONLY ONE who sees it?

Having made her way back to her Grosvenor Road home by back roads and a circuitous route—with the children and nanny in tow, for goodness' sake—Diana closes the door behind her, leaning up against it as if she could keep trouble at bay simply by her presence. The thought isn't so laughable when she considers it. For years, she's managed to keep Mosley and the BUF afloat through her connections to the Nazis and, if she's honest with herself, has managed to tie Mosley to her through the same means.

But her confidence that she can keep Mosley and the boys safe and together wanes by the day, as the BUF increasingly becomes a public scapegoat and the British government cracks down on proponents of fascism, real or imagined. As soon as war was declared last month, the Emergency Powers Act gave permission to the Home Secretary to detain "enemy aliens," a broad, far-reaching definition that seems to include everyone from those fleeing fascism and the Nazis to those who hailed from Germany or Austria, no matter how many years they'd been living in Great Britain and without heed of their beliefs. Thousands of British citizens have been placed in internment camps despite the fact that they are not fascists or Nazi supporters. Why does Mosley think that he and the BUF members will escape such a fate?

A single chink in her armor could mean the downfall of Mosley, particularly since he seems blind to these risks. *Damn Nancy,* she thinks, *for her comments today.* She's widened the already existing hole in Diana's shield.

Of course Diana feels sick about Unity. She'd be inhuman not to feel concern and remorse. But she can't do as Muv requests or risk opening herself and Mosley up to even more scrutiny. Most importantly, the outreach might lay bare her only remaining method of communication with Germany, if British intelligence is already watching them.

"Diana, is that you?" Mosley calls to her.

"Yes, darling, just back from my parents," she calls back, as she walks toward his voice.

As usual, he won't ask after them or Unity. No, the moment she steps into the library, he will redirect her attention to him. Diana is too enmeshed with Mosley and his selfish ways at this point to voice objections. But she is aware.

When she enters the mahogany-lined library, cozy with a blazing fire in the outsized hearth to take away the chill on this brisk autumnal day, she sees that M isn't alone. A barrel-chested behemoth of a man stands at Mosley's side at his desk. The chap looks vaguely familiar, but Diana can't quite place him.

"Darling," Mosley says with a most unnatural smile on his face. He almost resembles a wolf baring its teeth, and Diana feels afraid. Have her fears come true? Is this man from British intelligence? Has the inquisition begun? By God, why hasn't she burned the documents from the German radio deal? She'd been holding on to them like a talisman, hoping that somehow the arrangement would progress despite the war.

"Please meet Jonathan Sims, the official solicitor for the trust that benefits my children with Cimmie. As you know, she left the children a considerable trust created from her Curzon family inheritance."

"Pleasure to meet you, Lady Mosley." He nods in her direction, then turns back toward Mosley without even a lingering glance at Diana. How unusual. Clearly this man doesn't want to be diverted from whatever conversation he's been having with Mosley. What's happening here? Finances have been very tight because Mosley uses his personal funds for the BUF, and the trust of his first three children has been covering the costs of Wootton and Grosvenor House. Her stepchildren do visit them from time to time, after all.

"As Lord Mosley just mentioned," the man continues, " I am here about his children's Curzon trust. Lord Mosley has been using the trust income to finance the costs of Wootton Lodge and this house as well. As this estate is not the children's family home—Savehay Farm in Denham is their formal, registered residence—those funds may not be applied toward Wootton Lodge or Grosvenor Road."

Why is the solicitor raising these objections now? After all, Mosley has been engaging in the practice of using trust money for a variety of residences for years without inquiry. Is the British government or intelligence initiating this as a way to bring pressure to bear on Mosley and, indirectly, the BUF?

The fear that began to build when she stepped into the library begins to grow. Either this solicitor is operating as part of his formal duties, in which case she and Mosley are in even greater financial difficulties than they believed and will have to give up their homes. Or this man's audit of Mosley's spending has been prompted by governmental forces determined to dismantle the BUF—and possibly Diana and Mosley along with it—in which case their very lives are at stake.

The room begins to sway, and the debate over the propriety of Mosley's spending begins to recede. "Will you gentlemen excuse me for a moment?" Diana says, and Mosley's eyes widen. Her presence at his side will help soften the solicitor, and he counts on her for this.

"Are you quite well?" he asks, although from his tone, she can tell he isn't actually concerned about her health. It is a private message: illness is the only acceptable excuse for deviation from his desires. Otherwise, she should remain at his side, helping to defuse this bomb disguised in solicitor's clothes.

Control is slipping away from her grasp, but one matter remains in her dominion. Slowly, her hand firmly gripping the railing, Diana mounts the stairs to her study. Closing the door behind her, she removes the little key from its hiding place within a hollowed-out book and slides it into the lock of her secret drawer. She takes the stack of papers hidden there and tugs them out. Then she walks to the fireplace and tosses them into the flames.

# CHAPTER SIXTY-FOUR
# NANCY

*January 3, 1940*
*Wycombe, England*

T HE TRAIN IS DELAYED AGAIN, AND I SIT IN ANGUISH AT
Old Mill Cottage, the sole remaining structure belong-
ing to Muv and Farve near Swinbrook, their only property left
outside of Inch Kenneth in fact, as they'll soon give up the
Rutland Gate lease for good. I know I can't complain of the
hours of waiting. I didn't have to undertake the actual travel;
Debo had been enlisted to accompany Muv. The journey from
London to Berne, Switzerland, and back again has been nothing short of horrific, according to the telegrams. Train connections were missed, a boat passage across the English Channel
was delayed by two days, and even the ambulance broke down
at one point. Not to mention that the specter of wartime violence loomed over the entire journey, and reporters hounded
Muv and Debo every step of the way. But there was no other
way to bring Unity home.

The wait for her return since we learned Unity was in hospital has been arduous. The time has seemed to drag, particularly since the change in my posting from Air Raid Precaution

group to a First Aid post near Paddington Station meant I had even more long, empty hours at my disposal. Although *Pigeon Pie* has kept me distracted from some thoughts of Unity, writing about the capricious young aristocrat and wartime volunteer Sophia and her struggle with the spies in her midst has made me fixate on the nature and scope of Diana's sedition. Not to mention her culpability in Unity's "self-harm." Is the book too autobiographical for my current situation to ever publish it? And if I am worried enough to write about her actions, albeit in a veiled way, then what is stopping me from giving the radio documents to Winston? Hope that Diana will change or become marginalized enough that I needn't? Loyalty to a sister that I fear has lost all sense of loyalty to her family and country?

Rolling bandages and creating fictional German spies while perseverating how to handle real-life espionage, this was how I passed the hours. Until Christmas Eve, that is. The phone call from Janos von Almasy over Christmas pudding was the best possible gift. He'd rung my parents at Rutland Gate to tell them that Hitler had arranged for Unity to be transferred from Germany to a hospital in neutral Switzerland. Even better, Unity was finally well enough to come home.

This was the first definitive news we'd had about Unity since that October telegram. After an outpouring of happy tears and the quaffing of many celebratory glasses of wine, Farve awoke to the possibility that Unity might be arrested when she stepped on English soil. Would she be considered a war criminal for her allegiance to the Nazis? Farve sent an urgent inquiry over to an old acquaintance, Oliver Stanley, who was serving as the secretary of state for war; if prison was Unity's destination, then she might as well stay in Switzerland, he'd pronounced. Assured that her compromised physical condition would prevent trial and imprisonment, travel arrangements were made.

———

Dusk casts the snowy landscape in pink before I hear the rumble of tires on the gravel approach to Old Mill Cottage. I stop fussing over the hospital bed I'd set up in the front room so Unity would not have to mount the stairs, and I race to the door. Sliding on my heaviest wool coat to wrap off the biting chill, I step outside. The ambulance slows, then stops to allow Muv, Debo, and the driver to scramble out of the vehicle, after which Farve—who had joined them en route—emerges. The wide white door at the back of the vehicle swings open, and I rush out to help.

Muv and Farve hover at the door alongside the ambulance driver and a nurse I hadn't seen at first, but when Debo exits the ambulance, she holds back. Her eyes are red-rimmed, and black circles smudge the underside of her eyes. I've never seen my even-tempered, joyful youngest sister look so miserable. What happened on this journey? Or is it Unity and not the travel that's causing Debo's despair?

She reaches for my hand and grips it with an intensity I do not usually associate with her. "If only Decca could be here. She's always been so strong, and she can reach Unity when no one else can," she whispers, and I too long for Decca's presence, wishing that the loss of her little daughter and her disgust with European politics hadn't driven her to America. But I confess to relief—and a modicum of disgust—that Diana has begged off, claiming that the hectic schedule of their patched-together families and the idiosyncrasies of their changing residences made it impossible.

"Is it that bad?" I whisper back.

"Worse that you can imagine."

Debo's description sends a shiver through me. She is not known for hyperbole.

Muv and Farve finally part, and I am afforded a glimpse in the back of the ambulance, where the professionals are readying the stretcher to be moved indoors. At first, all I can see is a heap of white bedclothes on the pallet.

But then the driver and nurse lift the stretcher, and I realize that a body lies beneath the sheets. As they carry it past me, Unity's face appears from amid the tangle. At least I think it's Unity.

Sunken, hollow cheeks. Matted, shorn hair. Yellowed teeth. Lifeless, vacant blue eyes that seem incapable of meeting mine. How can this be Unity, my imposing, determined sister? The girl who always knew her mind and adhered to it, even if it led to expulsion from two schools. The debutante who'd never been fearful of embracing her uniqueness, even if it meant bringing a pet rat to a ball. The woman who forged a relationship with Hitler, however ill fated, through sheer tenacity and persistence. The sister whose familial loyalty was boundless, transcending even her beloved politics.

I stare over at Debo, in disbelief and horror. She nods and holds my hand tighter. "I know," she says, uttering the only possible consolation.

"It doesn't even look like her."

"It isn't her, Naunce. The Unity we knew is gone. As soon as she shot that gun and the bullet lodged in her brain, our Unity disappeared." Debo makes a choking sound, and I think she's trying to hold back a sob. "A nurse told me that she tried to kill herself again in the hospital by swallowing that damn gold swastika badge of hers."

My hand flies to my mouth. "Oh God."

Then she adds, "Would you believe that Hitler himself arranged for her to be transferred to Switzerland? And paid her hospital bills?"

"It's the least he could do," I seethe.

Tears stream down my face, growing icy as they trickle. I am despondent, but anger begins to supplant that emotion. Would this have happened to Unity if Diana hadn't brought her to Munich in the first place—knowing her proclivity toward extremes—and then prodded her along in her mad obsession for years, even benefitting from it? Who else might Diana lead down the destructive path of fascism if left unfettered? Could Diana and Mosley and their despicable BUF destroy not only Unity but Great Britain, by laying the foundation for a puppet state for their precious Hitler?

My resolve hardens along with my tears. I will take the step I hoped to avoid. A step far beyond simply passing over the lists I created of Unity and Diana's trips to Germany, the Nazi officials with whom they'd met, and every single thing they'd had to say about Hitler. More extreme than setting up one of Diana's own nannies to spy on her and keeping records of the tidbits she shares, which I pass on to Winston's men. I will hand over the damning radio-station documents to Winston.

# CHAPTER SIXTY-FIVE
# DIANA

*January 3, 1940*
*Staffordshire, England*

A SINGLE SNOWFLAKE ADHERES TO THE WINDOW. SOME might describe the tiny crystal as lovely, but Diana sees a quality far more crucial than beauty. Although seemingly delicate, intricate, and utterly unique, the snowflake must be strong to have survived the rigorous transformation from landlocked water to cloud-born ice.

Her gaze shifts, and her two oldest boys come into view. Jonathan and Desmond, bundled from head to toe in woolens, are ruddy-cheeked from cold and giggling. They glide down the hill on their toboggans with merry abandon, and she thinks how fortunate she's been in the temperament of these boys. Despite the constant shuttling between their mother and father's different homes, they remain even, polite, flexible, and good-natured. With his pleasant disposition, Bryan is, in part, to thank for this. Will young Alexander and this new baby be different, born to a very different father in a time of war and a tumultuous stretch in their parents' lives?

Witnessing her children's happiness, it pains her to take

Jonathan and Desmond from their last holiday at Wootton Lodge. Whatever or whoever prompted the investigation by the official solicitor of her stepchildren's Curzon trust, the worst had come; they could no longer use any of the trust's income to defray the costs of Wootton Lodge or Grosvenor Road, which meant they have to give both of them up as Baba would never agree to change their principal residence to Wootton Lodge. Now, they will be forced to use Savehay Farm in Denham— Cimmie's home—as their primary residence, save for a small flat in London. They cannot afford anything else; Diana's money from Bryan won't stretch any farther, and Mosley has mortgaged the rest of his assets for the BUF.

Trunk lids thud, papers rustle, furniture slides, drawers slam. The sounds of packing invade her pleasant contemplation of her eight- and nearly ten-year-old sons. Scolding follows, echoing throughout the cavernous Great Hall. *What have the servants done now*, Diana wonders about the few staff members they have left. Mosley is berating some poor soul, undoubtedly some farmhand hired to assist in the monumental job of packing but who is untrained in the art of service. She will have to intervene.

As she steps into the great hall, she sees that three servants stand immobile in front of M. Of the three, only Mary is part of the regular staff at Wootton; the other two are temporary hires, as she suspected. They've even had to let most of the nannies go. The three staff members look relieved at her arrival, and she knows that she alone can right the ship before they say farewell to this magical place.

Mosley throws up his hands and says, "Somehow they

are confused as to the future of the gray curtains." He points to the vast folds of silvery silk that she'd commissioned to frame the outsized windows, the same drapery she hopes to repurpose at Savehay Farm to replace Cimmie's oceans of chintz. "I've got better things to do than bicker with staff," he announces as he strides out of the room. Then he pauses and, without turning around, yells out, "Diana, we've got to leave within the hour."

Diana is left to clarify the staff's instructions and settle a misunderstanding with the sole remaining nanny. Only then can she finalize one last task—a private one. Ascending the staircase to her bedroom, she settles at the little writing desk that looks out at the vast wilderness around the lodge. She pulls out a single sheet of paper and her fountain pen, and begins writing: "Dear Peter."

This inquiry she's making of Peter Eckersley, one of the premier radio engineer experts in Great Britain, who also happens to have fascist sympathies and is on the board of their radio venture, is awkward. Diana struggles to finesse the language. Although Hitler had hinted that the radio station might not proceed in the event of war, she wants to check. After all, she hasn't received specific word from Hitler that the deal is off, and she still has a few means of communication at her disposal, no matter what she told Muv.

Using intentionally vague wording, she inquires into the status of the radio-station construction in Osterloog, in the northwest corner of Germany, from which broadcasts could reach East Anglia and the southeast of England. The Germans were meant to do the initial financing, with the British investors contributing later, along with Radio Variety, the separate entity formed to provide programming. Technically, British and German companies can no longer conduct business, but she'd been careful from the start to shield the German and British identities of the company founders. Even with these layers of protection, however, their business partners would have to have a certain appetite for risk. Do they? This is what she needs to know.

But she can't let Mosley discover the uncertainty in the radio deal. Not at the moment, anyway. She's been assuring him for some months that the transaction will proceed and the money will start flowing, that this removal to Savehay Farm is a temporary measure only. Diana cannot risk diminishing Mosley's dependence on her with Baba so close again; they'll be living together at Savehay Farm, after all.

Anyway, it is worry enough that Unity returns home today. The specter of facing her little sister, paying witness to her physical and mental ruin, provides dread enough.

A maid interrupts these unwelcome thoughts. "Ma'am, the trunks containing clothes and supplies for the next three weeks are fully packed and ready to be loaded. The rest will follow."

"Wonderful," Diana answers, staring out the window at the red blur of her boys' woolens as they race each other up the hill again, toboggans trailing behind them. "I suppose I should fetch the boys," she says almost to herself, her tone as heavy as her mood.

Tucking the letter into her sleeve, she descends the staircase one last time. She hands the missive to her most trusted employee, whispering instructions that he mail it from the post office one town away, Ellastone in Staffordshire. The letter cannot be traced back to Wootton Lodge.

It is time.

Opening wide the French doors to the back lawn, she calls out, "Come now, boys! We must ready to leave!"

"One last toboggan, Mum!" Desmond calls back. "Please!"

Diana laughs; how can she resist them? Even though it will cost them five minutes, even though Mosley will be angry. "Oh, all right!"

As she watches her delicious older boys sled down the snowy drifts, a strange sadness takes hold of her. Why does she feel as though a great, happy period of her life is coming to an end?

# CHAPTER SIXTY-SIX
# NANCY

*February 2, 1940*
*London, England*

I STEP OUT OF THE DISCREET BLACK AUSTIN INTO THE alley beside the majestic Admiralty House. A uniformed soldier awaits me, and without a word, he ushers me through a nondescript door cut into the yellow-brick side. I follow him through a winding service hallway that empties out into the grand foyer, where he gestures for me to wait on a bench upholstered with bold blue-and-red seahorse fabric. Anywhere else this pattern would look preposterous, but I suppose the marine theme is acceptable in the official home and workplace of the lord of the admiralty.

If I avert my eyes from the blackout curtains and pretend I didn't witness the hub of activity of naval-uniformed officers in the converted ballroom, it could nearly be peacetime. But it isn't, even though bombs aren't currently raining down on London. The so-called Phony War no longer seems so counterfeit. I keep abreast of the quieter developments, and I know that the Nazis are on the move and we are preparing naval patrols, air force surveillance, troops, and the discreet shipment of some divisions to France. Just because the war isn't apparent to our citizens, that doesn't make it any less real.

Even from Old Mill Cottage, where I've been holed up with Muv and Debo helping Unity, I could see the imminent conflict. In fact, every time I changed the bed linens for poor incontinent Unity or spoon-fed her mashed foods or retrained my childlike sister in words she'd forgotten or took an overnight shift in place of Debo or the surprisingly cheery Muv, war between Great Britain and Germany seemed just around the corner. When I watched Farve pack up and leave Old Mill Cottage for Inch Kenneth because he couldn't bear the sight of his broken daughter and he couldn't listen to Muv's ongoing admiration for Hitler, I longed for war to commence in earnest. If it were up to me, it would be. I'm dying to exact revenge on the Nazis for what happened to my sister, no matter the role she played in it herself.

The only phony thing that's happened in these terrible weeks since Unity returned was Diana's brief visit to Old Mill Cottage. From the moment she stepped inside the small, white stucco and timber-beamed house and spotted Unity in her hospital bed in the front room, her desire to flee was evident. Although she spouted words of kindness and verbiage of support, she started her exit from the moment she entered. She couldn't bear to stare headlong into the damage she'd wrought upon Unity. After no more than thirty minutes, she gave her enormous belly a slow caress and announced that she had to leave, "for the baby's sake." At least she had the decency not to bring Mosley.

"Lady Churchill will see you now," a military aide says, and I follow him up the central staircase to what appears to be the Churchill's private quarters. Settling on a homey sofa before a crackling fire, I warm myself while I wait for Cousin Clemmie.

When she'd rang Old Mill Cottage and asked me to pop in when I returned to London, I understood the nature of her invitation. Clemmie hadn't simply reached out to check on Unity or Muv, although she made the proper clucking on that account. No, Clemmie was sending a message from Winston. If I was ready to share the information I'd gathered, he was more than ready. A pop-in at the Admiralty House "to visit family" could mask the clandestine nature of the get-together.

The bitter cold of February has seeped into my pores, so I stand and move closer to the fire to warm myself while I wait. As I remove my gloves and rub my hands together before the flames, I hear footsteps behind me. Before I turn, I call out, "Afternoon, Cousin Clemmie."

"That's a hell of a compliment, Nancy," a gruff, deep rumble sounds out behind me. It's Winston. "No one has ever mistaken my heavy thud for Clemmie's delicate tread before."

He always has a way of making me laugh. Muv finds him impossible, and Farve finds him too single-minded, but I appreciate his intellect and humor. "Anything to please the lord admiral."

Winston puffs up a little at the mention of his title. After so very long in political exile, it must feel magnificent for him to assume this central role, vindicated in all his assertions. Certainly he has taken to the Admiralty stage with relish, giving rousing speeches around the country.

"How is Unity?" His voice is now humorless as he makes this dutiful inquiry as we settle next to each other on the sofa. He knows, better than most and undoubtedly better than the journalists who constantly cover Unity's fall from grace, the nature of my sister's injuries. I've guessed that the policemen guarding Old Mill Cottage have been handpicked by Winston and keep him well informed—of that I have no doubt. I believe that is their true purpose, although ostensibly they're protecting us from the angry masses and Great Britain from a Nazi.

"She is no longer Unity."

"Another tragedy of war," he sighs.

"So I am inclined to believe."

"And our shared beliefs have brought us to this juncture." He does not pose this as a question.

"Yes, but I think you know that."

He smiles as he puffs on his cigar. Reaching into his pocket, he pulls out a silver lighter and asks, "Care for a smoke?"

I nod, opening my purse and pulling out a cigarette. As I hold it out for him to light, he plods over to my side, flicks open the lighter, and presses the flame toward me. "I won't ask what drives you to share the information you've given to my man so far. I imagine Diana gave you any number of reasons. Perhaps Unity did as well in the past."

"You imagine correctly," I say, taking a drag of my Dunhill, thinking about the snippets of information I've passed on from Diana's former nanny. The most damaging details she'd gathered—beyond Diana's assertions that the Nazis' arrival was imminent—were dates and times of BUF meetings, which I suppose may have proven useful to Winston's network.

I continue. "But I've only been ready to give you the most damaging documents since I saw Unity's face upon her return from Germany."

"Ah," he says and begins pacing in front of the fire. "Right. I suppose that would drive one to patriotic deeds."

I am tiring of this little dance. This decision has weighed heavily on me for longer than I care to recall, and I am ready to hand over the burden. Not that I believe I will ever truly leave this choice behind me. It will haunt me forever.

Opening my purse again, I pull out the documents I took from Diana's locked desk drawer. "It is no easy matter giving you these," I say, placing them in his outstretched hand.

"I know. That is why I didn't press. I sensed there was more, but this is your sister and you are my cousin, of sorts. So I gave it time. Until I couldn't wait any longer." Without glancing at the papers, he asks, "What are they?"

"I am no expert in German, but from what I've been able to translate, they are contracts. It seems Diana and Mosley have created a series of entities to enter into an agreement with the German government to create a commercial radio venture on German soil that will transmit to parts of Great Britain."

Winston's eyes widen, and he looks down at the documents.

"Is it really as bad as all that?" I ask, even though I know the answer.

He stares at me with his piercing blue eyes. "Nancy, this so-called Phony War is about to come to an end. Hitler's military will soon be on the move again. Our intelligence suggests they'll turn to Scandinavia first, then to France. And in a country like Norway, where you've got party leader Vidkun

Quisling, who is openly anti-Semitic and pro-Nazi like Mosley, the way could be eased for Nazi conquest. Quisling could usher the Nazis in with open arms, creating a puppet government."

"My God."

"Yes. And then the Nazis will turn to Great Britain, and we need to take very seriously the possibility of a German attack on British soil. Certainly bombs will rain down from the sky in the streets of London, but we might even face a full-scale invasion. Imagine what damage a radio station in enemy hands broadcasting across England could do—creating easy communication between the enemy within and the enemy without, as well as sending out propaganda and false information to the British people. This makes plain the absolute necessity of routing out and trouncing our enemies within—those damnable fifth columnists you read about in the papers—or they will make short work of the German takeover of our country."

# CHAPTER SIXTY-SEVEN
## DIANA

*March 2, 1940*
*London, England*

L OOK AT THE SUCCESS QUISLING IS POISED TO HAVE. IT'S the sort of success we might secure for ourselves," Mosley says to the private BUF meeting at London headquarters.

Diana inhales sharply at the mention of the infamous Quisling, but when people turn in her direction, she keeps her mouth shut and eyes fixed straight ahead. As if she had heard nothing at all.

But she is flabbergasted. How could he utter such a clearly treasonous statement aloud, outside the confines of their own home? Never mind that they are in a restricted conference with only the top BUF leaders, behind closed doors and blackout curtains. One never knows when a traitor is in one's midst.

"Hear! Hear!" General Fuller concurs, and a round of clapping follows.

Even the mention of Quisling rouses these men to cheers. According to Mosley's sources, Vidkun Quisling, the leader of a conservative political party in Norway, has been in contact with Hitler about a pro-Nazi takeover of Norway. Quisling hopes to smooth the way for Hitler from the inside, a plan that appeals to Mosley and his inner circle. It isn't as though Diana objects to this Quisling approach; it has essentially been their objective all along. She just finds fault with this rather indiscreet discussion of this plan.

Why does Mosley think he can act unilaterally here? She's the one who labored hard and long to secure the relationship with Hitler, without which the future of the BUF would be tenuous at best. Shouldn't she be the one, or at least among the ones, to decide what risks they take now? Hasn't he read the news about the frantic focus on routing out fifth columnists, the groups within England that are sympathetic to the Nazis?

*Keep calm*, she tells herself, as she runs her hand along the rise of her belly. Only one more month until this little one enters the world. *He'll face tumult enough when he arrives, being born in wartime*, she thinks. *We should give him peace until then.* She takes a calming breath and decides to only half listen to the rest of the discussion.

Her thoughts drift to the excuse Mosley had offered her to skip the event tonight. "You are tired, darling," he insisted. "Allow me to handle this one. I couldn't bear it if my politics made you fall ill, like Cimmie." Mosley holds the belief that the speeches and travel that Cimmie did on his behalf contributed to her illness and subsequent death, but he only trots this out when he doesn't want Diana to join him. He certainly never bothered about her many arduous trips to Germany.

The very fact that he provided her with leave to skip the meeting meant that she needed to attend. Even though she'd much rather be nestled in their snug London flat on Dolphin Square, while the small children remained at Savehay Farm with the nanny and her older boys at boarding school. It's the only private space they can afford, and it takes the last of her Guinness money.

Then another unpleasant notion nags at her: Eckersley's lack of response to her letter. Why has he not replied? Has there been an interruption in mail service such that he never received her missive? Or has some problem occurred on his end?

"Victory is in sight—" She hears a snippet of M's speech.

An appreciative murmur emanates from the men, and she cannot hear what Mosley says next, until his voice raises. "Two years at most."

"Hear! Hear!" There goes damnable General Fuller again.

A terrifying thought occurs to her. Could Eckersley's failure to reply mean that her letter was intercepted? *No*, she thinks, *if someone in the British government or intelligence—or French intelligence, for that matter—got their hands on my letter, all they'd see were polite inquiries about Eckersley's health and that of his family.* If the authorities actually had the letter and read something more into it, she wouldn't be sitting here right now. Rumors abound about fascist sympathizers and suspected Nazis being rounded up.

The sound of Mosley's fist banging the podium startles her. "We need to continue to give people alternatives for the present government—and the hope of peace."

*That's more like it,* she thinks. Urging peace? No one would arrest Mosley for simply advocating that. After all, he's also requested his followers serve loyally in the war as first aid volunteers, constabularies, and Air Raid defense volunteers. Without the commercial radio venture documents, of what treason could the authorities possibly accuse them?

# CHAPTER SIXTY-EIGHT
# NANCY

*May 23, 1940*
*London, England*

THE PHONE RINGS WITH AN UNEXPECTED JANGLE. EVEN though I'm in the garden, hanging Unity's laundered bedsheets on the line to dry, I can hear it through the kitchen door, as it's opened to allow in fresh air on this balmy spring day. Winston had not been exaggerating. Once the war began, it moved quickly indeed. Each country on the chessboard advanced squares in rapid succession, until Germany brought out its rooks and bishops and invaded Belgium, France, Luxembourg, and Holland. In reaction, of course, Great Britain felt it necessary to bring out its strongest, craftiest player onto the board—the queen, ironically—and Winston became prime minister upon Chamberlain's resignation. Soon after he was sworn in on May 10 on the heels of the massive German invasion in continental Europe, Winston brought a new weapon to the game—Defense Regulation 18B, an amendment to the Emergency Powers Act that gave the government the power to detain anyone deemed a threat to the nation's safety or subject to foreign influence, without formal charges or a trial, including those who held beliefs sympathetic to the Nazi ideologies. Still, we felt the danger everywhere.

The phone stops ringing, and I hear Muv's voice. "Diana, darling, is that you? I can barely make you out," Muv says, and a pause ensues. "Take a breath. Calm down."

I pause in my task of hanging Unity's laundered bedsheets on the line to dry. What is happening? No one ever needs to tell Diana to calm down as she's always preternaturally calm.

"The police did what?" Muv asks. "Right in front of you?"

"Did you organize a solicitor to meet him?" Her voice quavers just a little.

A solicitor? Meet who where? Are they talking about Mosley? Has he gotten himself into another scrape at a rally? Earlier in the month, he'd been physically attacked for his views.

"What do you mean, no one will take the case?" Muv is practically shouting now. "What about Mosley's regular lawyer, Sweet?" After the shortest pause, "He declined?" Muv has cast aside all pretense of calm. She's furious. "The whole list declined? How dare they!"

She is silent for a long moment, then asks, "Sweet said what about this new law?"

Muv's heels clatter on the floor as she paces. "How can a regulation possibly allow the government to indefinitely imprison suspects without a trial? Without a charge? This suspension of habeas corpus will not sit well with the British citizens. Not to worry, Diana. It'll be overturned in a jiff." Muv tries to placate her beloved daughter.

Imprison? Is Mosley in prison? A wave of nausea takes

hold of me, and I sit down on the step outside the kitchen door. While I have no doubt that Mosley deserves to be jailed, that he cannot be allowed to roam freely and sow the seeds of sedition while invasion is imminent, it is heart-wrenching to witness the impact on my sister. Even secondhand. Even when it's possible that the information I gathered might have helped jail him, since his name was all over those radio-station documents as well. And the information provided by Diana's former nanny may have led Winston's men to the BUF meetings.

More quietly, Muv remarks, "You are quite right. As soon as the police search through Mosley's things at Savehay Farm and your London flat and find nothing, they've got to release him. New regulation or not. It's not a crime in this country to hold a differing view."

A brief pause in Muv's chatter, and then she asks, "Where is he being held?"

"But, Diana, Max is only five weeks old, and you are nursing him!" she exclaims, then adds, "Please tell me your new nanny is willing to stay on and look after Max while you take Mosley's things to Brixton Prison. Surely she hasn't quit as well?"

"That's one saving grace, I suppose," Muv says, the despair plain in her voice. I can only imagine how desperate Diana must sound, and I do hope she has some good staff in place. Jean left to help in the war effort several weeks ago, and I admit to feeling relieved. I was in constant fear that she'd blurt out to Diana our secret conversations where she reported on the fruits of her spying.

As Muv and Diana discuss the location of Brixton Prison

and the practical items Diana should bring to her husband, I wonder how much of a hand I had in this. I know that MI5 had Mosley and Diana in their sights before I began sharing information with Winston. But Mosley has not done himself any favors in recent weeks either. Even though the Germans broke through the Allied lines only four days ago and British forces are falling back on Dunkirk, Mosley, whose allegiance to fascism and ties to Hitler are well known, has continued to give public speeches about peace. All at a time when citizens are on high alert for spies, whether dropping from the sky in parachutes or brewing up bombs next door, and the government has in place a regulation that allows them to detain at will.

I hear the handset being returned to the cradle and then the unmistakable sound of Muv crying. Should I go into the cottage and embrace her? Consolation is not a language she and I speak. Do I even have a right to offer comfort?

Taking a deep breath, I step inside. My guilt, however private and secret I keep it, has to be faced sooner or later. After all, I suppose that it will become my life's constant companion.

# CHAPTER SIXTY-NINE

# DIANA

*June 29, 1940*
*Denham, England*

D IANA FINISHES NURSING SWEET MAX, THINKING HOW
sturdy he seems for eleven weeks. Placing him gently in
his pram so as not to wake him, she lowers the cover to block
the sun's rays and strolls him around the garden of Savehay
Farm for a few minutes. Finding a shady spot with a bench,
she parks the pram and settles herself with her book, Lytton
Strachey's *Elizabeth and Essex*.

Closing her eyes, she breathes in the smell of the sweet
peas blooming nearby alongside the irises and dahlias and
almost enjoys the brilliant day. But how dare she luxuriate
in a perfect summer afternoon, while Mosley sits in a dark,
vermin-infested prison, rotting away.

To ease her shame, she thinks about what she should take
for Mosley on her next weekly visit to Brixton Prison. Is there a
particular book that would bring him comfort or at least amuse
him? What clothes should she bring? She'll have to rummage
through his old threadbare items—the ones he used for fishing
at Wootton Lodge or romping through the forest—because

on her last visit, he asked her to stop bringing country squire outfits. Apparently, the attire was causing him "a bit of trouble" with the fellow prisoners. No matter how he begs, however, she will not bring him newspapers. The headlines about him are excoriating, and she cannot bear to think of him reading them, alone in that dreadful place.

She reminds herself to pack another box of books from Savehay Farm's extensive library. Last week, the military informed her that the estate was being commandeered for war purposes. Certainly other houses have suffered the same fate, but those owners had other homes to which they could retreat. Diana and her boys have very few options—particularly since she and Mosley are social pariahs. Even Baba didn't offer them a safe haven. Diana was thankful when a family member finally made a generous offer; Pamela and Derek will be hosting them at Rignell House, their farm in Berkshire. Diana supposes that, given Pamela and Derek's vocal support of fascism, Diana and her boys can do them little harm as their guests.

"Lady Mosley?" A housemaid peeks around a stone wall bordering the garden, in the direction of the main house.

"Yes?"

"There are some people at the door to speak with you?"

"Who is it? I'd rather not disturb the baby unless it's urgent."

"They did not give me a card, ma'am."

That's odd, Diana thinks. Everyone leaves a card. Then she wonders whether they could be journalists. Reporters have hounded her since Mosley's arrest, even out here at Savehay Farm. "What sort of people? They aren't journalists, are they?"

"They don't look the part, ma'am. There's a woman with three men."

Diana's heart begins racing. Reporters occasionally appear in pairs, but never a gaggle. The visitors could be police, although the presence of a woman is odd. Are they here to conduct another search? In the days after Mosley's imprisonment, they tore through Savehay Farm. Diana knew they wouldn't find anything—she'd already burned the most incriminating documents—but it was unnerving nonetheless. Would they undo all the items that she and the maids painstakingly packed?

This blasted new law of Winston's gives the authorities unlimited power without a single piece of evidence to support their intrusions. Leaving Max with the maid, with instructions to quietly wheel him to the nursery where Nanny is watching eighteen-month-old Alexander, she crosses the garden and enters the house. The visitors await her in the foyer.

"May I help you?" she asks, studying these four strange people. From the contrast between their air of authority and the shabbiness of their clothes, she supposes that they are indeed police.

"We have a warrant for your arrest," says the tallest of the men, wearing a crumpled fedora.

Arrest? Her? Diana had concerns for some time about Mosley's safety, what with all his careless speeches, but she hadn't really been involved in the BUF except as a supportive wife. The most damaging activity in which she's engaged was the commercial radio-station negotiations, of course, and there's no longer a paper trail of that. Is it a crime to have had a friendship with Hitler?

But what about the locked drawer in which she'd stored the contracts? Hadn't there been scratches on the lock and the drawer appearing slightly ajar? Had MI5 been in her study, after all?

"On what grounds?" she asks, doing everything in her considerable power to keep her voice calm and her posture erect, to stop the quivering of her limbs and lips.

"We don't need grounds," the man answers with a smug smile.

The woman chimes in. "I'll go with you up to your bedroom. You can gather up your essentials and enough items for a weekend."

A weekend? *That's a relief*, Diana thinks. *Sort of.* Perhaps the authorities merely mean to feed the public's appetite for a scapegoat. Even the basest of English citizens wouldn't want to separate a mother from her children for longer than that. *Imagine the headlines*, she thinks.

The female police officer follows Diana as she starts up the main staircase toward her bedroom. Diana calls back to her, "I'll have to pack some things for my baby as well. I'm nursing him so I cannot be separated from him for a weekend. He'll have to come along."

"No babies in Holloway prison," the officer replies.

Holloway Prison? By God, that is the largest women's prison in western Europe, where criminals of all sorts are incarcerated. Holloway is *not* the local Denham constabulary's holding cell. Images of iron bars with a central pen where the guards stare out at the prisoners as if they're animals in a zoo flood her mind.

Diana pauses on the stairs and turns back to her. "But my baby is only eleven weeks old! He cannot be parted from his mother. He'll starve."

The woman shrugs. How can she be so unfeeling about an infant? Even if the separation lasts only a weekend? Diana wants to swing at her, push her down the stairs, even though the officer didn't cause this catastrophic situation. Instead, she looks away and continues up the stairs. "Then we will have to stop in the nursery. I'll have to inform Nanny that she'll be in charge of both boys—my eighteen-month-old Alexander and my eleven-week-old Max." Diana emphasizes the boys' ages.

"You have five minutes." The officer is unmoved.

Diana strides up the second set of stairs to the nursery, the vast play space into which the boys' bedrooms and Nanny's empty. Little Alexander toddles about, a stuffed animal rabbit clutched in his right hand. Nanny perches on a rocker with the comparatively tiny Max in her arms, rocking him while keeping an eye on his older brother.

Diana kneels next to Alexander and says, "Mummy has to go on a little trip. Can you give her a big kiss and promise you'll be a good boy for Nanny?"

Alexander leans toward her, bestowing a wet, sloppy kiss on her cheek. She places her hand on it, pressing it into her skin. *It's only a weekend*, she tells herself when the tears threaten to come. *I've left him for far longer to travel to Germany*, she reminds herself. She says a silent prayer of gratitude that her older boys are in boarding school and will be unscathed by her departure. They needn't even know. She'll be back long before their next school break.

Pushing herself up, she tussles Alexander's blond hair as she walks over to Nanny, who stands as she draws near. Diana stretches out her arms to hold little Max, leaning down to smell his sweet baby scent. Then she whispers the unfathomable words, "I am being taken to prison."

Nanny gasps, then begins to cry. Diana consoles her, along with herself, by saying, "Not to worry. They tell me it's only for the weekend, and I am comforted that the children will be in your care until I return. Of course, it will be challenging for poor Max as he's nursing, so I suppose we will have to shift him to baby formula."

Nanny sobs at this new bit of information.

Diana says, "Now, Nanny, I am counting on you to be strong for my boys. And I'm hoping you will be extra strong in this transition for Max. I'll send out one of the maids for bottles and formula right now so you'll be situated."

Dabbing her eyes with a handkerchief, she says, "You can count on me, Lady Mosley."

"You will be rewarded for your efforts. I promise."

Diana gives Max a last kiss before handing him back to his caregiver. A single tear escapes her iron will, and then she reassembles herself into the calm, serene, enigmatic, and powerful woman with whom Mosley fell in love. Because, in the end, this has all been for him.

# CHAPTER SEVENTY
## NANCY

*April 20, 1941*
*London, England*

I ALMOST DIDN'T COME TODAY; I OPENED AND CLOSED THE door to my house over and over in my indecision and apprehension. The specter of seeing Diana in prison has haunted me for months. Will witnessing my perfect little sister debased by my hand, in part, put lie to the narratives I've told myself about Diana and Unity? The stories I've been knitting together about their lives and motives and misbehavior for years?

Are Diana and Unity really as I imagined them? Unity. I've told myself tales about her headlong quest for attention, her blatant efforts to stand out in a powerful way from our pack of whip-smart siblings, however sordid those means. Yet it is ultimately an account in which she was led by the hand to her natural destruction by her own sister. But is that story really true? Did Unity lead Diana instead? Did Hitler? Or do I simply want Diana to be the instigator as a means of assuaging my own guilt about her ultimate fate?

Diana. The sister for which I feel the most love and the most envy. Could she truly have sought out and manipulated the monster Adolf Hitler for her own gain? Disregarding the harm to Unity and the world in the process? What if the story I conjured in my thoughts—the one that propelled me forward in my spying—turned out to not be true? What if Diana wasn't a woman of her own mind, but instead was exploited by her husband, and that influence clouded her mind as to the harm she was doing? Or maybe, just maybe, there was nothing nefarious happening at all. Maybe Diana and Unity simply enjoyed taking tea with Hitler, and he gave them apartments and money and radio stations out of sheer admiration and friendship?

Was nothing as it seemed to me? Could the long-standing rivalry that exists between us all and my jealousy over Diana's easy fertility have permeated my decision? Did a mix of my own childish pettiness and long-harbored familial assumptions and present-day motives fog the lens through which I saw this drama evolve? What role did my hatred of fascism play in my perception? What was fact, and what was fiction?

It occurs to me that all these things could be true at once. I could be motivated by my loathing of fascism and also jealousy. Diana and Unity could wholeheartedly believe in the Nazi cause and yet also be propelled by a longing for fame or by infatuations with the wrong men—whether Mosley or Hitler. Does it matter as long as we think we are acting on the side of right and truth? Or must we be on the actual side of right? Even as I ask myself these questions, I am reminded of Diana's intentional choice to not inform our family of Unity's stated plan to kill herself on the declaration of war. That's a fact that cannot be ignored. But what role did that disturbing fact play in the mix of emotions and motivations and events? I wonder if I will ever know for certain.

The door to the visitation room opens with a screech. In walks my undiminished sister, her shoulder bones visible under a once-luxurious camel cardigan, now stained and worn. But her visage is still undeniably lovely, and her carriage is as formidable as ever. And she still has that unearthly air of confidence, which she wears like a fur mantle in this frigid, desolate place. Prison hasn't taken those assets from her.

"Nancy," she says, as she settles in the scuffed, hard wooden chair that faces mine across the table. On closer examination, I see dark undereye circles and dry patches on her ivory skin.

"Diana," I say, unsurprised at how my voice quavers. "I was so pleased when the prison rules relaxed and you were allowed more visitors." What a lie. That couldn't be further from the truth. It had been a relief that Diana's visitors were very limited initially. When the rules softened right around the same time that she and Mosley were granted leave to be incarcerated together in a little house on Holloway Prison ground, I knew I had to come soon. Mosley would likely block any of my requests to visit his wife, and Diana, always in Mosley's thrall, would undoubtedly agree.

"Yes, it was rather bleak when I was only allowed two letters and two visitors per week. Those visitors, naturally, were Nanny and the children and the letters were from Nanny and Mosley. I usually reject the special privileges that Winston offers"—her face hardens when she says his name—"out of guilt, I assume. It simply isn't fair. After all, most of the women here have been imprisoned because of their affiliation

with the BUF. But in the end I could not decline more visitors or the opportunity to be with M." Her face softens at
the reference to her husband, then she looks at me with her
piercing blue eyes. "I cannot tell you how much I appreciated
the woolen sweaters and hot water bottles you sent in with the
boys. Not to mention the bread and cheese and wine."

Her older two son, Jonathan and Desmond, came to stay
with me from boarding school on the days they visited their
mother. Although I wasn't permitted to see her even when I
drove them to and from the prison, I always made certain to
send in packages of necessary supplies for her. The icy temperature of the prison has been her primary complaint, that
and being separated from her children, I suppose, the youngest
two in particular, who often didn't know her when they arrived
with Nanny from Pamela's where they live.

"I wish I could do more," I say out of habit, before I stop
myself. In part, it is true, but it sounds disingenuous, knowing
what I know and having done what I've done. The imprisonment of Diana had not been my intention. My goal had been
to prevent Mosley and the BUF—and to a lesser extent Diana
and perhaps Unity—from treasonous acts of which I knew they
were capable, from the harm their handiwork might inflict not
only on our country but on my loved ones, Peter and Tom in
particular. Or is this just a lie I tell myself? Because, if I am
honest with myself, as I am when I'm alone in bed in the dead
of night, I knew when I handed those documents to Winston
that this outcome was possible. And I'd believed my sister capable of nearly anything.

"You cannot deliver my babies here to me." Her eyes well

up with tears, but she forbids them to fall. So they cling to her lashes, sparkling in the fluorescent light of the visiting room. How is it possible that my sister remains beautiful in this horrific place?

"How are their visits?" Politeness requires that I ask, but I am not sure I can bear to hear the answer.

"Hard. When Nanny brings them in from Rignell Farm, they don't always remember me at first, Max especially. Just when they've finally warmed up and recalled that I am their mother the guards tromp in and tell them visiting hours are over. Then the crying commences." She inhales deeply. "For all of us."

I reach for her bony hand, noticing that her usually perfectly manicured long fingernails are ragged. I have to stop myself from recoiling. Why does this unkemptness upset and surprise me?

"The only time I allow myself to cry in this god-awful place is when my fury over the illegal detention becomes irrepressible." Her expression morphs from sadness to anger. "Mosley and I are convenient scapegoats, stand-ins for the enemy and seized upon by the gutter press to satisfy their need for stories. But if due process had been done, we would have been found perfectly innocent, never mind my friendship with Hitler. Just because I desire a fascist state and want peace instead of war doesn't mean I would act against my country. I have not done a single thing against Great Britain, other than long for a different government."

I can't reply. Quite literally, I cannot form words. Has Diana convinced herself of the statements she's uttering? If I didn't know what she'd stored in the locked drawer in her study, I might have believed her. Perhaps she's written a more palatable history for herself as well.

"How do you pass the time? Is there anything I can bring to help with that?" I ask, unable to tolerate more of this line of conversation.

"More books are always welcome. Reading helps pass the time more than anything. That and talking with my fellow prisoners."

"I'll bring some on my next visit," I say, wondering if Mosley will even allow another visit and praying that no one has been so unkind as to send her a copy of my recent release, *Pigeon Pie*. I would hate her to read my novel of Nazi spies and their use of radios, and make the connection between her incarceration and me. Although I know that one day I may have to make amends for the role I've played.

Changing the topic, I ask, "What do you chat about with your fellow prisoners?" I ask out of politeness and to guide the conversation away from painful topics. I find it very difficult to imagine the imperious Diana chitchatting with average women, BUF members or no.

"The books we are reading. The bits and pieces we can glean about the war. Our families in the outside world. Oh!" She half laughs, and then says, "Everyone wants to know about Hitler, of course. What he is like? How he managed to rise up and take control of Germany, lifting it out of its economic slump? I tell them that people don't go from out-of-work painter to become leader of an enormous country like Germany unless they carry a special spark within them. I always share how perfectly charming and gentlemanly he is." She pauses and adds, "Of course, many of my fellow prisoners are BUF members, so they are especially curious about—and sympathetic to—my friendship with Herr Hitler," she says, and I notice that she calls her hero *Herr Hitler* instead of *Führer*. Is that shift difficult for her?

A small, self-satisfied smile appears on her face, and I wonder if she's reminiscing about a particular dinner or fireside chat with Hitler. How could those memories bring her pleasure now? *Look at where those strange, special encounters landed her*, I think. Not to mention that we are at *war* with Hitler, that his soldiers are putting our military and our civilians at great risk, including our brother, my husband, and countless young men that we know. But then, perhaps it isn't Hitler but Mosley who is to blame for Diana's current situation. Or perhaps, me.

Here I go again. In the narrative that runs through my mind, I've stitched together the threads of my sisters' lives to form a tapestry that is flattering to me, one that supports my decision. But could the threads have just as easily been embroidered to form a different image? I do not inhabit my sisters' minds and spirits, after all, and I need to believe my actions are for a larger purpose, that they'll reverberate positively throughout time. We all do.

Just then, the door to the visitation room swings open, and I feel immense relief at the thought our time together might be over. Instead of a prison guard, however, Sir Oswald Mosley steps into the room, bedraggled in his shabby work clothes and thin but unmistakably his cocksure self.

"Your husband's transport date was moved up," the guard says by way of explanation.

Diana's eyes meet Mosley's, and they rush into each other's

embrace. Though their arms are still wrapped around each other's waists, they pull away a bit to stare at each other in disbelief. Their long separation is finally over, even if they'll stay in prison for the foreseeable future. As far as Diana and Mosley are concerned, they are alone in the room. Their reunion is all that matters.

Diana cries out, tears coursing down her cheeks, "I can't believe it's really you."

"It's really me, my darling," he assures her. "And we will never be parted again."

"Never," Diana says with a fierceness that shocks me. Although I suppose it shouldn't. How well do I really know her?

I watch as my sister bestows upon her husband a wide, knowing, secret smile, and it is clear she remains entirely in his sway, just as I believe Unity was in Hitler's. In that moment, I know with utter certainty that Diana could sacrifice everything—country, family, her own life—for this man and his cause. Whatever fiction I've been writing in my head about my sisters, that part, at least, is true. Whether it justifies my actions remains to be seen—or perhaps I'll never fully know.

*How personal is the political in the end*, I think. It turns each one of us into authors of our own histories; we become patriots and heroes and, where necessary, spies and traitors. Which of these, I wonder, am I?

# AUTHOR'S NOTE

I stumbled across the rarified, mesmerizing, often peculiar world of the Mitfords during college, when a dear friend and I backpacked across Europe after a semester abroad in England. Before we departed, I'd picked up a couple books for the long train stretches from country to country, and one was a trade paperback containing the two best Nancy Mitford novels, *The Pursuit of Love* and *Love in a Cold Climate*. I became immediately hooked on the semi-hilarious, semi-tragic, always singular world of Nancy Mitford, a stand-in for her own upbringing, familial universe, and social realm, and that fascination continued over the years as I turned from practicing law to writing.

I recently dipped into some research about the Mitfords that I'd started back then, as well as some research about the Mitfords I came across while writing *Lady Clementine*, which focused upon their cousin, Clementine Churchill. As I scampered down the rabbit hole into the historical documentation of those interwar years, I was gobsmacked, to use Mitford lingo. I'd expected to discover a light-hearted romp through the past alongside these aristocratic "it" girls—perhaps shot through with the occasional deeper musings and issues—but what I actually found shocked me.

These well-heeled, pedigreed sisters had placed themselves at the epicenter of scandal and political intrigue in the lead-up to World War II, dabbling in and then embracing fascism, communism, and Nazism. Given the access they had to the upper echelons of society and leadership of most European countries, their actions were at the core of potentially world-changing events. In the case of Diana and possibly Unity, their decisions threatened to alter the trajectory of their times, had incarceration and catastrophe not befallen them.

Uncovering this dark chapter in the Mitford story was personally challenging—I found it very difficult to look at the monstrous Adolf Hitler in a positive light through the eyes of Diana and Unity—and prompted a slew of questions as my understanding of these sisters changed dramatically. What possessed these affluent, intelligent, and otherwise well-established women to veer so far off the expected political path? What was it about these extremist political movements—fascism and Nazism, in particular—that attracted them? How far would they go to fulfill their perceived destinies? When would their loved ones feel they'd stepped over the line of acceptability? What on earth would—and should—their friends and families do to stop them, if anything? What role should loyalty play in that decision? And how do we know what thoughts, beliefs, and plans really inhabit peoples' minds?

The more I examined this lesser-known piece of the Mitford lives and lore, the more familiar the scenario seemed, particularly the idea that the political is so very personal. In our own times, we are dealing not only with a worldwide pandemic but also with wide-ranging political views, divided families and communities, and unexpected military actions and invasions. And I began to think that perhaps the questions evoked by *The Mitford Affair* might well be questions we could ask ourselves and others—after reading the novel and in book discussions. Maybe, just maybe, in the safe space of those conversations, we might begin the process of avoiding the terrible pitfalls faced by the Mitfords and draw one step closer to understanding one another and healing those divides.

# READING GROUP GUIDE

1. Before reading *The Mitford Affair*, were you familiar with the famous (or infamous, depending on your perspective) Mitford sisters? If so, how has your understanding of these eccentric, beautiful, aristocratic sisters changed, if at all?

2. Nancy is concerned that Diana is considering divorce, particularly because her new partner will not be leaving his own marriage. Why is Nancy so concerned? What is behind Diana's decision?

3. Unity thinks that the only thing that distinguishes her from her sisters is her awkwardness. What are her strengths? Why don't others notice them?

4. Nicknames abound among the Mitford sisters. What purposes do these names serve?

5. What was the appeal of fascist rhetoric for people in Britain, and people like Diana and Unity in particular? What promises did the BUF make? Had they attained power, would they have been able to keep those promises?

6. Diana and Unity are reprimanded for attending the Nuremberg rally wearing bright lipstick. How were German beauty standards shaped by fascist ideas? What social issues are reflected in our modern beauty trends?

7. How do Nancy's concerns about privacy, reputation, and loyalty affect her conversations with her sisters? What finally goads her into taking a more active role against their dangerous beliefs?

8. While waiting to hear if she'll see Hitler during her time in Berlin, Diana has a moment of self-reflection and doubt that startles her. How do you think the events of the book would be different if she questioned herself more?

9. On a couple of occasions, as she tries to make sense of her sister's decisions against the complicated, incendiary developments happening across Europe, Nancy observes that political decisions are often based on personal motivations. What do you think this means in the context of Diana and Unity? Do you think that observation applies in modern times?

10. Though Nancy is clever enough to understand the danger of the radio station documents, her loyalty to Diana wins out for a long time. How does that compare to Diana's treatment of Unity?

11. Nancy asks herself, "Does [a single motivation] matter as long as we think we are acting on the side of right and truth? Or must we be on the actual side of right?" How would you answer those questions?

12. In the final chapter, Nancy suggests that she may have misapprehended her sisters' actions and the reasons underpinning them. Did this make you reassess the chapters attributed to Diana and Unity throughout the book? Is it possible that those accounts do not reflect what actually transpired (in the fictional world of *The Mitford Affair*) but Nancy's presumptions and projections about her sisters' activities based on her own, very personal beliefs?

# A CONVERSATION
# WITH THE AUTHOR

**It's clear that despite her own beliefs, Nancy found it very difficult to act against her sisters, especially before the outbreak of war. When writing a character like Nancy, are you ever tempted to add more fiction or push her into a more active role than she took in real life?**

Yes! In actuality, while the record reflects that Nancy did report about her sister's activities to MI5 and that report played a role in Diana's incarceration, I was not able to locate documentation that Nancy engaged in the more active spying activities that I depicted in the book, although she *must* have been collecting information on her sister's whereabouts and companions informally for years, particularly as the political landscape shifted. Consequently, I did add more action than I was able to verify in the record, in part because I found Diana and Unity's behavior so unbelievably appalling and Nancy's inaction in those earlier years difficult to fathom, aside from the obvious internal conflict. That said, hindsight is twenty-twenty, and of course, Nancy would not have been privy to everything we know now—but still! I didn't want to stray too far, however, from what the record reflects, and the book reflects that compromise.

**What kinds of sources did you consult to learn about the
Mitford sisters and their world? When looking at writing
they published more broadly, like Nancy's books or Unity's
articles, does the intended audience change the way you
interpret their perspectives?**

In some ways, the Mitford sisters are the best chroniclers of
their own histories and the most crucial sources, even though
there are myriad books written by others about them. Between
them, they've penned many books and countless shorter pieces—a mix of biographies about each other, biographies about
others, autobiographies, non-fiction on a variety of topics, articles, and, of course, Nancy's famous semi-autobiographical
post-World War II novels, *The Pursuit of Love* and *Love in a
Cold Climate,* and her less famous novels as well. Each of these
books, in its own way, shares different slices of the Mitford
sisters' lives. That said, given the sisters' penchant for larger
than life tales and the way their writings shifted depending on
the nature of their audiences, those writings need to be taken
with a grain of salt—and often, I found myself turning to their
actual letters to one another as a rich and engrossing source of
information about them.

**Diana and Unity seem to get involved with fascism largely to
further other agendas in their personal lives. Can we divorce
our politics from our personal lives? Should we?**

In part, the way in which politics and political figures
affected the Mitfords and their relationships with one another
drew me to this part of their history; it is so very timely in some
ways. The further I delved into the almost unbelievable manner

in which Diana and Unity became fascinated, even obsessed, with fascism, the clearer it became that, for these two sisters, politics was intensely personal. This notion, in fact, is a theme in Nancy's writings. And the more I considered it—the more I examined the world around me through that lens—the truer it seemed to be for most people; did people really land on a polit-ical belief system first and build a worldview around it as I'd sort of always thought, or did they have a personal worldview and select a political perspective based on it, I began to wonder. Throughout the writing of this book and beyond, I've specu-lated as to whether it's even possible to divorce the personal from the political, and I haven't yet arrived at an answer.

**Unity's suicide attempts drastically altered Nancy's perspec-tive. Do you think she would have been so willing to assist Churchill without seeing consequences that hit so close to home?**

As I was investigating Nancy's life and her sisters' actions while building this story, I found Nancy's inability to act for so long—knowing what she knew—so frustrating! But then I thought about my own siblings, and I realized that it would take something truly momentous for me to put them and their futures at risk by reporting any questionable activities to the authorities (not that they engage in questionable activities, mind you!). I am not surprised that it took the nearly fatal suicide attempt by Unity to push Nancy to act against Diana, but that doesn't mean I didn't find Nancy's passivity disheartening. I do think that, even if Unity hadn't taken that drastic, terrible act of shooting herself, Nancy would have eventually disclosed Diana's plans as the war progressed and the scope and scale of Hitler's evil revealed itself. I hope so, anyway.

**Between the three sisters, did you have a favorite perspective to write? Who was the most difficult to understand from the inside out?**

Without question, I found Unity's point of view the most challenging to comprehend and write about. Even without the benefit of hindsight, I wondered how she could possibly be intrigued by a politician as odious and evil as Hitler! I found it extremely difficult to look at him and the Nazis through Unity's eyes and see anything other than wickedness. But as often happens while writing historical fiction, I have to remind myself that she didn't know all that we know—even still, I found it incredibly difficult to adopt her mindset, no matter how fictional. I probably enjoyed writing Nancy's story the most, although there was something appallingly compelling about stepping into Diana's world. But boy, was I happy to step out of it!

**One of the big questions throughout the book is, to whom do we owe our loyalty. Do you think there is a way to remain loyal to someone without supporting their ideas and ambitions?**

Loyalty must have its limits, I think, particularly if remaining loyal to someone will put others—particularly large numbers of others—at risk of harm. Of course, we all have to draw our own lines around our loyalty to those individuals and institutions holding very different beliefs from our own and acting upon those beliefs. I think that, in *The Mitford Affair*, Diana crossed Nancy's line when her actions (and inaction) nearly killed Unity—and Nancy realized that many, many more people might be similarly impacted if Diana's plans reached fruition. But, of course, as the book posits, how well can we really know someone's beliefs and decisions? How certain do we have to be before we put aside our loyalty?

**What's next for you and your writing?**

I hope to continue excavating from the past the most important and fascinating women of history—women whose stories deserve to be told and legacies celebrated—until such novels are no longer necessary because both modern and historical women are no longer in the shadows.

# ACKNOWLEDGMENTS

*The Mitford Affair* would not have emerged from the depths of those important, yet often overlooked, years between World War I and II without the assistance and encouragement of so many people. First of all, I must express my gratitude to Laura Dail, my wonderful agent whose insightful advice and support made this book possible. Second, I am indebted to the amazing people at Sourcebooks, whose expertise and wisdom helped bring this book to life and to shelves, especially my fantastic editor, Shana Drehs; the amazing leader of Sourcebooks, Dominique Raccah; the tireless, brilliant marketing and publicity folks Molly Waxman and Cristina Arreola; not to mention the astonishing Todd Stocke, Valerie Pierce, Heather Hall, Margaret Coffee, Beth Oleniczak, Tiffany Schultz, Ashlyn Keil, Heather VenHuizen, Kelly Lawler, Brittany Vibbert, and Danielle McNaughton. And I am beyond thankful to the booksellers, librarians, and readers who've chosen to read and share *The Mitford Affair*, as well as my other novels.

My family and friends cheer me on behind the scenes, and for that and so many other things, I am beholden to them, including my supportive parents, Jeanne and Coleman; my champion mother-in-law, Catherine; my many marvelous siblings and siblings-in-law and their children; not to mention my tremendous friends, the Sewickley crew, Illana Raia, Kelly Close, Laura Hudak Daniel McKenna, and Ponny Conomos Jahn. Yet, always, it is Jim, Jack, and Ben—*my boys*—for whom I am eternally grateful.

If you'd like to learn more about the larger-than-life Mitford sisters, I can heartily recommend a slew of nonfiction books, including but not limited to Laura Thompson's *The Six: The Lives of the Mitford Sisters* and *Life in a Cold Climate: Nancy Mitford, The Biography*; Charlotte Mosley's *The Mitfords: Letters Between Six Sisters*; Anna de Courcy's *Diana Mosley: Mitford Beauty, British Fascist, Hitler's Angel*; David Pryce-Jones's *Unity Mitford*; Lady Diana Mosley's *A Life in Contrasts: The Autobiography*; Harold Acton's *Nancy Mitford*; Duchess of Devonshire Deborah Mitford's *Wait for Me!*; and Jessica Mitford's *Hons and Rebels*. But nothing quite compares to the novels of Nancy Mitford—*Highland Fling, Christmas Pudding, Pigeon Pie, Wigs on the Green, The Blessing*, and, of course, her famous *The Pursuit of Love* and *Love in a Cold Climate*.

# ABOUT THE AUTHOR

Marie Benedict is a lawyer with more than ten years' experience as a litigator at two of the country's premier law firms and Fortune 500 companies. She is a magna cum laude graduate of Boston College with a focus on history and a cum laude graduate of the Boston University School of Law. She is also the author of the *New York Times* bestsellers *The Mystery of Mrs. Christie* and *The Only Woman in the Room*, as well as *Carnegie's Maid*, *The Other Einstein*, *Lady Clementine*, and *Her Hidden Genius*. Her books have been translated into multiple languages. She lives in Pittsburgh with her family.